G000153571

BORNE ON THE TIDE

Also by Julia Bryant

WAITING FOR THE TIDE
WRITTEN ON THE TIDE

For
Louise my daughter
and
Jack my grandson
with love

ACKNOWLEDGEMENTS

My thanks are due to many people who generously gave me their time and advice.

Mr Don Baker, of Mead Mill Water Gardens, Romsey
Mr James Cramer, police historian
Dr Francis Keane, Portsmouth GP for over fifty years
Dr Chris Lawrence, Southampton GP and doctor to the Southampton (Saints) football club
Denise Spendlove, RGN, RM Portsmouth Midwife
The staff of Portsmouth City Libraries
Everyone at Portsmouth Record Office
The staff of Portsmouth Naval Library
As ever, Peter Rogers, Local Historian
And Chris and Margaret Seal of Sealpoint Computers

PROLOGUE

26 May 1856

Peace in the Crimea threw the whole of Portsea Island into a ferment of excitement. On the common near Southsea beach, scarlet-coated soldiers, blushing maidens and their vigilant mamas rejoiced. At one moment the sun was glinting on the bandsmen's bugles, and the next, lightning rent the sky. Thunder cracked overhead and the rains came, turning the ground into a morass and creating a stampede for carriages.

To the south-west in the churning waters off Point Beach a man in an open boat struggled to bring his craft ashore. The sail had been swept away. Shivering with fever he locked one arm round the tiller while the other clasped a ragged bundle tucked inside his jacket. A wall of green water swamped the boat and drove it against the base of the Round Tower. The force of the impact of timber against shingle holed the vessel and the sea began swilling through the hole in the planking. He had reached the shore. What happened next was out of his hands.

Chapter One

Dr Obadiah Pragnell walked through the Sally Port and on to the beach. After several glasses of victory champagne at the George in the High Street his head was buzzing. He breathed in the salty air and began to feel more alert. The rain-washed stones glistened like molten toffee and the sea lapped at his boots. This little stretch of shingle in the lee of the town walls had been his haunt since boyhood. Often he had stood here, hand in hand with his father, watching the ships of the line pass in full sail out into the Solent. The violent storm had abated and the beach was deserted, even the soldiers at Point Battery were only watching with half an eye.

Obadiah sauntered to the water's edge and tossed a stone into the sea. Turning to his right he noticed a boat aground at the foot of the Round Tower. He called to the figure sitting in the stern of the craft. There was no response, so he hurried towards him across the shingle. The man was dead, his face raw from exposure and hands badly blistered. Sea water swilled through a hole in the planking steadily covering his legs. One arm was locked round the tiller and the other clasped a bundle poking out of his tarpaulin jacket. Obadiah leant over the side and took charge of the mysterious bundle.

God Almighty!

It was a baby and barely alive at that. His headache forgotten, Dr Pragnell pressed his ear to the infant's chest. He could hear nothing. Rarely had he saved a baby in such a grey, flat condition. One-handed he tore at the buttons on his shirt and with the other held the infant. After much cursing he managed to slide it beneath his shirt and next to his skin. He rushed back through the Sally Port into the arms of Constable Norris.

'What's amiss, Doctor?' asked the policeman.

Pointing to the beach, Obadiah gasped, 'There's a dead body on that boat by the tower. I have a babe here near death.'

'My wife, she'll help you. Over there! Seven White Hart Row! I'll fetch a handcart, get the man away decently. Details can be got later.'

Obadiah took to his heels, crossed Broad Street and ran around the curve of the Row until he reached number seven. He thanked the fates that it had been the clear-sighted Norris on duty rather than his young officious colleague. Hammering on the door, he swept aside the young girl who opened it and gasped, 'I am a doctor with a babe, here, near death.'

The smell of baking and hot jam assailed him as he burst into the kitchen.

'You and I must save her,' he cried to the ample rear of the woman bending at the door of a black-leaded range.

'Ma, Doctor's got a dead baby,' shouted the young girl, tugging at her mother's apron.

Mrs Norris was no more than a blonde blur to Obadiah as he pulled the bundle from his coat. By the time he had laid the baby down, limp and stone coloured, on the floury table, she had set her baking aside.

'Merciful heavens!' exclaimed the woman, clutching her plump hands together as if in prayer.

Obadiah hoped fervently that she was not going to give way to hysteria. Her co-operation was vital.

Instantly she began undressing the infant, stripping off the ragged blanket. 'May! Quick! Fetch that towel off the chair and bring it here,' she commanded her daughter. Swiftly she undid the tiny button at the neck of the infant's gown then peeled off the vest and napkin. 'Put them in cold water in the bucket out in the yard.'

The stench of ammonia was overpowering.

'By the smell of its water it's many hours since this babe was fed,' Obadiah observed.

May pulled a face.

Again Pragnell held his hand over the chest. Was it wishful thinking or was there a faint heartbeat beneath his fingers? He judged the baby to be about ten pounds or so in weight and in the first few months of its life. Taking one of its tiny blue hands and curling the fingers round his thumb, he tested the baby's grip. The hand fell back immediately and the limbs were flaccid and without response to his pinching.

'Dear little maid! Look at that mop of black hair and those eyelashes! A little beauty, if we can just get her warmed into life. All your testing can come later,' said Mrs Norris, wrapping the child in the towel and sitting by the range with her. She lay the baby across her lap and began rubbing its back. 'May! Don't stand there looking 'mazed. Upstairs, chop-chop, fetch those baby things from the box under my bed,' she snapped to her daughter. Tendrils of blonde hair escaped from the pins beneath her lace cap. Impatiently, she brushed them aside. 'Doctor, kneel down beside me and chafe some warmth into these little feet,' she commanded, her face flushed and purposeful.

Another medical man would have protested at being ordered about by a constable's wife but Obadiah was grateful for her quick appreciation of what was needed. 'I don't know how we will get liquid into her. She's too weak to suck,' he said as he settled himself on the rag rug as instructed.

'Don't you fret about that,' said Mrs Norris. 'The little nestling can lick, most likely, once her lips are wetted and she gets the smell of milk in her nostrils.'

'It will be a long, slow business.'

'We'll not let her slip away,' she said. 'I wonder where the little maid is from and who are her kin? Her mother must be frantic with worry.'

'I found her in a wrecked boat at the Round Tower. She was nestled in the jacket of a young seaman. I'm afraid he is dead, poor fellow. His face was raw from the sun while his hands were dreadfully blistered. As to her mother, she may have been swept away. He kept the babe alive and for that we must be thankful.'

'It must have been the storm. Terrible it was. Lucky you chanced on her. Sweet Jesus! a little foundling. Well, she'll have every ounce of my strength behind her,' said Mrs Norris, fiercely.

May thumped down the stairs with a heap of tiny garments.

'There's a good girl,' said her mother, approvingly. 'Now, you pick out a little gown, a vest and a square of muslin and set them down by the fender to warm.'

Little May did as she was bid then knelt beside Obadiah and looked fondly at the baby. 'Can we keep her, Ma? Please, oh please say yes.'

'No, child. Someone will come forward to claim her most likely.'

'Oh, Ma!' protested the girl, glowering into the fire and chewing the end of one of her pigtails.

'Don't be pettish, May!' snapped her mother. 'You're ten years now, too old for sulks! Fetch a cloth and get the tarts out or they'll not be worth eating. Doctor, step aside, if you will.'

Obadiah's mouth began to water as the fragrance of the warm pastry filled the kitchen.

All the while she had been talking, Mrs Norris's hands had been constantly rubbing and turning the infant on her lap.

'Her feet seem a better colour,' observed Obadiah, resuming his place on the rug, 'but once a baby has become as chilled as this one I don't hold out much hope.'

They both stared down at the child as the clock on the mantelpiece chimed the hour.

'By Jove! It's after six. Augusta will be vexed,' gasped Obadiah. 'My wife is at home nursing my boys with measles. She will berate me soundly.'

'Don't go yet, Doctor,' Mrs Norris coaxed. 'You could send a note with May. Let's just try a little milk. Half an hour will not change things with your wife but a note may soften her temper.'

'You may be right,' he said doubtfully, remembering the promise to hurry home given earlier to his harassed wife.

'There's pen and paper on the dresser shelf. Never did get book learning myself, but folk set great store in letters.'

'Quite, quite,' said Obadiah distractedly. 'Your skills have saved the day,' he said, taking up the pen and dipping it into the ink.

Mrs Norris turned to her daughter who was absorbed in curling the baby's fingers around her own. 'May! Fetch a knife,' she said, 'and ease those tarts out onto a plate.'

Unthinkingly, after he had blotted the note and sealed it into an envelope, Obadiah reached forward and took one, biting eagerly into the rich sweet centre. The boiling jam scalded his lips and brought tears to his eyes.

Mrs Norris was all concern. 'May! Fetch a cup of water this instant! That's it, Doctor, drink deep. I've some hazeline cream, it will soothe your mouth. May! Fetch it from my medicine box in the dresser.'

With his lips still smarting, Obadiah exchanged the note with May for a small brown pot of ointment. 'Take it to number two, St George's Square, over in Portsea,' he instructed.

May turned round as she reached the door, 'Can she sleep in my dolly's crib?' she asked.

'You run like the wind, child, there and back, and then we'll see.'

The front door slammed shut behind her. Dr Pragnell and Mrs Norris once more studied the baby in their care. They stripped off the towel and examined her carefully. A pink tinge was creeping into the infant's flesh. Obadiah would have been grateful for a whimper or the twitching of an eyelid; any faint sign that recovery was in sight. While he continued his observations, Mrs Norris busied herself heating a mixture of milk, water and sugar in a saucepan then rinsing out a little blue jug and silver teaspoon.

How fortunate he had been to bump into Constable Norris and thereby find this capable woman! Into how many houses could one trespass, he wondered, with such favourable results? With the infant gaining strength, Obadiah allowed himself a glimpse of his surroundings. The kitchen was a model of cleanliness and a testament to Mrs Norris's homemaking. On the clothes-horse were two freshly starched shirts and over the mantelpiece an embroidered picture of a galleon in full sail. Above the door into the scullery was the cross-stitched text 'Jesus saves' which he took as an admonition against medical complacency.

As Mrs Norris poured the milk into the jug, he said, 'I think she is still too weak.'

'Oh do let me try, Doctor,' she begged.

He looked up into the rosy face of the plump young matron and considered Constable Norris a fortunate man indeed! Smiling at her, he nodded his permission.

She swaddled the baby firmly in the towel, dipped her finger into the small jug and then stroked it across its lips. The milk dribbled down the tiny chin and was instantly wiped away with a snowy handkerchief. Again she tried, to no avail. 'You're going to take your vittles if I have to stand here all night,' said Mrs Norris firmly.

'Her colour is better, certainly,' said Obadiah looking at the baby's face, which had turned from a grey-white shade to a healthy pink. He felt the tiny chest once more. 'Yes!' he said smiling. 'A definite beat.' It was not as fast as Obadiah would have liked but it was there throbbing beneath his fingers.

'Try her grip again,' said Mrs Norris.

He curled the tiny fingers around his thumb and tugged

gently against them. Was it his imagination or did they keep hold of him for just a fraction of a minute?

Skilfully Mrs Norris repositioned the baby and the spout of the little blue jug. The tiniest drop of milk touched the child's lips again. They waited almost breathless for some response. The lips parted and the pink tongue licked experimentally.

'Oh, glory be!' exclaimed Mrs Norris. 'I don't know when I've been so excited.' She tilted the jug carefully and then righted it. She repeated the action several times. She and the child began the delicate process of feeding. Laughing delightedly she said, 'Look at her! She's lapping it up like a kitten.'

They were both so intent on the child that they didn't hear Constable Norris come into the kitchen.

'How is the little mite?' he asked.

'Oh, Thomas.' Mrs Norris turned to her husband, her eyes shining. 'She's roused herself, the little treasure. I think she may be saved.'

'Good, good,' said the constable, smiling down at the child. 'Now, Doctor,' he said as he began to unbutton his uniform jacket. 'Did you form any impression of the fellow in the boat?'

'I only looked at him briefly once I realised that he was dead. A man of about thirty years, I would have said. From his weathered face and tarpaulin coat, I thought him to be a seaman. Naturally, once I had discovered the babe in such a perilous condition, I dismissed the mariner from my mind completely.'

Thomas Norris removed his top hat and carried it out into the passage before responding to Obadiah's words. 'His clothes were sodden and the papers in his pocket fell to pieces in my hand. There were a few coins: French centimes, I think they were. Of course, if there'd been a proper guard kept at the tower, likely one of the soldiers would have seen the boat earlier and a rescue might have been possible. What with all the parading on the common, there was only a handful of men at Point Battery and not one of them looking out to sea. I've sent for their doctor to make a more thorough examination for the coroner. The cause of death doesn't look to be foul play.'

'The moustache, now I recollect,' said Obadiah. 'Rather points to his being a Frenchman – only a young fellow – pity!'

'Her little gown is finest lawn,' said Mrs Norris, 'and the embroidery is beautifully worked. I noticed there was the letter "B" in satin stitch. Could the babe's name begin with a "b" or is it just for baby, do you suppose?'

'The boat is done for. A tender to a larger craft, I think. The name of "*Beatrice*" is written on her stern. I've contacted the coroner's clerk and there'll be an inquest tomorrow. I'll send a note round to your house as soon as the time and place are confirmed. Will that be convenient, Doctor? As first on the scene, your testimony will be invaluable. Lucky you were down this way; don't often see you in Old Portsmouth.'

'Yes, Portsea keeps me well occupied,' said Obadiah, looking wistfully at the tarts but not wanting to risk another scalding. 'Of course, I shall attend the inquest.'

'Seeing as you found the babe,' said the constable also looking at the pastry, ''tis fitting you should name her.'

'Well,' said Obadiah, 'I think your wife has been equal partner in her revival. She should name her.'

'Beatrice,' said Mrs Norris flushing with pride, 'after the boat that bore her to safety.'

'How about Weymouth,' teased her husband, 'after the little jug what's bringing her nourishment?'

Mrs Norris chuckled and her fresh, plump beauty again struck Obadiah.

'Anne,' said her husband, reaching forward and taking two tarts, 'that Mrs Salter who lost her babe last week. Couldn't she be persuaded to nurse this little mite for a day or so while proper arrangements are made?'

'My stars! Thomas, you're speaking out of turn,' snapped his wife. 'It would be wanton cruelty to expect her to take on this child with her own barely cold in the ground.'

Her husband chewed thoughtfully before answering. 'Once she'd put the infant to the breast she'd soon grow to love it. Could be the answer.'

'You've vexed me now, good and proper. Fancy talking of her as if she were naught but a pair of udders. And what happens if she takes to the child and some of her kin are found to claim her?'

Obadiah was struck by the frankness of their speech. He couldn't imagine the word udders passing his own wife's lips.

Mrs Norris's eyes filled with tears. 'Do you think I could have nursed another baby after our Matthew was taken?'

Her husband studied his stout black boots.

Dr Pragnell was in a dilemma. He could see the sound sense in the constable's words. A mother's milk was vital to an infant's survival, and yet he felt disloyal to the good woman in siding with her husband.

'Could I take the child while you make me a cup of tea, Mrs Norris?' he asked. 'I feel quite parched.' He smiled at her and said, 'You have truly brought her back from the dead.'

'It has been a joy to me,' she said, simply, before settling the infant in his arms. Turning to the dresser she took a black lacquered caddie from the shelf and after warming the pot she shook in three heaped spoonfuls of tea. 'Can I see little Beattie safely through the night, then see how she is in the morning?' Must be more certain before we take her anywhere.'

A thin cry came from the baby in his arms and its eyes opened. They were slate blue! It was a rare, rewarding moment. Infants so often failed to take a hold on life – born to malnourished parents in damp, insanitary homes without a hope of survival. He watched the baby turning its head and looking curiously around the room. Perhaps the child was older than he had supposed.

'Here, Doctor, a cup of tea,' said the constable, spooning sugar liberally into a cup of mahogany liquid and setting it before him on the table. 'Give the young maid to me.'

Obadiah drank thirstily. It was hours since he'd sat in the George quaffing champagne. He watched the broad-shouldered man speaking tenderly to the baby in his arms and felt his spirits lift. As he drained his cup there was the sound of running feet in the passage and May burst into the room, her face red from running.

'I bin to your house,' she said to him. 'Cook says to come quick. Your missis bin took badly.'

Obadiah's spirits plummeted. All the euphoria at the baby's recovery was quenched. He began to put on his coat. 'You know what's needful, Mrs Norris. It's between God and your good care. I will call tomorrow.'

'May! You set the table and fetch the pie from the larder,' said her mother. 'Thomas! See the doctor out. Give me the child. I'll finish its feeding, then May and I can dress and settle the little maid. Now, Doctor, you should find a hansom in Broad Street it'll get you home in no time!'

Obadiah was plunged into anxiety as he hailed the waiting cab. Please God, let Augusta be safe! She was everything to him. As he bowled along towards St George's Square, all thoughts of little Beatrice vanished from his mind.

Chapter Two

Pain skewered through Augusta's temples and her body was slippery with sweat. Was this the beginning of measles? When it started with the boys they had certainly been fretful and feverish. Little Albert's eyes had rolled back in his head showing only the whites and his skin had burned beneath her touch. But surely she had had measles as a child? Augusta bit her lip and her eyes filled with tears. There was no one to ask. Mama was in India and Nanny Groves had died when she was twelve. She yearned to be back in her childhood home in Nursling with the picture of the angel over her bed, sitting on Nanny's lap, being cuddled into her pillowy bosom and rocked to the rhythm of her songs. Tears leaked under her lashes. Her mouth was too dry and foul-tasting to sing, so she hummed the tune in her head. 'Toora loora loora.' The words comforted; they were words for rocking, words from childhood. She tried to rouse her spirits by moving her head in time to the lullaby, but each turn of her neck set up painful vibrations.

Someone leaned over her and draped a wet cloth over her forehead. It smelled of eau de cologne. Oh, she was dry, so dry she could drink an ocean. Augusta forced her lips apart. 'Water,' she managed to whisper.

Mildred, her maid, leaned towards her helping her into a sitting position against the pillows. She held a glass to her lips and Augusta saw the anxiety in the young woman's face. Was she really so ill? As she looked up at her, Mildred's face was ringed with a painful dazzle of light. Having emptied the glass, she nodded towards the jug. The sound of the water being poured was magnified in her head. As she raised her arm, the smell of stale perspiration wafted towards her from the maid's dress making her want to vomit. She steeled herself to gain control. Her throat ached and, if she were sick, it would be even more painful.

'I'll get the master,' gasped Mildred, rushing from the room. The sound of the door slamming reverberated in Augusta's head. She pressed her hand to the cloth on her head, then held her fingers to her nose, taking in the sharp stinging scent of cologne. How had she sickened so quickly? Was it only this afternoon that she had been singing to Sammy and Albert, rejoicing at their recovery and looking forward to Obadiah's return? It seemed a lifetime ago. Dear, dear Obi, where was he? She so wanted to see him. He set everything right. He laughed at her foolishness and drew out the best in her. 'Obi, Obi,' she shouted in her head, but no sound came.

Augusta began to shiver. Draped over a chair near the window was her Paisley shawl. With her head pounding and legs trembling, she made her way across the room. The little gilded French chair had been a present from Papa. Now the golden legs seemed to glitter in sharp stabbing points. Augusta leaned forward and pulled the shawl towards her. It left the chair in a slithering sinuous movement that frightened her. The red and green spoon-shaped swirls of pattern turned into hissing snakes. Terrified, Augusta dropped the shawl. Backing away from it, she tripped against the table holding a vase of daffodils and irises. It rocked and fell, the vase shattering into jagged slivers. A stale green stench of flower water made her retch. She slithered over the flower stems and glass fragments. Beads of scarlet crisscrossed her feet. 'Obi, Obi,' she cried out, as the room spun and she dropped into a dark void.

'Oh, praise God you're home, Doctor. We been so worried. Mistress took bad this afternoon. She's prostrate with fever, likely she's got the measles from the boys.'

'Thank you, Cook. I'll go straight to her.' He thrust his coat and hat at her and took the stairs two at a time.

Augusta lay in a tangle of shawl and nightgown between an upended table and overturned chair. 'Gussie, darling, I'm here. Your Obi's here. Let me get you back to bed.' He knelt beside her and smoothed her long dark hair away from her face and kissed her. Augusta's skin was pale and clammy to his touch and her breath fetid. Her blue eyes looked at him unseeingly.

All his professional detachment deserted him. Sweet Jesus! His Gussie could die if he didn't act swiftly. His heart pounded as he knelt beside her and tried to gather her into his arms. Only as he was about to slide her legs under the covers did he see the cuts on her feet. Swiftly, he tugged the bell-pull behind the bed, dipped his handkerchief into the carafe of water on the bedside table and began to bathe her feet. Fortunately, they were only surface cuts and after careful inspection he was certain that he had removed all traces of glass.

'Come in, quickly.' His voice was sharp with anxiety. 'Mildred' – he turned to the maid, standing anxiously in the doorway – 'I want hot water, fresh linen and towels. The

17

mistress has a fever and I need to give her a sponge bath. All that can wait.' He gestured impatiently to the upset furniture. 'Go! There's no time to lose.'

Obadiah turned back to Augusta. Thank God her skin was a better colour now and her eyes more focused.

'Thirsty,' she moaned.

'Of course, my darling. You must drink. Here, let me help you.' He poured the water into the glass and held it for her while she drank. Augusta trembled as she gulped, then pushed the glass away after only drinking half of it. Obadiah tried to calm his fear. The cook had spoken of measles and it was the most likely cause for the soaring temperature. His mind fastened inescapably on the possible complications, rushing ahead to the most serious: inflammation of the lungs!

'You shall be well, Gussie, I promise,' he said, with forced conviction. He lay her back against the pillows and held her wrist as he withdrew his pocket watch from his waistcoat. Her pulse was rapid. He counted the beats – one hundred and ten! 'Listen, dearest, we need to make you cool and comfortable. I'm going to give you a sponge bath and fetch you some medicine from my bag, to take the fever away.'

Augusta stared at him, her eyes full of fear. Obadiah smiled reassuringly – yet he too was frightened. Never, even in childbirth, had he known her to be ill. He had taken her boundless energy and enthusiasm so much for granted. She must not be taken from him. 'Your Obi will make you well again, I promise,' he said, taking her hand and kissing it before going to the door and opening it to Mildred. 'Set down the jug and linen. I shall attend my wife. Could you fetch up my bag, please? I left it in the hall.'

He poured the water into the bowl in the wash stand and

cooled it with some from the ewer. Taking a sturdy chair from his dressing room, he put it beside the bed and set the bowl on it along with the sponge and soap-dish. Mildred tapped on the door again.

'Thank you,' he said, taking his bag and making to close the door.

'Doctor, I've got the brush and dust pan to sweep up the glass.'

'Quickly then,' he snapped. Dismissing the maid from his mind, Obadiah began to undress his wife. He was sponging her face and neck when he became aware of Mildred standing beside him, fidgeting with her apron. He realised that she was discomfited by him assuming the role that was hers. 'I shall manage on my own. Thank you, Mildred. You can retire for the night.'

'Yes, sir,' she mumbled.

'Keep your mistress in your prayers,' he said as he picked up the towel.

'Good night, Sir and Madam,' Mildred said backing out of the room.

'Gussie, darling, I'm going to bathe you and make you comfortable. Then I shall give you some laudanum to help you sleep.'

Augusta looked at him, her face flushed and eyes fever bright. 'Head! My head!' she moaned.

Slowly, tenderly he began to wash her. The sight of his wife's naked body was a rare one. In other circumstances, he would have been aroused at the sight of her full breasts and long white thighs. Tonight, he was moved to pity. Poor Augusta! So beautiful and so fettered by her mother's narrow views on loving! So at a distance from the pleasure that could be hers!

Lovemaking was conducted in silence, in the dark and beneath the covers. It was difficult not to feel furtive and ashamed. Fleetingly, he wondered if Anne Norris was as reticent and dutiful. Guiltily, he thrust the thought of her plump charms aside, picked up the wet sponge and stroked it down Augusta's arms. She was so hot the water seemed to evaporate before he could dry her skin. Obadiah sponged her back with long sweeping strokes.

'My head, my head,' she moaned again, into the pillow.

He dipped a handkerchief into the cold water jug and wrung it out, before plastering it cross her forehead. By the time he had completed bathing her, he was exhausted. Gussie was fretful and shivering as he wrestled to get her into her nightgown. After administering a few drops of laudanum to his wife, Obadiah refilled her carafe with water and turned down the lamp. He lay down fully dressed beside her. Closing his eyes, shutting out the floral swags on the curtains and the pink and white fussiness of the bedroom, he remained wakeful throughout the night.

At seven o'clock he rang for Mildred to clear away the bed linen and to fetch him some shaving water.

'Obi, is that you?' cried Augusta.

'Yes, my darling, your Obi is here.' He sat on the bed and held her hand in his, turning it round so that he could feel her pulse. His watch was on the table on the other side of the bed but, even without being able to count them, the beats seemed rapid. He tried to reassure her with a smile. 'You have the measles, my love. It will be a while before you are well.'

'I feel so tired and far away,' she said. 'I dreamed I was a child again in Nursling with Nanny Groves, then I awoke not knowing where I was. Obi, are the boys all right? Have they come through the fever? I fancied that I had been playing with them before Nanny took them away for their bath. Then the rest of the day was lost.' She turned to him. 'I called and called for you but you could not be found.' Augusta began to cry. Where were you? I needed you so desperately.' Her eyes were bright with tears and accusation.

'My darling,' he said soothingly, as he took her into his arms. 'Had I known that you needed me, I would have been here posthaste.'

'Where were you, Obi?'

'I rescued a young baby from drowning. It was all quite desperate for a time but immediately she was better I flew home to you.'

Augusta showed not the slightest interest in his words. 'Are you sure my boys are better?'

'They are quite recovered, my darling.'

'I must see them. Have Nanny bring them to me, at once.'

'First you must have some tea and perhaps a little porridge.'

Augusta screwed up her face in distaste. 'Just water, Obi, please. The thought of anything thick and creamy is nauseating. Perhaps later, some beef tea.'

Obadiah touched the bell-pull. 'I'll get Mildred to bring you some barley water and to wash and tidy you for the day. I shall breakfast and come and see you later, my love.'

'The boys – can I see them, Obi? Just for a moment or two to quieten my mind.'

Obadiah smiled at her. I'll fetch them to you when I've had my tea and a glance at the paper. You will be refreshed then and ready for the little imps.' He raised his finger in warning. 'Only a few moments, Gussie. Sleep is what you need.'

As he sat in the dining room trying to concentrate on the

article in *The Times*, Mildred came in with a letter. Distractedly, he slit the envelope with his paper-knife.

> *Dear Dr Pragnell,*
> *The babe has survived and Mrs Norris is taking her to the young woman at 10 Golden Lion Lane. Perhaps you could meet her there at half past one, examine the child and then proceed to The Bell for the inquest at two o'clock?*
> *Thank you for your assistance.*
> *Yours respectfully,*
> *Constable Norris.*

Obadiah sighed. How he regretted straying on the beach yesterday and not going straight home to Augusta! He would be glad to be done with young Beatrice. She had taken up too much of his time already.

Chapter Three

Ruth Salter dragged herself from the couch to answer the loud knocking on her door. She had no interest in who might be calling. Since the death of Sarah, nothing mattered. The time with her child had been cruelly short. All night she had held the tiny body in her arms, feeling the warmth seep away. Then in the morning she heard Jacob talking in anxious whispers to the lying-in woman. Mrs Norris had bathed the infant and Ruth had dressed her in the little gown that she had sewn for her.

'We must christen the child, Ruth. You don't want your baby missing out on heaven,' Anne Norris had said. 'There's no time to call the parson. Couldn't bear to think of the little maid a wandering in limbo land.'

It was all nonsense to her. She wanted her child to stay in the circle of her arms. Limbo or heaven, they were both meaningless. What did she care where her baby was taken if she could not accompany her? But Jacob, the firm believer of the two, had got a cup of water and knelt down beside her, making the sign of the cross on the baby's forehead.

He turned to her. 'Shall she be Sarah?'

Ruth nodded. She had looked at the baby with such an intensity of love, trying to impress on her mind every detail of her face. Tracing her blonde eyebrows with her fingers, she kissed her tiny mouth and then her hands.

Again Jacob dipped his fingers into the cup. 'I baptise thee, Sarah Salter, in the name of the Father, Son and Holy Ghost.' He bent and kissed his daughter then ran from the room.

Ruth knew that Sarah was dead but she could not yet be parted from her.

Jacob returned with a few ragged daisies torn from a clump of grass. He put them in an eggcup and set them on the table before kneeling down beside her and taking her hand.

'Ruth, my dear,' said Mrs Norris, 'give the child to me. She's gone now. Your little one wasn't meant for this world. You must be brave and let her go.'

'Just a few more minutes,' she'd begged. But later, when she had fallen into an exhausted sleep they had stolen the baby from her. Ruth bit her lip as the pain of their treachery stabbed afresh. Why couldn't the strength of her love have kept just a spark of life inside that tiny body until her milk had come? Now her breasts were hard and painful in their fullness.

Poor Jacob had to go and see the parson and arrange the funeral. She had been too exhausted. The thought of seeing the little coffin or watching it being covered in earth was beyond bearing. She had spent the day in bed staring at the pathetic little bunch of daisies still clinging to life while her Sarah was beyond saving. To compound the cruelty, Jacob had been posted early to India. She was alone with only her grief for company.

Yesterday he had held her close, his eyes red-rimmed from

frequent tears. 'Oh, Ruthie, it breaks my heart to leave you. Bear up, my love. Please God, I shall be able to send for you in a year or two.'

'Jacob,' she had cried, clinging fiercely to him, 'why is He so cruel to us?'

Her husband nodded, sadly. 'I don't know. Ruthie, I look at the nippers around here in the stinking courts, living on scraps, turned out all day by their sluts of mothers and I can't find answers. Our Sarah would have been so precious to us.' He held her tear-stained face between his hands. 'Listen! You rest and get well. Mountains and mountains of time yet, you're only twenty.'

Ruth had shaken her head.

'I know we'll never forget little Sarah, but when you come to me in India, you'll be well and we can hope again.'

She turned away from him. 'I'll never, ever forgive Him, that gentle, bloody Jesus.'

'He gave us each other,' Jacob reminded her. 'Please, my Ruthie, get well for me.'

Her eyes filled with tears as she remembered standing at the door watching him walk away from her his figure getting smaller and smaller until he was quite gone. In the space of five days she had lost everything. How was it that her body went on living? In spite of herself the blood continued to pulse through her veins. Doubtless her fingernails were growing and her hair lengthening. Why couldn't the force that was keeping her so unwillingly in this world strive with equal force for Sarah? Angrily she became aware again of the knocking on the door.

'I'm coming, I'm coming, hold your racket,' she called as the flung a shawl around her shoulders.

It was Mrs Norris and a doctor by the look of the bag in his hand. The lying-in woman was holding a bundle in her arms her apple-cheeked face creased with anxiety.

'Mrs Salter,' she said, 'may we step inside? The matter is urgent, or we wouldn't have troubled you.'

As the doctor moved towards Mrs Norris, the bundle in her arms shifted and a pink fist thrust itself free of the blanket.

Ruth gasped and drew her arms protectively across her body. What could they mean by it? Bringing a baby into her house when her own infant was so lately buried!

The kitchen was in chaos. Dirty plates covered the table and by the door into the scullery was a heap of unwashed garments. Careless of the slovenly impression they created she sank back into a chair, leaving the visitors standing uncertainly before her.

'Well?' she demanded, staring angrily at the doctor.

'I deeply regret the loss of your child, Mrs Salter,' he said quietly as he took off his hat and placed it on the dresser between a sticky spoon and a pot of jam. 'You will think me insensitive in what I am going to ask of you, but it is a matter of life and death.'

She shook her head, refusing even to think about it. He was asking too much. Ruth glared at Mrs Norris. How could she rub salt into her grief? No! She would not consent. If she shut her ears to the cries emerging from the bundle in the lying-in woman's arms and the demands of those little fists they would have to leave. Yet her body yearned traitorously for the infant. Her breasts tingled beneath the binder and her womb tightened but she would not look.

'Mrs Salter, for pity sake. We couldn't save your Sarah, try as we might, but you could feed this little one and give her a start in life. Just for a few days till Doctor Pragnell goes to the workhouse and sees what can be arranged.'

'The child was found on the shore in a seaman's jacket. Poor fellow, he had died in the effort of bringing his boat to safety and keeping little Beatrice warm.'

'What's that to me?' said Ruth, sinking back onto a chair and feeling her womb clench and blood surging onto the towel she'd pressed inside her drawers.

'You have the means to save her. I know that she cannot be a replacement for your child but her need is desperate. Will you not take her for just one night while I cast about for somewhere else?'

If only she felt stronger she could rush to the door and hustle them through it. As it was she could feel her energy ebbing away. They would wear her down. She knew it. Ruth sat staring into the fire willing them away, wanting only rest and silence.

'Mrs Salter,' pleaded Anne Norris, 'you can save this little soul and give her a start in life. I'll see to the house for you and make you some vittles. Please, Ruth, I beg of you, just for a few days. There's a bout of measles at the workhouse or we'd have taken her there.'

They took her silence for consent.

'I'll want paying,' she said, glaring at the doctor. 'I'll not spend Jacob's money on another man's child.'

Mrs Norris looked away from her in embarrassment.

'Certainly, Mrs Salter,' said the doctor. 'That is only fair and reasonable.' He put his hand into his waistcoat pocket and drew out half a crown from a leather purse. Putting it on the mantelpiece over the sulky fire he said, 'I shall find out when the child can be taken to the workhouse. I believe it is possible for a small weekly payment to be made to you by the authorities in the meantime – non-resident poor relief – I will send a note to the workhouse. As Mrs Norris said, there is the matter of the measles outbreak – even my wife has been stricken. I left her this morning in low spirits.'

Ruth glared at him, without a word of thanks. What did she care? What were his wife's low spirits compared to her own? 'By the sound of things,' she said, 'you're looking to palm this brat off on me for a deal longer than one night. That poor relief had better be got soon.'

The doctor met her gaze unflinchingly. Ruth felt that in other circumstances she would have taken to the man. His dark eyes were kindly and he had none of the disdain she had met with in others of his profession.

'Mrs Salter,' he said, 'I shall call tomorrow to ensure that you are both in good health and meet any further expenses deemed necessary. Now, I must bid you good day as I have other urgent calls on my time.'

She sat, mute and unresponsive while Mrs Norris saw the doctor out and returned with the child. She placed it in her lap. As if she were helpless, the older woman took Ruth's arms and folded them around the baby. It was only idle curiosity, she told herself, as she stared into the baby's slate blue eyes. It wrinkled its face and licked its lips with a pink pointed tongue. A tiny hand flew towards its face and then away again. Near and far the hands waved and then some inner discomfort caused the legs to draw themselves up to the stomach and a flicker of pain crossed its face.

Milk leaked from her breasts, milk that was meant for Sarah. The baby began to wail and turned its head back and forth bumping against Ruth's tender breasts. Listlessly, she changed the baby's position so that it was lying in the crook of her arm. Unbuttoning her nightgown, she shifted around so that she could push her nipple into the little seeking mouth. The pressure of the gums was like wire piercing through her. Ruth gritted her teeth and tears welled in her eyes. Gradually the pain eased. The baby suckled vigorously and stared intently at her as she continued to feed. The milk from the other breast trickled onto her gown and Ruth changed the infant around to the other side. Again, she winced as the baby attached itself to her. It closed its eyes and Ruth studied the shock of black hair, forming a widow's peak on its forehead and sticking out in silky tufts. Her eyebrows were straight as ruled lines and her lashes long and thick. It was curiosity, not interest, she assured herself. Anything more would be disloyalty. At least the suckling had relieved the tautness in her breasts and, if Mrs Norris were to put the place to rights and cook for her until she'd regained her strength, some benefit could be got from the situation. But, she promised herself, I will not love this child.

Chapter Four

Constable Norris tramped across the beach to check that the *Beatrice* had not been tampered with before proceeding with his other inquest duties. Since yesterday's storm the shore was littered with the usual flotsam and jetsam: timber, great swathes of rubbery brown seaweed encrusted with shells and crabs, old candles, a sea boot and tarred rope ends. Once the sun warmed the seaweed it would begin to stink, attracting flies and gulls. Norris left the beach and crossed Broad Street to the Camber fish quay to further his enquiries.

He nodded to a trio of old salts sitting on the bench outside the Bridge tavern. 'Anyone here know anything of the tender called the *Beatrice*, that fetched up on the shore by the Round Tower yesterday?' he asked.

'Boat could have come from the Isle of Wight, along at the Witterings or even further eastwards, Shoreham way. Ain't there a scrap of cargo on board, bits of coal or flour sacks?' asked one of them, squinting up at him through bleached blue eyes.

'The vessel's badly holed. Anything aboard was likely washed out,' said Norris.

'What do the body show you?' asked another weathered old man shifting his position on the bench outside the tavern.

'Precious little,' answered Norris warily. Any word of the contents of the seaman's pockets would be richly embroidered into a tale of the constable stealing from the dead. 'I shall be up at the Bell if you come across anyone as can give any news. Inquest's at two,' he said, leaving the old mariners to watch the boats and yarn among themselves. As he passed further down the quay a woman in sea boots and a large coarse apron threw a fish to a one-eyed cat.

'Were you here yesterday, Madam?' he asked, watching the cat leap off the boat and bear the gift away to a nest of kittens in an upturned bucket on the dock.

Putting down her gutting knife the woman said, 'Got in from Langstone afore six this morning.'

Norris raised his hat and went on his way to the Bell tavern. There was much to arrange if the Coroner's Court were to be held there.

The landlord was less than pleased. 'Takes up me best room and a good scuttle of coal for the fire. Then there's the back room for the body that'll stink out the place for days after. All for half a crown.'

'I don't make the laws,' said Norris with some sympathy, 'just enforces them. See you at one. I've a jury to find and the body to fetch.'

Strolling down the High Street he looked about him for likely victims. By eleven he had secured nine men: three soldiers, the sexton of St Thomas's Church, a schoolmaster, the butcher's apprentice, two fishermen and the gravedigger. By noon he had made up the requisite twelve with a trio of sailors.

Back at the Bell, promptly at 2 p.m., through a fog of pipe smoke and ale fumes, came the coroner. He nodded to the constable, as his officer, to begin the proceedings. Norris cleared his throat. 'All manner of persons having anything to do at this court before Her Majesty's Coroner for the Borough draw near and give your attention,' he said.

There was a scraping of chairs and the assorted jurymen, Dr Pragnell and another medical man got to their feet.

'And you members of the jury who will be duly sworn and empanelled to enquire how and by what means this unknown man came by his death severally answer your names as you shall be called.'

'Present,' was answered promptly by all the men.

The sexton, their elected foreman, was quickly sworn in. Passing the Bible from one to the other the jurors repeated the oath. 'I swear by almighty God that I will diligently enquire on behalf of our Sovereign Lady the Queen into the death of the man unknown and give a true verdict according to the evidence.'

The next stage was the viewing of the body. Norris led the doctors and jurors along the low dark passage to an unused storeroom. As he opened the door the stench was over-powering. The body was lying on a trestle table loosely draped in a sheet. From a small dirt-encrusted window the sun glared onto the seaman's face. Holding a handkerchief to his nose the landlord shoved his way to the back of the room. After a struggle he lifted the latch and forced the window open. The benefit of the meagre draught of air was negated by the entry of a large fly.

Owing to the confines of the room each person had to wedge themselves between the dingy brown walls and the table, getting far closer to the body than they wished. A young sailor turned pale and vomited out of the window.

Norris felt both pity and revulsion. The dead seaman could not be above thirty years old. His face was white and his lips a dark blue. He had a black drooping moustache and his hair, of the same colour, was pulled back into a seaman's queue. The combination suggested that he was not a British sailor. That and the centimes in his pocket led Norris to think him a Frenchie. It was possible, even in his present state, to see that he had been a handsome, well-muscled fellow. The knuckles of his hands were grazed and the fingernails broken, indicating hard usage. One foot was red and swollen with a suppurating wound adding to the foul odour in the room. The jurymen hurried back to the other room and left him to shut the door on the deceased. Glancing back at the body he was struck by the stillness and the finality of death.

Always after such a viewing he had an urgent need to take his Anne to bed and release the tensions of the day in her plump accommodating flesh. He checked himself. The inquest was by no means over. Dr Pragnell had yet to speak.

Wearily Obadiah took the oath and gave his evidence. 'I was walking on the beach and saw the deceased sat in the boat at the foot of the Round Tower. I gave him only a cursory inspection.'

'And why was that, Doctor Pragnell?' asked the coroner briskly.

'I found a bundle wrapped in rags in the seaman's jacket. It was an infant near death. All my attention was then focused on the child.'

The jury began to murmur among themselves. Mention of a baby had sharpened their interest.

'Has the babe survived?' asked the coroner.

'Yes,' said Obadiah. 'She is temporarily lodged with a young nursing mother and appears to have recovered.'

'Good, good. I am assured, Doctor Pragnell, that you will be in contact with the authorities about this infant and will keep them informed of its progress.'

'Certainly,' answered Obadiah.

'Relatives may yet come forward to claim her, but that is outside the authority of this court.'

Obadiah sat down relieved that his part in the proceedings would soon be over. He thought of his recent visit to Ruth Salter and the seaman's child. The young woman seemed exhausted and on listening with his stethoscope he had heard a faint murmur consonant with aortic incompetence. She had likely suffered from rheumatic fever as a child. Having a hungry baby foisted on her when she had so lately lost her own was just the sort of strain she should avoid. Obadiah sighed. At least the baby had benefited. Perhaps in time she would come to love her. And then he thought of Augusta and became impatient to leave.

'Doctor Abernathy,' called Constable Norris.

'Present,' said the dapper little man in the starched wing collar and black suit.

The constable handed him the Bible to take the oath.

'You were called, I believe, Doctor Abernathy, to Penny Street Station to examine the body of this man and to ascertain the cause of death?'

'Yes, that is so,' replied the doctor.

'What were your findings?' asked the coroner.

'The man was in the early stages of rigor mortis. The deceased had been a strong fit man in his thirties, I should say. His face showed signs of exposure and his hands were badly blistered as if he had been rowing a boat for some hours. Exhaustion, exposure and possibly lack of food and water were certainly contributory factors in the cause of death.' The doctor paused and the jury looked at him expectantly. 'But I am certain the main cause of death was septicaemia.'

'Explain yourself, Doctor, for the laymen among us,' commanded the coroner.

'You will have seen the wound on his left foot caused by a nail or other rusty implement having pierced the skin. On my examination his clothing and boots were removed. The left boot had to be cut away due to the swelling of the foot caused by the infection. Inside the boot the warmth and moisture were the perfect breeding ground for bacteria. The infection spread to his blood stream and the principal cause of death in my opinion was septicaemia or blood poisoning.'

'And so, Doctor Abernathy, you would rule out any likelihood of foul play?'

'Certainly. The causes of death are sad but straightforward. Exposure exacerbated the earlier neglect.'

The coroner nodded, then turned to the policeman. 'Constable Norris, have you been able to glean any information as to where the boat had come from or whether any other persons had earlier been aboard?'

'No, your honour. I have questioned the guards at the Point Battery and the fishermen at the Camber Quay. The boat would appear to be a tender belonging to a larger craft, but nothing is known of her.'

There was a pause and the coroner shuffled his papers. He

turned to the foreman of the jury, the sexton from St Thomas's, and said, 'I am directing you to consider the matter carefully and to bring in the verdict of death by natural causes.'

There was a shuffling of feet and the jurors went out of the room for a hushed confab in the passage. The coroner had suggested they could confer in the storeroom, but they all agreed to stand in the passage.

Obadiah didn't blame them, the ripe condition of the corpse was not conducive to cool reflection. Poor fellow, how had he come to be in such desperate straits, he wondered? What was his connection with the baby? Again he felt guilty at foisting the child on Mrs Salter. However, the few shillings a week from the workhouse would be useful to her, and the constable's wife had promised to keep an eye on her. His thoughts were interrupted by the return of the jury.

'Are you all agreed on your verdict?' the coroner asked.

'Yes,' said the foreman.

'How say you?'

'Death by natural causes.'

The coroner nodded approvingly and after scraping away with his pen he looked up and said, 'This court is now dismissed.'

After a nod to Constable Norris, Obadiah hurried out of the tavern and stepped into his carriage. 'Away, Dapple,' he said to the pony as he took up the reins. He was anxious to see Augusta. Hopefully, he was now done with Beatrice.

Chapter Five

Once Mildred had taken away the remains of her tea, Augusta crept across the room and stood at her dressing table. The room was in shadow due to the closed curtains. Impatiently she pulled them aside and looked at herself in the mirror. Her eyes were watery and red rimmed and her face still covered in rusty coloured spots. If only she could find some scissors she would slice off her hair. It hung around her shoulders in a hot im-penetrable blanket. What a vile pathetic figure stood before her. How tired she was of being ill.

Obadiah had warned her that sunlight would hurt her eyes. To her intense aggravation he had been proved right. Closing them she knelt down on the floor and let the breeze from the open window play on her face. The scents of the garden – lavender, stocks and honeysuckle – wafted up to her. Last week she had cut some roses and shaken the raindrops from them, revelling in their fragrance. How she loved them. When Samuel was expected she had even taken to eating their petals. Papa loved roses. Augusta sighed. Only a couple more years and they would be home from India. She would be able to take the boys to Nursling and give them a country holiday away from the clamour of Portsea.

It was a military town and they were close to The Hard, the area around the harbour and the dockyard. She hated the rough language of the soldiers and sailors; the hard-faced women touting for trade; the drunkenness and the sudden eruption of violence which was a feature of their neighbourhood. And then there was the sea. Its sound, its strength, its size, its wildness were foreign to her and she had no wish to learn its language.

Reluctantly she closed the curtains and got back into bed. She must have slept for at least an hour, for when she opened her eyes again the room was in darkness. Someone was tapping on the door. 'Come in,' she called softly.

'Gussie, my love, how are you feeling?' Obadiah tiptoed across the floor and drew up a chair beside her.

'Hot and thirsty and weak as a kitten,' she said.

'I'll get Mildred to bring you something,' he said, ringing the brass bell on her bedside table. 'Would you like me to brush your hair and plait it for you?'

Augusta smiled. 'Yes please, dearest.' How kind he was to her. She did love him, truly she did. If only he would stop wanting to be so warm with her. Augusta's mind slid away from the word intimate. Mama had said it was her duty to bear her husband's 'invasions', for without them there would be no children. Now that they had their boys, couldn't she somehow do her duty in some other way?

'Take the jug away, Mildred, and bring Madam up some more barley water, if you please.' Obadiah turned the covers down and helped her to the chair by the dressing table.

Augusta closed her eyes, soothed by the lulling rhythm of the brush. He took up the comb and divided her hair into three sections.

'I don't like being ill,' she said. 'It's hot and tedious and lonely.'

Obadiah smiled ruefully. 'Gussie, it won't be for long. Think how much you'll appreciate being well again. After the boys have visited I shall read to you. What would you like to hear? There's *Nicholas Nickleby* or *Jane Eyre*.' He picked up a green ribbon and holding the end of the plait in his teeth secured it in a tight bow.

'I've read *Jane Eyre* already, but I did love it.'

'That's what it shall be,' said Obi, smiling at her. 'I'll just pin this hair up away from your neck. There now, that should be considerably cooler.'

'Oh, thank you, my love.' She kissed him on the cheek and stood by the bedside as he plumped up the pillows and smoothed the sheets.

A tapping on the door and an excited rattling of the handle interrupted any further conversation.

'Come in,' called Augusta.

Nanny Hobbs stood in the doorway with Albert in her arms and Samuel clutching at her skirt. 'Good evening, Madam,' she said, nodding her head and making the strings on her cap jiggle about. 'How are you? Fit to see your young gentlemen?'

'Mummy,' implored Albert, holding out his arms to her.

'A little better,' she sighed. 'Yes darling, Nanny will sit you on the bed beside me. But you must be quiet as a mouse.'

While Nanny was settling Albert beside her Samuel launched himself at his father.

'Nanny,' said Obadiah, 'you can get Mildred to bring up Madam's supper and come and fetch the children again in half an hour.'

With another jiggling of her ribbons Nanny Hobbs closed the door.

Albert nestled against her shoulder and began sucking his thumb.

'Saw the big ships, Papa,' said Samuel, tugging at his father's sleeve. 'Lots and lots of sailors. One sailor had a parrot in a cage and 'nother one had a monkey with a collar.'

'Did you, my man,' said his father, 'and would you like to be a sailor?'

'I want to be the captain with lots of gold on my hat and a big telescope,' declared his son.

Obadiah smiled at him. He seemed to have grown in the last two weeks since being ill. All that was needed was some sunshine to put some colour in his cheeks.

'Soddgers,' contributed Albert. 'Soddger fall down.'

'And why did the soldier fall down, my pet?' asked Augusta, drawing him into her arms.

'Nanny said he was very thirsty,' said Samuel. 'Then some more soldiers came and said, "The silly young bugger's soused", and carried him away.'

'I think we should hear more about the sailors,' Augusta said hurriedly.

Obadiah had turned away to hide his amusement from his little son, but Augusta knew he was laughing by the shaking of his shoulders.

'Do you know what Papa found yesterday?'

The boys were all attention.

'A pirate?'

''Nother soddger?' offered Albert.

'Neither a soldier nor a pirate. It was a little girl washed up on the beach in a broken boat. She was wrapped up in a bundle and tucked in a sailor's jacket.'

'Was he her papa?' asked Samuel.

'I don't know,' said Obadiah. 'The sailor has gone to live with Jesus.'

'What has happened to the child?' asked Augusta, mildly curious.

'A mere babe of three months or so. She has gone to a woman who has recently lost her own child. Hopefully she will form an attachment to the little one.'

'P'r'aps she's a mermaid,' ventured Samuel. 'Did she have a tail?'

Obadiah laughed as he lifted his son on to a chair beside him. 'No, she is not a mermaid, though she came to us from the sea.' He turned to his wife. 'I almost brought her home with me. Would have done certainly had it not been for the boys having measles.'

'Why?' asked Augusta greatly alarmed. 'Why would you think of such a thing, Obi?'

'Because she was a foundling,' he answered simply, 'in need of a home and a family.'

She felt a great surge of anger. 'You have a family, Obi: a wife and two little boys. There is no need to drag in strays from the seashore.'

'Have you no pity, Augusta?'

The use of her full name made her turn and look at him. Rarely did he call her Augusta and when he did she knew that she had overstepped some invisible line between them.

Why did he have to care so much for these sick, hopeless

people? They were always knocking on the door or sidling up to him outside church. Why couldn't he take a room somewhere else for his surgery and dispensary?

'Of course I have pity,' she retorted. 'But where would you stop? Every week there are babies found neglected or children orphaned.'

'Come along, Samuel and Albert. Let Papa take you back to Nanny,' he said, 'Mama is tired.'

'Good night, my precious,' said Augusta, kissing Samuel and ruffling his hair.

He left her with no regrets. Already he had become his father's child.

'Tiss, Mummy,' insisted Albert.

Augusta held out her arms. 'Sleep tight, my lambkin,' she murmured into his neck.

'Night, night,' murmured Albert, giving her a wet open-mouthed kiss.

She smiled at him. What a beautiful child he was with his light brown curls and large grey eyes. Soon he would grow up and leave his baby dresses and curls behind like his brother. 'Take Samuel and come back for Albert,' she said to her husband. 'He needs more time with me.'

'Very well,' said Obadiah.

'Thank you, dearest,' said Augusta, watching his face. She hated it when he withdrew from her. Even anger would be better than this weary defeat.

'Will you read to me later?' she asked.

'We'll see,' he said. 'I will send Mildred with your supper, she can take Albert back to the nursery.'

The door closed behind him.

Albert snuggled up beside his mother and slipped his thumb

into his mouth. She stroked his cheek. His eyes closed and in seconds he was fast asleep.

Augusta sighed. She was hurt by Obadiah's implied criticism. Of course she felt pity for the baby on the beach, but that was a world away from wanting to take the child into her family.

Chapter Six

For six weeks now the babe had been with her. Six weeks on the workhouse register as a foundling child on non-resident poor relief. Ruth had deliberately not spoken the name that Mrs Norris had given the child. There had been no petting and smiling, no opportunity for the little one to charm her way into her heart. But on the other hand there had been no neglect. The infant had been fed and made dry and comfortable whenever her cries required it. She would be glad, yes glad Ruth told herself, to be free of the obligation.

Without the babe to suckle, her milk would have dried up and she would have gone to Hay Street and got some sewing from the corset makers. In the last couple of weeks she had begun to feel better, to move away from the sofa and notice how drab and unkempt the room had become. She would brighten it up, hem those curtains that Mrs Norris had given her. They were too long for the windows but she could make a cushion cover from the excess cloth.

The babe began to cry – a monotonous wail that Ruth

knew was not from hunger or discomfort. Was it sadness? she wondered. Did this child grieve for her mother as she grieved for Sarah? No, she could not afford sympathy. If she ignored her crying it would pass. Earlier she had set the crib in the yard by the lavender bush. The movement of the stems in the breeze seemed to interest the babe, who waved her hands at them and watched their tossing back and forth. Not that she had any interest in pleasing the child.

No, she would not attend to her. Once the infant was gone she would write to Jacob and tell him that she was well again. With the babe in the house and Mrs Norris calling every day, Ruth had not felt settled enough to put her thoughts on paper. It was Jacob who had taught her to read and write. He had been so patient with her stumbling efforts and as thrilled as she was when gradually the black marks on the page had begun to have sense and meaning. It had been her greatest pride when she signed her new name in full on her marriage certificate – Ruth Mary Salter. Her mother and father had each scratched a cross in the space for their names, along with Jacob's parents. It was a sergeant in the Marines who had given Jacob book learning. But in order to write to him there needed to be absolute peace and quiet. It took her many false attempts before she could form the words correctly and she had a little notebook in which were written words that Jacob thought might create difficulties. In spite of herself Ruth looked out into the garden. The crying had stopped and the babe was still.

She picked up the basket of clean washing and took a bowl of water and began to damp down the sheets ready for ironing. As she took the block out of the fire and set it in the iron she felt almost well again. The heat from the metal transferred itself to the cotton sheet and the scent of lavender rose up around her like a blessing, giving her hope. Perhaps she would be well again and happy. Jacob was right, she was only a young girl, with most of her life still to live. They had talked of her going to join him in India but her pregnancy had changed their plans. Maybe next year she could go out on the troopship to join him. Other wives would be going, there would be no lack of company. Ruth folded the sheet and smoothed the other side. But what about Sarah? Who would put flowers on her grave? Kind as Mrs Norris had been at Sarah's birth she could hardly be expected to take on the task. If Ruth went out to India her daughter would lie cold and forgotten. She dried the sudden tears on the sleeve of her dress.

How long would it be before she had another letter from Jacob? She had been so comforted by the letter he'd managed to post from Gibraltar. Again she took it from the pocket of her apron.

My own dear Ruth,

How desperate and sad I was to have to leave you in your sorrow. If it had not been for the fear of being clapped in irons for desertion I would have let the army go to the devil.

Bear up my love. Our Sarah will never be forgot. She has a firm place in my heart along with her mother. I will write more from Calcutta.

I am writing in haste to tell you that you are ever in my thoughts.

Best Love

Your Jacob

Ruth sighed. With the three months it took to reach Calcutta she would be lucky to get another letter before Christmas. She wondered if Jacob was busy writing letters for any of the other soldiers or sailors aboard the *Eastern Monarch*. They had decided that if he wrote their letters the other men would likely give him a halfpenny for his trouble. These he would save and when he came home from India they would look for rooms to rent in a street away from a tavern. They had not fully realised when they took the rooms in Golden Lion Lane how rowdy it was, in spite of having St Thomas's graveyard nearby. The lane was always swarming with soldiers and sailors ashore for the night. In a room upstairs was a young girl hardly more than sixteen, living on her own, pretty but starved-looking. How did she manage for food? Ruth had wondered, until one night she had seen her in the back alley with a sailor, her dress all torn. Another time she'd been begging for fish heads from the men at the Camber. How could she condemn the woman? It was had enough surviving on a private soldier's pay. Without a husband it must be a nightmare keeping her head above water.

Putting Jacob's letter back in her pocket she decided to go to the churchyard later and take a bunch of marigolds for Sarah's grave. First she would eat up the remains of the soused herring and the egg custard Mrs Norris had brought over yesterday. As she was folding away the ironing blanket, a sudden scream alerted her to the baby out in the yard.

The cries intensified. Ruth slammed the iron down in the grate and ran out of the kitchen. As she bent to pick up the screaming infant a bee flew out of the crib. With trembling fingers she examined the baby and found a pink swelling on its

47

hand. In that moment it was as if she too felt the hot stab of the sting in her own hand. Holding the baby tightly in her arms she rushed back into the house. 'Oh, don't cry, don't cry, my pet,' she urged as tears ran down her own cheeks. The infant was red-faced and hysterical. Swinging her onto her hip Ruth searched her work basket for a needle and, pinching the flesh of the baby's hand between her fingers she managed to probe the sting to the surface. Still the child screamed. With heart thumping in panic she found an onion on the floor in the scullery and sliced it in half before rubbing the cut surface across the tiny wound.

Again she gathered the baby up into her arms, resting her hot wet face against her own. 'I'm sorry, I'm sorry,' she sobbed as she paced about the room. Every now and again she stopped to kiss her face. 'Beattie, Beattie, please, please stop.' That cry had unlocked something within her. For the first time she was mindful of the child's loss as well as her own. Back and forth, back and forth, half whispering, half singing she went until the crying ceased. Sinking down into the old sofa by the window Ruth settled Beattie on her lap, unbuttoned her dress and gave her the breast. The little girl gazed up at her as she suckled, the tears still wet on her cheeks. Her eyes continued to watch her as she fed.

Ruth looked down at the child. 'What are we going to do, you and me?' she said. 'How are we going to mend ourselves?'

Beattie turned her head away from the breast and studied her face intently.

Ruth looked at her with equal intensity. There were, she realised, minute changes in the child. Her eyes had darkened to a shade somewhere between grey and brown. Her face was now rounder and rosier. In spite of herself she had enabled the little girl to live and thrive. 'Hello, Beattie,' she said smiling down at her.

They continued to look at each other for some moments and then Beattie's lips curved upwards in a returning smile.

Chapter Seven

'Margaret Sankey is my name,' said the tall woman in the plaid shawl and frilled bonnet. 'Good afternoon to you all.'

Dr Pragnell and the other members of the Mariners' Orphanage Committee awoke from their lethargy. This astonishing figure was their last candidate for the post of matron.

Without waiting to be invited, the woman sat down and smiled at everyone. 'I am glad to be here,' she said.

She was a raw-boned, oddly dressed woman, but her smile exuded confidence. The large army boots peeping from beneath her long black dress fascinated Obadiah. For the first time that stifling August afternoon he had found a candidate that he would willingly endorse.

'The children have shown you around, Miss Sankey?' said the secretary, a thin, tired ex-naval officer. 'As you will have seen we have a large, well-run establishment.'

'Large, certainly,' said Margaret Sankey.

The secretary was startled by the woman's combative tone. 'And what was your impression of the children?'

'Too docile and well behaved,' was her blunt reply. 'They

will have to make their way in the world with very little assistance. What they need is spirit and properly fitting footwear.'

No one was dozing now.

Two of the committee ladies' lips were pursed in disapproval.

Miss Sankey, without any invitation, got to her feet and went over to the tea trolley and helped herself to a cup, heaping in the sugar and stirring the tea vigorously.

Obadiah smiled as he looked at those large boots reflected in the polished floorboards. She is no fool, he thought, warming to her championing of the children.

'What changes would you want to make here, should you be given the post of matron, Miss Sankey?' he asked.

'I would hope to change the name from "The Mariners' Orphanage", to "The Mariners' Home for Children". I want my charges to find sanctuary here – to have a sense of belonging and loyalty to each other. They need to develop their talents and to learn to laugh. They've had a deal of sadness in their lives, a pinch of fun would not be out of place.'

Obadiah wanted to stand up and cheer.

'What fits you for the position, Miss Sankey?' demanded one of the ladies.

The committee waited impatiently for a reply while Miss Sankey finished her tea and returned the cup to the trolley. 'I know what it is like to be an orphan,' she said. 'The cold, sanctimonious charity, the lack of kindness, the stigma of bastardy.'

The lady who had asked the question blushed angrily under Miss Sankey's gaze.

'But perhaps, you were thinking of my medical credentials?'

'Of course,' said the lady, greatly discomfited.

'I have lately returned from the Crimea where I was nursing at the Balaclava hospital.'

'You met Miss Nightingale?' asked another committee lady, eagerly.

'No,' said Miss Sankey. 'As I said, I was at Balaclava where the survival rate among our soldiers was infinitely better than at Scutari. My nursing superior was a Mrs Elizabeth Davis.'

Obadiah frowned. If Miss Sankey wasn't careful she would thoroughly antagonise her future employers. Florence Nightingale was the heroine beyond criticism among the committee.

'Could you give us an impression of your life in the Crimea?' he asked.

'Waking and dragging on our clothes, snatching something to eat before going on to the wards. We worked from dawn to dusk scrubbing floors, cooking, catching rats, dressing wounds, holding down a soldier while the surgeon sawed off his leg, changing soiled linen, washing the dead and writing letters home. I think that caring for your children will hold no terrors for me.'

'You realise that you will be responsible for the children's spiritual as well physical welfare?' asked the chaplain. 'They are taken to church twice each Sunday and we expect the matron to take prayers with them each day.'

Obadiah caught her eye and tried to signal to her the importance of her reply.

'I shall try to demonstrate to them the love of God, certainly,' she said, quietly.

'What about your needlework skills?' asked a thin sour

woman who had not spoken before. 'The girls will need to know how to sew before they go into service.'

'Well, there you have me,' laughed Miss Sankey. 'However, I know you have a school here and, I am sure, a capable teacher of sewing. Looking at the quality of the embroidery on your blouse I am sure you would give her some valuable assistance.'

'Well, I don't know whether I have the time.'

'Purse-string charity is so much easier, isn't it?' said Margaret Sankey. 'It avoids human contact. Getting involved face to face with the poor is a different matter entirely.'

The thin woman gave Miss Sankey a look of undisguised hatred.

Unperturbed, the prospective matron turned to the secretary. 'Will you tell me what my salary will be and is there a trial period?'

He scanned his ledger, spread out on the long oak table. 'You will receive £20 a year and will be here on a three-month probationary period. Of course, you will have a home with us, a bedroom and your own sitting room and we require you to wear a uniform.'

'That seems quite satisfactory to me,' said Miss Sankey. 'Uniforms are useful, I find. One doesn't have to waste time deciding what to wear. Well,' she said, getting to her feet. 'I have brought such possessions as I have and will start immediately if that meets with your approval?'

'Don't you want to see your quarters first?' asked the secretary.

'My needs are simple and I have made a home for myself in far less appealing surroundings.'

'Miss Sankey,' snapped the sour embroideress, 'you may

well have decided to take the position advertised here, but we have not yet decided whether we wish to offer it to you.'

'I take that you have checked my references from Lord Shaftesbury and Sir Edwin Chadwick?' asked Margaret Sankey smoothly.

The committee looked at one another askance. They had received no such testimonials, but if Miss Sankey was so well connected how could they fail to employ her?

'May I show you out into the garden?' Obadiah said, getting to his feet.

Together they walked down the corridor.

'Soap, cooked cabbage and furniture polish,' said Nurse Sankey sniffing. 'The typical institution smell and that other indefinable odour.'

'What is that?' he asked.

'Unhappiness,' she said.

Obadiah nodded. 'This institution badly needs some fresh air blown through it,' he said quietly.

'Oh, I shall be a veritable tempest, Doctor Pragnell, have no fear,' said Miss Sankey.

'I was surprised to hear of your illustrious supporters,' Obadiah said dryly.

'So was I, Doctor,' she replied chuckling to herself. 'I was driven into a corner. When in difficulty I feel that the big lie is called for, don't you?'

'I have never thought so before,' he said, smiling at her and feeling, suddenly, light-hearted.

'We could, I think, make a profitable exchange. I will give you a scruple of daring and you can give me in return a dram of caution.'

'We will debate the matter when I return with the committee's decision,' said Obadiah.

'I suppose I should send my champion into the lists with a ribbon tied on his sword,' said Miss Sankey, teasingly.

'I should love to hear of your Crimean experiences and your opinion of the Sanitary Commission. That will suffice.'

'That you shall have in full, but please go back into the lists. I have at present no home and little money. I am anxious to know before nightfall whether I shall have a roof over my head.'

'I think she is a most unsuitable woman,' one of the ladies was saying as Obadiah went back into the dining room.

'She comes to us highly recommended,' he said, amazed at his own duplicity, 'and the fact that she is prepared to commence her duties immediately is a great advantage. It means that we can turn our minds to other matters such as the autumn sale of work.'

'Are we ready to take a vote?' asked the secretary.

'I am somewhat dubious about her spiritual standing and influence over young minds,' grumbled the chaplain.

'A bit of a battler,' said the secretary. 'I like that.'

'Miss Sankey will have three months in which to demonstrate her suitability. Long enough for her shortcomings to have become evident as well as her virtues.' Obadiah got up and made to pick up his bag. 'I have patients to see and I would appreciate us taking a vote now. A show of hands will suffice, surely,' he suggested.

'I'm not at all sure,' sighed one of the ladies.

'Perhaps you could take a turn of duty here, while we wait for someone better to appear,' said Obadiah, greatly daring.

'I seem to be a voice in the wilderness,' she snapped.

'We must observe the proper procedure,' said the secretary, fussily distributing voting slips.

Obadiah fumed. The two old harpies, as he had secretly named them, fidgeted in their handbags for pencils. Couldn't they see the woman's qualities: humour, courage and common sense?

'Eleven to one, I think that is a most satisfactory result,' said the secretary, entering the votes laboriously in his ledger. 'Dr Pragnell, could you ask Miss Sankey to come back in, please?'

He found her sat on a tree stump near the vegetable plots, eating peas from a pod she had just picked and deep in conversation with one of the boys.

'They want you to come back in, Miss Sankey,' he said, 'so that they can congratulate you.'

Margaret Sankey burst out laughing. 'I must have been the best of a very bad lot for those old crones to have voted for me.' She stood up and thrust out her hand. 'I thank you, Doctor, very much.'

They shook hands. Obadiah looked up into her face, at her large nose and nutcracker jaw so very like a picture book representation of a witch. He smiled into her fine brown eyes and felt that he had met an ally. 'My name is Obadiah,' he said.

'Margaret,' she said. 'I think we shall be firm friends.'

Still smiling to himself, Obadiah walked out into the yard.

'I like your 'orse, Doctor. Wouldn't 'alf like a ride with 'im,' said a young boy.

'Good gracious, it's Freddy. You've shot up like a beanpole. Like horses, do you?'

'Not 'arf,' said the whey-faced boy who was wearing a jacket far too small for him.

'How old are you, now?'

'I'm nearly nine, Doctor. Can I give her that pear under the tree, over there?'

'Certainly you may, Freddy. That's it, hold your hand out flat.'

The little grey pony snaffled the pear from the boy's outstretched hand. He smiled at her. 'Ain't she gentle. You gotta good'n there.'

Obadiah smiled.

Freddy looked over to where the new matron had been standing. 'Who was that funny looking woman, scoffing the peas? Cripes, Doctor, she weren't half ugly.'

'Well now, Freddy, I think you are in for a surprise,' said Obadiah, stepping into the trap, and taking the reins.

Chapter Eight

May 29 1857

Dearest Jacob,
Almost a year to the day since you went off and what a
long weary time it do seem. I am famished for a letter. Your
tale of the voyage put fear in my heart what with the ship
rolling, your sickness and the poor wife what broke her arm
with falling about. Fancy them poor women stuck down out
of the way of good fresh air for days on end. Do not make
me want to make the journey but if you are there to meet me
s'pose I would risk all, dear husband.
But now Jacob I have news that will maze you.

Ruth could imagine Jacob seated on his bed in some stifling
barracks scratching his head in wonderment at what she was to
tell him. But she was certain in her mind of what she wanted
and the sooner he knew her plans the better.

You know I told you of the infant what the doctor and Anne
Norris palmed off on me before ever our Sarah be cold in the

*ground? A mirrakle have happened. The little one was stung
by a bee and her cries so pitiful they melted somethin' in me
and now I love her like my own. Her name is Beattie and
she is a very taking child. She do smile and chuckle now and
have me winded round her finger. I think she puts me in
mind of your brother's child having a mop of black hair strait
as pump water and great dark eyes. Nothin is nown of the
sailor who she was found with or where they came from.
And no enkwirees have been made for little Beattie. Jacob
could you think to us taking this babe and making her our
own. She have brought such happiness to me and would
make the time that we are parted from each other so much
easier to bear. If you are in agreement I am wanting her
chrissend Beatriss Sarah so that our dear baby won't never be
forgot.*

Please write as soon as you can to tell me what you think.

Ruth turned to look at Beattie, seated in the laundry basket,
shaking a bunch of bobbins in her chubby fist. The child looked
up at her and smiled. How pretty she was with her rosy cheeks
and big dark eyes. Surely Jacob would love her, wouldn't he?
Ruth again took up her pen.

*I hope you are keeping well and not too fagged with the great
heat of India.*

Do be shore to wear the kidney belt what I made you.
You must keep well my darlin as you are all the world to me.
All my best love,
Your Ruth.
*P.S. I am most faithful in taking flowers to our dear
Sarah.*

Ruth sealed the letter in its envelope and stuck on a penny stamp. 'When we go out, my lamb, we'll post a letter to your daddy,' she said. Beattie continued to shake the bone bobbins on their thread of string. Not for the first time Ruth wondered how old she was and where she had come from. If Dr Pragnell's estimate was correct, when he first brought her from the beach, Beattie must now be at least fifteen months old.

'You must have a birthday, lambkin,' she said. Why not the same as her Jacob on 10 January. That would bind them together. She wondered about a certificate of some kind to say that the babe was their child, come what may. Well, she would be seeing Anne Norris today and her Thomas would be sure to know about such things.

'Mumma, Mumma,' Beattie cried, holding out her arms to be picked up.

Ruth swept her up onto her lap, untied the ribbons on her dress and fed her.

'Gracious me, you're not still nursing her after all this time,' Anne Norris had exclaimed when last she saw Ruth with Beattie at the breast. 'She'll have to bid goodbye to the titties now she be a little maid. Besides, it'll likely sap your strength.'

'It do soothe her so,' Ruth had said, 'gets her off to sleep like magic. In the morning while she's feeding I sit there gathering myself together, sorting what I'm going to do with the day.'

'Precious moments, I'll not deny,' Anne had said. 'I used to cuddle little May to me and think the world with all its fripperies and enchantments well lost. Didn't envy the Queen of England with all her golden sovereigns.'

Ruth smiled down at Beattie. How she loved the child. She leaned over behind her and tugged the curtain aside. The early sun and the smell of the sea poured through the window. Soon, next door at the Golden Lion, there would be the thumping of beer kegs, the stamping and neighing of horses at the stable and the yelping of the publican's dogs, but at this moment she and the child had the July morning to themselves.

'Mumma, Mumma, tuddle,' she murmured turning away from Ruth's breast and slipping her arms around her neck.

'My little daughter.' There, she had said it! Ruth kissed Beattie's neck and twisted a tendril of hair around her finger. She so hoped Jacob would consent to her proposal. 'Lots to do today,' said Ruth, tidying her dress. 'We're going round to see Auntie Anne and little May.'

Beattie laughed and clapped her hands. May was a favourite of hers.

'Yes, we must get washed and in the rig of the day. Mumma must take those stays what she have finished around to Hay Street and then we'll see our friends, my pet.'

Ruth set Beattie down again in the basket with a fistful of spoons. She was shaking her mat at the front door when the postman approached with a letter in his hand.

'Mrs Salter, good morning. You've been waiting for this many a day, I'll be bound,' he said, handing her a longed-for letter.

'Oh! Bless you, bless you,' Ruth cried, a great surge of joy welling up in her as she snatched the envelope from the postman's hand. 'And I have one for you. I won't be but a moment.'

'Quickly now, Mrs Salter, I can see the old dames along at number fifteen a peering out the casements at us. We'll be grist for their gossip if I don't look sharp.'

She set the letter in her apron pocket, sped into the kitchen and snatched up her letter to Jacob and rushed out into the lane again.

'Thank you for your kindness,' she said, handing over the envelope.

The postman smiled. ''Tis all smiles I get when I bring glad tidings and scowls when Jack or Tom are tardy with their love.'

Ruth hurried back into the house alerted by Beattie's loud cries of pain. She found her with a red mark on her nose and a tablespoon flung across the room. 'What a silly thing you are,' she cooed. 'Spoons is for eating, *shh* now, Mumma get you a little bowl of stewed apple. Come on, my darling, let's dry your tears. We're going to have such a day of rejoicing. Mumma's got a letter and we're taking tea with your friend May.'

Beattie rewarded Ruth's efforts with a watery smile and allowed herself to be set down once more in the basket and fed some pudding. She was then cajoled into shaking a box with dried peas in it, while Ruth settled to her letter.

Cawnpore January 31st 1857

My Dearest Ruth,

 How thankful I was to get your letter, and to know that you are feeling better and not so terrible sad. We shall never forget our little maid, but, we must trust in the Lord to help us.

Ruth sighed. She wishes she had Jacob's firm faith in God. Her belief was like a flickering candle and easily blown out.

You asked me to tell you what India is like. My Ruthie it is more than my poor powers of telling. I think it best to start at the Hooghly River that carried us up to Calcutta. My

*sergeant was telling us that it is very dangerous with shifting
shoals and sandbanks, the worst one is called the James and
Mary where many boats have been sucked down and the
passengers never seen again.*

Ruth shivered and tucked her shawl more tightly around
her shoulders.

*But the banks were full of bright flowers that I couldn't give
a name to. I got my first sight of coconut, date and banana
trees with the fruit hanging in the branches. And then we
docked safely in Calcutta.*

*Oh my Ruthie, I wish you had been there with me. I
was breathless with the wonder of it all. There are great
numbers of people here, with faces of every shade from almost
ebony to ivory whiteness. As you pass them there is a great
babble of words that sound like nothing you've ever heard
before. The women here have clothes, of such a dazzle of
different colours and then, on the market stalls, comes
another dazzle with green and yellow orange and purple
fruits and vegetables. Hanging over all this is a smell that is
made up of all of us people sweating in the heat, the stench
of rotting stalks and leaves from the stalls, strange spices from
cooking pots and women's perfumes and flowers.*

*Everything is different and though I have always liked
seeing new places how I do long to see Portsmouth again and
you standing at the door in Golden Lion Lane. I would give
up all my adventures to hold you close and see you smile.*

Reluctantly Ruth folded up the letter and put it among all
the others in the wooden box Jacob had made for her. Only

four years and yet she could but dimly remember her time before he came into her life. The boredom of that tiny cottage she had shared with her mother, brothers and sisters near Colchester. Her bullying, red-faced, farm labourer father and the endless scrimping and scraping, the hunger and the cold. How good Jacob had been to them all, helping her parents with money for new clothes for the wedding and mending a broken window. With what thanks? she thought bitterly.

'Mumma, Mumma.' Beattie held out her hands to be picked up.

'We must hurry, my little lamb, if we're to be at the Norrises by twelve. Mumma will just riddle the fire and set the kettle to boil then we must set things straight, wash the pots and tidy ourselves.'

Ruth looked around her. Everything was patched and makeshift. The two wooden chairs didn't match and the table had a rickety leg. In spite of the hours spent hemming Anne's yellow curtains and making the cushions the room looked what it was, a private soldier's temporary lodging. Would she ever have furniture of her own, she wondered, or pictures on the wall? Anne had promised to show her how to sew a sampler in coloured wool and to make over some of her May's frocks for Beattie. Oh, everything was better, so very much better than last year. Ruth picked a bunch of lavender from the yard and tied it up with a pink ribbon she'd found in the lane.

The sun was hot on her face and she put Beattie down every so often to walk a few steps. After crossing the High Street, she paused. The pain in her chest which had awoken her that morning had returned. Could it have been the raw onion she had eaten the night before? Was that the cause of her discomfort? Again she set Beattie back on the pavement and turned into White Hart Row, where her friend was waving to her from the doorway.

'Morning Ruth, my word, you look so bonny in that shawl and bonnet. Come in, come in,' said Anne Norris, 'and you, little maid. Let's carry you out to May, she's made a dolly for you.'

'What a lovely smell, what you been cooking, Anne?' gasped Ruth. 'It do make my mouth water.'

'Stewed rabbit and pot herbs. I must remember to plate up a dinner for Thomas; he's gone over to Cosham to see his old father. Sit down now the girls are busy in the yard. I'm bursting with news.'

Ruth looked at her friend's face flushed with more than the heat of the fire. 'Oh, Anne,' she said, 'tell me quick, I can tell it's something joyful.'

'I am to have a child.'

'Oh! I'm that pleased for you,' said Ruth, her pain instantly forgotten. She got up from the chair and threw her arms around her friend. 'What do Thomas say? He must be like a dog with two tails.'

'I've yet to tell him,' said Anne, 'and May, of course.'

'She'll be that excited,' laughed Ruth. 'Look how she do make a pet of my Beattie.'

'Please, Ruth, keep it all to yourself. I'm going to tell them both tonight.'

'Of course, Anne, I shan't breathe a word.'

'Here, was my ears deceiving me or did you say "my Beattie"? When did you make her yours? Months and months you been going to take her up the workhouse.'

Ruth blushed. 'I think you knew that soon as you put her

in my lap last year when I was so broken-hearted. Knew as I'd come to love her, didn't you?'

'Well, I nearly wore out my knees with praying for it to be so, Ruth. Your sadness cut me so, reminding me of my own little babe, my Andrew. Have you wrote to Jacob and told him your plans?'

'I gave it to the postman just this morning. I shall be in a fever waiting for his answer.'

'You can't doubt but that he'll say yes? He do worship you, you know that.'

'But p'r'aps he won't want a foundling child. P'r'aps he will only want a child of his own. 'Twould only be natural and he's never set eyes on little Beattie. He's not come to love her like I do.'

Anne chuckled. 'You can have the best of both worlds. I'm sure when Jacob do come down the gangplank and set eyes on the maid he'll be proud as any natural father. And the pair of you can make another baby to keep Beattie company, with no hesitating.'

Blushing, Ruth put her arms around her. How good she had been to her, almost a mother in her kindness. 'Anne, I don't know what I would do without you,' she said.

'You been a true friend to me,' said Anne, 'listening to all my troubles. It do cut both ways.'

'Come and look quick,' called May from the yard, her face flushed with excitement.

Ruth and Anne stepped outside into the June sunshine. Beattie was sat on a knitted blanket holding a rag doll around the neck and kissing its face with great fervour.

'I never did think she'd be so taken,' laughed May delightedly.

'It's a lovely doll,' said Ruth, slipping her arm around May's slim waist. 'That great mass of black hair just like little Beattie's and those little rosebud lips. She'll love it to death.'

'I do so care for her,' said May, twisting her apron in her hands.

'And she do love you too,' said Ruth. 'This morning I said we're going to see May, and her little face lit up like a candle.'

'Come on, you two, the dinner's spoiling. May, fetch that blanket. Baby can sit on the floor while we eat. Ruth, sit yourself down. Here you are, take a sip of this blackcurrant cordial what I put by last year.'

The rabbit stew and potatoes were rich in flavour and Ruth felt her pain ease away. May washed the pots while she and Anne sat in the yard laughing and talking.

'We'd best get in out of the sun,' said Anne, tapping her on the shoulder. 'You look like a lobster, my dear. Must have been that wine; you've been asleep for the last hour or so.'

Ruth got to her feet and had to sit down again, feeling sick and dizzy. She smiled at her friend's concern. 'Got up too soon,' she said. 'Be right as rain in a minute.'

Anne fetched a glass of water and she began to cool down. Half an hour later she was ready to set off home.

'I'll likely not see you till next week,' Anne said as she kissed her goodbye. 'Thomas is bringing his father up from Cosham to stay a few days. If I find that bit of green cloth we was speaking of I'll send May along with it.'

'I have enjoyed myself, Anne, and so have Beattie. That little dolly will be her treasure,' Ruth said and was rewarded by May's happy smile.

Beattie was tired and fell asleep in her arms. By the time she stopped to fit the key in the lock, Ruth too was exhausted.

Carefully she stepped inside and slid Beattie onto the bed and lay down beside her. The pain returned, making her gasp. Tomorrow she would call on Dr Pragnell and see if he could give her some pills. Perhaps he could advise her about a certificate for Beattie.

Getting the child washed and ready for bed that evening took all her strength. She abandoned the idea of sewing and decided to have an early night. At eight o'clock Ruth fell into an uneasy sleep. Early in the morning she was awoken by another fiercer pain in her chest. With difficulty she sat up and looked about her. Beattie was fast asleep. Breathing carefully, Ruth pushed her hands down on the bed and tried to push herself up onto her feet. Gasping, she lay down again. What could she do? Ruth began to feel frightened. She was alone with a dependent child. Perhaps if she lay completely still, in time the pain would go away. Beattie rolled over towards her and Ruth took her hand in hers. The contact comforted her. She closed her eyes and gritted her teeth as the pain clutched at her chest. 'Aaaaahhh!!!' she gasped and pulled her hand from her daughter's grasp.

Chapter Nine

Augusta picked up the fat cream envelope from the hall table. She recognised Mama's large decisive handwriting and prepared herself for what Obadiah called 'a sermon from the Memsahib'.

Augusta laughed. Nothing could spoil her day. She had just returned with the boys from taking tea with Major Spooner's wife in Lombard Street. Samuel had delighted the major with his questions about swords and soldiers, while Albert had smiled shyly at Lavinia Spooner and by the end of the visit was sitting contentedly on her lap.

'They were angels, Nanny, and all credit to you,' she said as she stepped from the carriage and gave the children back into her care.

Nanny Hobbs glowed. 'Thank you, Madam, I'll take them up for their baths.'

'I'll see you boys at bedtime,' Augusta said, as they trooped up the stairs. After taking off her jacket she settled herself in the sitting room to read her letter.

Cawnpore   February 28th 1857

My Darling Daughter,
    How I rejoiced to receive the book of sketches from you,
especially the drawing of Samuel and Albert – what splendid
little fellows. By the time your father and I return to
England they will be young gentlemen.
    Poor Damaris Mowbray is quite distraught after sending
her son off to boarding school at Sherbourne. That would
have been a decision for you to face had you married
Sheridan Franklin.

Augusta's heart lurched uncomfortably at the mention of
Sheridan. How handsome he'd been in his Hussar's uniform,
and so attentive to her. She remembered sitting in the palm
room with him, eating raspberry water ices, while the music
from the ballroom drifted across the lawn. He had set down
their sundae glasses, shut the glass door and drawn her deeper
into the room. It had been frightfully hot and she had felt giddy
with excitement. And then he had been horrid to her: kissing
her roughly, thrusting his tongue into her mouth and pinching her breasts. She had struck him across the face with her
parasol and he had been furious.

'You stupid little virgin,' he'd hissed at her, snapping the
parasol over his knee and striding away, leaving her alone and
in tears.

Mama had been ecstatic when the invitation had come for
her to attend the spring ball at Test Manor, high on the hill
above Romsey. Sheridan's father, a brigadier, had been with
Wellington at Waterloo and was a hero to everyone. The
family served as the local gentry for lack of anyone else. Mrs
Franklin was gracious, in a faded genteel way, and a complete

contrast to her roistering menfolk. Augusta sighed. Mama's ambitions had run away with her. She had had her daughter married at the abbey and settled in Test Manor with a brood of children, all on the strength of that invitation card.

Papa had been less enthusiastic. 'Oh, yes, Sheridan,' he'd said. 'An impatient fellow, with a streak of cruelty in him; there was talk of having a horse put down, after he'd ridden it to exhaustion.' He had looked at Mama. 'It's not a hap'orth of good you shaking your head, Gwendoline. Seeing how a man treats his animals is a pretty accurate measure of how he'll treat people.'

They had left the party early. The three of them sat in the carriage in silence, Augusta in tears, Mama furious and Papa thoughtful.

But he had warmed to Obadiah from the first. Augusta, not wanting to go to India, had clung to him. Her father had been impressed at how hard Obadiah had had to struggle to set himself up in practice in Portsea. Managing on not much more than bread and water to start with, letting out a room to an old soldier so that he would have someone to answer the door to his patients and be there when he was out on calls. He'd even started without a carriage. They had laughed as he told them of almost being driven to putting a banana skin outside his front door in the hope of a rich woman tripping on it and needing his services.

Mama had smothered her outrage at throwing her daughter away on a penniless medical man, after her husband had spoken to her in a tone he had never used before.

'Gwendoline, the boy has a good heart and I am convinced that he will take great care of Augusta. I am only concerned that she will be a credit to him. She has a lot to learn about people. You have filled her head with nonsense. Obadiah is a gentleman, in the true sense of the word.'

Was she a credit to her husband? Augusta chewed her bottom lip thoughtfully. Sometimes she could be quite gracious to his patients: take their messages or hand them their medicines with something very like kindly interest. On other occasions, she was bored or disdainful.

Did she love him? Augusta fidgeted with the braid along the edge of her little nursing chair. Sometimes she felt a great surge of tenderness when she thought of him. How kind he was to her, so concerned for her happiness, so gentle with her. He told wonderful stories and could make her laugh with his imitations of his patients: the gruff old lance-corporal and the admiral's wife who reduced her husband to a jelly with her rages. Obadiah was a good man and she was – what? I am my mother's daughter, a greedy little girl impressed by titles and grandeur. Mama and Papa were like the two opposite poles on a compass. She recognised that her father had a truer sense of what was right, and never faltered. Poor Mama was always seeking, but never finding, the acceptance she sought. Augusta knew that Obadiah loved her, even her vanity and silly fears and fancies. Yet there was more to her than foolishness. When Obi was dispensing sometimes she would sit and talk to him about the various pills and mixtures. She liked the weighing, measuring and counting, the different coloured liquids and the ceremony with the hot wax that secured a paper parcel. It wasn't just playing at being an apothecary; Augusta was interested in what each medicine was prescribed for and how effective it was. In those moments, in the dispensary, she felt closer to Obi than anywhere else. He spoke to her as if she were a medical colleague, even asked her opinion. There was no pretending or seeking to impress. Afterwards she felt a glow of satisfaction, of happiness, as if she were following her true path. There was more in her than lace and frippery. But pursuing that course meant forsaking others. To be of real assistance she would need to study and to apportion her time differently. No more cultivating officers' wives, going to tea parties, or spending hours at the dressmakers. She fidgeted with her wedding ring. The trouble was she wanted both: the admiration of what amounted to society in Portsmouth and the respect of her husband. Given a crossroads she always took the easier path. Sighing, Augusta returned to her mother's letter.

Speaking of Sheridan brings me to a most unfortunate episode, involving that young man. It seems that he had a servant bearer who displeased him in some way and Sheridan lost his temper and flogged the man. Had your father not intervened the fellow might well have died. Papa wanted to have him court martialled but Sheridan resigned his commission and is on his way home. We are out of favour, in some quarters, as the boy was so popular with the mamas wanting him to pay court to their daughters. However, the servants consider your father a hero.

Soon we will be packing our traps for the long trek to Mussoorie. I love the climate in the hill stations but dread all the heat, and dust, and shaking about involved in getting there. It's wonderful, after the parched aridity of the plains, to see little streams and greenness everywhere. The flowers are like old friends. Outside Mrs Templeton's cottage there is always a trellis, covered with sweet peas. I love their pastel shades of pink and lemon and lilac. They make me feel so homesick for Nursling. Please darling, could you write to

73

your Aunt Susan and ask her how the garden is faring.
Better still, if you could persuade Obadiah to take you and
the boys out, one Sunday, to see that all is well. You asked
in your last letter what I would like for my birthday. What
would please me most would be some of your sketches of our
old garden.

Somehow I seem to have lost my enthusiasm for foreign
climes and yearn for England. However long one is here, one
is always the foreigner, in a strange and sometimes
frightening land.

Fondest love
Your devoted Mama.

Augusta felt a gleam of satisfaction at the downfall of
Sheridan. Would he have whipped her? she wondered. Those
disappointed daughters may well have had a lucky escape. She
was disturbed by the sadness in Mama's letter. Usually it was
full of wonderful word pictures of life in the different canton-
ments: the balls with the splendid uniforms and gowns; the
odour of sweat beneath the perfume; the war waged against
mosquitoes and awful diseases; the arrival of the 'Fishing Fleet',
that cruel nickname for the boatload of hopeful spinsters that
arrived each autumn. Of course, she always asked about home
but not with quite this intense longing.

A tap on the door distracted her. 'Come in,' she called, slipping the letter back in its envelope.

Samuel and Albert rushed into her arms.

'Hello, my darlings,' she cried.

'Shall I call back for them in half an hour?' asked Nanny
Hobbs.

74

'I'll bring them back to the nursery and put them to bed,' she said. 'Dinner will be late tonight. The master is out at a meeting.'

'Thank you, Madam, I'll get off to chapel then.'

'If you are back by nine o'clock that will be splendid.'

Bathed and in their nightgowns, the two little boys sat one on either knee. 'Story, story,' they pleaded.

'What shall it be, Sinbad the sailor – Rumplestiltskin?'

'Made-up story,' demanded Samuel. 'Get the magic box.'

'All right then, the two of you sit down on the carpet and close your eyes.' Augusta went into her bedroom and brought out the little mother-of-pearl box from her dressing-table drawer. 'Aha,' she cried, when she returned to her chair, 'what have we in here today?'

Samuel chewed his hand and Albert's eyes were large in expectation.

She took off the lid and spilled the contents on the floor.

'A little key and a button,' said Samuel, 'and a fevver.'

'Soddger,' said Albert, pointing his finger at a battered lead Hussar.

'Once upon a time there was a brave Hussar,' began Augusta.

'And, and he lost his button and . . . ?'

'Major General Ponsonby was furious and said to him . . . ?'

'"Buzzfuzz, you are a worm. Lower than a snake's belly."' Samuel said the words that were a part of every story and could be guaranteed to result in a tickling from Mama.

After the giggling had subsided Augusta continued. '"Search the barracks from top to bottom, and if you don't find that button, by sunset gun, there will be the devil to pay."'

'Buvfuvv,' said Albert

'Poor Buzzfuzz,' said Augusta. 'He searched high and low but he couldn't find the button. But under his pillow he found this small, brown feather.'

'Who did it b'long to?' asked Samuel.

'It was the wise old owl, sitting in the oak tree, outside. Buzzfuzz opened the window and called to her. "Mistress Owl, I have your feather?"'

'"Twit-twoo, I shall fly down to you. I need the feather to line my nest. My little owlets will hatch out soon." She flew down onto the window ledge and sat with her head on one side, staring at Buzzfuzz. "Twit-twoo," she said, "what's wrong with you?"'

'"I've lost my button and Major General Ponsonby will be furious if I don't find it."'

'"Is it bright and shiny?" asked Mrs Owl.'

'Buzzfuzz nodded.'

'"Well," said Mrs Owl, "I think I may be able to help you."'

Samuel and Albert looked at her expectantly.

'"I was up in the top of the oak tree this morning, and I saw something bright and shiny in the magpie's nest. Would you like me to fly up there and take a look?"'

'Yes, yes. Oh, please, Mama,' begged Samuel.

'So Buzzfuzz asked the owl, very politely, and he flew high up into the tree and came back with the brass button, and before the sunset gun Buzzfuzz had it sewn back on his scarlet jacket.'

'What about the key?' asked Samuel.

'Now, that belongs in another story, which I will tell you on another occasion.'

Hand in hand, the three of them trooped up the stairs to the nursery, at the back of the house. Augusta stood at the open window looking out over the garden. The scent of stocks and Albertine roses floated up to her on the still evening air. She stood there, her arms around her sons, thinking about poor Damaris Mowbray, having to wave goodbye to her little boy, and the many miles and long years that would separate them. No, she could not ever be parted from Albert and Samuel.

'The need will never arise,' Obi had assured her. 'I would miss them too. Besides, I'm poor as a church mouse, so we would never be able to afford to send them away.'

'Where's the moon?'

'Moon, moon,' echoed Albert.

'It will be along later, my lambs,' said Augusta, drawing the curtains. She set the boys on their chamber pots before letting down the side of Albert's cot. Soon Samuel would leave his cot behind and have a proper bed. Obi had been talking of having his son's hair cut and buying him a sailor suit. She sighed. They were babies for such a short time. Why rush them into boyhood with all its noise and roughness? Returning to her sons Augusta tucked them in and heard their prayers before setting the nightlights on the nursery chest of drawers.

'Mama,' said Samuel, 'we didn't say God bless the owl and the magpie.'

'Buvvfuvv,' murmured Albert.

'God bless Mrs Owl, and the Magpies and Buzzfuzz,' said Augusta, kissing Albert and moving over to Samuel's cot.

'What about the mermaid?' he asked as she bent towards him.

'Who is that, my darling?'

'The little girl Papa found on the beach.'

Augusta felt a stab of guilt that she had so easily forgotten the child. 'God bless the mermaid,' she said before kissing him and leaving the nursery.

Chapter Ten

Beattie opened her eyes and touched Ruth. She touched her own face. 'Mumma, Mumma,' she said, then patted her own face again and that of her mother. 'Mumma, Mumma,' she shouted in Ruth's ear. Climbing on top of her, Beattie stuck her fingers in Ruth's eyes and then into her mouth. She began to rock back and forth wailing, 'Mumma, Mumma.' Repeatedly she smacked the still white face with the flat of her hand. Her rocking turned to trembling and her wailing to screams of terror. 'Mumma, Mumma, Mumma.' Beattie began hitting the still figure repeatedly with her bunch of bobbins. The child was now sodden with tears and urine. At some time in the long dark night, she became exhausted. Beattie's screaming had now become a whimper. She put her arms around her mother's neck. 'Tuddle,' she whimpered, 'tuddle.' There was no response, no warm returning cuddle. Beattie fell into a fitful sleep only to awaken later to the same cold, still figure beside her. Again she began to scream.

★

Upstairs, Lizzie blinked into the darkness. Was that shrieking inside her head? Where was it coming from? Could it be that mangy cat from the fish quay? She rolled into the dip in the mattress and pulled the sheet over her head. Again the cries invaded her sleep. It was a child. With eyes still closed, she swept her hand across the floor until it came in contact with a jam jar. She raised it to her lips and drained the last dregs of last night's ale. A piercing scream had her leaping off the mattress and scrabbling for her petticoat. It was that babe downstairs, belonging to the soldier and his missis. She hurried down the stairs. That woman wouldn't never leave her nipper to cry like that. 'What's up, Missis?' she called, tapping on the door. The cries intensified.

She stepped inside. Through a gap in the curtain, she could see the little girl on the bed, crouched over her mother's body, waving a bunch of bobbins back and forth. Her heart thumping, Lizzie drew closer. The child's voice sounded hoarse with continued shouting. Sweat plastered her hair around her face. Her body shook. 'I gotcha,' Lizzie said, picking her up and holding her tight. Still the child trembled. 'I gotcha. *Shhh, shhh, shhh,*' she whispered, against her neck. 'Jesus! You're soaked, my little lamb. Stink of wee, you do. Best get you out of them clothes.'

All the while she had avoided the silent figure on the bed. Nerving herself, the young woman edged forwards to get a closer look. 'Christ! Oh, Jesus!' she gasped, then clamped her hand over her mouth. Her neighbour lay on her back, eyes staring up at the ceiling. Quickly, she grabbed the corner of the sheet and flipped it over the dead woman's face. Clinging to the child, Lizzie hurried down the passage and into the kitchen. She peered at the clock on the mantelpiece – six o'clock of a

Sunday morning. The neighbours would all be sleeping. Besides, what could they do for the poor cow? It was all over for her. No, she'd find something fresh for the kid to wear and see what there was in the way of vittles.

'Mumma,' croaked the baby.

The sound stabbed at her, bringing tears to her eyes. How long had the little one sat alone in the darkness, howling with fear? Lizzie knelt at the hearth, with the child still clinging to her, and tried one-handed to rake the embers into life. 'I'll 'ave to put you down, my babes, or we'll get nothink done,' she said. On the table was a heel of bread, wrapped in a cloth, beside a pot of jam. She tore off a corner of bread and dipped it into the jam and handed it to the child before setting her down on the floor. Her dark eyes stared blankly at her. 'Mumma?' she grizzled. Next to the loaf was a jug. The woman dipped her finger into it. 'Mmm, lemon barley.' She put the jug to her mouth, drinking thirstily. Looking about her she found a cup, and half filled it for the child. She knelt beside her holding it to her lips. The child shook her head, her cheeks bulging with bread.

Lizzie turned her attention back to the fire. She laid a few fresh sticks of wood on top of the embers and some nobs of coal that she found in a bucket. In the chair by the fireplace was a newspaper, which she held across the grate. Soon there was a roaring sound behind the paper as the fire crackled into life.

Scouting around the room, she found a fresh set of clothes for the child on top of a basket, filled with newly ironed sheets. Lizzie thought of how the baby's mother had set them there in readiness the night before, and tears welled in her eyes. Impatiently she dashed them away with her knuckles, and then set a pan of water to boil on a trivet, over the fire. In the scullery was a bar of soap on a saucer, a basin and a towel. Lizzie looked at the little girl. Her face was smeared with jam and encrusted with snot. Poor nipper, she was now too exhausted to make any noise but, every so often, she gave a half-hearted whimper.

As soon as the water was decently warm, Lizzie poured it into the basin and, taking up the child, stripped off her clothing and began to wash her. Still the little one clutched her bunch of bobbins. It was with difficulty that she was persuaded to let them lie on the floor while her hands were washed and dried. All the while, the little girl stared at them and clutched them to her, directly the washing was completed.

'There, my lamb, ain't that better?' said Lizzie, rubbing her vigorously with the towel.

'Mumma,' whispered the little voice.

She laid the child down on a square of muslin and knotted it together either side of her waist before drawing a pink cotton dress over her head. As she lifted her back into her arms the child nuzzled its head against her breasts. Could her mother still be nursing her? she wondered. If so, it showed extraordinary devotion. The child was well over a year from what she could tell. Lizzie rinsed the cup in the washing bowl and found a large pitcher of water in the scullery. After an initial shaking of her head the little one drank thirstily.

'Mumma?' she asked, then rubbed her eyes.

The young woman took the ironing out of the basket and wrapped the child in a small clean sheet. 'Hushabye, hushabye,' she crooned, pacing slowly round the room until the little one's eyes closed. She grew heavy and the woman knelt down slowly and slipped the child into the basket.

Lizzie, too, was exhausted. She stood at the table and helped herself to the remains of the bread, washing it down with the lemonade. The clock chimed seven. What should she do? The babe was settled, and her mother beyond help. Did she want any further involvement? Christ! She could barely feed herself, let alone keep a brat. No, she would look outside, see if anyone was stirring and make sure they found the child before she went on her way. Standing at the front door, Lizzie spied a young constable approaching on the other side of the lane. Quickly she fetched the basket and set it on the pavement. Pausing to look at the sleeping child she noticed that the bobbins were missing. She ran back into the kitchen, picked them up off the floor and set them in the basket where the child could find them.

Chapter Eleven

'Sorry, Doctor, but Mrs Pethick have asked for you,' said Mildred apologetically.

Obadiah sighed. He had only that moment set his bag down in the hall after a gruelling day with his patients. The last thing he needed was to patch up the results of a fracas in the next-door lodging house.

'Very well,' he said resignedly.

'Oh, and this letter come for you this afternoon.'

He took the envelope from Mildred, recognising his father-in-law's handwriting. Why had Major Morrell written to him? He had no time to find out. Slipping it into his coat pocket he left his home and knocked on the door of Rosa Pethick's lodging house.

'Oh, thankee, Doctor,' Mrs Pethick said, drawing a shawl around her shoulders. 'Sticks have had a fall and bin took badly. Would you take a look at him?'

Obadiah stepped into the dimly lit hall and followed the landlady's ample form up the stairs and down a narrow passage. He always felt as if he were entering a gravy boat, for the house seemed totally brown and sticky, from the door handles to the rag mats and threadbare blankets.

He heard the wheezy bellows of Sticks Malone, the old Royal Marine drummer, before he saw him. 'Good evening, Sticks,' he said, standing in the doorway of the poky room, acclimatising himself to the compound odours of sweat, urine and unwashed bedding. 'I hear you have been in the wars.'

'Thankee, Sir, for troublin',' gasped the old marine, his face flushed and eyes bright with fever. 'I was wantin' air. Stands on table. Comes off it arse over 'ead.' His face crumpled. ''Urts sommat cruel,' he wailed, tears leaking down his sunken cheeks.

'Fetch me something solid to stand on,' barked Obadiah, disregarding a flimsy chair. 'We must have this window open at once.' He perched on the edge of the bed and helped Sticks out of his nightshirt. A large bruise covered the left side of his chest, probably caused by his falling on the table. Fortunately the ribs were unbroken. His breathing was laboured and pulse rapid. Obadiah tapped the old man's chest with his fingers and listened intently. There was a dull sound as he struck against the lower lobes of the right lung. It was pneumonia. He pulled the nightshirt down again and met the old man's unflinching gaze.

'I'm about ready to be crossing the bar,' he wheezed. 'Had more than me due portion. Served with Nelson. Fell at me feet, 'e did.'

'You're in a bad way, certainly,' said Obadiah, quietly. 'I'll try and make you comfortable and give you something for the pain.'

'Ready,' the old man gasped, 'to meet me maker, me kit is packed.'

They were both silent as Rosa Pethick came in with a more substantial chair. Obadiah stood on it and wrestled with the window sash. He pulled it up one inch and then it slid down. After much banging, pulling and shoving, he was able to lower the top half of the window sufficiently to allow a rush of breeze into the room. There was an immediate sweetening of the air.

'Don't go away,' said Obadiah, briskly, to the landlady. 'I need you to fetch more pillows and empty this chamber pot, if you will. Also, I need hot water and a basin to wash my hands. Is there someone else in the house that can assist you? Sticks will need a jug of water and a glass.'

Rosa Pethick attempted to protest but was forestalled by the expression on the doctor's face. 'S'pose me husband will lend a hand,' she said, grudgingly.

'This man needs care and kindness. Anything less and I shall contact the authorities.' Obadiah didn't quite know what his powers were over the landlady, but he was determined that Sticks should have what he deserved.

'Knowed your pa, I did,' the old man said. 'Gent of the first water. Knowed your Merle – pretty maid she were.'

The mention of his sister pierced him like a dart – little Merle, the country name for blackbird. He was drawn back to that terrible afternoon when he had come back from playing on the beach to find his sister gasping for breath. Together he and his mother and father had stood by her bed watching help-lessly as she fought for life. Obadiah had been sent for the doctor and had fallen and hurt his knee in his anxious rush down the street. By the time he had got to the house the man had left on another call. He had left a message, but by the time the doctor had eventually come it was too late. How he had loved her, and how bitterly he had reproached himself over her death. Was that the moment, he wondered, when he had first wanted to take up medicine? Only Sticks and I remember her, he thought, and soon it will be only me.

'Thank you,' he said as the Pethicks returned with all his requirements.

He took two fusty pillows from the landlord. 'Now, if you will assist me a moment we will make Sticks more comfortable.' He plumped up all the pillows and between them he and the silent Pethick managed to lift the old man into a sitting position.

'Have the goodness to send a message to my house, telling them not to wait dinner,' Obadiah said. 'And the chamber pot, if you please,' he said bending down and handing it to Rosa Pethick. 'Rinse it well before you bring it back.'

'Bloody skivvy, what I am,' she muttered. Finding no response, she left the room slamming the door behind her.

Obadiah poured some cold water into the basin, and soaked his handkerchief, before wringing it out and plastering it across Sticks's forehead. He held a glass of water to the old man's chapped lips. Opening his bag he took out a teaspoon and filled it with water, then suspended it carefully over two cracked vases on the mantelpiece. Striking a match he held it under the bowl of the spoon to heat the water, then stirred in some grains of opium with the other end of the match. He drew up the mixture into a hypodermic syringe. Rolling up the sleeve he injected the fluid into Sticks's arm. Soon the old man's eyelids fluttered and then closed.

Obadiah sat on the chair and took his father-in-law's letter from his pocket.

Do not show this to Augusta.

The words were written inside the flap of the envelope and startled Obadiah. With a sinking heart he withdrew the letter and another smaller envelope with the words *My Darling Daughter* inscribed on it.

Lucknow   April 30th 1857

My dear Obadiah,
    I am anxious that you receive this letter as soon as possible and have entrusted it to a colleague taking the overland route from Egypt.
    I am not a fanciful man, Obadiah, but events here lead me to have the gravest misgivings as to our future safety. I had hoped that Gwendoline would have been safely at Mussoorrie by now, but the continuing cool weather has delayed the move to the hills.
    There have been the most curious incidents over the past few weeks. Everywhere these little floury cakes, known as chapattis, have been left on desktops and verandas with no explanation. Also Lotus flowers were passed among the Sepoys with this ominous slogan: 'Sub lal hogea hai.' (Everything has become red.)

Obadiah frowned. Major Morrell was the most cool-headed of men and a seasoned soldier. It was not in his nature to be fanciful. He pulled the bedclothes up around Sticks and returned to the letter.

You may have read, by now, in The Times, *of the rumour raging here that the cartridges for the new Enfields are*

88

*greased with beef suet. This, if true, would be an anathema
to the Hindoo Sepoys. Since the state of Oudh has passed
into British control there has been fierce resentment among
the native regiments at being disbanded.*

*Now, with no means of earning their living, they have
flooded into Lucknow and the town is a hotbed of discontent.*

*Without the loyalty of these soldiers we are lost. This
would be grave enough, but we have also the added burden
of the protection of the women and children under our care. I
have been furiously engaged in ordering my engineers to dig
protective earthworks and persuade their families to come into
the residency.*

Obadiah thought about what he had read recently in the
papers of events in India. It was most alarming – the murder of
an English captain and the subsequent hanging of the native
ringleader. There had been mention of the offending cartridges
and emphatic denials of the use of animal fat. Poor Augusta; he
thought she would be distraught if anything happened to her
parents. Only recently she had spoken eagerly of her father's
imminent retirement and return to England. Fortunately she
seldom read the political pages of the papers, but living as they
did in a garrison town it was impossible to avoid discussion of
military matters.

Obadiah looked at Sticks. His colour was better but his
breathing still short and shallow. Poor old fellow holed up for
years in this ghastly room. He remembered as a young boy not
much older than Samuel, visiting him with his father, being
thrilled at the tales of Trafalgar and the Battle of the Nile. The
marine would beat out the naval commands with his drum-
sticks on a table-top. Occasionally, Pa and he would walk with

him along to the Hard and he would point out the ships in the harbour. Sometimes his old sailing cronies would take him to a nearby tavern and he would stagger back across the cobbles full of rum and good cheer.

'The country smiles and beckons its young men when war's afoot,' Pa had said. 'Once glory fades they're cast off like so much spare cargo.'

Obadiah pulled up the blanket around the old man's shoulders and returned to the letter.

I hope that what I propose to you will prove an unnecessary precaution' [Major Morrell continued]. *'Should we meet with an untimely death, I wish you to sell our home in Nursling, and use the money to set your practice on a more secure foundation and ensure that Augusta is well provided for. Do not concern yourself unduly over the details. I have written to my solicitor in Romsey and enclose his address. Call on him should it be necessary.*

Obadiah, I have every confidence in you. I liked you instantly, and that liking has grown into a firm affection. Augusta has a good heart but has been too influenced by her mother's desire for outward show and social ambitions. She will need your strength and love and belief in her better qualities. Encourage her to be your partner in all your endeavours. She has intelligence and needs to use it and not fritter her time in tittle-tattle and frippery. Win her to your side with gentleness and patience.

Give my best love to Samuel and Albert. I had so looked forward to making their acquaintance and to being an attentive Grandfather.

I hope, soon, to write again instructing you to destroy this letter and to prepare the home at Nursling for our return.

Ever my deepest affection.

Arthur Morrell

Obadiah sat with the letter in his hand listening to the old man's laboured breathing. He shivered. How hopeless it all seemed and how powerless he felt. It would not only be Augusta who would miss her father. Yawning, he went over to the window and drew the curtains, so that air still filtered into the room without leaving his patient in a draught. He lit a candle and placed it on a saucer on the table, and crept out of the room.

'I shall call in again at eleven, Mrs Pethick,' he said to the landlady, who shuffled out of her room as he reached the foot of the stairs. 'Please be good enough to fill his water jug.'

The landlady sighed.

Obadiah took out half a crown and gave it to her.

'I shall see you at eleven,' she said, pocketing the coin in her brown apron.

Chapter Twelve

Something terrible had happened to Beattie – May was sure of it. It was a week now since she had seen the little girl or her mother, and Ma and Pa wouldn't tell nothing. It was like when her brother died. They had clung to each other and shut her out, as if they were the only ones to be hurting. May was desperate to see little Beattie. Such plans she'd made for the pair of them: showing her the sea; learning her to skip; building sandcastles together; even reading and figuring. Oh, she was so eager and quick and loved May as much as she loved her. Well, she was going round to see them today, whatever happened. When Ma was out in the yard, pegging out the washing, she'd sneak out the front door and away down to Golden Lion Lane and find out for herself. Whatever it was couldn't be worse than not knowing.

She heard the kitchen door open and her mother's voice called up to her.

'Your porridge be getting cold.'

May hurried down to the kitchen.

'Oh, there you be, child. Sit you down and eat up hearty.'

'Ain't you 'aving none, Ma? You looks ever so pale; you sick or sommat?'

Her mother's smile did not reach her eyes that were red-rimmed from crying. 'Just a bit tired, my love. Having your grandpa here takes a bit of getting used to. We shall all have to be extra patient with each other.'

'Is he going to live with us forever?' asked May.

'You know he is, child. Your Pa told you; it's all too much for him on his own.'

'But he's so sour and looking to find fault all the time.'

'Honour thy father and mother the good book do say.'

'But he don't honour us one iota,' said May, using one of Pa's favourite words.

'That's as may be. We'll just have to make the best of it,' said her mother, passing her the sugar.

May summoned up her courage for a last bold throw. 'Something's happened to Mrs Salter and Beattie. I know it has. What is it, Ma?'

'She 'ave gone up to Colchester with the little one to see her kin.'

May knew that her mother was lying. Ruth always said how she was finished with her family. Even the last time they were all together she'd said it. 'My Jacob be all the kin I need – him and little Beattie.' She felt angry and betrayed. Ma never lied to her. There were things she didn't tell her, mostly about her father's work. 'That doesn't concern you, Madam,' she would snap when May questioned her. But that was different. For a moment she considered challenging her, but her nerve faltered. She watched her mother as she stared out of the scullery window, screwing her apron up into a little ball. If only they could have that day back with Ruth and Beattie and everyone laughing and happy.

'Annie girl, Annie where are you?' It was Granddad, shouting from the top of the stairs.

Ma wiped her face with her apron then got a cup and saucer from the dresser. 'Here, May, take this tea up to him and say I'll be up with his washing water in five minutes.'

May walked into the bedroom that had so recently been hers.

'Thought you'd all died down there,' the old man complained as he held out his hand for the tea.

'Morning, Granddad,' said May, sliding past his wooden leg resting on a chair.

'No kiss for me then?' he demanded.

Sucking in her breath, she leaned forward and pecked his whiskery cheek.

'Tell your mother to look sharp. I'm half starved up here. Never mind the washing water. Bring up my porridge and don't stint the sugar.'

May hurried away.

'I heard him,' said her mother wearily. 'Please take it up to him, as a favour to me, while I put out the washing.'

This was her chance.

'Here you are, Granddad,' she said, fixing a fake smile on her face, 'all sugary and sweet.' May settled the tray on his lap, took away the empty cup, and tried not to look at his moist moustache.

She hurried to her room and put on her lace cap and shawl before picking up the dolly Beattie had left behind. Quietly she sidled down the stairs and out of the house.

*

Anne Norris knew at once where May had gone. She sighed. It was wrong of them to have deceived her. Better to have faced her with it from the beginning. The world was full of sadness; there was no avoiding it. Lying didn't help one jot. Almost every day there was somebody suffering. Thomas had spoken of an old sailor burned to death after knocking over a candle. There was the woman found lying on a bed of seaweed in a derelict house with her children naked and starving. Poor souls, she thought, I pity them. But Ruth, she was my friend.

A picture of her waving and smiling with Beattie jiggling in her arms moved Anne to tears. How could it have happened? Ruth had borne such sadness over little Sarah. And now to be struck down, just as she was making a new family for herself. What could have been going through the little mite's mind when she found her mother lying still and cold beside her?

'Must have been her cries that woke the girl upstairs,' the young constable had said when he called to see Thomas and told him the news. 'Seemingly, she took in the babe, washed and dressed it then left her in a basket for me to find.'

''Twas lucky you chanced by,' Anne had said. 'Poor little maid could have been there for hours on end.'

''Tweren't luck,' said the constable. 'I reckon the girl spied me coming and left the basket out there of a purpose. Flitted now. A whore she was, begging your pardon, Mrs Norris. Took to her heels afore I got to her door.'

'But not before she'd done a kindness to little Beattie,' Anne had said, angry at the young man's dismissal of the girl. 'Thomas, we must take the child. Ruth would want it so and

95

May will be heartbroken when she hears of it. That little maid can't be left at the workhouse.'

'We'll speak when I get home,' her husband had said.

'There's no need to speak at all. May and I can go to the workhouse and explain as it's all been a mistake. She can sleep along with May.'

'Woman, be quiet,' snapped her husband. 'I will not be contradicted in my home.' He glared at her and then turned to the young constable, who was standing uncertainly by the front door.

'But, Thomas . . .'

'Woman, will you let me be about my business?' Thomas had snapped before slamming out of the house.

That night there had been bitter words between them.

'Beattie is a bonny babe, I grant you, Anne, but she's no kin to us. We have a duty to my father and the child to come.'

'Ruth wanted to raise the child as her own. I know she wrote to Jacob telling him of the little maid. What if he writes home saying as he wants the child?'

'How's a soldier with no wife going to fetch up a child?' he asked.

'We could help him, Thomas,' she pleaded. 'Ruth were a dear friend of mine. Dearer and kinder to me than ever your father as is snorin' up there,' she'd shouted. 'For all the years I been traipsing up to see him and taking up little dainties – never a word of thanks. I promised Jacob as I'd keep an eye on her.'

'My mind's made up Anne, and there's an end to it,' Thomas had snapped as he leaned out of bed and snuffed out the candle.

'I shall never forgive you and neither won't May when she hears of it.'

'Well you best not tell her.'

'Merciful heavens! How d'you think I'm a going to hide it?' Anne had cried. 'She loved little Beattie, even made a dolly for her.'

'She can make summat for her new brother or sister then, can't she?'

'What you're asking is that I lie to her?'

'God Almighty woman you'll do whatever is needful. We are not having Ruth's child under our roof. Now, do I have to sleep in the scullery to get any peace?'

Never had they been so at odds with each other. And there was May watching the pair of them, knowing something was amiss. She'd seen through that lie, about Ruth going to Colchester, of course she had. Any moment she'd come running back grief-stricken at what she'd found.

'Where in God's name are you? I need to go to the privy,' roared a voice from upstairs, dragging Anne back to the present.

Clenching her teeth she set off upstairs. *Why, God? Why could you not take him in place of my dear, sweet Ruth?* she asked angrily.

'What are you doing? They're Mrs Salter's things. No, stop, stop,' May cried to the man outside Ruth's house, busily tossing her clothes and ornaments into a handcart.

'In arrears she was, the goods are in lieu of payment.'

'Where is she and her baby? Where's little Beattie?' May demanded of the group of neighbours, clustered around the cart. 'What happened?' she asked.

'She took badly and died, babes. Little tot got took to the workhouse.'

All the breath was punched out of her body and she sank down onto the pavement. Mrs Salter dead, but she had been so happy, and waving to her. But Beattie, Beattie was alive still. Her shock and hurt transferred itself to the man loading the cart. May sprang at him, kicking and screaming.

'Leave her things be, you bad bugger. Leave them, leave them,' she screamed, raining blows on him.

'You touch me once more and I'll fetch you such a clout,' roared the man, thrusting her from him.

'You hit that kid and it'll be you and me. Fancy your chances, do you, gainst someone yer own size?'

'Go on, Jack,' the gaggle of onlookers urged the sailor.

While the two men were squaring up to each other May looked at the things in the cart. There was Ruth's bonnet thrown in with a milk jug and a pair of her husband's braces; a rag doll and a little wooden box with 'R' on the front picked out in brass nails, inside were letters bound in pink ribbon. She hooked the doll over one arm and bundled the other things together with one of Beattie's little dresses.

Clutching her finds to her chest, along with Beattie's dolly, she ran away, just managing to hang on to her tears until she turned the corner. It was a wonder she was not mown down by a carriage or didn't go smack into a passing stranger, for she rushed heedlessly on, tears pouring down her cheeks. Beattie, they must get Beattie back. She didn't know how they would do it, but Ma would know. On reaching her front door May hurtled through it and into her mother's arms.

Anne Norris sat down with her daughter and held her tight. Thomas would be in for his dinner at any minute, but he would have to wait. Thank God his father had hobbled away to the tavern, leaving her to give her whole attention to the child. 'There, my pet, your ma's got you,' she whispered.

'Mrs Salter's dead, Ma? How could she be dead? It ain't fair. We gotta fetch Beattie back and keep her with us.'

'Life isn't fair, my lamb, 'tis cruel and hurtful.' Anne closed her eyes and continued to hold her daughter close, as much for her own comfort as for that of the child. She felt weary to the bone with all the upset. She had never wanted old Reuben living with them. She hated the man. He watched her with eyes like hard grey pebbles, making constant demands and finding fault with everything. If he weren't with them she might have been able to persuade Thomas to make a home for Beattie.

'They was throwin' all her things on a cart. I saved her letters and Beattie's frock. I shall keep them and the dolly till I sees her again.'

Anne Norris nerved herself for a battle between her husband and her daughter.

At the sound of footsteps in the hall May got up from her mother's lap and waited for her father to join them in the kitchen.

'What's all this? he asked, smiling at his daughter. 'No food on the table and my May in tears?'

'Pa, Mrs Salter be dead and little Beattie gone to the work-house. We must fetch her home.'

Thomas took his daughter on his lap and glared at his wife. 'That's not possible, my child. We got your grandfather to care for; besides, your mother is ailing and it wouldn't be fair to her.'

'Why couldn't Grandpa go instead? None of us don't like him and—'

'Silence!' He stood up horrified by his daughter's lack of respect.

''Tis true,' she screamed from the door. 'If we can't 'ave Beattie, I'll go and live wiv her in the workhouse, and you won't never see me again.'

Her father rushed across the room and slapped her leg. 'Get upstairs,' he roared, 'and don't come down till you're sorry. You can forget about Beattie. She's not our concern. She'll be fed and clothed and cared for. Go anywhere near that work-house and I'll lock you in your room on bread and water.'

May picked up the doll and the little wooden box and tore up the stairs. She got into her bed fully dressed and pulled up the blankets. Burrowing her head into the pillow she sobbed and sobbed. How could Ma let Beattie go to strangers? And Pa hitting her, he'd never done that before.

May picked up the doll and tucked it beside her, under the covers. She knew in her heart that she was helpless to change things. But Pa was wrong, she would never ever forget Beattie. One day they would both be grown up, and she would find her.

Chapter Thirteen

Augusta stepped out of the carriage and up the steps with Obadiah and the children. It had been freezing in St Thomas's and she was eager to warm herself indoors by the fire. 'Nanny,' she called; 'bring the boys down in half an hour, please.' Samuel and Albert had been bribed into good behaviour in church with the bait of opening their presents before dinner. The sprat to catch the mackerel, Obi called it.

She handed her coat to Mildred and hurried into the sitting room. Every wooden surface had been burnished with lavender polish; scattered about the room were pomanders and little bowls of potpourri, their rich mingled scents released by the heat from the fire. Oh, it was splendid! All her preparations over the last few months had blossomed. The ornaments on the Christmas tree were her personal triumph. The star on the topmost branch had taken hours of patient gluing. She had unpicked Mama's old evening bag and stuck the silver sequins, interspersed with crystal beads, onto a crisscross of spills. There were red velvet hearts and green paper crackers. Best of all was the tiny figure of Private Buzzfuzz complete with whiskers from Obadiah's shaving brush. Beneath the tree was a mountain of presents and across the room by the window sat one huge, lumpy parcel.

'Darling, I must just drop in next door and check on Mr Pethick. He fell downstairs while we were out at church.'

'Obi, not today, surely,' she protested, as eager as the children for Christmas to begin.

'I shan't be more than a moment. Do not open anything,' he warned with mock severity, 'except, perhaps the sherry.'

Augusta plumped up the cushion in her husband's chair and picked up a scrap of paper concealed beneath. Idly curious, she began to read. It was an old page of *The Times* with an article entitled 'The Indian Relief Fund'.

Day by day ladies were coming into Calcutta with their ears and noses cut off . . . Children of the tenderest years have been reserved to be put to death under circumstances of the most exquisite torture.

The words terrified her. She rushed into the downstairs cloakroom and vomited into the lavatory, then tore the paper into shreds, and dropped them into the bowl, watching them swirl away with the remains of her breakfast. What was she to do? She couldn't stop trembling and crying. It had been months since she had heard from her parents in Lucknow. Fear beat against her ribs like a caged bird. I must not give way, she vowed to her chalk-faced reflection in the cloakroom mirror. It's Christmas day. At any moment Obi and the children will be waiting for me. I cannot, I cannot. She dipped her handkerchief into the water jug on the wash stand and dabbed at her eyes. After several slow steadying breaths, she collected

herself. Please God, don't let it be true, she prayed as she
stepped out into the hall.

'There you are,' said Obi, smiling at her from the doorway
of the sitting room.

She wanted to rush into his arms and for him to make her
fears dissolve. But it could not be done. There were gifts to be
given to Cook and Nanny and Mildred. The whole household
was depending on her. Augusta followed him into the sitting
room. 'Happy Christmas, everyone,' she managed to say.

'Mama, Father Christmas has been,' cried Sammy, taking
her hand and leading her towards the tree.

'Did you see him, Papa? asked Albert.

'No, I didn't Albie, I was fast asleep like you. Now, ladies,'
he said, setting four glasses of sherry on a silver tray. 'Let me
give you all a drink before the festivities begin.'

Cook and Nanny sat on the edge of the horsehair sofa and
Mildred perched on the piano stool.

'A Happy Christmas to us all,' said Obadiah, smiling at
everyone.

The three women sipped genteelly while Augusta
swallowed hers down in one gulp. Perhaps she had panicked
unnecessarily. Perhaps it was going to be all right.

'Now, Albert,' said Obi, 'your little mountain is over there,
between Mama and Nanny. Samuel, you and I will see what
we can find among these mysterious packages, and perhaps
Cook and Mildred will help us.'

'Buvvfuvv,' shouted Albert, as he caught sight of the little
Hussar.

How splendid they look, thought Augusta. Samuel was
in a new sailor suit and shiny button boots and Albert was in
a blue smocked dress and matching pantaloons. Sammy

immediately tore into his presents, scattering paper all around him, while Albert watched and waited. Was it because he was the youngest that he was diffident, or was he naturally more of an observer? she wondered.

'A farm,' shouted Sammy, his face red with excitement. 'Oh Papa, let's find all the animals.' Augusta and Nanny Hobbs smiled like successful conspirators. 'I'll set up the hedges and you find the pigs,' said Obadiah.

'Farmer,' said Albert, holding a rosy-cheeked figure with mutton chop whiskers and checked waistcoat in his hand.

'He's just like Mr Merryweather the fishmonger,' said Augusta. 'Don't you think so, Nanny?'

'The very spit of him, Madam,' said Nanny, her brown eyes gleaming with merriment.

'Look, Pa, here's the sow and the piglets and a horse.' Samuel tumbled the box of animals onto the carpet. He and his father became absorbed in setting out the farm.

'Come on, Albert, let's see what Santa has for you,' said Augusta, taking her small son and leading him over to a huge lumpy parcel. She so wanted him to love it, as she had. Oh! It was so novel and so exactly suited to him.

Experimentally he tore off a strip of paper at one end to reveal the pointed prow of a bright green boat. 'Oh,' he gasped, his eyes widening in surprise. Again he tore backwards and upwards to find a little foothold made of coiled rope and then a seat just like a sailor's sea chest. He stood back and thrust his thumb into his mouth, and then the excitement seized him. 'Albie do it,' he said, pushing Augusta's hands away. Red in the face he stripped away at his prize.

A few feet away, Obadiah and Samuel were still setting out the farm, oblivious of Albert's discoveries.

'Sails,' he exclaimed, 'sails,' as he tore the paper up as high as he could reach. 'Mumma do it,' he eventually conceded. When his present was revealed in all its splendour, Albert shouted. 'Oh, gracious me!' and ran around it laughing and shouting.

'Have a ride, darling,' said Augusta.

The little boy hitched up his dress and, taking hold of the rope handle, swung himself up into the seat of his rocking boat. He sailed up and down over the painted waves and leaping fish, his brown curls dancing.

How beautiful he is, she thought, wanting to hold the moment. Soon he would be four years old and a baby no longer. She had promised Obadiah that he would have his hair cut then, and leave his infant dresses behind, but today he was still her baby.

The words of the newspaper article came back to her with dreadful clarity. Those poor little children, she thought, as fear leaked beneath her shaky defences. If anyone hurt my boys I'd want to kill myself, she thought. She stared at the candles on the Christmas tree, the yellow flames dancing in her tears. Surreptitiously, she drew her handkerchief from her sleeve and dabbed at her eyes. Nobody was looking, they were all so taken up with the children's excitement. Augusta clenched her teeth to stop herself from screaming.

'Come and look at my farm,' said Samuel running up to her.

'Oh, it's wonderful, darling,' she said, rising with difficulty from her armchair. 'What a lot of animals. Do you think the pigs and sheep like to be in the same field?'

'Papa is going to make some sheep pens and some sties for the pigs,' said Samuel, 'but for now, they must just grin and bear it.'

Mildred giggled and Cook smiled.

'We're forgetting ourselves,' said Obi, turning back to the presents. 'Nanny, here is something for you from the mistress and myself. Here you are, Mildred and Cook. Happy Christmas to all of you.'

'Oh, Sir, thank you. And you, Madam. Just what I could do with.' Nanny Hobbs forced her bent fingers into the fur-lined gloves. 'They'll ward off the chilblains.'

'I'm much obliged,' said Cook, unwrapping a woollen scarf.

'Oh my!' exclaimed Mildred, 'it's beeootifful,' her normally chalk-white face flushed with pleasure, as she held the string of glass beads up to the light. 'Thank you ever so much.'

'Beg pardon, Madam,' said Cook. 'I must attend to the goose.'

When dinner was announced, Albert would not be parted from his boat.

'You can come back in here with Mama and Papa after-wards,' said Obi later, taking hold of Albert and prising him, red faced and furious, from his perch.

'Albie not want dinner,' the little boy shouted. 'Albie want his boat.'

'Crackers,' said Samuel to his brother. 'After pudding we will have crackers.'

'Albie not want cackers,' roared little Albert.

Augusta went over to the tea trolley to fetch her box of liquorice comfits, but Obi shook his head. 'He can't have everything his own way, darling. We don't want him becoming spoiled and brattish.'

'Master Albert, get off that boat at once,' said Nanny firmly.

'Upstairs with your brother and let's get you both looking ship-shape.'

'Boat,' said Albie sorrowfully as he followed Sammy.

Augusta opened the door into the dining room. The table was laid with the red Christmas cloth that her mother had given her, and the Waterford glasses that Papa had bought as a wedding gift for both of them. Another trickle of fear swilled in her stomach. Poor fussy Mama, nothing must happen to her, she couldn't bear it. Augusta looked at the table and the crisp starched napkins and sparkling glasses. The goose glistened plump and golden on the silver platter. In the vegetable dishes were the sprouts, carrots and crisp roasted potatoes. Gravy waited in the Wedgwood boat. Looking at it all Augusta felt sick.

'What a feast,' said Obi, taking her hand and squeezing it. 'How sumptuous. Mildred, do give Cook our compliments and you have all worked very hard. I do thank you most sincerely.'

Beaming, Mildred and Nanny closed the doors and left them to their meal.

How kind he is, thought Augusta, once more near to tears. It's all so effortless and natural, while I have to force myself to remember all the little courtesies. She took her napkin from its ring, and tried to make some impression on the food Obadiah heaped on her plate, but her stomach was churning with anxiety. He and the boys laughed and chattered, making short work of their dinners.

Now and again he smiled anxiously at her, and Augusta shook her head, trying to signal her desire to be ignored. She stared at her plate. One more gentle enquiry, one more tender glance, and I shall scream, she thought. But what happens if I can't stop screaming?

'Pudding on fire,' shouted Albert, banging his spoon on the table as Cook carried in the flaming pudding.

'Albie,' said Obi, 'put down your spoon, please.'

'Lots of custard, please, Papa,' said Samuel, holding out his plate.

At last they left the table and went back into the sitting room. Albie leapt back onto his rocking boat. The afternoon dragged on and by the time Nanny called for the children at five o'clock, Augusta was exhausted.

'I'll read their story tonight, darling. Why don't you go upstairs and lie down for a while. Once I've settled the boys, I will fetch you up some supper.'

Augusta nodded.

'Shall I send Mildred up to you?'

She shook her head. In her room she struggled with the fastenings on her dress. How hot she was in all her finery, trussed up like the Christmas goose. It was all so petty and interminable. Would she never be free of all these garments? Breaking a fingernail, stubbing her toe against the foot of the bed, Augusta tore at her buttons. Almost weeping with frustration, she realised she could not undo the fastening at her waist.

She rang the bell and waited for Mildred.

As she helped her out of her crinoline and petticoats, her maid kept up a ceaseless stream of chatter.

'Master Albert was so excited, wasn't he, Ma'am? Oh, he do love that boat, I never did see the like.'

Augusta smiled and nodded. Her nerves were taut as piano wires. Mildred prattled on as she drew the pins out of her hair and brushed it down around her shoulders. 'No, I shan't require that blouse; I am going to bed now. The master will bring me up my supper later.'

'Oh, Ma'am.' Her maid frowned with kindly concern. 'You bin took badly; anything I can fetch for you?'

'No, please, please just go and leave me to rest. I shan't need you until tomorrow.'

The silence and privacy she had earlier craved was now oppressive. Please, please, Obi, hurry up, Augusta begged. She could hear him laughing and chatting with the boys. Come on, come on: she ground out the words with clenched teeth. By the time he eventually came into the bedroom, all control had fled.

'Darling, whatever is the matter? Gussie?'

He took her in his arms and she clung to him, overwhelmed with anxiety.

'*Sh, shh*, Obi's got you safe. Darling, you're trembling. Whatever is it?'

'I think they're dead,' she gasped. 'They must be.'

'Who, my love? What are you talking about?'

'Ma and Pa,' she said, pushing her hair away from her eyes and blinking away her tears. 'Obi, please tell me, do you know anything?' His silence panicked her and she began to scream.

'They're dead, I know it – cut to pieces. Tell me, tell me,' she raved at him.

He put his arms around her and she fought him, kicking and scratching. He grabbed her arms and forced her down into a chair. She bit his hand and he gave her a stinging slap across the face. She gasped, and in that moment knew that they were dead. 'No, no. Oh no,' she wailed.

Obi carried her back to bed. 'Oh Gussie, my love. I'm sorry, I'm so sorry.'

Augusta clung to him and wept.

Obi held her till she could cry no more.

It was almost a relief after all the terrible uncertainty. 'How, Obi? I want to know?'

He helped her into bed, then sat at her side, holding her hands in his. 'It was in the *Gazette* yesterday. Your mother died of cholera a month ago.'

'Poor Mummy, would she have suffered much, Obi?'

'I think it would have been very quick, my love. She wasn't a strong woman.'

'What about Papa?'

'A cannon ball hit him and he died instantly.'

'Oh!' she gasped. 'I don't think I can bear it.'

Obadiah took her in his arms. He kissed her face and stroked her hair. When she was too exhausted to cry any more, he bathed her face and tied back her hair.

'I found a piece of the paper telling me about torture and mutilation. I was so frightened that Mummy had been horribly injured. Oh, Obi! I can't believe I'll never see or hear from them again.'

Obadiah went across to his side of the bed, took out an envelope and handed it to her. 'Gussie, please don't be angry. Your father sent me a letter for you, but made me promise not to give it to you, until now.' He kissed her hand. 'You read your letter. I will get you some milk and a sleeping draught.'

Augusta took the paper from the envelope. She could hardly bear to read the familiar handwriting.

Lucknow   April 1857

My Darling Child,

   How can I convey in one letter all that it has meant to be your father? From the very first moment of seeing your angry pink face, and feeling your fingers curling around mine, I was captured. It has been a delight to watch you transform yourself from a little country sparrow into the elegant young swan that I gave away seven years ago, into Obadiah's keeping.

'Oh, Daddy,' she sobbed, wounded by his tenderness.

Darling, you are far more than a beautiful woman. You have intelligence and a loving heart. Don't get led away from your true nature by all the gauzy flim-flam of rank and social position. Be the woman it is in you to be, that will be my best remembrance. No memorials with pompous sentiments, please, Augusta.

   It is painful to think that I shall not see you again or watch my grandchildren grow to manhood. But I know that I shall be always in your heart and perhaps some of the things that I held dear you will pass on to Samuel and Albert.

Augusta nodded. There would be so much to tell.

On my desk before me I have the picture you painted for me when you were eleven. Dear old Jupiter, such a faithful dog, he was the dearest friend and companion, wasn't he?

   What a talent you had for drawing; don't let it slip away, Augusta. Perhaps you could, if it won't make you feel too

sad, journey out to Nursling one day and make some
sketches of our home. Let them be our memorial.

Augusta remembered her mother's letter, all those months
ago, asking for the very same thing. Poor Mummy, she had
sounded so homesick.

I hope you will not be unhappy with the decision I have
made about the house. I want it sold and the money to be
shared between you and your husband. Life goes forward
darling. Your future is with Obadiah and your children. He
is a good man, who loves you, as you deserve. Not
flatteringly or indulgently, but seeking to encourage the best
that is in your nature.

Mama has been failing of late. The doctor says that her
heart is not strong. I must treasure the time we have left
together. What a sweet, silly woman she has been, and such
a dear companion. How she loved you.

Goodbye, my dearest daughter and thank you for all your
love and kindness.

Papa

She could not bear to be parted from the letter. After Obi
had brought her the milk and sleeping draught, she laid in his
arms, exhausted from grief, the envelope still in her hand.

Awakening in the early hours, Augusta thought guiltily of
the little foundling that Obadiah had wanted to bring home.
Now it was she who was the orphan.

Chapter Fourteen

Beattie knew that the pictures in her head would go away when she opened her eyes. In spite of Gertie's fingers trying to open her eyes and Mabel pinching her, she clung to the picture. She could hear herself laughing and the wind rushing past her face. Up in the air she was, up and down. Someone was calling to her and they were laughing too.

'Gerrup or you won't get nothink,' insisted Gertie.

'Come on B,' urged Mabel. 'if you don't, we'll eat yer bread.'

Beattie was hungry, but she didn't want to leave it. All her laughing was locked up behind her eyes and once she opened them, everything would be empty. All the colours would creep away as soon as she woke up. But there was an empty hole in her belly and her mouth felt dry. Her head itched and her face felt stiff.

Gertie and Mabel got hold of a leg and an arm each, and hauled her off their shared bed.

Crack, went her head as it hit the wooden floor. Beattie's tears were for far more than the bump on her forehead. The picture had gone, taking all that wind rushing through the air, all the sun on her face, and the faraway lady with her arms open.

The two girls ran ahead of her down the stairs to breakfast. Beattie dragged the chamber pot out from under the bed and sat on it, while she dug the sleepy dust out of her eyes. Mabel and Gertie had left it half full. She hated using it after them and getting her bum wet. Knowing they would not save her any bread, she hurried into her clothes: a rough grey dress and lisle drawers. Her button boots she would worry about later.

She was just about to go down the stairs when the cleaning woman clutched at her shoulder. 'You emptied your po and rinsed it out?'

Beattie shook her head.

'Back you go,' she demanded.

She lifted the metal chamber pot and carried it out to the stone sink, trying not to breathe or spill the wee over her bare feet. The tap was stiff, and she could only force a thin trickle of water into the pot. Her nose wrinkled as the pong from the sink wafted up to her. She went back to the dormitory and slid the chamber back under the bed.

Rita scattered wet tea leaves on the floor before sweeping them up with a broom. 'Take yer boots wiv yer,' she demanded.

Beattie carried them down the stairs. She hated the boots. They were too big and rubbed against her heels, giving her blisters. The buttons were hard to do up without a hook and, since one could never be found, she either slocked about with them undone or walked barefoot. By the time she reached the dining room, Gertie and Mabel had left for school. Knowing she would likely get a clout from one of the women clearing the table and gossiping, she crept away. Beattie sidled up to the kitchen door and peered round it. Inside, it was all steam and clanging saucepans. At the sink, a red-faced girl was washing the porridge bowls and shouting over her shoulder to her friend, stacking clean plates onto a trolley.

'I reckon it's my birthday tomorrer.'

'What, August the ninth?'

'Yeah, 1860. Christ I must be thirty.'

'How old you reckon to be?'

'Old enough ter know better,' the other girl cackled, rubbing her belly.

They had their backs turned away from her. Holding her breath, Beattie pattered into the open larder and looked around her. At eye-level, on a marble shelf, was a jug. She took it in both hands and drank greedily. The milk was cold and thick on her tongue, not like the watery stuff she was used to. Beattie recognised the square white box with the lid on as the bread bin. She lifted off the lid; inside was a whole new loaf. Breaking off a corner, she stuffed it up the leg of her drawers and stood in the larder doorway, waiting her chance to sneak away.

'When d'you reckon to drop the brat?' the girl at the sink asked.

'Well,' said the other, 'it's quickening; prob'ly afore Christmas.'

Still their backs were turned.

Beattie scampered out. She found herself a hiding place under the steps leading to the laundry. The bread was fresh, and the crust crisp and chewy. Perhaps she would miss her breakfast again. Licking her lips to garner any stray crumbs, she slid out from under the stairs and looked about her. Soon she would have to go to the workhouse school. Mabel said she had to be five years old. Someone had said that she was four. Beattie

didn't know what four meant, except that she wasn't as big as
Gertie and Mabel, who told her they were six. But then, what
did six mean? She knew that her name was in a big book along
with her friends'. It was Beattie Salter, and she was a foundling.
She thought it was like being a stray. Gypsy, the master's dog,
was a stray. Nobody knew where he had come from, or about
his ma and pa. They didn't know where she had come from
either, p'r'aps it was the same place as Gypsy had lived in.
Beattie felt thirsty again, but didn't think it worth the risk of
going back into the kitchen. There was a wall that led to the
road and the porter's lodge. Beattie knew that she must not go
outside, or she risked a slap from Mrs Figgis, who dosed them
up when they were sick and bathed them, sometimes. Hanging
over the wall was the branch of an apple tree. Temptingly, just
out of her reach, was a shiny red apple.

How could she get at it?

Beattie looked up at the branch. Could she climb up there?

'You give me a kiss, my little moppet, and Charlie will pick
you that apple.'

The man was smiling at her. His shirt was spattered with
food and his teeth were brown. He stood by the wall, reached
up at the branch and twisted the apple free of its twig.

Beattie frowned. Already her mouth was watering. Could
she hold her breath, peck his face, grab the apple and run away?

'Not so fast, my pretty.'

Beattie screamed. He had her held fast, one arm locked
across her chest. With the other hand he was lifting up her
dress, his fingers grabbing at her drawers. The apple had fallen
to the ground.

Panic-stricken, she thrashed about kicking out at his shins.

He had her drawers halfway down, his breath hot on her neck when she bit his hand.

'You little cow,' he roared, slapping her across the face with such force she fell onto the ground.

The window of the porter's lodge was opened, and the big man in the blue uniform poked his head out. 'Shut your noise, out there,' he called.

Charlie slunk away, mumbling to himself.

Beattie sat on the ground with the apple in her hand. It weren't no good crying, no one took no notice. Her cheeks were red and stinging, and her body felt all itchy like when she'd had the fleas. Charlie had made it dirty. Yet, when she pulled up her frock, and looked at herself, Beattie couldn't see nothing different. Somehow the apple had changed. It seemed smaller, and not such a bright red as it had from a distance. It was the colour she had wanted almost as much as the juice. When she bit into the apple she cried with disappointment, it was sour and maggoty.

'What 'appened ter you?' asked Mabel, when they met up at dinner-time.

'Cripes! Who walloped yer?' asked Gertie.

'Weren't nothin',' she said, sucking at the meat bones on her plate. Mabel and Gertie would tell the master, and he would make a big fuss, and go and find Charlie. And it was her fault for lettin' him kiss her.

It was bath day, and Mrs Figgis rubbed at her with the towel. She had washed her hair in green soap and said she was infested. Beattie sat trembling in her nightgown, while Mrs Figgis got a razor and shaved off her hair. Her head felt cold and bare. She wanted to sneak up to bed, pull the blanket over her and have the mattress to herself, without Gertie's feet in her face or Mabel's stale breath.

'That'll see the back of them nits for a month or so,' said Mrs Figgis, briskly. What's this bruise on yer face? That Gertie bin fightin' again? You hit her back.' The big lady looked at her and smiled. 'You got to get in the first blow. It's sink or swim, should know that by now.'

That night, when she and Mabel and Gertie were wedged together on the straw mattress, the other picture came. There was a clicking sound and screaming. Beattie woke up with her heart banging against her ribs. Now she was afraid to close her eyes. Where was the picture she had woken up with? She wanted it back.

Chapter Fifteen

'Beattie Salter, I been traipsin' all over the place for you. Got ter see the doctor, get yer arm pricked.' Mrs Figgis hurried across the yard to where Beattie had been watching the big girls skipping.

They went into the grown-ups building and down the long corridor to the nurses' room, next to the children's ward. Beattie was filled with dread; she didn't like doctors. They poked at you like you was nothing, and made you take your clothes off. The last doctor had bony fingers and powder down the front of his jacket that made her sneeze. He'd got out a tin and sniffed something up his nose and then he sneezed, too, all over her. Last time, that doctor made Mrs Figgis scrape all her hair off with a razor and paint her head with purple stuff just because she had the ringworm. Mabel said they was lying, the only worms she seed was in the garden. Beattie rubbed her hand over her stubbly hair.

'Good morning, Mrs Figgis. Vaccination, I believe?'

'Yes, Doctor. This one we got as a tot so missed out on the pricking. Nurse Hobbs been through all the susstificates and

Beattie's not got one. She's off out this morning takin' a child to Cosham. Asked me to get it done.'

The doctor took a book out of his bag and set it on the table next to the inkstand, it was followed by two small bottles, a glass square and a shiny knife. He turned around, picked Beattie up and set her down on the high bed in the corner. 'Hello, young lady, and how are you?' he said, smiling at her.

Beattie looked at the knife and swallowed hard. She didn't know how she was. It wasn't a question anybody had ever asked her before. 'Don't know,' she murmured, staring at her boots.

'Let me see, what is your name?'

'Beattie Salter,' she mumbled.

'Merciful heavens!' he gasped, 'little Beatrice.'

'Do you know the child?' asked Mrs Figgis, looking cross.

Beattie was startled. Nobody knew nothing about her. Whenever she had asked her, Mrs Figgis got all narky, and said as she was lucky to have been found, and should be grateful. Some words had a nasty taste to them and grateful was one, like orphan and charity. She looked at the doctor. He was tall with a big nose and dark hair and smelled of soap. His eyes were brown like Gypsy's, and just as friendly. He was looking at her and smiling, like he was really seeing her. 'Name's Beattie,' she said.

'That is an abbreviation of your full name, which is Beatrice.'

'Beatrice.' She said the word in her head and liked the shape of it. When she was on her own again she would say it out loud.

'Just roll up your sleeve, Miss, and be quick about it. Doctor's not got time to waste.' Mrs Figgis stared at the doctor. 'You looked as if you knowed this child.'

Beattie felt her mouth go dry; did he know her? He had looked sad when he'd said, 'Merciful heavens,' like he was going to cry. When Mrs Figgis got on to him he changed the look on his face, like he'd pulled a curtain across it. Had she been in a family once, like Mabel and Gertie?

The doctor shook his head. 'I was mistaken, there was a passing resemblance to a child I once treated, but she would be five years old by now.'

'Beattie will be five next January, it's here in the records.'

'I am surprised that this child is that age, Mrs Figgis.' The doctor looked cross. 'She is severely underweight. I hope, when I return in ten days to check her vaccination scab, that she will look considerably healthier than she does at present.'

Mrs Figgis's face went a blotchy red colour. 'Just small made, she is. I'll pour out the water and wash her arm for you.'

While she scrubbed at Beattie with a rough wet towel, the doctor got some cloth and dabbed something from one of the bottles onto it, and wiped it over her arm. She wrinkled up her nose; it had a sharp clean smell.

'Perhaps you could fetch me a cup of tea and some biscuits. I neglected my breakfast this morning.'

'I was going to do that, after the pricking,' said Mrs Figgis.

'I can manage perfectly well on my own,' said the doctor, pouring a tiny drop of liquid from the other bottle onto the glass square. 'If you would be so good as to fetch the tea.'

Mrs Figgis shut the door noisily behind her.

Beattie gulped as the doctor struck a match and lit a lamp before passing the blade of the knife through the flame.

'Now, Beatrice,' he said, smiling at her, 'I need to scratch your arm very lightly with this knife, but first I need to rub this liquid, from the glass, onto the blade.'

She tensed as he took hold of her and pinched a fold of skin between his fingers.

He was right; it didn't really hurt but left a circle of pink marks.

'It will be uncomfortable for a few days and then you will be protected from a bad illness.'

Beattie looked at him. 'Can you say that other name?' she asked.

'What name would that be?' he asked, smiling at her.

'Beetiss,' she said.

'Ah! Beatrice, your Christian name. Let me teach it to you – Be-a-triss. You have been called Beattie for quickness,' he said as he began to wrap a piece of white cloth over the scratches. 'I have two boys, and their names are Samuel and Albert, but I call them Sammy and Albie. In the register you are Beatrice.' He helped her down from the bed and pointed to something in Mrs Figgis's book, open on the table. 'That line there says your name, Beatrice Salter.'

She stared at the black squiggles on the paper. At the beginning there was a bigger, swirlier bit and then another further on. Her face felt hot and there was a fluttery feeling in her belly. Reaching up, she traced the pattern with her finger. 'My name is Beatrice,' she said.

'Now,' said the doctor, 'I must write your name in my book.' He sat at the table and took up the stick, made of a bird's feather, and dipped it into the inkwell. There was her name again, with the same beginning and middle swirls.

Beattie stared at it, trying to make the shapes jump into her head so that she could remember them later.

'Would you like me to write your name down on a piece of paper for you to keep?' he asked.

Beattie nodded. She stood beside him as he took a card from his pocket, turned it to the empty side, and dipped his quill back in the ink. He rolled the blotter over the card and gave it to her. She closed her fingers around it and nodded her head in thanks, afraid to speak in case she blubbered.

'Somebody gave you a beautiful name and wanted you to be happy, Beatrice; I know it.' He shook her hand, like she was a lady. 'I shall be back to look at your arm in a few days.'

'Most kind,' he said, as Mrs Figgis came back into the room with a tray. 'Here you are, Beattie,' he said, handing her a biscuit. 'You have been a brave girl. Off you go now and don't get that arm wet.'

Mrs Figgis looked all sour and vinegary. She didn't never like people giving you things.

'Grateful,' said Beattie, smiling at the doctor as she took the biscuit from the plate and slid it over the card. The doctor smiled back at her and she knew that he understood that the card was a secret between them. She ran quickly up to the dormitory and wriggled under her bed. Nibbling only the tiniest bit of the biscuit, she made it last as long as she could, while staring at the card. The doctor's words wrapped around her like a blanket: 'Somebody gave you a beautiful name and wanted you to be happy.'

Obadiah sat in his trap, the reins held idly in his hands. Little Beatrice; he could hardly believe it. The last time he had seen the child she was toddling along beside Mrs Salter, a bright eyed, laughing infant. When was that? Great heavens it must be at least two years ago, if not more. Now she was a pale, thin waif of a child. But there was still a spark of curiosity about her, in spite of the deadening regime of the workhouse. How had she come to be there, after such a promising start with Mrs Salter? He had thought her well settled with her new mother. Constable Norris had said as much when last he spoke to him. Something about the woman writing to her husband out in India, wanting to make the child her own. How had things gone so badly wrong? The sight of the shaven head, pinched face and stick-like arms of Beattie haunted him. What had been the good of rescuing her from death, to the half-life she was condemned to now? He must find her somewhere better. Fleetingly he thought of taking her home, but dismissed the idea almost as soon as it entered his head. Augusta was still in a delicate state of mind after the death of her parents in 1857, given to tears and groundless anxieties. In a few days they were going up to Nursling, to pack up the house and take away any books and furniture that Augusta might find a use for. It was now 1860 and had taken all this time for her to nerve herself to the task. No, bringing four-year-old Beatrice into his family was not the answer.

He berated himself for letting her slip from his mind. His practice in Portsea and the medical demands of the Mariners' Home took nearly all his waking hours; then there were Augusta and the children. Obadiah straightened up and flicked the reins. 'We'll go and see Mrs Norris, Dapple,' he said, to the restive pony. 'She will put us in the right path, if anyone will.'

'They left about a year ago,' said the woman who opened the door at White Hart Row. 'Her husband got some sort of step-up in his job. Went off to Cosham. You could get her address off the constable at Penny Street station. Was you a relation?'

The woman stood in the doorway with a flat iron in her

hand. How often, on his calls, he surprised his patients in the midst of their tasks. It was not unusual for a mother to come to the door with a knife in her hand, or a colander of peas, or a piece of sewing.

'I said, was you a relation?' the woman repeated.

'Oh, no,' said Obadiah, collecting his thoughts. 'I am a doctor and had some business with the family.'

'Mrs Norris was took badly and lost her baby and the Constable's old fellow died. I think she was glad to go. She said that a new home might change her fortune. There was a young girl – May, I think she was called.'

'Thank you, Madam,' said Obadiah, 'I'll detain you no longer. I shall call at the station, as you suggested. Thank you again.' He tipped his hat and stepped up into the trap.

At Penny Street, Norris's protégé was now in charge. 'Family named Salter, you say, living at Golden Lion Lane? How long ago did the child live there, doctor?'

'I found her on the beach on 26th May 1856 as a baby. How long she lived with Mrs Salter I don't know. I had thought her well settled there.'

'Here we have it,' said the constable. 'Sunday, 30th May 1857. Child found on pavement outside 10 Golden Lion Lane, in a basket. On searching the house a dead woman was found in the front downstairs room. The child was taken to the work-house. No relatives have ever come forward, as far as I am aware.'

'Mrs Norris must have been greatly upset,' said Obadiah, thinking of her efforts at bringing the baby back to life. He felt sure she would have taken the child herself, but perhaps her own pregnancy prevented her, or had her husband refused to sanction the idea? He would never know.

'Yes, I do remember the case now you bring it to mind. Cause of some dispute between Constable Norris and his wife, I believe. Afterwards, she came to the station with a note, giving details of the child's name and birthday. Nothing was ever heard from Mrs Salter's husband, a soldier in India, I believe. I took the letter up to the workhouse myself, but what they did with it, who knows?'

Once more Obadiah sat in the trap deep in thought. He'd set Dapple's nosebag in place and the pony munched contentedly at her feed. Who could he turn to for sound advice? He had an hour before tea, and needed to be able to offer Beattie more than sympathy. Getting down from the trap he removed Dapple's nosebag, climbed back on board and set off for the Mariners' Home. The decision was instinctive. Since Margaret Sankey's arrival as matron, a friendship had grown up between them, based on mutual respect. As he drew up at the Home, he could hear a lot of shouting and cheering. Almost immediately Freddy came out with a bucket of water for the pony. ''Ello, Doctor, you looking for a tiger?'

Obadiah was startled. 'Why would I need a tiger, Freddy, I'm not looking to start a circus?'

'You mistake me, Doctor. Ain't it what they calls a young lad as takes charge of a gentleman's horse? He picks her up in the mornin' from the stables, and takes 'er back of a night. Keeps 'er looking spry and nippy.'

'That would be useful to me, certainly Freddy, but where would you live? We are packed quite tightly together in St George's Square, you know. What with the family, plus Nanny and Mildred, and Mrs Frostick our cook, we are bursting at the seams.'

'I weren't reckoning on livin' with yer,' said Freddy. 'I got my place here, as Matron's right-hand man. I was lookin' on it as a bit of a supplementary post, while I'm waiting for a proper job, in racin' or military stables.'

Obadiah smiled. He could hear Margaret's voice behind Freddy's words. Well, he thought, one good turn deserves another.

'Be around at my house at six o'clock sharp this evening, and you can take Dapple back to her stables at the Kepple's Head. We will have a month's trial and see how we suit each other.'

'Right you are, Doctor,' said Freddy, and shook him firmly by the hand. He then rushed back up the steps and into the home whooping at the top of his voice.

It would be futile to ring the bell, thought Obadiah, as he walked round to the side of the building and through the garden gate. Matron Sankey was with the children who were sitting around her on the grass. They watched her every move with rapt attention. She was juggling. Obadiah was astonished. He realised the objects flying through the air were coloured eggs. Every so often she stopped the threw one of the eggs to a child, amid hearty cheers, and then resumed her juggling. Her skills did not stop there, for she began a series of conjuring tricks involving coloured flags, handkerchiefs, and a top hat filled with liquorice comfits; the whole fantastic performance was brought to an end by Freddy ringing a bell. 'Tea's ready in the hall. Don't all rush,' he said.

'Doctor Pragnell, you find us celebrating,' said Matron smiling broadly.

'Celebrating what?' asked Obadiah, feeling his spirits lifting.

'Lionel and Horace Stebbings are joining the navy. They're off to *HMS Ganges* in the morning, and now, with Freddy's new position, it's a triple celebration.'

'What position?' asked Obadiah, feigning innocence.

'Surely you gave him the position as your Tiger? I cannot believe you would have let such an opportunity slip you by.'

'Yes, Margaret, I gave in to your and Freddy's combined scheming.'

'Good, now, let's have tea in the sitting room. You have an official look about you.'

After they had settled themselves at either end of a small table, covered with a starched cloth, she said, 'Fire away, I can see you have something on your mind.' Obadiah was familiar with the room from visits during the previous matron's tenure. It had been transformed from a dark, cluttered place to a homely sitting room. The furniture was well polished, there were fresh flowers in a vase on the desk, and the walls were hung with the children's paintings and first efforts at embroidery.

'Do you remember me once telling you that I had rescued a baby found half dead in a boat some while ago?'

'Oh yes, I do,' said Margaret, pouring him a cup of tea. 'She was cared for by a woman who had lost her own child, and was thriving the last time you saw her.'

'That was my impression. However, I was called to the workhouse to do a vaccination, and who do I find but the child herself, in the most wretched state.'

'Why is she there?'

Obadiah told her in as few words as he could.

'Naturally, you want to rescue her.'

'I don't think Augusta could be expected to.'

'No, that would not answer. She would always be second best to your own family, whether you wished it or no.' Margaret stirred her tea thoughtfully. 'She must come here quickly, Obadiah, before another child is brought in. We're dangerously near capacity in the infants' dormitory.'

'You know the children have to come from military families? Beattie is an orphan, her parents unknown. I doubt if any letters exist from Jacob Salter, even then, it would be too much to hope. Should we find them, it's unlikely that there would be any mention of Beatrice.'

'That is where we have to be somewhat inventive,' said Margaret.

'What do you mean?'

'What regiment was this soldier in and whereabouts in India did he serve?'

'I don't know. I think it was Cawnpore; I'm not sure.'

'Capital! He's most likely dead, which gives us carte blanche to find a letter overlooked somehow.'

'Margaret!'

'Don't look so sanctimonious, Obadiah, the ends well justify the means. I have friends in the army. Anyone who nursed at Balaclava can rely on their support.'

'Just give me the relevant details. Now, the next board meeting is in a fortnight, by which time the letter will have been found, and the case of Beatrice Salter placed on the agenda. An orphan of Cawnpore will elicit all the necessary sympathy.'

'Margaret, I never thought forgery was one of your accomplishments,' said Obadiah with mock severity. 'It will be lock-picking next.'

'No,' she said dryly, 'I think poisoning may be a skill worth acquiring. Go home, Doctor Pragnell, I want to rejoice with my family.'

'How was your day, dearest?' asked Augusta when he stepped in through the door.

'One of mixed fortunes,' he said, kissing her on the cheek.

Chapter Sixteen

It was a hot, dusty, clanking journey, with the sun blazing through the windows. Augusta gazed out at the towns and villages, green and golden in the September sun, as the train steamed past them. Harvest workers toiled in the fields building ricks: the women in bonnets with floppy brims; and men in their shirtsleeves. Cows sought the shade under the trees, swishing the flies off with their tails.

'Boat, Nanny look!' urged Albie, his face pressed against the window as they passed Fareham creek. 'Only a little one, big boats at home.'

Sammy was more intent on spying out the different animals. 'When will we see Uncle Hector's farm?' he asked. 'We've been on this train for ever and ever.'

'A few more stops yet,' she said, smiling at his eagerness. 'We have the mill to see at Botley and the trains at Eastleigh before we stop at Romsey.'

'Uncle Hector will come to meet us with his wagon and then we shall have a picnic, somewhere in the shade, with Nanny,' said Obadiah.

Albert turned to her. 'Mama, are you coming with us?'

'Later, Albie, I have to go and see Grandpa and Grandma's house and say goodbye to it.' Augusta bit her lip, and stared out of the window. What a void there was between saying and doing, she thought. Obadiah had been so patient with her, even offering to go and pack up Meadholm himself. But she must go herself and lay the past to rest. Papa would expect it of her.

'Nanny,' she said. 'Why don't we all have a glass of barley water? It will refresh us before we step out into the sun. Obadiah, will you get down the hamper?'

'What else is in there?' asked Albie, peering over the edge of the wicker lid.

'Never you mind, young sir,' said Nanny, pulling out the bottle from its nest of straw. 'Sit you down in that corner with your brother, and your papa will fetch out the glasses.'

Could she do it? Was she grown up enough? Sometimes Augusta caught sight of herself in a mirror at a tea party. She was indistinguishable from all the other women laughing, talking and nibbling little cakes. But then, sometimes with Obi, she felt that she hadn't grown up at all. He was so serious and purposeful. What was her purpose? With Sammy and Albie, she had no doubts. She was their beloved mama and they had such fun together. But life was supposed to be more than fun, wasn't it? Lately, she had begun to help Obi again in the dispensary and he had praised her efforts. Nevertheless his words failed to satisfy her. They were like a pat on the head to a willing child. In the bedroom, she felt her failure even more. They would kiss and caress one another and she would even begin to feel a stirring of desire for him. Obi would kiss her breasts, and then it was all haste and confusion with him panting and

132

thrusting at her. Worse, was his apology for troubling her, which humiliated both of them.

'We're here, darling,' he said, breaking into her thoughts. 'Look, over there by the railings – Uncle Hector.'

'Gussie, my girl, does my eyes good to see you,' he said, holding out his arms. 'Too long it's been, too long.'

She hugged his dusty brown farm coat that smelled of grass and sweat. 'I'm sorry about Aunt Susannah,' she murmured into his chest.

The old man nodded gruffly, his blue eyes moist. 'My Susannah was a rare, good woman. Passed off peaceful like a babe. Not like your folks.' He shook his head. 'Tarrible that was, tarrible.'

Augusta gulped.

'Good to meet you, sir,' said Obadiah, hurrying forward with the boys.

'Are you really a farmer?' asked Sammy, looking up at his red-faced Toby jug of an uncle.

'That I be, young master, and who might you be?'

'I'm Samuel Pragnell, and this is my brother Albert.'

'Would you like to ride up the front with me, or in the shade with your ma?'

'With you, Uncle; yes, please,' they said, climbing eagerly either side of him.

'Ladies, that's clean sacks on the seats and I thought to bring two sunshades.' 'Twon't be long afore we gets to the farm.' He turned to his niece. 'I'll drop you and Mister up at the top of the lane, and you can come down to the farm when you've conducted yer business.'

'Thank you, Uncle,' she said, settling herself on the rickety plank seat between her husband and Nanny. Augusta was glad she had doused a handkerchief with lavender water and brought Mama's old ivory fan. By the time they had reached Nursling she and Nanny were sweltering. Obadiah helped her down onto the flagstones, in front of her home, and she waved to the boys until the wagon was out of sight.

Augusta turned around expecting her father to appear, his arms open in welcome, but the house was silent. The lion knocker was dull from lack of polish, and the white-pillared porch was filled with dead leaves. She looked up at the sagging roof, noticing gaps where the terra cotta tiles had fallen off. Yellowing muslins hung in the windows and the horseshoe above the door slewed drunkenly from one nail. Meadholm had died of neglect. Obadiah took her hand in his and Augusta could feel his anxiety pulsing between their fingers. The weight of his concern was too much. 'Obi,' she said, 'you go on down to the farm. Leave me our picnic bag, I only need a scone and a drink. The boys will want to show you everything. Please, darling. I need to do this on my own.'

'But darling . . .'

'No, I won't be moved on this. When I am ready I shall join you. Please go, Obi, I need to do it for myself.'

Obadiah kissed her before walking off down the lane leading to Dovecote Farm, while Augusta turned back to the house. She looked up at the withered *Passiflora* vine around the porch. It reminded her of her tenth birthday, that far-off August, when she had won the prize at Sunday school. Then, she had held a passion flower in her hand, and recited all the religious features of the plant: How the ten petals and sepals represented the disciples, leaving out Judas, who betrayed Christ, and Peter who denied Him: the corona stood for the crown of thorns, and the five stamens for Christ's five wounds; there were three stigmas representing nails on the cross, and the tendrils resembled the scourging whips. What a serious little girl she had been.

Taking the key from the envelope in her handbag, she eventually got it to turn in the lock. The door creaked open. Her home smelled of damp plaster, soot and dust. Augusta tried to remember the scents of her childhood as she drifted through the rooms. Mama would have had all the windows open on such a day and the blinds drawn. The house would be wonderfully cool: with the combined scents of lavender and honeysuckle, wafting in from the garden, mixed with the beeswax furniture polish, Papa's tobacco and the smell of baking from the kitchen. Best of all was the green fragrance, when Damson, their pony, was hitched up to the mower and Papa walked him back and forth across the grass. What had delighted her, as a little girl, were the leather boots the pony wore to avoid leaving hoof marks on Papa's lawn.

Augusta wandered through the house: picking up a paperweight and setting it down again; touching the yellow keys on the piano, hearing their clicking dissonant sound and her footfalls echoing in the empty rooms. The curtains were faded and thick with dust. Papa was right: she could not go back. It was as if the house knew of her parents' death and had entered into a period of mourning. She had intended to be methodical and make a list of items to be brought down to Portsmouth, but her mind refused to settle to the task.

Feeling hungry, she decided to picnic at the kitchen table, and dusted off a chair with her gloves before sitting down and unwrapping her picnic. Spreading the napkin out she took out a scone and bit into it before taking a swig of barley water from the bottle Nanny had packed for her. There were moments still when she forgot that her parents were dead. Emerging from sleep sometimes, she would plan a letter only to be pierced with the pain of remembering. If only there had been a funeral, she thought, with coffins and black horses – a proper leave-taking.

It was the cracked pudding-basin on the dresser that made her cry. The inside was stained with blackberry juice. Summer pudding, a favourite of her mother's, was served always on her birthday, on the first of October. That dear face would be shiny with joy, as Cook carried her treat to the table. 'I declare this is the best one yet,' she would say. 'It's those Angelina Burdett plums, they give it a rare piquancy.'

The dam of her grief burst out. 'Mummy, oh Mummy,' she sobbed. The sun had left the window, when with aching head and parched throat she dried her face in the napkin and took another gulp of barley water. Almost instinctively, Augusta took her sketchpad from the picnic bag. She drew the cracked basin, surrounding it with blackberries and plums. 'Happy Birthday, Mummy', she wrote underneath. For a moment she stood in the doorway before closing it behind her. Each room evoked a particular memory and an appropriate drawing. Still hanging on the hallstand was a lead and collar with the name 'Jupiter' stamped on a brass label. Augusta sat on the stairs making a sketch of her father's dog, standing on his hind legs, the lead in his mouth. 'Jupiter, dearest of companions', she wrote at the bottom of the page. In the drawing room it was hard to see what to record. The furniture was draped in sheets and there were bare patches on the walls, where the pictures had been taken down before being shipped to India. Here, at some time, a bird had fallen down the chimney and flittered frantically around the room showering everything with soot, before collapsing exhausted on the window-seat. Mama – I haven't placed you yet, she thought. Returning to the sitting room she uncovered her mother's writing desk by the window. There she had sat so often, pen in hand, gazing out of the window, writing to her husband. *'Darling Arthur, the garden is looking glorious today.'*

Augusta climbed the stairs and stood in the doorway of her parents' bedroom, looking around her. Her eyes were drawn to the brass galleon fire screen by the grate, and Papa's stud box on the dressing table. Sitting on the faded pink nursing-chair she sketched a quick impression of him, sat in front of the mirror, wrestling with a starched collar. *'Dratted invention,'* she wrote.

In the nursery, at the back of the house, she found a box of bricks and the picture of the angel she had loved as a child. Augusta closed her eyes and Nanny Groves' round face with its black eyebrows and red cheeks swam before her. She made a rapid impression of her round figure and hands busy darning a sock by the nursery fire. In the nursery cupboard, she found Nanny's sewing basket. Augusta knew every item inside it, from the wooden darning mushroom and tartan pincushion to the ivory lace-bobbins. Nanny had threaded them together for her to use as a rattle. The click, click, click of the bobbins; the hissing and crackling of the fire, and Nanny's singing were the sounds of her childhood. Augusta slid the bobbins into the pocket of her skirt before leaving the nursery, and shutting the door behind her. Looking into her own bedroom she felt as if a stranger had inhabited it; the girl that had slept and dreamed there was no more. Her home was with Obadiah and the boys. Standing looking down the garden beyond the hedge to the distant cows in Uncle Hector's fields, Augusta felt a small measure of peace. The drawing had healed and finalised that part of her life and she was now ready to leave Meadholm behind. Taking a large hessian bag from the back of the kitchen door, she packed up the collar and lead, the angel picture and the stud box.

Augusta left the house by the back gate and strolled towards Dovecote Farm.

In the distance she could see Sammy and Albie sat up on Beauty, Uncle's black Clydesdale. They were laughing and Obadiah had the bridle in his hand. Uncle Hector was in the field beyond, supervising the building of a hayrick.

'Hello, Madam.' Nanny Hobbs was stood at the gate to the first field, a large cabbage leaf tucked into the back of her bonnet. 'Come over into the cool, under the oak tree. Let me help you with they things.'

'Oh thank you, Nanny,' she gasped, taking her hand and stepping over the stile. 'A strange assortment, and not worth tuppence of a rag and bone man's time,' she said, settling down on the rug under the tree.

Nanny smiled at he. 'Rich with meaning for you, Madam,' she said.

Augusta touched her arm. 'Oh yes, how right you are.'

'It do put me in mind of my mother's passing. My sisters and me went to her cottage, gathered up all her things and shared them out between us. I took her paring knife what she had used all her married life. The blade were worn all thin and narrow, but, now, every time I pick it up I feel her hand upon it and it do comfort me. Going to her place set a seal on the past, and carried sommat forward into the future.'

Augusta wanted to fling her arms around the homely soul with the cabbage leaf hat. She thought of all the letters of condolence that she had received, soon after her parents' death – each beautifully written with sentiments elegantly expressed. None compared with the simple kindness of Nanny's words.

'Thank you,' she said, 'that's most comforting.'

'Darling, finished so early?' Obadiah came towards her from the other end of the field with Albie on his shoulders and Sammy skipping along behind.

'Yes, Obi,' she said, 'I've finished entirely. The new occupants are welcome to every stick and stone.'

'That is good, Gussie,' he said putting his hand on her shoulder, his face tender with concern.

'Mummy, Uncle Hector says I can come and stay on the farm next spring, and help with the ploughing. Isn't that stupendous?'

Augusta looked at his flushed, dirt-streaked face and dusty boots. 'Yes, Sammy, that is truly stunning news.'

'A cow licked my face, Mama. Its tongue was ever so rough,' laughed Albie. He thrust a piece of paper at her. 'I drawed you a picture.' It was on an old envelope that had been cut and flattened out to form a page.

She spread it on the rug and was astonished at her son's depiction of a corn stook. It was a wonderfully, well-observed picture for a six-year-old. The stalks all converged towards the centre at different heights, bound together with twine. Each ear hung down, heavy with grain, and the whole bundle stood firmly balanced n the field. 'That is wonderful, Albie.' She glimpsed Sammy watching her. 'And you, Sammy, are going to be a proper farmer, one day.'

'Let me take your bag, Gussie. Uncle Hector says we are welcome to go up to the farmhouse and have tea with him and tidy ourselves. One of the women from the village has got things ready.' He took out his pocket watch. 'Four o'clock, we have an hour and a half before we need catch the train.'

Augusta took his hand and squeezed it. The two boys leapt and tumbled over the field, and Nanny Hobbs walked behind them with the folded rug. She held her parasol and Obadiah carried the picnic hamper and her bag from Meadholm. 'Gussie,' he said, 'your father would be so proud of you.'

'I feel quite proud of myself,' she said, 'but now, darling, I want to go home.'

Chapter Seventeen

My Dearest Ruth,

I hope you are well and little Beattie. Your idea of making the child our own makes me so happy. After the loss of our Sarah, God has sent us a new daughter to love and care for. I give you my blessing.

Give my regards to Constable Norris and his family. I pray God that I will return safely to you and little Beattie.

You are ever in my thoughts and prayers,

Your loving husband,

Jacob

Silently, Obadiah congratulated Margaret Sankey on her inventive skills, while the secretary turned to her and said, 'What are your wishes in this matter, Matron?'

'The home was brought into being for the care of children from military families. As the daughter of a soldier, this child deserves a place here.'

'Our duty is quite clear,' said the Commander. 'We accept this little girl, and meanwhile ascertain what we can of Corporal

Salter. What does the committee think of this?' he said turning to Miss Parsons.

'I believe, Matron,' she said, 'that the infants' dormitory has fourteen beds. You have told us that they are at present occupied.'

'The eldest infant is now seven years old. She can go tomorrow to the Frobisher dormitory, where her sister will welcome her.'

'Perhaps we should put the matter to a vote?' asked the Commander.

Matron Sankey looked at Obadiah, her eyes signalling him to do something.

'Beatrice Salter is pale, listless and underweight. Frankly, I would be ashamed to tell Corporal Salter how ill his daughter has been treated.'

'A show of hands, please,' said the Commander. 'Six in favour and one against,' he noted. 'Matron, I will expect a full report next month on our new infant's progress.'

Light headed with relief Obadiah took his leave. They had done it.

Beattie just had time to slip the card into her pocket. She couldn't even say goodbye to Mabel and Gertie.

'You should be grateful, getting a chance like this; be the making of you.'

She gave Gypsy a quick hug and nodded to Mrs Figgis before climbing up into the trap with the doctor. If he hadn't smiled at her she would have made a run for it.

The boy who was holding the pony turned round and said, ''Ello, Miss, pleased to meet ya.'

The trap bowled out of the gates and the pony's feet clip-clopped along. Beattie looked around her. Perhaps this was a venture like the ones in the Bible. Mabel and Gertie had told her about this man called Noah what had a message from God to build this boat and fill it with all sorts of animals. Gertie said it rained like buggery and the boat ended up on top of a mountain. Then, when the water went down, there was a rainbow and a bird with leaves in his beak. Mabel said it was true or strike her dead. Beattie turned to the doctor. 'Is this a venture?' she asked.

'Yes, Beattie, I rather think it is,' he said, smiling at her.

'Will it be the making of me?' she asked, parroting Mrs Figgis's words.

The doctor burst out laughing. 'I think you are very well made already, my dear. At the Mariners' Home you will make friends, learn to read and write and even have some fun.'

She didn't know what fun was, but writing was that swirly stuff on the card in her pocket. 'One day,' she said carefully, 'will I write Beatrice Salter?'

'Yes, you will write your name and address and much, much more.'

'Will I have to say grateful?'

The doctor looked angry, not with her, but at something she couldn't understand. 'No, Beattie,' he said, 'I promise you. You can forget that word this instant.'

They trotted past the graveyard with its iron gates, and down a long road. At the bottom was a big church and its tombstones. Dr Pragnell said that soon they'd be at Fratton Bridge and pass over the railway line.

'I ain't never seed a train,' said Beattie, feeling excited at the prospect. 'I heard them rattlin' past the bottom end of the yard.'

'You shall see one, I promise you,' the doctor said, smiling at her.

A great big wagon rumbled past, full of beer barrels, drawn by huge black horses. All sorts of shops, there was, with striped shades over the windows. One of them had dead pigs hanging up off shiny hooks, then a fish shop, with a man in a straw hat scooping cockles out of a barrel with a tin cup. Up at the bridge everything seemed to be happening at once. There was a shrill whistle, and loads of smoke and a great green engine rushed underneath them, pulling lots of carriages with people inside looking at her out of the windows. On the pavement was a lady in a shawl and straw hat, with buckets of flowers all around her. Over the bridge they were in a smaller street. Two women in aprons talked to a man sharpening their knives on a grindstone. Boys and girls hopped and skipped over chalk marks on the pavement, while an old man scooped up some horse muck into a bucket.

'What's he want that for?' said Beattie, in surprise.

'For his garden,' said the doctor. 'He'll put it on the soil, to make the flowers grow.'

Beattie wrinkled her nose. 'Wouldn't want my garden ponging of horse shit.'

'You must call it manure,' Dr Pragnell said.

'Won't make it smell no different,' she declared.

The roads got bigger, lined with white stone buildings and big red brick ones.

'This is Queen Street, Beattie, the gateway to Portsea and the home of the navy.'

There were people everywhere and it smelled of beer and cooking. Strangely dressed men, in straw hats and blue collars with white stripes, and funny wide-legged trousers; Dr Pragnell called them sailors. There were brown shiny buildings, with curly golden writing on them and a picture swinging on a stick outside. The children had no shoes and the women were shouting at them, and cuffing them round the head. Beattie noticed a red brick wall running all the way down one side of the street. At the end were two gates with golden balls on top. A policeman stood beside it, looking everywhere at once.

'That is the Royal Naval Dockyard,' said Dr Pragnell, 'and here is The Hard.'

It was an open space with more shiny buildings, lots of carriages and tons of sailors. There were women with painted faces, shouting and carrying on. But, on the other side of The Hard were little boats pulled up on the stones. When Beattie looked beyond them there was a space filled with water and great big boats with sails fluttering high above her head. There didn't seem to be an end to this water, for it stretched as far as she could see out of the window of the trap.

'That's the sea.'

The sight of the heaving green space, moving about all the time and slapping itself against the stones, excited her. Beattie licked her lips and tasted salt on them. She would like to have got down from the trap and taken a closer look, but Dr Pragnell said that when they turned the next corner they would be at Kettle Street, where the Mariners' Home was. I'll see you again, she promised the sea, before it disappeared from view.

Freddy jumped down and helped her onto the pavement. Beattie stood at the bottom of the steps and looked up at the Mariners' Home. There was the high tower, in the middle, with windows, then lower sides. In front was a patch of grass, then trees at one side and, at the other, hankie patches of garden. In one of them a girl in a check dress and apron was pulling up some stalks and throwing them into a basket. She looked again at the front door, with its shiny knocker and letterbox. It opened as she was about to mount the steps. A tall lady with a blue dress and a white cap tied under her chin, in a big bow, walked towards her.

'Beattie Salter, I am delighted to make your acquaintance,' she said, holding out her hand. 'I welcome you to your new home.'

Beattie held up her hand. The lady had a deep voice that sounded like singing. Her face was like Mr Punch, then she smiled, and the knot in Beattie's belly undid itself.

Margaret Sankey recognised the fragile pride, in the squared shoulders and fierce expression on Beattie Salter's face. Her hand slipped away from her grasp like a wriggling fish, and her eyes darted everywhere. Normally, the task of settling in a newcomer would have fallen to Miss Swift, the Infants' mistress, but not today. She and Obadiah had schemed to get this child accepted. Nothing must go wrong.

'Come with me,' she said. 'We must find you some new clothes and settle you into our routine.' Beattie followed her up the main staircase to the girls' quarters. At the clothes' store she selected a white camisole, drawers, black lisle stockings and a regulation red and navy check dress. She also took out a sewing box and two pairs of black boots. They went from there along the echoing corridor to the bathroom.

As she ran some cold water into the bath she said, 'Every child that comes here must be washed and dressed in our clothes. You will find, Beattie, that I am a stickler for cleanliness.'

'What's a sticker?' asked Beattie, standing in the doorway, looking as if she might run at any moment.

'A stickler is someone who likes things done their way. Now arms up, let me help you out of these things.' The child allowed herself to be undressed, and sat on a chair while Matron donned an apron and poured hot water from two huge enamel jugs into the bath. After testing the temperature with her elbow, she helped Beattie into the bath.

'We shall have to get rid of these, I'm afraid.' Matron tried not to hold the workhouse clothes at arm's length.

'Gotta get summink out the pocket,' said the child, kneeling up in the water and holding out her hand. Margaret went to help her, but Beattie glared. 'Secret, you gotta shut yer eyes.'

Holding the dress just beyond her reach, she paused and looked down at the set expression on the four-year-old's face. It was unfair of her, the child was powerless, but Margaret knew she must gain the upper hand. 'What do you need to say for me to do what you want?'

'Please,' she whispered, staring at the dress.

Matron closed her eyes.

'Can open them, now.'

'Thank you, Beattie,' she said, taking back the dress. After she had been thoroughly washed with carbolic soap from head to foot, Beattie obediently stepped out of the bath and onto the mat. Matron dried and dressed her, studying the child's thin body, noting the bruises on her shins and the corns on her toes from ill-fitting boots. She measured some tape around the child's thin legs and quickly stitched a pair of garters. Beattie seemed swamped by her clothing, and it took several tryings on to find the right footwear. Obadiah had thought her to be five years old but the workhouse had recorded her birthday as 10th January 1856, which made her just over four and a half. Whatever the truth, she badly needed feeding up.

'Why do yer skin get all creased up in the water?' Beattie asked, studying her fingers. 'Then when yer not lookin' it smooves out again.'

'I don't know,' Margaret answered, taken with the child's curiosity.

'I fort grown ups knowed everythink.'

'Nobody knows everything, Beattie,' she said, smiling in spite of her efforts to be stern. Beneath that urchin exterior was a keen intelligence, Matron was sure of it. Heavens, she chided herself, I must not make a favourite of this child.

'Do you want to have a look at your new self?'

The child nodded. As they left the bathroom she suddenly let go of her hand and darted back inside. 'Forgot summink,' she said. A few seconds later, she came out again, patting her pocket.

Beattie stared into the mirror that was held out for her. 'You won't change me name, will ya?' she asked. 'It b'longs to me.'

'Certainly not; Beattie Salter is who you are.' She watched the child looking at herself in the mirror, and wondered what she was thinking. It must have been a bewildering day, so far, and there was more to come.

'What 'appens now, Matrin?'

'Today, you can go and play with the others and then it will be dinner time.'

Once downstairs Margaret sent for Clara Stiggant, a robust seven-year-old. 'Clara, this is Beattie Salter. I want you to take her out to meet the other girls, then sit next to her at dinner.'

'Yes, Miss Sankey,' said Clara. She turned to the new girl and held out her hand, 'Want to play skipping?'

'If yer like.' Beattie let go of Clara's hand and followed her into the Infants' yard.

Matron was called away from her vigil at the window, and did not see Beattie again until mealtime, in the large dining hall. It was one of the things she wanted to change, this long, high-ceilinged room with its parquet flooring and large brown tables. She wanted a small bright place for the infants, with chairs of the right size and pictures on the walls, but she had to be careful. She was already sailing close to the wind with Matilda Wendover, the Commander's sister. She must let things lie for a while before she battled for the next improvement.

'For what we are about to receive may the Lord make us truly thankful,' she said, taking her place and removing her napkin from its ring.

Beattie had obviously not been used to cutlery. Her hand hovered over the potato, then picked up the fork and put it whole into her mouth. She was a quick learner, she would give her that. By the end of the meal the child was managing her knife and fork at least as well as the other children.

Other duties claimed Matron until evening prayers in the Infants' dormitory. Fourteen nightgowned figures knelt at their beds.

'Lighten our darkness, we beseech Thee, O Lord, and by thy great mercy defend us from the perils and dangers of this night; for the love of thy only Son, our Saviour, Jesus Christ.'

The girls mumbled and stumbled over the words, then climbed into their beds. She tucked them in, and made sure that the nightlight was securely fixed in the saucer, away from any draughts before bidding them all 'Good night all of you and God bless you.'

Beattie stepped down from her bed, onto the shiny wood floor as a shrill whistle blew.

'All done wiv whistles here,' said Molly. 'Gotta go an' wash yerself, then 'nother whistle for breakfist.'

Everything was different. The windows had railings on the bottom and the top was open, making the red curtains flutter in the breeze. Smells were different too: flowery going up the stairs, in the bathroom soapy, and, in the dining room, smells what made your mouth fill up with water. At workhouse everythink had ponged of cabbage or wee. Here it was hot cheese or sausages. Then the sugary scent of rice, and the jam what you could dollop on your puddin', and swirl it around makin' it go all pink. Eating was a palaver with knives, forks and spoons. There were different plates for dinner and afters. It was nice not having your pudding tasting of gravy.

Cleaning mad they was. The clothes was nice and the shoes fitted a treat. Best of all was a bed all to herself. She wondered if Gertie and Mabel was missing her. Probably the only one wanting to see her would be Gypsy.

The girls in Frobisher dormitory was all right. Course, they had to treat her proper, 'cos there was always someone watching them. Clara was not bad, but she liked the girl in the bed across the way from her, called Molly. Her hair was orange coloured and all tight curls. There was rusty spots all over her face called freckles. She had winked at her, and Beattie was sure they would have larks together.

That matron said she would be going to school in the morning and would learn her to read and write. Sliding her hand under the pillow she took out the card that Dr Pragnell had given her. *I am Beatrice Salter,* she whispered to herself.

Chapter Eighteen

'Carry on with your copying, children,' said Miss Swift. 'I have to see Miss Sankey for a moment. Clara, I shall leave you in charge. Remember to put the date at the top of the page. January the 9th 1862. What are the numbers? That's it, Molly, nine, one, eight, six, two.'

Beattie dipped her pen in the inkwell and tried to get a proper grip on it. Writing had been such a disappointment to her. However hard she tried, the marks forming beneath her fingers never looked anything like the ones set out for her in the copy-book. In spite of the cold, her hands were sweaty, making the pen slippery and difficult to control. Just as she was dipping the nib back into the inkwell, Clara sneaked up on her and snatched her book.

'Give it back,' she yelled, struggling to reach it, as Clara held the book high above her head.

The bigger girl stood on a chair and held open the pages. 'Look what Beattie done. All scribbles. Stupid, like big Aggie.'

Beattie grabbed the back of the chair and pulled it towards herself until it rested on two legs. 'Give it back,' she screamed.

Clara climbed onto a desk, out of her way. 'Stupid, stupid,' she crowed.

'Stupid,' chanted some of the girls.

Her heart racing, Beattie leapt after her and knocked Clara to the ground. The girl fell over backwards onto the floor. Furiously, Beattie set about her, kicking, punching and pulling her hair. The copy-book was forgotten. What she wanted was to wipe that mocking smile from her face, and stop her saying that word.

'Stupid,' gasped Clara, tugging Beattie's plaits.

'Stupid, stupid.' The words were like nails stabbing at her. She writhed out of the bigger girl's grasp, made a fist, and punched at her with all her strength.

'Ooh,' Clara roared, blood pouring down her face.

Triumph and fright whirred in Beattie's head. On the floor was her book. As she bent to pick it up, still roaring loudly, Clara snatched it, and rubbed it on her face before throwing it back at her. It was now all splattered with blood. 'You cow,' screamed Beattie, leaping at her in a fury. 'You blooming cow.'

It was a while before either child realised that the room had grown silent. There was a sudden slam of a desk lid and Beattie looked up into the eyes of Matron Sankey and her teacher.

'Go to my room at once, the pair of you. Clara, hold this handkerchief to your nose.'

'Miss Swift, I leave you to settle your class.'

Beattie stood in Matron Sankey's room watching Clara, snivelling and dabbing at her nose. She wasn't sorry. Behind her back was the copy-book, now a mishmash of blood and ink.

'Be quiet, Clara. Let me see; there now, I have cleaned you up. It doesn't look too serious,' said Matron. 'You will have a bruise and some swelling, but there are no bones broken. Sit down and hold the wet cloth to your nose.' She turned to Beattie and glared at her.

'I am ashamed of you, Beattie. Your behaviour was that of a savage, nothing could excuse it. What possessed you to behave in such a manner?'

It was that word that did it – that and the laughing. It wasn't fair. She had tried so hard. Why couldn't she make the letters do as she wanted? Beattie stared down at the mat, the pattern going all wobbly through her tears. The word burned in her heart. 'Stupid, stupid.' She winced as she remembered all of them chanting and laughing, even Molly. Oh, she hated Clara, and at this moment she hated Matron Sankey.

'Beattie, I am waiting, what have you to say for yourself?'

'I didn't do nothing,' whined Clara.

'That I doubt, Miss. Now, I am going to sit here and wait, I have all day. Beattie, I want the truth. Clara, while she is speaking, you will remain silent.'

'Took my book.'

'No, I never she got it behind her back.'

'Silence!' Matron turned back to her. 'Beattie what made you behave so badly?'

'Called me . . .' She couldn't say it.

'What did you call her, Clara? . . . I did not hear that, speak clearly now. If I have to go back to your classroom and find out what you called Beattie, I shall do so. But I want you to tell me. Have the courage of your convictions.'

'Stupid,' whispered Clara.

'Why did you do that?'

''Cos she can't write.'

'How would you feel if I called you stupid? Would you like it?'

'No.'

'So you wanted to hurt Beattie, to make her unhappy?'

Clara shook her head.

'What did your classmates do? Did they laugh? Yes,' said Matron, 'I should think that they laughed and that made you feel tremendously clever. Now, Clara, do you know the one thing that I hate above all other faults?'

Clara shook her head.

'It is deliberate unkindness. You set out to hurt Beattie and make her feel foolish in front of everyone.'

Still holding the hankie to her nose, Clara began to cry noisily.

'And you, Beattie,' said Matron, ignoring Clara, 'you must learn to govern your temper. The world is full of girls like Clara, who delight in hurting others. You must grow a tougher skin. Striking out at everyone will get you into serious trouble.'

The dinner-time whistle shrilled out.

'Both of you are hungry, I am sure. Shake hands and say sorry to each other.'

'Sorry,' Beattie mumbled, letting go of Clara's hand as soon as she could.

'Sorry,' said Clara, in a pretend way that made Beattie want to hit her all over again. 'Clara, I shall inform Miss Swift of the tasks I wish you to perform. Beattie, I will see you directly the afternoon whistle has sounded. Leave your copy-book here, if you please.'

Clara flounced out of the room and shut the door behind her.

'You too, run along now.'

Beattie could not run along, the handle wouldn't turn. Again, she felt her fingers slippery with sweat as she wrestled with the doorknob. Why could she not turn it? She couldn't learn her hand to go the way the handle wanted.

'Allow me,' said Matron, opening the door. 'Beattie, you sit on that temper of yours, and sit as far away from Clara as you can.'

Margaret Sankey rang the bell. One of the older girls, on kitchen duty, answered it promptly. 'Jane, please will you bring me my dinner on a tray. I will have it in here. Oh, and a glass of water, please. Tell Miss Swift to sit in my place in the dining room.'

She picked up the battered copy-book. As she turned the pages she reminded herself that the child was not six years old, until tomorrow. She had had only a year of handwriting practice. The letters were large, with shaky lines, and it was very difficult to identify one from the other. It was the child's distress about her failure that worried her. Beattie was a puzzle. Miss Swift had praised her mental arithmetic and her quickness in answering Religious Knowledge questions. She seemed to have a remarkable memory and the ability to skip and run. Beattie could thread a needle, handle a trowel, and yet she struggled with the door handle. There must be a way out of the impasse and she would find it.

As for Clara, she could help the maid strip the beds on Saturday morning. The slightest lack of co-operation and Aggie would deal with her. Clara's lust for power and popularity would meet its match in Agnes Yerbury. She had thought of getting her to copy out the story of the Good Samaritan from the Bible, but hated the thought of those wonderful words being used as a punishment. No, the Bible was strong meat for small stomachs. It should be used sparingly. She wrote a brief note to Miss Swift and handed it to Jane, along with her dinner tray.

The afternoon whistle blew and Margaret Sankey watched Beattie walking towards her along the garden path. She opened the window and called to her. 'Catch,' she ordered, tossing a ball of wool at her. Instinctively the child reached out with her left hand and caught the ball.

'Open Sesame,' said Miss Sankey, with satisfaction. She crossed the room and opened the door ready for Beattie. 'Come in and sit down, here on this chair beside my desk. I have put a cushion on it to raise you up to the right height. We are going to set about your handwriting, you and I.'

Beattie swallowed hard, and stared at the big yellowy jug that stood on the shelf above the desk. It had come from somewhere called Bakalarva and was a present from a Turkey soldier 'cos Matron had looked after him. She wondered if the soldier had feathers like a real turkey, but then she had seen a picture of him, and he was just an ordinary soldier but with a big black moustache. Beattie wished he had been called Aladdin, and the jug was a magic lamp, specially when Matron opened her writing book. Then she could wish her scribbles and blots away and have a neat row of letters marching across the page.

'I think we should make a fresh start,' said Miss Sankey, taking her book and handing it to her. 'Here, tear it up and put it in the basket; that's it.' She drew up a chair and sat beside her at the desk. 'Now, I want you to tell me, Beattie, what you find hard about writing. Here is a piece of scrap paper. Let me dip the pen in the ink. Just write a row of big "A"s and little "a"s and say, as you are doing it, how it feels.'

Beattie stuck out her tongue and tried to make the line go up to the point of the big 'A' and down again. 'The pen's all slippy,' she said.

'Aha,' said Miss Sankey. 'Now, what I would like you to do is to hold the pen in your other hand.'

Warily, Beattie changed the pen over and continued shaping her letters.

'How does it feel?'

'Don't know yet.'

'Try and write with that hand and see if it's any easier for you.'

'Gertie got hit fer using that hand back at workhouse,' said Beattie, doubtfully.

'If I had met the person who had struck Gertie, I would have been very cross with them.'

Beattie was astonished.

'Now, I will write you a set of "A"s again and you can be getting on with them. I am going up to the stationery cupboard to get you a new copy-book.

Beattie began to write. The pen felt different, more comfortable, between her fingers, but would it make her learn better? She was frightened. The card Doctor had given her with 'Beatrice Salter', written on it was getting all crumpled up. What would happen if it fell to bits? If she didn't never get to write proper, would she forget that she was really Beatrice?

It had been a rotten day. She could still hear the word 'stupid' in her head. Worse was having to say sorry to Clara.

It had been so hard to say, like having to tear the words out of herself and leaving holes behind. Beattie sighed and tried to turn her mind back to her writing.

At first she couldn't believe it. The pen was doing what she wanted. It was going up and down and making letters. They wasn't nearly as good as Molly's or Clara's writing but you could see what they was meant to be. She tried to remember the letters of Beatrice Salter. Sticking out her tongue she wrote the letter 'B' and the pen followed the two big swirls and then the 'e' and the 'a', on until all the letters had been done. She couldn't hardly stop for excitement. There on the page her name was coming out from under her fingers. It wasn't like she wanted it to be but it was tons and tons better. '*Beatrice Salter.*' She had a name and she could write it on her own. As she laid down her pen she was startled by the sound of clapping. Turning around she saw Matron standing behind her, face all smiley and glad.

'Well done, well done, Beattie,' she said. 'You see, it was there all the time, we just had to try something different.'

'Can I keep writing wiv me other hand?'

'Of course you can. With lots of practice you will be able to write as well as anyone.'

'My stars!' Beattie gasped.

'My stars indeed,' said Miss Sankey. 'Off you go now and take your new pen and copy-book with you.'

'Can you write sommink for me ter copy?'

Miss Sankey sat back at her desk. 'What shall it be?' she asked.

'"I will learn to read and write,"' said Beattie.

'You are halfway there,' she said, setting down the words on a scrap of lined paper. 'Determination is half the battle.'

★

Beattie held up her arms and smiled up into that face, then everything melted away just as she was going to say the lady's name. Each time she had the dream, her disappointment on awakening was worse. For a long time it went away and then it came back. It had been so real. She couldn't remember the name. Was it 'Mummy'? She hoped it was. Beattie hit her head with the flat of her hand; then dashed the tears from her eyes. No, she wasn't going to cry – not on her birthday.

This morning she was going to make rock cakes with Molly and Susan. She looked around the dormitory. Was she the first one awake, or were they all pretending? Beattie pattered out to the bathroom. When she came in they all sprang on her. 'Birthday bumps,' they shouted, 'birthday bumps. One, two, three, four, five, six.'

Beattie was laughing and giggling with the others when Miss Swift came in. She was in a long blue nightgown and her hair was all wavy and loose about her shoulders. 'Girls, girls,' she protested, holding a finger to her lips. 'It's only seven o'clock. You will wake Matron.' She stood in the doorway while they piled back into their beds. 'Wait until the morning whistle; until then, quiet as mice, now.' Miss Swift turned to her and smiled, 'Happy birthday, Beattie,' she said, before closing the door.

Lying there in the early-morning gloom Beattie thought about what it would be like to be six. Being five had been better than four; she could do more things, like whistling and skipping, and she was the only one in the dormitory who could climb the pear tree. And now she could write her name. 'Happy birthday, Beatrice,' she whispered to herself.

The breakfast porridge was hot and creamy and there was honey out of the vicar's beehive. Afterwards, it was time for Clara to help change the beds. Beattie and Molly got their skipping ropes, and swept out like duchesses, leaving Aggie to boss Clara about. Today Molly was her best friend, and Cook said the rock cakes was fit for royalty.

'Happy birthday, happy birthday, Beattie,' they shouted.

Everyone was looking at her and smiling. She smiled back and straightened her paper crown. There was a funny feeling in her belly when they sang to her. Part of it was wanting to hide, and the other bit might be being happy.

Chapter Nineteen

Obadiah rejoiced in Albie's enthusiasm. He was so whole-hearted in what he did, especially if it concerned the navy. They could have watched the illumination of the fleet from the top windows of their house, with a telescope, but the boy so wanted to be with the crowds on Victoria Pier. Welcoming the French fleet into British waters and toasting Napoleon, it seemed incredible. But this was August 1865 and perhaps – with the Crimea debacle safely in the past and the mutiny in India beginning to fade in people's minds – perhaps there could be peace among the nations at last.

'I've memorised the order of things, Pa,' Albie said. 'Fifteen minutes before the start, two rockets will be fired from *Victory* to tell the sailors in Spithead to get their long matches lit, and then there will be a third rocket. This will be followed by a nineteen-gun salute from *HMS Hull.*'

Obadiah looked around him at the crowd, packed together on the beach and the pier. There were fathers with children riding on their shoulders and some with their trouser legs rolled up, standing in the water. There was scarcely a ripple on the sea and not a breath of air. He sighed; it was so calm and beautiful as the sea reflected a three-quarter moon in its dark bosom. He looked towards the Round Tower and thought of another occasion, almost ten years ago. How well things had turned out for the little foundling he'd snatched from the Frenchman's jacket on that day. Beattie was now a tall, dark-eyed nine-year-old full of energy and intelligence. 'She is a credit to you, Margaret,' he had said to Matron Sankey only yesterday.

'A credit to herself, Obadiah,' she had answered.

When had they become Obadiah and Margaret to each other? He couldn't quite remember. She was the dearest, yet most eccentric, of friends. With who else could he have discussed the germ theories by Pasteur, or the works of Darwin?

'All that miasma cloud theory was bunkum; Pasteur has proved it, and so did we at Balaclava. The cleaner you kept everything the better the survival rate. One of the men from the sanitary commission, he even cleaned the water closets himself. And look at Owen Chadwick, a voice in the wilderness pleading for a clean, piped water supply. Look at the fall in cholera figures in Portsmouth since his recommendations have been implemented with proper piped water.

Yesterday, they had come close to severing their friendship, on the subject of the existence of God and the word of Genesis.

'Why has a day got to be twenty-four hours, and why has God to be an old man with a white beard?'

'How many hours would you have in your day, Margaret?'

'It's quite irrelevant. The seven days of creation could be seven thousand years or a million. You have only to look around the world to see that natural selection is in operation.

The poor do not inherit the earth, and the cunning get clean away with everything.'

'And what of God?' he asked, almost in a whisper.

'I don't know. I like the words in the first chapter, don't you? "*And darkness was on the face of the deep. And the Spirit of God moved on the face of the waters.*"'

'What do you mean?' he asked, fearfully.

'I think God is the prime mover of creation, but I don't think he can be seen as a person. Rather, he is apprehended in the movement of the sea, the sound of the wind and the sting of rain on the skin. I can be happy with that.'

'But what of a personal God?'

'I don't know, Obadiah. I think we are all born with different gifts and instincts. We come nearest to God's intentions for us when we use our talents to the full, or help others to do the same. Our instinct for good is God-given, but as to evil . . . ?' She shook her head. 'It is certainly present in the world. Evil has a glamour that good cannot compete with, but that doesn't mean we have to throw in the towel. We must have vision. Just remember: when one of your patients survives against all the odds, or one of my children gets a real opportunity to show what's in him, we can chalk it up to the angels.'

Obadiah had been deeply disturbed. Goodness knows what the committee would make of her beliefs.

'Ain't them little boats lovely, Percy, with those lanterns on their masts?' said a voice from behind him.

'Bloomin' dark, can't hardly see nothin. Hurrah! Hurrah! Hark at that rocket.'

'Did you count the shots, Pa? It was a nineteen-gun salute.'

'By Jove,' exclaimed Obadiah, as the whole harbour and Spithead Fleet was suddenly illuminated.

'Oh Pa, isn't that splendid? Red, then white, then blue.'

'Here, Albie, take the telescope.'

'Hurrah, hurrah.' The crowd cheered wildly, as bouquets of rockets leapt into the night sky.

'Wouldn't Sammy have loved this? said Albie, sweeping the horizon with the telescope.

Obadiah wondered if that were so. At this moment he was probably sound asleep after a day of harvesting on Dovecote Farm, with Uncle Hector. His strong blond eldest son was becoming a young man to be proud of. Not that Albie wasn't a credit to him also, but Albie was more complicated, less open than Sammy. Albie shared more in common with Augusta than with him.

'It's all over too soon,' said his son, taking his arm. 'I could have done with a ton of rockets. Next time I might be on one of those ships, Pa. I will be a midshipman on the *Britannia* next year.'

'Come on, Albie, I'm shivering. It will take us a while to get through this throng.' They're growing up too quickly, he thought, pulling his coat collar up against the cool September night.

'I hope Cook has left us something for supper,' said his son, taking his arm. 'I could eat a horse.'

Augusta was enchanted with herself. Her blue silk dress was a triumph. The square neckline sat at the point of each shoulder and skimmed the top of her breasts. Never had she exposed so much flesh. Silver ribbon encrusted with ruby beads and fringing emphasised the neckline, the edges of the bell-shaped sleeves and the frill around the skirt. Mildred had spent an age making matching ribbon rosettes to pin in her hair, which was dressed for the occasion in ringlets. The finishing touch was the ruby and pearl necklace given to her by Papa on her twenty-first birthday.

'Oh, Madam, you looks ever so pretty,' said Mildred now, as she stood by the side of the cheval mirror, holding her evening bag and ivory fan.

'Gussie, my Gussie.'

She saw her beauty reflected in her husband's eyes. Poor Obi, he worshipped her, and she was so undeserving of his love. Sometimes, Augusta hated herself for her lack of generosity. But tonight he was not a provincial general practitioner; he was her handsome prince, whirling her off to the ball. They drove up to Governor's Green in a hired carriage. Obi looked so handsome in his dinner jacket and tight black trousers with satin edges.

Augusta held the white and gold invitation cards. They had the crest of the Duke of Somerset embossed on them and the 'N' and 'V' of Napoleon the third and Queen Victoria. She looked out of the carriage window at all the shops illuminated with gas jets and tricolour bunting in the High Street. Even the tower of St Thomas's Church was bedecked with flags.

The carriage stopped at Governor's Green, transformed from the military parade ground to a brilliantly illuminated and tented space rivalling the Vauxhall Gardens. Obadiah helped her down the steps, and they walked through a vast, triumphal arch. The central portion was for carriages and either side for foot passengers. Augusta looked up at the painted pediment depicting the fleet at Spithead mounted on crimson drapery and gold fringing.

'Who would have thought this was once a drill shed, and

will be again in the morning when the tented ceilings are taken down,' Obadiah said.

Gussie took his arm. 'But for this one evening it's paradise. Obi, I hope we won't meet anyone we know, and then we can pretend we have just met, and you can pay court to me.'

Laughing together, they entered the tented ballroom. The grandeur of the burgundy carpet, the banks of flowers, and the chandeliers, high up in the vaulted ceiling enchanted Augusta. Obadiah handed the invitation cards to a man in a powdered wig.

'Wine, Madam, or fruit cup?'

No, she didn't need wine she was already intoxicated. The last thing she wanted was to be befuddled, every moment must be engraved on her memory. Events like this were scarce in their calendar. She felt a sliver of disloyalty to Obi, so kind and loyal. What would her life have been like had she married one of Mama's well-connected young men? Would she have found an evening such as this commonplace? she wondered. 'Please, kind sir, will you dance with me and save me from the attentions of the French admiral?' Augusta enquired of Obi.

'Madam, I am at your service,' he said, bowing deeply. 'Let me whisk you away to my castle.'

They whirled around beneath the candelabras: he the duke and she the countess. Augusta felt dizzy with excitement. One dance followed another: quadrilles, polkas and then the waltz.

The duke was most attentive, holding her close and whispering pretty compliments. 'Madam, let me escort you to a couch, and bring you some nectar from the Elysian Fields. For you I would swim the Hellespont.'

'Sire, I would not want to tire you. I need your youth and fire for another purpose.'

Oh! It was all such wonderful nonsense. Augusta sat on a velvet couch at the side of the ballroom and sipped her fruit cup, while Obi helped her to a strawberry meringue from the buffet table. Red, white and blue, the colours of the tricolour, were much in evidence in the women's gowns. The men were either in navy or military scarlet, and each with flashes of gold braid. She studied her husband as he walked towards her. At forty, Obadiah was still tall and lean, and the grey streaks in his hair gave him a look of distinction.

Why could she not love him as he deserved? She touched Papa's necklace and wished that she had more of his nature and less of her mother's tendency to sudden whims and dis-satisfactions.

'Why so serious, my countess?' he asked, as he handed her a plate and spoon. 'Remember, gravity is my department.'

'I was thinking,' she said, smiling at him, 'these are called *fraise* in French. I do think the English strawberry is a much better name, don't you, Obi?'

And then the band struck up another waltz. As they whirled around together Augusta became aware of someone waving to them from one of the tables. It was Commander Wentworth, from the orphanage. No, she would not respond. This was her evening, hers and Obi's, they would not be dragged down into the tedious doings of the Mariners' Home.

'Darling,' she said to him at the end of the waltz, 'let's walk home now, instead of waiting for the carriage. It's such a beautiful night.'

'What about your dancing slippers, they will be ruined?'

'Just indulge me, Obi,' she pleaded.

'When do I ever do otherwise?' he said.

'Perhaps, a little later, it will be my turn to indulge you,' she whispered as he bent to kiss her. She steered him away from Wentworth's table. While he left a message for the cabman, she collected her mantle from the cloakroom.

They walked away from Governor's Green and the press of people, back through the triumphal arch and into the Grand Parade. At one side of her was the town wall, and beyond was the water, shifting and dangerous.

'Shall we look at the sea?' asked Obi.

'Let's not,' said Gussie with a shiver. 'I want to see all the lamps lit along the High Street.' She squeezed his arm. 'It has been a splendid, splendid evening, hasn't it?'

'Quite superlative, Countess,' he said, making her a mock bow.

'It seems a different town when it's like this, all the ugliness is hidden away. And this evening, I have had you entirely to myself,' Gussie said.

'There were several hundred others in attendance,' laughed Obi.

By the time they had walked to St George's Square, and their own home, it was midnight. They crept upstairs like conspirators.

'Will you help me off with my dress?' she asked, as they stood together in the bedroom. He kissed her and she returned his kiss. Obi helped her out of her hooped petticoat, and she stood there in her chemise and drawers, her arms wound around his neck. She kissed him again. Beneath his cologne, Augusta drew in the smell of male sweat. Somewhere, beneath her mother's teaching was a freer self that responded to his body.

He looked at her questioningly, and she nodded. 'I must just brush my hair, Obi. You get into bed, my darling, and I shall be with you in a moment.' She pretended to be busying herself at her dressing table, unpinning her ribbons, but she was watching her husband undress. Obadiah had his back to her and she studied the bones of his spine as they curved down the centre of his body. His hips were narrow, and his buttocks, round and tight. He turned and reached for his nightshirt and she saw the whole of the front of his body in one tantalising glimpse. He was like the marble statue she had once seen in a museum, but Obi's skin would be warm and soft, unlike the statues. Gussie had never given a name to the male organs that she glanced at, before his shirt covered them. Oh, she had read the words in Obadiah's books on anatomy, and seen her sons' bodies countless times, but never before had she seen Obi naked. Never had she touched his body. How beautiful he is, Gussie thought, feeling a tender pain for her husband and wanting to kiss and stroke him. She desired him. It was a new emotion for her. How would it feel to run her hands over his body, to hold his penis between her fingers? Hastily she un-buttoned her chemise and unfastened her corsets. How encumbered she was. How long it took to free herself of all her fussy garments. Leaving them in a heap on the floor, she walked naked towards the bed.

Obadiah lay on his side with his eyes closed. 'Good night, my sweet, turn down the lamp, will you?' he said.

Gussie lay beside him staring into the darkness. Obi was sunk in sleep and she had never felt more wakeful. The moment had gone, and she had not the courage to call it back.

Chapter Twenty

Everyone waited for the collector to unload the leftovers, sent to them after last night's banquet at the Naval College. Only the day before they had been deluged with food from the ball at Governor's Green.

'It's either a feast or a famine,' Miss Sankey said. 'In a few weeks we may well be down to bread and scrape.'

Beattie would love to have gone out with the collector on his rounds of the ships and naval establishments, asking for money and bringing back whatever the sailors chose to give. Sometimes the collecting tin would be full of money, and at other times the boys would come back with exotic food from naval parties. Once they'd brought a bag of socks and a bundle of sheets. What would be in the metal mess tins today, after the latest French festivity? It could be anything.

'Beattie Salter and Molly Horrabin, go to the kitchen and help Cook, if you please.'

They needed no second telling after hours spent tacking new school dresses, ready for the older girls to sew.

'Cripes,' gasped Beattie as she took the silver lid from an

oval plate. She was immediately eye to eye with a large pink fish.

'Leave that to me,' said the cook, deftly transferring the fish onto a china platter. 'You two, go to the sink and start washing up these tins, while I get the vittles put away. Do the job proper and, Miss Sankey says, you can go with Fred when he takes them back to the college.'

'What's it called?' asked Beattie, tying an apron round her waist.

'It's a salmon – the king of fish. Now, Miss, you keep your 'ands to yourself,' she said, whacking Molly's hand with the back of a ladle.

'Ooh it ain't 'arf good,' said her friend, spooning up a mouthful of a crisp snowy white stuff, with strawberries on top, from a glass plate.

'That's meringue made with sugar and white of egg. You whips it till your arm is fit to drop off,' said Cook. 'For your cheek, Molly, you can help Aggie skin the rabbits fer tomorrer's dinner. Only needs one girl to go back with Frederick.'

'Mean old cow,' whispered Molly, as Cook carried the salmon across the kitchen to the larder. 'I'm goin' to 'ave another bit. 'Ere, Beattie, open your gob – quick!'

'Ever so sorry,' she wailed, tipping the plate onto the floor as she heard Cook returning.

Beattie bent over the sink, her mouth crammed with the meringue. It was crisp, yet chewy, and flooded her mouth with sweetness, followed afterwards with the juicy contrast of the strawberries.

'Since you've made the mess, Molly, you can clear it up and wash the floor when you've finished.'

'Can't take the meringue back what we've eaten, can yer?' snapped Molly, when she was safely out of range of Cook's ladle. Her face was red with temper as she flounced out to the scullery to get the bucket and floor cloth.

Beattie felt guilty at profiting from her friend's theft, but not guilty enough to own up to her part in it. She wanted the outing with Fred. The dishes piled up endlessly.

'Port wine jelly, duck paté, Chantilly cream, Boudoir biscuits – a right royal feast,' said Cook naming the dishes, as Fred carried them onto the table.

'Town's gone mad,' he said, sliding a sandwich into his pocket. 'The place is smothered wiv flags and bunting. Blue Jackets and Frenchies walkin' about together arm in arm.'

It took many journeys back and forth to the doctor's carriage, to get all the mess tins safely stacked. Beattie was in a fever to be off, but she knew that Freddy would not move an inch until he had eaten his dinner.

He was popular in the dining room, especially among the older boys. As she forked up a mouthful of cottage pie she heard him holding forth on the nearby table.

'Was goin' along one day wiv the doctor and this sailor hollers out to us. He says, "I got a job fer you, your reverence."'

'"I am not a man of the cloth," says the doctor. "I'm a medical man."'

'"Don't matter a row of beans, so long as you got a sharp pair of scissors."'

'"How can I assist you?" says the doc, raising his hat, all polite like.'

'"Nelson needs 'is nails clippin'."'

'But 'e's dead,' said one of the boys, scornfully.

''Sides what would a admiral be doin' in a blue jacket's gaff?'

'So 'oo d'you think it was then?' asked Fred, not in the least abashed.

''Nother old sailor?'

'His missis?'

That brought a roar of laughter.

'Well, yer both miles out, 'cos it was a parrot. It flew all round 'is room a cursin' and carryin' on, then it settles on me shoulder.'

'Was you feared?'

'Out of me wits. Had to stand there while doc trims its 'orrible black nails. Thought 'e might take a fancy to one of me ears.'

'Probbly thought 'twas a slice of bacon,' said one of the boys. Their laughter was drowned out by the shrill note of the afternoon whistle.

'Don't take all day, Fred,' Miss Sankey cautioned. 'Doctor Pragnell wants you back by five and you, Beattie, have sewing to finish.'

'There ain't an inch to spare with all them pots inside. You'll 'ave to sit on top with me.'

Beattie almost leapt up the steps, so eager was she to make the most of her freedom.

'What we'll do is get shot of the stuff over at the college,' said Fred, twitching the reins, 'then we'll 'ave a look around the town.'

'Can we see the sea?'

'After the dockyard, we'll gallop smart right off up the High Street, on to Point Beach and chuck a few stones in the water.'

Beattie was astonished. Every shop and tavern was hung with flags, ribbons and flowers. The Hard was thick with sailors, some with black moustaches and a red pom-pom on their hats. Coming and going from *Denby and Shanks* the naval tailors' shop, with uniforms in the window, were officers in tricorn hats, their jackets smothered in gold braid. They stepped straight into carriages and were borne off towards the High Street. Women with painted faces and gaudy clothes tugged at the sailors' sleeves and swore at them if their attentions were ignored. They crept as near to the dockyard gate as possible and were then driven off by a constable who roared at them, his face ruddy with rage. Fred handed him a letter from Matron Sankey.

'Go through there, to the right. That's the college, with the clock on the front. Go round behind it to that big tent.'

Beattie looked up at the gates. On each pier was a star and anchor and there were strange metal letters strung in an arch between them.

'Don't look like nothing now but when it gets dark it's all lit up. Gas jets they are. All round 'ere at night it's like fairy-land.'

It was a whole different world behind the dockyard wall. Beattie was twisting and turning around looking up at the different buildings, at a big pond with masts floating in it and another with a beautiful boat bobbing up and down on the water.

'Port Admiral's barge,' said Freddy, as they rattled over the cobblestones, between sailors and dockyard men hurrying to and fro. There was the noise of hammers, whistles blowing, shouts and curses. 'Where are the ships?'

'They're way down the other end at the yard, at the Kings Stairs and South jetties. We got to shift the pots and then out. They don't let yer hang about, in here.'

'What's that building over there with the mast on top?'

'Semaphore Tower.'

'What's semaphore?'

'Blimey, Beattie, you ain't 'alf nosey,' laughed Freddy. 'Remember other day when Miss Sankey was out in the garden with them flags? She was sending the lads messages, what was up on the roof, and they was writing the messages down and wavin' flags back at her.'

'Yeah?'

'That's called semaphore.'

'Does a sailor stand up there, then, and wave flags to the ships?'

'You've got me there. Dunno' how it works. Now, give yer brainbox a rest, and look after Dapple while I gets unpacked. Don't want no Blue Jacket scarpering with Doc's horse.'

Beattie looked up at the great balloon-like tent at the back of the college. What would it have been like, she wondered, to arrive there in a ball gown, and sit and eat all those dainty dishes that she and Molly had seen? Fancy staying up until after midnight, with all the lights shining bright as day.

'Where was yer?' asked Freddy, making her jump, as he leapt up into the cab and flicked the reins. 'Miles away you was.'

'Thinking about how the rich get to do things, and we just watch and clear up afterwards.'

'Yeah, Doc and his missis was out other night at Governors' Green, cavorting at this Naval Ball. They was all dressed up in their finery. Course, she, her ladyship, loves all that gadding about, but the doc, he 'ates it.'

'How d'you know?' asked Beattie, sceptically.

'I gets to spend lots of time wiv him trotting about here and there and everywhere. I watches his face. Loves bein' a doctor he do, and people what he sees, they loves him. Ever so clever he is too. Got this old soldier livin' in a cellar, wiv no proper vittles. Well, all his old scars, what 'e got in battles, they started to open up again. Doc hikes him out of there to another gaff, and buys him bags of oranges, and them wounds closes up again, sweet as a nut. But I reckon what he likes best is crossin' swords with Miss Sankey. He do rarely enjoy that.'

'I never seen a sword in Matron's room. You're making it up.'

Freddy laughed out loud and Beattie couldn't help joining in.

'It's just a manner of speaking; means a good old argie-bargie. He says something and she won't wear it. Then she pipes up with 'nother notion, and he sets up in opposition. They knock sparks off each other. Where I am, in my little caboose tucked behind 'er sittin' room, I gets to hear every-think. Course, she's sweet on 'im, stands out a mile. But he's only got eyes for his Augusta.'

Beattie was astonished. How could Miss Sankey be sweet on anyone; she was ugly. 'I don't believe you, you're joshing.'

'Just 'cos she looks like a boot, don't mean she ain't got feelin's, still a woman, ain't she?'

Beattie felt guilty. She loved Miss Sankey, how could she be so unkind about her? It was she who got her reading and writing so well. Miss Sankey had sat up with her, when she had had the whooping cough, and told wonderful stories about

Persephone, Pandora and Hercules. 'Inside there, Beattie,' she had said, tapping her on the forehead, 'is the world of your imagination. You must feed it as you feed your stomach. Ideas are the food of the mind. It is in reading, listening to music, watching people and listening to them that you find out what your talents are. In that head of yours, you are the equal of royalty. And even in the deepest dungeon your mind would still soar above its petty confinements.'

Beattie wanted to know things and be clever like Matron; but she also wanted to be pretty and have bright colours around her. Her latest project was what Miss Sankey called elocution.

'Just because you have not had many material advantages, does not mean that you must automatically speak like a pauper,' she had said. 'You appreciate the beauty and subtlety of your native language from the books you have read, Beattie.' She picked up an exercise book. 'Your writing shows that you are beginning to have a facility for written English and now I want you to take equal care with your speech.'

'I don't want to sound all toffee-nosed,' Beattie had said, doubtfully.

'I am not talking about affectation. What I want is for you to take up your birthright and use the English language expressively and grammatically.'

Her efforts had not been appreciated in the dormitory or the dining room.

'Ooh d'you think you are?' Molly had demanded. 'Duchess of bleedin' Devonshire.'

'Miss Hoity-Toity,' Clara sneered when she caught her reciting poetry to herself.

'Beattie, you died or sommink?' Freddy said, nudging her in the ribs and startling her back into the present. 'I wanted to know if you was ready for a gallop up the High Street and a sight of the briny?'

'I thought we was going to see the sea,' said Beattie, feeling a stab of disappointment.

'Another name for the sea, it is. You know what brine is, don't ya?'

'Course, it's water with salt in it.'

'It's what the sailors call the sea, that and the oggin; got all sorts of names for stuff, 'av sailors, different lanwidge altogether.'

'You're getting really clever, Freddy,' she said, admiringly.

'I looks and listens. You'd be surprised, Beattie. When yer standin' holdin' the horse people treats you like you're invisible, and you hears all sorts.'

She looked around her, as the pony and trap rounded the corner into the High Street, and began to read the names of the shops on either side. There were two big houses joined together, belonging to a Mr Clark, called the 'Berlin Warehouse' and 'Hessian Haberdasher'. She used Berlin wool in tapestry work with Miss Swift, and hessian cloth. They passed a bootmaker and barber's, and then the George Hotel.

'That's supposed to be where Nelson spent his last night, before Trafalgar,' said Fred. 'Then he went through this archway down to the water where we're going.'

'My stars,' gasped Beattie filled with excitement.

They reached the end of the High Street and Freddy leapt off the cab steps and tethered Dapple to a railing by the side of the Garrison Church. He and Beattie walked towards the town walls. The Square Tower was high, white and solid, with a niche high up on which was set a golden bust of a man with long curly hair.

'Who's that?' asked Beattie.

'Old King Charles the First; he landed here and married an ugly Portugee Princess, over in Garrison Church.'

'My stars!'

'Now cut your cackle,' said Freddy, 'and let's go see the briny.'

The town wall continued down the street, with arches at intervals, and ended with a gate that shut off another part of the town, guarded by soldiers in red jackets.

'That's Spice Island. You wouldn't want to set foot down there. All the doxies and cut-purses and villains lives there. Sailors lying drunk in the street and fighting and cursin' from dawn till dusk. No place for a respectable girl to be seen dead in.'

Beattie was immediately curious. She had been about to ask him what a doxie was when he'd called her respectable. Miss Sankey talked about respect – treating people right and having a good opinion of yourself.

'Here we are – the Sally Port,' he said, taking her arm. They walked through an arch in the wall onto a wooden landing stage and there, below, was the sea.

Beattie rushed to the railing and looked down at it. She listened to the sound of the waves breaking on the shingle and was entranced. Back and forth they went, casting up stones and dragging them away again. The sound of the sea filled her head. She tried to slow her breathing to the rhythm of the waves.

'This is Point Beach,' said Fred, walking down the steps and lobbing stones into the water. 'Over there's the Round Tower and back, where we was before, is the Square one.'

Beattie watched the water lapping around her boots. She bent down and scooped some into her hand. It wasn't green when you held it, but no colour at all, until it joined back with the rest of the water and it was moving all the time – moving and sighing. Oh, she was filled with the wonder of it. If only she could sit here, on her own, and just watch and listen until she sound of it lulled her to sleep. She cast about for a stone to take with her, as a memory of this day. Molly had said that if you held a big shell to your head you could hear the sea.

'Likes it, don't ya?' said Freddy, grinning at her.

Beattie nodded.

'P'r'aps it's your 'ome.'

'What are you on about?' she asked.

'P'r'aps you was a mermaid and they cut off yer tail.'

'I don't know where I came from,' she said. 'All I remember was this place called the workhouse.'

'I ain't got much else to 'member either. You know my name's Frederick Street, don't ya?'

'Yes, what about it?'

'That's where I was found, in Frederick Street, as a little nipper, all wet and snotty nosed, in ragged trousers, sleepin' in a doorway.'

'How old were you?'

'Dunnow. Might 'ave bin two or three.'

'You ever been there?'

'Where?'

'Frederick Street.'

'No,' said Freddy, throwing another stone into the water. He shrugged. 'Lucky in a way, I was.'

'Why?'

'Could have been called Blossom Alley?'

'Or Unicorn Gate,' laughed Beattie.

'Don't you know nothin' 'bout yourself?' he asked.

'They said, at the workhouse, that I was brought in when I was a baby,' said Beattie, her heart thumping. 'But I don't know who took me there.'

'P'r'aps it was the doc. He gets all over the place. Why don't you ast 'im. It was 'im and me as brought you to the Mariners' that time when you was little.'

Beattie closed her eyes and tried to think back five years. It was all chopped up in her head. Freddy smiling at her, the clip-clop of the pony's hooves, the billowing smoke and shrill whistle of a train. She had been frightened and excited, but not too frightened, because the doctor was with her. Then there was the great big Mariners' Home with the steps, and Matron Sankey waiting for her. 'You was the first person, ever, to shake my hand,' she said, smiling up at him.

'I bet the doctor knows things about you.'

'What things?' Beattie dragged her eyes away from the sea to look at Freddy. Her mouth felt dry and her heart began to thump in her chest.

'P'r'aps he was the one what took you to the workhouse.'

'But that doesn't sound right; he was the one what took me out of there.'

Freddy threw a stone into the sea. 'Wonder what it's like 'aving a family,' he said. His face was turned away from her, so that she couldn't tell what he was thinking.

'Don't know.' Beattie thought of the families she saw sat in church, when they trooped in on Sundays. Mother always fussing, and the children sat between her and a stern-faced man. There was so much that was different about them. The children didn't wear a uniform, and sometimes the little ones carried a doll or a book in their arms. When they were tired or sleepy their mother took them onto her lap. Once, she had seen the doctor with his family: two boys, and a pretty woman with golden hair poking from her bonnet. When his wife wasn't looking the doctor had waved to her, and then the smaller boy had smiled in her direction. Later, as they left their pew, the mother had smiled at her son. Beattie had wanted that look for herself. It was as if her boy was the only person in the world that mattered to her. She wanted to matter that much to somebody. But then she thought of other families she'd seen sometimes out on the streets near The Hard. The children were barefoot, in ragged clothes and the mothers were thin and sharp-faced with hunger. They alternated between hugging and cuffing. Knowing who you were, and where you came from, to belong, that's what she wanted.

Above her head the seagulls clamoured, and there were shouts from the Round Tower where the soldiers were patrolling. She knelt down and sorted through the stones and shells for something to add to her meagre treasures.

The shells were a disappointment, nothing like the ones she'd seen in books. These were nearly all the same size and shape, like toenails. Then when you turned them over there was a little seat like a rowing boat at one end. Beattie tossed them aside for a streaky, grey and white stone, a bit like a hammer. It fitted snugly in her hand and there wasn't another one anything like it. She turned and saw Freddy a few yards away from her, with his back turned, peeing into the sea.

Stowing the stone securely in her pocket, she stood up and brushed the sand from her coat. She gazed again at the sea, watching a gull bobbing on a wave: how mysterious it was. The water that was now lapping at her feet might be miles away tomorrow, and somewhere in the distance was a wave that was meant for Point Beach.

'Beattie, hurry up, we're adrift. Got to get back or Miss Sankey'll skin us and the doc will be pacin' about, wanting his cab.'

'How d'you know we're late,' said Beattie, 'you haven't got a watch or nothing?'

'I asked that man over there, he got one on a great gold chain 'cross his waistcoat,' said Freddy, pointing to a figure in cloak and top hat, hurrying up the shingle towards the High Street. 'It's nearly four; poor old Dapple will be dying for a drink and her nose-bag.'

'It's been the best day of my life,' said Beattie, as they rattled back to the Mariners'.

Freddy smiled and flicked the reins. 'You're my best pal,' he said. 'We'll go again when we gets the chance.'

Beattie awoke early the next morning, before Molly and Clara were awake. She took her diary and pencil from the tin under her bed, and knelt by the windowsill with the curtain open.

September 1865

I have seen the sea today; Freddy took me there. It is big and always moving and what I like best is the noise it makes. I can get my breath to be in time with the waves; in and out in and out. It smells clean and salty. I live on the edge of the land and I can look out far away to an island.

The sea is like a bit of green silk that wants ironing badly. I think I could stand and look at the sea without ever getting fed up. I made a promise to the sea that I would come back and look at it again, soon as I can. Next time, I will be on my own. When I miss the sea I can take out my stone hammer to remind me. The end, for now, Beatrice Salter.

Chapter Twenty-one

Full of excitement, Obadiah hurried home with his prize. Gussie would be thrilled. He had acquired three tickets for an evening of readings from Charles Dickens' novels by the author himself. What was even better, he had been assured that *David Copperfield* was on the programme. It was, for both of them, their favourite book.

He glanced again at the tickets, Friday, 26th May 1866. The event would fall on his forty-first birthday. He was glad it was early in the year as Albie would be able to accompany them. In September, he was due to join the navy as cadet on the *Britannia* at Dartmouth. Already, Sammy had left them in order to work with Uncle Hector on Dovecote Farm. He was even speaking of going later to Canada. By the end of the year they would be on their own, save for Cook and Mildred. Nanny Hobbs had gone to live with her sister in Devon, when Albert was six years old. Their children were grown.

As he strolled down Queen Street, towards St George's Square, he thought about his early years of marriage to Augusta. She had been so young, and pretty, and petted by her parents. After her childhood, spent at Meadholm with her dogs and her paintings, she had found the life as a poor general practitioner's wife, in a seaport town, a harsh contrast. Spoilt and wasteful, Augusta had reminded him of Dora the child-bride in *David Copperfield*. Another cloud had been the physical side of their marriage. Lovemaking had been an activity surrounded by acute embarrassment for both of them. The fact that it was the only route to childbirth was, he was convinced, the only reason Augusta submitted to the indignity of it all. Now? Obadiah sighed. They seemed to be forever out of step with each other. When he was stirred by desire for her, and the necessary courage to make advances, she was tired – or worse – simply dutiful. He then retired to the bath-room, shamed and frustrated. Since her mother's death, Augusta had, sometimes, initiated lovemaking or at least embraced him more warmly, from time to time, than had been her habit. These displays of affection always found him ill prepared: he was either on the verge of sleep or would misinterpret her affection for passion, causing her to draw back in fear or distaste – he never knew which. They were, at times, as ill matched as Jack Sprat and his wife – he could not stop wanting her, and she could not begin to desire him. He chided himself for this sudden attack of the glooms. In all other aspects of their marriage Gussie had drawn closer to him. She would never have the same concern for his poorer patients that he had, but now she was kinder and less censorious. Her interest in the dispensing of medicine had grown. Augusta was now becoming quite knowledgeable and of real assistance to him. What account of their marriage would she give? he wondered.

If she had sometimes disappointed him, how much greater

must be her regret at his shortcomings as a husband. How often had he been snappish to her when she had wanted to show him some new purchase she had made, or share with him some incident from her day. He must have been a far too solemn companion for his lively young bride. Augusta's girlish prettiness had now become womanly beauty. And their boys – two fine young men. How time rushed on, he thought, as he raised his hat to a naval acquaintance and hurried up the steps of his home.

He sniffed the air appreciatively – lamb cutlets, if he was not mistaken. The clock in the hall struck six, half an hour before dinner. He looked in the sitting room and saw his wife in her chair by the reading lamp, immersed in a letter.

'Close your eyes and hold out your hand, and see what God has given you,' he cried, as he kissed her on the forehead.

'Darling, I didn't hear you come in. I've had such an interesting letter from Sammy. You shall read it later.' She smiled up at him. 'Now what is this nonsense about closing my eyes?'

'Surprise, surprise,' he said. 'Do as I say and fortune will attend you.'

Obediently she closed her eyes and he dropped the tickets into her hands.

'Oh!' she gasped, blushing with excitement. 'Obi, how wonderful! What a treat, and on your birthday, too.' She got up from her chair and hugged him warmly. 'Albie will be thrilled when he comes n. He's been trying out that telescope you gave him. What does he call it? A funny name that the old marine taught him.'

'A "bring 'em near" was old Sticks's name for them,' said Obadiah, putting the tickets on the mantelpiece.

188

'How appropriate,' she said. 'That poor old man. I miss him sometimes.'

'So do I,' said Obadiah; 'he was the last link to my pa and to little Merle. I dreamt about her only the other night; strange, isn't it? Thirty years or more since she's been gone and yet I still think of her from time to time. She would have been an aunt to the boys, they might even have had cousins.'

'Thank heavens they never got diphtheria,' said Gussie; 'measles was bad enough.'

They both turned as the door burst open and Albie rushed in with the brass telescope on his shoulder.

'Evening, Ma and Pa, do I smell lamb? I'm as hungry as a hunter. Do you know, I have been down at Point Beach and I could see the Isle of Wight as clear as crystal.'

'Perhaps you could bring your powers of observation to bear on the three tickets on the mantelpiece,' said Obadiah, pouring himself a sherry from the decanter on the sideboard. 'Gussie, can I bring you a glass?'

As if the cards were miles away, Albie stood back against the opposite wall and raised the cumbersome telescope to his eye, and focused it on the mantelpiece. They both watched the curiosity change to excitement in Albie's face.

'Great heavens, how truly splendid,' he said, turning around and grinning at both of them. 'Fancy meeting Dickens! He's like a conjurer bringing all those people to life. Poor old Smike and the wicked Wackford Squeers, and my favourite, I think, Jo Gargery.'

'I can imagine his exact words at being given such a treat,' said Gussie.

'What larks, Pip,' they all cried in unison.

★

St George's Hall was crowded to overflowing, on the evening of the Dickens recital. Obadiah, Gussie and Albie had dined early and their promptness had gained them seats at the front. On a table were a jug of water, a glass and a wooden book-rest. There was an air of expectation. People kept looking towards the curtained door, in the corner of the hall, behind the table. And then, when Albie was fidgeting with impatience, the door opened the Dickens entered the room to tumultuous applause.

Obadiah would never remember who introduced him. From the moment the small man with the soulful brown eyes and colourful cravat began to speak everyone was captivated. Dickens's voice was mesmerising. He could assume a vast range of expressions and accents from the cultured tones of Mr Pickwick, to the lively speech of Sam Weller and Barkis the coachman, to the florid evocations of Mr Micawber, and the gentle voice of Agnes Wickfield.

The audience rocked with laughter at Dickens's depiction of the trial scene in Pickwick Papers, and drew out their handkerchiefs to wipe away mirthful tears. They needed them again when he read excerpts from *David Copperfield*. Gussie was openly weeping at the death of David's mother, and he saw Albie wipe tears from his eyes at the drowning of Steerforth. What affected Obadiah most were the simple words of Betsy Trotwood, when she advised David on how to treat Dora, his young wife.

It will be your duty, and it will be your pleasure too — of course I know that; I am not delivering a lecture — to

estimate her, as you chose her, by the qualities she has, and
not by the qualities she may not have.

It seemed to Obadiah that Dickens was looking straight at
him when he continued.

The latter you may develop in her, if you can, and if you
cannot, child, you must accustom yourself to live without
'em.

The words struck him with the force of a slap. For the rest
of the evening he was deaf to Dickens's oratory. Poor Augusta,
how selfish and demanding he was, and how hard she had tried
to please him. He took her hand and squeezed it. She smiled
at him and returned the squeeze.

'What a wonderful evening,' she said, as the three of them
walked back to their home just around the corner.

'He was quite amazing, wasn't he?' cried Albie. 'I was
somewhat disappointed when I first saw him. Just a little old
man in fancy clothes, I thought, and then . . . !' – Albie spread
out his hands – 'when he began to speak the hall seemed to fill
with all the people from his books. I think I could have sat there
for days on end just listening to his voice.'

Augusta smiled at him. What a lively companion he could
be, especially when he was in the grip of an enthusiasm. Samuel
was more immediately striking, with his blond hair and blue
eyes, but Albert had a charm and attractiveness peculiarly his
own. He was so responsive to others and had his father's natural
courtesy. How she would miss him.

How would she and Obi manage without the boys?
Perhaps, when they had more time, they would draw closer

together. Looking at her friends' husbands, there was not one that she would want to exchange for Obi. None had one ounce of his kindness or tolerance. Oh, he could be exacting at times and often she had resented his criticism of her delight in what he called display and frippery. But, since Papa and Mama had gone she had come to see things differently. Helping in the dispensary had, initially, been taken up to please Obi, but now she had become absorbed in the study of various medicines and their effects. Her new project of growing herbs in the corner of the garden for use in the dispensary was something she was proud of; how much more satisfying these pursuits had become than the tea parties and visits to the dressmaker. She would always love beautiful fabrics and jewellery, and the occasion to wear them, but now they were relegated to the special treat area of her life and no longer dominated her thoughts.

'Gussie, a penny for them?' asked Obi, turning to her from his talk with Albie.

'I was just thinking about treats,' she said, taking his arm. 'They have to be spread out between the everyday happenings or they cease to be so enjoyable.'

Albie laughed. 'So if I had treacle pudding every day and a sail in the Solent I would become tired of them.'

'Yes,' said his mother. 'What you require is more tapioca and trigonometry.'

'And what would you prescribe for me as a corrective?' asked Obadiah.

'Dancing lessons and a visit to your tailor,' she said with mock severity.

'I think Mama should spend more time with Miss Sankey. She might even begin to enjoy her company.'

Augusta did not join in Albie's amusement. She knew that

Margaret Sankey had worked wonders at the Mariners' Home. Wasn't Obi always singing her praises? Perhaps that was half the trouble. She resented the affection and respect that Obi showered on her. The woman was ugly – there, she had said it, albeit only in her thoughts. It was something she was ashamed of – this instinctive withdrawal from people whose appearance was displeasing. She knew it displayed shallowness in her nature. Margaret Sankey knew it too. Always, she came away from contact with the woman feeling that she had shown herself to be silly and trivial.

'Let's round off the evening with a sherry and some ratafias,' suggested Obi, turning his key in the front door.

They sat together in the sitting room sipping the sherry and reliving the evening.

'Your drink, Sir,' said Obi, giving a mock bow to his son and placing the glass at his elbow.

'Thank you, Cavendish,' said Albie in a wonderful imitation of an old captain at the yacht club. 'That will be most agreeable.'

Augusta and Obi laughed. For all his pretended sophistication Albie was still a boy at heart. He polished off far more biscuits than sherry, leaving his glass half full.

'Well, I don't know about you two,' said Obi, yawning as the clock struck midnight, 'I am for my bed before I turn into a pumpkin.'

'I will join you,' said Augusta, taking his arm, 'or we shall be two pumpkins.'

'Well, I am Prince Charming,' laughed Albie. 'I will not retire until I have found the glass slipper.'

Later, in bed, Obadiah took his wife in his arms and kissed her neck.

'Good night, darling,' she murmured, before turning away from him.

'I wish, I wish, oh never mind,' he said, pulling the bedclothes around his shoulders.

'What, Obi? What is it?' Gussie asked, turning towards him.

'I wish I could stop wanting you.' There, he had said it at last, the thought that had been fretting him all day.

The silence between them lasted so long that he began to think that he had offended her, and then she answered him.

'Sometimes,' she said, 'I want you, too.'

Obadiah was astonished. 'Truly, Gussie?' he asked.

'Once,' she whispered, 'I saw you naked when you were getting undressed and –' She hesitated.

'What did you feel?'

'I was surprised. I had never considered a man's body as beautiful but you were, you are, beautiful, to me. And then, when I wanted to tell you, Obi, you had fallen asleep.'

Obadiah sighed. 'We seem destined to miss the moment.'

'I feel that I want you when you are kissing me and holding me close and then . . .' her voice trailed away.

'Gussie, I am not a clairvoyant, you need to tell me.'

'When you want more than cuddles I feel rushed into something else.'

'Help me understand,' he said, taking her hand and kissing it.

'But I don't know if I do, myself,' she replied. 'When you cuddle me I know it's me you're cuddling. When you rush on to other things, I feel as if I'm just another woman, just a body.'

'Gussie, we live in our bodies, how could we not? You are all of a piece to me: heart and mind, spirit and body.'

'I think Mama made me afraid. She was so convinced that love between husband and wife was something to be endured.'

'It's that damn serpent from the Bible,' said Obadiah. 'The story has got so twisted away from its real meaning.'

'What do you mean, Obi? What has that to do with us?'

'Don't you see, my darling?' he said, holding her close to him. 'The sin that Adam and Eve committed was feeling shame about their nakedness. Dividing off parts of their bodies and labelling them as shameful. Causing that division.'

'But when you're told something, as a little girl, and everyone reinforces it you can't change your feelings overnight.'

Obadiah kissed her hand. 'There was something else you said, about rushing?'

'Don't be cross, Obi,' she whispered against his neck.

'Tell me, Gussie, help me understand.'

'I think that I could love you, and keep pace with you, if you didn't rush from kissing to the act so rapidly.'

'Meander a little?'

'Yes, darling, stroke my neck, whisper to me, wait for me to stroke you, too.'

'What you're saying is that I should take soundings on the way?'

'Yes,' she said. 'I think we need to enjoy the journey and not be so intent on the destination.'

'Why have we never spoken like this before? I wonder.'

'It was something Dickens said.'

'Charles Dickens?' said Obadiah in surprise. 'We have him to thank? What did he say, Gussie?'

'It was his Betsy Trotwood. I can't remember exactly, but

it was something about loving a person as they are, and not as you wish them to be.'

'God bless Betsy Trotwood,' said Obadiah, smiling in the darkness and drawing his wife into the circle of his arms. 'Dear, dear Betsy,' he whispered, as he stroked her neck.

Chapter Twenty-two

'It's him, my Charlie,' whispered Molly.

Beattie peered through the dormitory window, down into the garden. There was someone standing on the other side of the gate, under the street lamp. It was five o'clock on a January evening, and difficult to make out his features in the dusk, but she could tell immediately that he was no young boy. The man shifted his weight from one foot to the other, as if ready for flight, and his eyes raked the windows, probably looking for an easy entry to the building. 'Can't see much of anything,' she said.

'Charlie Mabs,' breathed Molly, pulling aside the curtain.

'How'd you meet him?' Beattie whispered.

'Works on the Camber. He's a fisherman. 'Appened to pass his boat, accidently of a purpose, you might say.'

'But the Camber's over in Old Portsmouth. What were you doin' there? It's not on the way to anywhere.'

'Met 'im in the street, if you must know,' said Molly. 'If it's any of your business. Nearly run me down wiv his barrow, he did. We got to talkin' and one thing led to another.'

'When was that?' asked Beattie, fixing the last hairpin in the back of her head.

'Weeks ago it was. We're steppin' out together.'

'Does Miss Sankey know?'

'You breathe a word to that old boot and I'll cut ya.' Molly drew a knife from a pocket in her skirt, and jabbed the blade at Beattie.

'You wouldn't Molly, I'm your best pal,' gasped Beattie, shocked by Molly's fierceness.

'I ain't foolin',' she said.

'Who gave you that?' Beattie gasped.

'My Charlie. Charlie says I don't need pals now I got 'im.'

How could she say that — standing there in her best white blouse and black skirt, looking like butter wouldn't melt in her mouth? How could she toss their friendship aside so easily? Ever since she came to the Mariners' she and Molly had been partners in crime: stealing cake, climbing trees, shaking salt over the food Cook sneaked out to her gentleman friend. She'd even let Molly read bits out of her diary, had almost shown her the card the doctor had written her name on all that time ago. And now it was all tossed aside.

'No one matters but 'im.'

Beattie was chilled; this was a Molly that she didn't recognise. 'What's he doing here now? We've got our celebration supper in ten minutes.'

'Don't you fret, I shan't miss out on me grub. But after, Charlie and me got other plans. The certificate? Well!' she scoffed, 'that's for the likes of you what toadies to old Sankey.'

'What plans?' she snapped, stung at Molly's disparagement.

Only yesterday she had been as excited as Beattie at getting her certificate and going out in the world.

'Dunno, yet,' she said, angrily, 'but we won't be hangin' around.'

Beattie looked again at Charlie Mabbs as he struck a match to light his pipe. In the sudden flame she saw his face. A black moustache hid his mouth and his eyes were flickering around, seeking an opportunity to take something not his own. Even in the few seconds of illumination, she could tell that he was far older than her friend, and a schemer to boot. After tossing the match away, he looked up at the window and gave a low whistle.

Molly whistled back and Charlie laughed softly to himself before walking away.

'I don't like him, Molly, he's shifty. No, please don't. Oh! You're hurting me, let go.'

'Hurt you some more if you don't keep yer gob shut,' snarled her friend, twisting Beattie's arm behind her back.

The whistle blew for the beginning of the Presentation Supper.

'You promise me you'll say nothin' or I'll 'ave ya,' snarled Molly, shoving her towards the door.

Beattie hurried down the stairs. She had been so full of excitement, now anger, fear and resentment boiled inside her. For weeks she had looked forward to dressing up, receiving the needlework prize and her certificate of domestic competence. It was the fifteenth of January 1870, just five days after her fourteenth birthday. Tomorrow she would go to the Servants' Registry and find herself a job. She was eager for new experiences, but Molly's path was not hers. Beattie was the first to admit that being a scullery maid lacked excitement, but at least she would be free to walk about the town sometimes, to go and sit on Point Beach, or listen to a band on the new Clarence Pier.

Molly's dash with Charlie filled her with dread. Men skulking in back gardens were not to be trusted, and as for being whistled at like a dog! Where was her pride? Only last week there had been a story in the paper about a girl running off with a married man. Later, when he returned to his wife, the girl had taken strychnine, leaving a baby that nobody wanted. Beattie shook her head. No, she wouldn't waste any more time thinking about Molly. This was her evening – she had earned it.

The dining room was transformed. Each table had a snowy cloth and a vase of flowers. Set out daintily on lace doilies were triangular potted-meat sandwiches, sprinkled with mustard and cress. There were little iced cakes and jam tarts and tall jugs of lemonade. The smaller children had made place-names and woven raffia napkin rings – hers, she knew, was made by Rosie Siddons, a pale, timid fairy-like seven-year-old. When Beattie had been made a monitor, to assist with the younger children, she had helped Rosie with her reading and been her protector ever since. Rosie was in the sick bay, with a troublesome cough, and Beattie had promised to sneak her up a jam tart and some ginger-bread.

She turned her attention back to the dining room.

Standing at the centre table in a starched blouse and jet necklace was Miss Sankey. Her face shone with pride. She was surrounded by her committee – all except Dr Pragnell. Beattie wished that he could be here to see her but he had sent a letter of apology, something about giving a talk to the Philosophical

Society. Looking at Miss Sankey she felt a surge of affection. Life in the Home was often a treadmill of routine and sameness, but she suffused it with colour and difference. Beattie would leave the Mariners' not only with her domestic skills, but with a love of reading and a questioning mind. The best proofs of Miss Sankey's success were the letters she received from old pupils and their visits 'back home' at Christmas. She would be back, too; often and often, wherever life took her.

After banging on the table with a little wooden mallet, Miss Sankey began her speech. 'Welcome, everyone, to the celebration supper of 1870. It has been a vintage year for our young people, setting out on their own adventure. I feel that they leave us well equipped for the journey ahead. What an abundance of talent we have here before us. I will try to list just some of the skills they have begun to acquire: carpentry, cookery, knot tying, knitting, sewing, laundering, navigation and seamanship – the list is endless. Above all, they are people to be proud of and I take great pleasure in calling on Commander Wentworth to present the certificates and prizes.'

Deaf to the Commander's well-chosen words, Beattie looked about her. From the other side of their table Molly gave her a warning glare. She and Miss Sankey had never shared the liking and mutual respect that Beattie had with her teacher. Where Molly harboured a grudge and delighted in paying back an insult Miss Sankey moved forward all the time, never looking back. She had striven to find something to reward Molly for and finally settled on a prize for ironing.

As it was announced, Molly walked up to receive it, all smiles and gratitude. How false she was.

'And now the prize for needlework and for most promising pupil – Beattie Salter.'

'Go on, it's for you. Hurry up,' whispered Clara, nudging her.

Beattie got to her feet and hurried over to the Commander, who was holding a book in his hand.

'Well done, Miss Salter,' he said, shaking his hand. 'You have obviously made the most of your stay with us. As is customary, we have started an account for you at the post office with a donation of one pound. You may put your address in it when you have found your new situation.'

'Oh, thank you,' she gasped. A savings account, it made her feel so grown up.

'And this is from me,' said Miss Sankey, handing her a new book with the gold lettering bright on its blue cover: *Adam Bede* by George Eliot. Beattie wanted to cry. To have a book that had not been read before, to turn the pages not touched by anyone else. She was overwhelmed. All she could manage was a nod to Matron Sankey before walking, head down, back to her seat. At first she was so caught up in her delight that she didn't notice the empty space opposite her, where Molly had been sitting. Perhaps she had gone out to the lavatory; a vain hope, Beattie knew. What should she do? That Charlie Mabs was a mongrel, anyone with a pennyworth of sense could see that. It was too late, Molly had made her choice, and even if dragged back to the Mariners' Home she would likely run off again. Besides, she would be fifteen, soon, and no longer Miss Sankey's responsibility.

Beattie sat with all her friends, watching them tucking in to the party-food. Her belly was filled with dread. Stupid little cow, she fumed, staring at the tablecloth while they chattered away.

'Where's Molly scarpered to?'

'Gone off with that cockle-man. You can bet your boots she have.'

'She won't 'arf catch it when old Sankey gets 'old of 'er.'

'Reckons as she's gettin' spliced.'

'All moonshine that is; Charlie just wants to get inside her drawers.'

'What do you reckon 'as happened, Beattie?' asked Clara. 'You ain't said nothin' yet.'

'It's all news to me,' said Beattie, pretending innocence. 'She never told me anything.'

'Liar. You and Molly was always thick as thieves.'

'Not any more,' snapped Beattie. 'I've got to go up to Sick Bay, I promised Rosie a bit of cake.' It was a heaven-sent excuse to get away from the questioning. Wrapping a tart and a piece of gingerbread in a paper napkin, she slipped it in her skirt pocket. Taking up her book, she hurried out of the dining room and up the stairs to the sick bay.

Peering round he door she waited an opportunity when Nurse Stuart's back was turned to creep into the room. The little girl lay on the bed holding her ears and whimpering. Hiding behind a screen, Beattie watched anxiously. She had seen her only yesterday, it had just been a sore throat and a tickly cough. How had it got so much worse so quickly?

She was just about to creep from behind the screen when Nurse Stuart returned, with a metal tray containing swabs and instruments.

'*Shh!* My little pet,' she said, as she set the tray down on the bedside table. 'Open wide, and let me wash that nasty stuff from your throat.' With a pair of forceps she took hold of a square of cloth, and dipped it into a pink liquid. Rosie protested weakly and shook her head. 'Just for a moment it will be horrid, and then you can have your drink. I have made you a lovely honey and lemon cordial. Let me take that nasty stuff away.' She grasped the child's jaw, held it open and swabbed inside. Swiftly she dropped the swab, coated with thick brown mucus, into a dish on the tray and then repeated the process. Rosie struggled weakly, choking and gagging. The nurse took the bowl of dirty swabs away and tossed them into the fire before going to the sink and scrubbing her hands.

Again Beattie attempted to creep round the screen but just in time spied Miss Sankey coming into the room.

'Nurse Stuart, how is the child?'

'I fear it may be diphtheria. Thank goodness there are no other patients. We shall be able to isolate her.'

'I think you should call in to Doctor Pragnell's on your way home and get him to call. I know it's ten o'clock, but better now than in the middle of the night.'

'Certainly, Miss Sankey,' said Nurse Stuart, gathering up her coat and bag. 'It will relieve my anxiety, too. I'm sure he'll come at once.'

The two women walked to the door and stood talking in the corridor.

Beattie took her chance.

'Rosie,' she whispered, peering round the screen and patting her on the shoulder.

The child was pale and listless, showing no interest in seeing her.

'Beattie, what you doing here?' she asked, her voice hoarse from coughing.

'I brought your cake like I promised.'

'Don't want it now.'

'Can I give you a drink?'

Rosie nodded.

Beattie put down the cake on the bedside table, poured some water from a jug into a feeding cup and held it to Rosie's lips. She heard the nurse's footsteps die away and the front door close behind her. At any moment Miss Sankey would return and find her. It was only a second or so that she had been distracted, but it was enough for Rosie to have drunk too much at once. The child began to choke.

Beattie was terrified. 'I'm sorry, I'm sorry,' she gasped.

Miss Sankey was instantly beside her. She grabbed some forceps and a swab and tried to force Rosie's mouth open and clear away the obstruction.

'Her hands,' she barked; 'hold them at once.'

The child flayed about the bed, her face turning blue.

'Roll her tightly in that sheet, arms as well. Bring her over here.' With one stroke Miss Sankey cleared the table of books and papers, and rolled up a small towel. 'Place this under her neck so that it's extended. Now, hold her head still between your hands and pray.'

Miss Sankey put her index finger low down at the centre of the child's throat, and placed her second finger and thumb either side. Taking up a penknife from her pocket, she followed the course of the index finger and made a vertical cut. There was a gasping sound and blood and a thick white mucus oozed from the wound. 'Crochet hook; there in that workbox,' she barked.

Still holding Rosie with one hand, Beattie reached across the bed to the needlework basket, open on a chair. As soon as she found it Matron snatched it from her hand.

Beattie was rigid with fear.

The knife was discarded and followed by the crochet hook,

with which she probed the wound, securing something inside the neck.

'Hold the handle firmly – that's it – while I find something to keep the wound open.' Beattie stood with the hook grasped in her hand, too terrified to move, while Miss Sankey took up a tiny brass funnel, like the one used for filling ink bottles in the school. She wiped it with a swab and then said, 'Thank you, Beattie, I have it now.' Somehow she manoeuvred the funnel into the hole in Rosie's throat and removed the hook. There was a hissing sound and blood bubbled out of the tube, soaking Rosie's gown.

'Quick, those swabs, dip them into that bowl of carbolic solution and pass them to me,' ordered Miss Sankey. 'One at a time – that's it. Turn your head away, and try not to inhale,' said Matron, wiping away the blood and mucus.

The room was in darkness save for the lamp on the nurse's table, the glowing coals in the grate, and the candle beside the bed. To Beattie, it felt as if the world had narrowed to the halo of light around Rosie's face. There was a battle going on between Miss Sankey's nursing skills and the demon diphtheria.

As she threw the swabs into the fire, Beattie realised that the sound of choking had ceased. Breathing peacefully, Rosie was settled back in her bed, propped upright against the pillows. They both scrubbed their hands after soaking the instruments in a tray of carbolic.

'Sit yourself down, Beattie, and I will make us both a hot drink. We've earned it.'

How had she stood there, while Rosie had her throat cut? Only Miss Sankey's absolute command of the situation made it possible. Now, she couldn't stop shaking. All the suspense of

the evening combined in her belly. Beattie barely made it to
the pot by the sink before vomiting up the remains of her celebration supper.

'Here, give that to me,' said Miss Sankey, holding out her
hand. 'Wash your face and sit down again. You've done
enough nursing for one night.'

The vomiting gave way to tears.

'Your visit was heaven sent,' she said. 'I'm not so sure about
the cake. If she had attempted to eat and begun choking, you
would have been in serious trouble. Now, Beattie, you have
had a shock. I think the best thing is for you to get into the bed
over by the window and settle yourself for sleep. There are
some nightdresses in the linen cupboard. You will have to stay
here for a few days in isolation, until we are certain that you
have not succumbed to Rosie's infection.'

Beattie nodded, too tired to protest, and went into the
bathroom with her nightdress.

When she returned, Miss Sankey was standing beside
Rosie's bed ensuring that the bandage around her neck was
securely in place. She moved about the room setting things in
order.

Before getting into bed, Beattie padded barefoot across the
room and picked up the book Miss Sankey had given her and
set it on the table. Beattie was almost asleep when she came
over to her with a glass of hot milk.

'A night of alarms and excursions,' she said, drawing up a
chair beside her. 'It seems a long time ago that we were celebrating your success, and yet it is only an hour or so since I
climbed the stairs to relieve Nurse Stuart.'

'Some days nothing happens and then, others, everything
goes on all at once,' Beattie said before taking a gulp of milk.

'A feast or a famine, that's what keeps life interesting, my dear.'

'Molly's run off with that Charlie Mabs.' She had blurted it out before she knew it. Aghast, she put her hand to her mouth as if to push the words back inside.

'I thought as much,' said Miss Sankey, calmly. 'Poor Molly, she is going to be schooled by a hard teacher.'

'What d' you mean?' asked Beattie.

'It is the school of life, my dear. She wants to experience all it has to offer, like a greedy girl and a bag of bonbons. The child will simply get the belly ache, while Molly will receive a far harsher lesson.'

'What can you do to stop her?'

'Nothing at all. Oh, I shall inform the constable of Molly's likely whereabouts, but the ilk of Charlie Mabs will have spirited her away hours ago.' She rose wearily to her feet. 'Constable Perkins usually calls in about this time, to have a cup of cocoa with Cook. I shall leave a message for the constable with her, once Doctor Pragnell has seen Rosie and checked that all is well.'

Beattie looked anxiously at the sleeping child.

'Provided her heart stands up to the shock, I think the little maid may well pull through. You have had a very worrying evening. A night in the sick bay and a quiet day tomorrow will soon restore your spirits.'

Beattie was almost asleep when she heard voices.

'Let me look at the child. Margaret – a tracheotomy! Thank God you were here. How in heaven's name did you perform it on your own? How did you know what to do?'

'I was not alone. Beatrice helped me. Providentially she had sneaked up to see the child. As to my surgical skills, they were honed at Balaclava.'

'Thank God for Balaclava,' said Dr Pragnell. 'I will just wash my hands and my tracheotomy tubes and then I will remove your temporary device. It was very resourceful of you, Margaret, but now I think we need something designed for the job. Have you a narrow length of bandage to thread through the sides so that we can secure it firmly to her neck? Four-hourly aspirations, Margaret, please; more, if necessary. With luck and a sound heart she may pull through. I will sit with her a while.'

'Thank you, Obadiah, for your promptness. While you're here I need to leave a message for Constable Perkins on another matter. I shall be back instantly.'

Beattie closed her eyes thankfully. Where was Molly, she thought, as she drifted into sleep? Wherever she is I hope she's safe.

Chapter Twenty-three

Beattie went up the front steps of 2 St George's Square and read the name on the brass plate – *Doctor Pragnell, FRCP.* It was him – her doctor at the Mariners'. She would be working for Dr Pragnell. The woman at the Servants' Registry had said there was a position for a scullery maid with a doctor and his family in St George's Square. She hadn't mentioned the name, just told her to go round to the back door and give her references to Mrs Frostick, the cook.

But Beattie was tired of standing in back yards and wanted to see more than kitchens and sculleries. In for a penny in for a pound, she thought, rapping the brass knocker. While she stood there shivering and waiting for the door to be opened she thought about the Pragnells. What did she know about them? Only what she glimpsed on Sundays in church. The doctor's wife was a pretty woman with blonde hair that hung in little tendrils from beneath her bonnet. Two boys sat between the parents. One of them was solid looking with fair hair who sat staring at his hymnbook. It was the brown-haired son that interested Beattie. He looked around him and smiled and talked to people when they left the church. Once, when an old man started singing the wrong hymn, he had smiled at her and for a moment they were like conspirators in a wonderful joke.

'Good morning, how may I help you? The patients' entrance is round to the back of the house.' Mrs Pragnell stood looking down at her.

Close to, she was even prettier than Beattie remembered, with a small heartshaped face and eyes that were startling in their intense blueness. She held a medicine bottle in her hand and had a long white coat draped over her gown.

Beattie blushed in confusion. 'I'm not a patient. I have come from the registry about the scullery maid's job. I've got my references,' she said, handing an envelope to her.

'Please step inside,' Mrs Pragnell said, smiling, before putting the envelope in her pocket. 'Mildred should have answered the door. Follow me, I have some tasks to finish in the dispensary, then I will attend to you.'

Beattie went behind her, up the stairs, fascinated by the thick golden plait of hair hanging down Mrs Pragnell's back. Accustomed to the brown and cream of the orphanage, this house was a feast for her senses. There were black and white tiles on the hall floor and a red carpet on the stairs. The curly banister reminded Beattie of a stick of barley sugar. As she reached the top of the stairs a grandfather clock chimed eleven. There was the smell of lavender polish. They turned right at the end of the passage and entered the dispensary. Beattie was consumed with curiosity. The walls were lined with row upon row of tiny wooden drawers. On shelves behind a marble topped counter were dark blue jars with gold lettering on them. The words were magical: *Tincture of Arnica, Belladonna, Syrup of Squills* and *Tincture of Benzoin*. She watched Mrs Pragnell, standing at the high desk, writing on a label in swirly script. When the ink was dry, she ran the label over a little sponge in a dish before fixing it to a bottle. There was a rhythm and grace to her movements which filled Beattie with admiration. Once the bottle had been wrapped in white paper, Mrs Pragnell took a stick of sealing wax, then turned on a tiny tap on a brass tube. There was a hissing sound and she struck a match and held the flame to the tube which burned steadily, melting the wax she held over it. After sealing the ends of the paper with the wax, she turned off the tap, and the flame disappeared. Mrs Pragnell set down the package in a square basket and opened Matron Sankey's letter.

Beattie waited, dry mouthed, for her response.

'That seems satisfactory,' she said. 'Now, Beattie, tell me, what are your accomplishments?'

'Well, I can wash and starch clothes; iron them and do running repairs; I can clean a room; polish silver and lay a fire. I been used to making my own clothes; and I can read, write and do arithmetic.'

'Good. I shall take you down to the kitchen and introduce you to Mrs Frostick. She will make you some chocolate, and will have the final say about your employment.' Mrs Pragnell handed her the dispensary basket to carry downstairs for her.

As they went into the kitchen there was a rich aroma of beef gravy. The cook was standing on a square box at the table, fitting a lid of pastry on top of a pie dish full of stewed meat.

'Mrs Frostick, this is Beattie, she is to be the new scullery maid; subject to your approval, of course.' Mrs Pragnell took the reference out of the envelope.

'Is she, Madam?' Mrs Frostick looked doubtful. Her deep,

gravelly voice was at odds with her small stature. When she stepped off her box and turned to look at her, Beattie saw that she was well under five feet tall. The cook looked her searchingly up and down, then grasped her hand in a firm floury handshake. 'Morning, Beattie,' she said. 'Stand over there by the window so's I can see you.'

'Mrs Frostick, I will read you her reference, and then I really must go upstairs and help Albie with his packing.'

'Fine words butter no parsnips Madam,' said Cook. 'When I've got this pie safely cooking, you and me'll have a talk,' she said, nodding to Beattie.

All the time they had been talking, Beattie had been aware of a girl stood at the other end of the table. She was using a goffering iron on the pleated sleeves of a white blouse. Mildred was dressed in a black dress and starched apron and cap.

'This is Beattie,' Mrs Pragnell continued. 'Mildred is my personal maid, and has care of all my clothes.'

The girl flushed with pleasure at what she saw as a compliment. She was a thin, colourless figure, with mousy hair and chewed fingernails. 'Delighted, I'm sure,' she said, looking anything but delighted, her hand slipping quickly out of Beattie's grasp.

Mrs Pragnell walked towards the door. 'Cook,' she said, 'send two cups of hot chocolate up to Albie's room, if you please.' She swept out of the room, leaving Beattie feeling abandoned.

Cook completed the pie and then kicked the box across the room to the stove. Turning her back on her, Mrs Frostick stepped back on her box, and busied herself with making the chocolate.

Beattie sat at the table, dry-mouthed with anxiety.

Ignoring her, Mildred continued ironing the blouse.

When the milk was heated Mrs Frostick came back to the table, spooned some chocolate powder into a jug, and poured the milk over it, stirring the mixture vigorously with a spoon. She set a doily on a silver tray and took down three cups and saucers from the dresser. 'Run this up to her ladyship will you, Mildred?' she asked. 'I'm like the cow's tail, today, all behind.'

The maid sighed. 'I got all this ironing to put away in Madam's room, and there's them hankies not done yet.'

'You take up them clothes, then, while I takes the cups. Beattie, put aside the goffering iron and pick up that flat one on the back of the range, there. After all them fine words in your reference, you'd make short work of that stack of hankies. When they're done, you can drink that choclit what I've poured for you.'

She wanted to run back to the Mariners', jump into bed and pull the covers over her head. Tears welled up in her eyes, and she wiped them away with her sleeve. Then she thought of the slighting look that Mildred had given her, and her temper was aroused. Skinny cow, she thought, what does she know about me? I'll show her. Testing the iron on the blanket spread over half the table, she picked up one of the handkerchiefs and began to press it on the wrong side. As she ironed the initial 'A', embroidered in blue satin stitch on each hankie, Beattie wondered whom they belonged to. When she had finished her task and laid them, neatly folded, on the corner of the table, she looked about her. It was a small kitchen with a well-scrubbed table, gleaming windowpanes and crisp white curtains. By the fire were two old wheel-backed chairs with plump cushions and on the floor a blue-and-red-rag rug. She wondered how it was made – it was so cheerful.

'I was looking for those,' said a voice behind her.

Beattie looked up and saw Dr Pragnell's brown-haired son standing there. She blushed and so did he.

'I'm Albert, I'm pleased to meet you,' he said, holding out his hand.

'Beattie, Beattie Salter,' she mumbled, shaking his hand. Albert had a firm grasp and he looked straight at her as if genuinely glad to know her. He seemed taller than she remembered and, in his naval cadet's uniform, more handsome. What drew her to him, were his grey eyes and his friendliness.

'It's a shame that you have been called Beattie,' he said. 'Beatrice is such a beautiful name.'

The word was like a gift. She was more than Beattie – she was Beatrice. 'I know it's my real name,' she said, 'your father wrote it out for me when I was little.'

'I am Albert, as I said, but everyone calls me Albie.'

'Do you like that?'

He smiled. 'It's fine in the family,' he said, 'but I like Albert when I'm on *Britannia*. Albie is the sort of chap to run a pleasure steamer, but to command a real, steam-powered destroyer requires an Albert.'

How different his smile was from that pasted-on twitch of the lips given her by his mother. His smile was warm, and crinkled the corners of his eyes. It was a shared thing that drew you to him and made you part of his amusement.

'Where were you when Pa wrote your name?' he asked. 'Please, Beatrice, if you would rather not say. That was impertinent of me.'

'The workhouse,' she said, staring down at his black polished boots.

Albert blushed. 'Well,' he said, 'if you would like, I shall always call you Beatrice.'

'Albie, darling, hurry,' called a voice from the hall, 'we need to close the chest. Pa will be here in five minutes and the train leaves at one.'

'Master Albie!'

Beattie could hear the affection in Cook's voice.

'Don't you look well set up.'

Albie laughed and said something that made Cook chuckle.

'Albie!' There was a note of command in his mother's voice.

Beattie realised she had forgotten to drink the chocolate, and took up the little flowered cup. How different it was from the orphanage cocoa; so rich and velvety on the tongue. In the bottom of the cup was a smaller pattern of flowers. As she tipped it to her mouth a tiny clover and buttercup revealed themselves. Beattie was charmed. She set the cup and saucer in the sink as Cook bustled back into the kitchen.

'Right, young miss,' she said. 'Tell me how you go about laying a fire?'

Beattie described the building up of layers of paper, sticks and coal. 'You holds a newspaper across the front of the grate and it makes the fire fairly gallop into action.'

'You got to be careful, miss. Young girl I knew was daydreaming and the paper caught alight, she dropped it in a panic and it set fire to the carpet. That was the end of her position in that household.'

'That wasn't fair,' said Beattie.

'What is fair, in this life?' snapped the cook, looking fiercely at her. 'What do you do with vegetable peelings?'

'Put them in a bucket and give them to the pig man when he calls.'

'What's the servant's worst enemies?'

'Dirt and muddle,' Beattie answered.

'You'll do,' said Mrs Frostick, smiling at her. It creased up her face and shone out of her brown eyes. 'What you best do is go back to the Mariners', and get your goods and chattels. I shall save washing and the vegetables for when you gets back.'

Beattie wanted to grab hold of Mrs Frostick and dance her round the kitchen. As Freddy would say, she had landed on her feet. There was so much yet to find out. How much was she to be paid? Where was she to sleep? How many hours would she work each day? But that would all be told to her in time. She had hit it off with Cook and that was the key on which everything else turned.

Excitement speeded her steps back to Nile Street and up the stairs. Beattie stood in the unnatural quiet of the dormitory and began gathering up her things into a bolster case. She took her copy of *Adam Bede* out of her locker, a tin filled with oddly-shaped stones and the card on which Dr Pragnell had written her name. It had been the first time she had felt that she was more than just Beattie – how much more she had yet to find out. There had been a difference in the way he had spoken her name and the way his son had spoken it. Dr Pragnell had informed her of what she was called, and Albert had bestowed it on her as a treasure.

What she knew, in fact, about herself was meagre; simply that she had been taken to the workhouse when she was a baby

217

because her mother had died. But Freddy had hinted that Dr Pragnell knew more about her than he had chosen to say to her or to Matron Sankey.

'Beattie,' she had said, 'I'm afraid the facts are scanty. I believe there had been a note given to the workhouse about the possibility of your birthday being January the 10th 1856 but beyond that we know very little. There was, I think, some vague idea of your father being a soldier in India, who died during the mutiny. I'm afraid I traded on the military link in order to entitle you to a place here. But nothing else is known.'

Was that true, she wondered, and if he knew more about her, why did he not tell her? Was their something shameful in her past?

'You seem in a great hurry to be gone from here.'

Startled, Beattie looked up to see Matron Sankey standing in the doorway. 'I hope you were not going to leave without saying goodbye.'

'Oh, no,' she said hastily. 'I was just putting my things together.'

'Come and take tea with me when you've finished up here.'

Beattie nodded.

Later, with the bolster bulging with all her possessions, she made her way to Miss Sankey's sitting room.

'Sit down, my dear, and stow your luggage on the sofa.'

Beattie did as she was told and took a cup of tea from the silver tray.

'We have travelled a long way together, you and I.' It was as if she had read her thoughts.

'I have been happy here,' said Beattie, 'and I've learned a lot.'

'High praise,' said Miss Sankey. 'I think I can take the credit for laying the foundations with very promising material. Now, Beattie, don't let this be the end of learning. Nourish your imagination; it will sustain you through many a dull patch.'

As she sat talking to Miss Sankey, Beattie's earlier excitement began to trickle away. Here she had been secure and knew exactly what to expect. What happened if she didn't fit in at Dr Pragnell's house? Where would she go then? She was neither a teacher nor a nurse, so there was no hope of returning here.

'Now, Beattie, I have a gift for you,' she said, taking a square wooden clock from the top of her bookcase; 'something to put in your new room. Punctuality is everything in a well-run household.' She handed her a little brass key. 'Wind it every night and you will always be on time.'

Beattie was overwhelmed. The little clock, she knew, was a treasured possession that had travelled with Matron to the Crimea.

Miss Sankey stood up and brushed aside her thanks. 'Before your courage deserts you, pick up your things and be gone. Remember my maxim; if you don't grow up to help other people, you are not worth the upbringing.'

Beattie stood at the end of the street and waved until Matron disappeared inside the Mariners' Home. She had wanted to put her arms around her, as if she were saying goodbye to her mother, but she knew it would have embarrassed both of them.

This time Beattie entered Dr Pragnell's house via the yard. It was tiny as most of the space at the back of the house was given over to a garden, which was bare of flowers, merely so much twigs, bushes and grass. She tried to imagine what it would be like in the summer when the rose bushes were in bloom. Passing an upturned bucket, with a floor cloth draped over it, she tapped on the scullery door.

'Oh, it's you,' said Mildred, without enthusiasm, standing in the doorway.

'Are you going to let me in or shall I go round the front and tell Madam that you sent me away?' said Beattie, her temper flaring.

Mildred pursed her lips as if there were a thread drawing them tight. 'You got a lot ter say for yourself,' she snapped, standing aside.

'Thank you, I'm sure,' Beattie said. You won't get the better of me, she vowed to herself, I'm as good as you any day of the week.

'Mildred,' said Mrs Frostick, 'take Beattie up to the nursery. She'll have to sleep in there, for the moment. Don't dilly-dally the pair of you. There's a stack of pots for you, Beattie, and Mildred you got to go and collect that ribbon what Madam ordered from John Dyer's.'

She followed the maid up the stairs onto the landing, then back up to the top of the house. The carpet changed to a faded green once the passage turned away from the front of the house. There were three rooms up at the top.

'This is mine,' said Mildred, holding the door open.

Beattie glimpsed inside. The room and bed linen were entirely white. The only splashes of colour came from a red curtain stretched across one corner where, presumably, Mildred hung her clothes. There was not so much as a hairpin on top of the chest of drawers. A tiny window opened onto the yard. The bareness and lack of any personal possessions depressed Beattie. The only attempt at decoration was a sampler in a carved wooden frame announcing that 'Jesus Saves.' Beattie sighed to herself. Jesus had not made much effort on Mildred's behalf.

'Next door's Mrs Frostick's, then the old nursery, where you're sleeping. You're beddin' down there temporary.'

Beattie was enchanted. There were pictures on the walls and even a curious blue and white rocking boat. Against the wall, filled with folded up curtains was a wicker cot. 'Oh,' she gasped at a wooden screen with pictures pasted all over it. 'That's so bright and pretty.' As an after thought, stuck in the middle of the room, was a narrow iron bed made up with one pillow and a faded patchwork quilt.

'It should be your room,' she said to Mildred, in an effort at generosity. 'It's so much bigger.'

'Shan't be here much longer,' sniffed Mildred, 'my feller's in the army. Soon as he's back from Egypt we shall get married and live with his ma.'

'I'm pleased for you,' said Beattie, still hopeful of coaxing a smile from the maid's mournful features.

There was the sound of a bell ringing. Mildred responded instantly. 'Got to go. Drop your stuff in the nursery and get back to the kitchen.'

In the scullery sink, the dishes were stacked from the cold luncheon eaten by the Pragnells and from Cook's pie-making. At the table Mrs Frostick was busy setting spoonfuls of cake mixture into a bun tin. Beattie put on a sacking apron in readiness to start the washing up. As she swirled some soda into the water she realised she was very hungry. Meals in the Mariners' Home appeared at the set times of eight for breakfast, one for lunch and five o'clock for high tea. She wondered what the routine was, here, for Mildred, Cook and herself. Feeling like

Oliver Twist, she said, 'Can I have something to eat? I haven't had anything since breakfast.'

'Doctor and Freddy'll be here about three, we'll have something then. There's a scrapin' of rice pudding in that dish, there on the side,' said Cook as she wiped some stray cake mixture from the edges of the tin before setting it in the range. The scraping amounted to about a dessertspoon of rice and rich nutmeg flavoured skin. Beattie had just finished washing the dish when Mildred came back into the kitchen.

'Ever so snappy she is. Can't do right for doing wrong. I put out the blue shantung, but she wants the cream cotton. Just as I unbuttons it she changes her mind and it's back to the shantung.'

'It's always the same when Albie goes away. He's the sun, moon and stars to her, you know he is. Never mind, tomorrow's your half-day – not long to go.'

Cook and Mildred prattled on as if she wasn't there.

After scrubbing the table and sweeping the kitchen floor, she looked up at the clock, counting the minutes till Freddy came in.

'Now, Miss, fetch your basin and I'll give you the veggies for peeling. Can't 'ave you clock watchin', that would never do. I'm going to roast them parsnips, so just cut 'em in half, and the taters. This knife will serve the purpose.'

Beattie returned to the square brown sink and began washing and peeling the parsnips. So much for all the fine carpets and curtains, she thought, this is going to be your corner. She was fetching a bucket in from the yard when Freddy bounded in through the gate.

'Blimey, what you doin' here?' he asked, grinning at her.

'I works here, now,' she said, grinning back, delighted to see a familiar face. The smell of hot cakes made her mouth water.

Cook set a wire rack on the table, picked up a thick cloth and took the buns from the range. She eased them out of their little hollows with a knife and set them on the rack.

'Beattie, make us some tea – four spoons and one for the pot. Don't forget to warm it first. Then set the table for four. I'll cut us some bread.'

Just as Beattie set the cosy on the teapot, Cook turned round suddenly and swiped Freddy on the wrist with the handle of the bread knife.

'Gotcha,' she snapped. 'You forgets I got eyes in the back of me head.'

'Ow!' Freddy yelled, tossing the stolen cake from one hand to the other.

''Ope it burns yer tongue,' laughed Mildred.

'Fww, fww,' he gasped, dancing round the kitchen.

'Right, Beattie, now you can fill yer boots,' said Cook, smiling at her as she put a dish of jam on the table.

She needed no second telling. It took four slices of thickly buttered bread and raspberry jam to fill her stomach. No sooner had she finished than there was more washing up. Beattie would like to have talked more with Freddy but he had to run some errands for the doctor. He rushed in again, and after a hasty mouthful of cold veal pie, he was off taking Dr Pragnell out on a call.

The washing up from the tea was followed by the dishes from the Pragnells' dinner and the kitchen supper. The fifteen minutes or so sat around the table with Cook and Mildred was a blessed relief from the scullery sink. The steak pie was a combination of crisp pastry and tender steak, contrasted with the sweetness of the roasted parsnips. A blancmange and blackberry syrup followed this. It was eight o'clock before she was finished. Cook and Mildred were sat in the easy chairs either side of the fire, busy with their mending.

'You'd best get up the wooden hill to Bedfordshire,' said Mrs Frostick. 'Here, fill your hot water bottle and I'll come behind you with a candle.'

Beattie was glad that it was Cook and not Mildred that was accompanying her. She sensed a warmth and sympathy in the little woman that was totally absent in the housemaid.

'You tuck down, soon as you can,' she said. 'You'll be up with the lark in the morning. Mildred will tap on your door at six. Be sure to study all she shows you 'cos you'll be on your own after that.'

Beattie must have looked downcast.

'Got to butter her up. Show her you're grateful for her help. Mildred's got religion and it makes her mournful. Not a bad girl at heart, just takes her pleasures sparingly.'

'Thank you, Mrs Frostick,' said Beattie, smiling at her.

'Oh, yes, your uniform is over on that little settee. Wear the Holland dress and the rough apron to start off with, in the morning, 'cos you'll be scrubbing the front step and then laying the fire in the dining room. There's a chamber pot under the bed; don't forget to empty it in the first-floor lavatory, at the bottom of the stairs. Never ever use the bathroom at the front, that's family only. Just give yourself a splash over with cold water first thing, then I'll let you have some hot just before breakfast. Night, ducks. See you in the morning.'

Beattie undressed and pulled her nightdress out of the

bolster. She used the chamber pot, blew out the candle and got into bed, too tired even to worry about all that she had to do and learn. Her last thought as she sank down into sleep was of Albert saying to her, 'If you would like, I shall always call you Beatrice.'

Chapter Twenty-four

Beattie shivered as she left the warmth of the kitchen to toil up the stairs to her bedroom.

'Bring down that mat you're making and we'll put in a few more rows before they gets back and wants their supper,' Cook had said, settling herself in the chair beside the fire. 'We got the afternoon to ourselves. You wasn't going anywhere, was you?'

Beattie pulled the bolster case from under her bed containing a piece of sacking and the mat clippings. No, she was not going anywhere. The April rain beat at the window, her head buzzed and her throat ached; besides, her one pair of boots was soaked through. All week she had looked forward to Sunday afternoon when she would be free to go to the Mariners' and see Miss Sankey and everyone. To sit and talk with her about everything and nothing; to have her tea on a tray in the sitting room and not have to wash up afterwards. Her mind was tethered all week to the routine of the house: sluicing soapy water down the front steps, swilling washing soda down the sink after the dish-washing or muddy water after the vegetables. 'Many waters cannot quench love.' The words from the Bible popped into her head. Going to the Mariners' quenched her thirst for ideas and talk other than kitchen gossip.

She trailed downstairs with her bolster and a wave of heat washed over her as she opened the kitchen door.

'That's going to be real cheery,' Cook said, as Beattie unrolled the piece of sacking with its rows of red and blue strips. She smiled and her cheeks pleated into wrinkles like the skin of a baked apple. 'Them old dresses of yorn: the tartan rug and flannel petticoat have mixed in together a treat. What you want ter do, the hookin' or clippin'?'

'Hooking,' Beattie said. Cutting up all the strips and making sure they were the same length was a tedious business. Drawing the strips through holes in the sacking with a crochet hook and watching the pattern grow beneath her fingers was much more satisfying. 'The first thing of my own,' declared Beattie; 'the mark of the invader in hostile territory.'

'You and your words, I don't know where you gets them from,' laughed Cook, as she poured them both a cup of mahogany-coloured tea from the pot kept warm on the back of the stove.

'Don't you want to have your things about you?' asked Beattie, who had never seen the inside of Mrs Frostick's bedroom.

'To tell you God's honest truth, by the time I gets to my bed I'm too fagged out to look around me. But I have got this drawrin' what a chap along the sea front did of my late husband, Clem.' The little cook chuckled. ''An'some he was, like an angel.'

'What happened to him? Was he lost at sea?' asked Beattie, blowing her nose in a piece of rag.

Cook slurped her tea appreciatively, then said, 'Lost at sea be buggery. When I said he was late, I was meanin' late getting home. Fact is, he never did come back. We was only wed a few months when he slung his hook, took up wiv another woman and left me potless.'

'What did you do?' asked Beattie, her matmaking forgotten. 'You must have been in dire distress,' amazed that Cook's life should have contained such drama.

'Dire's the word. You know, the world's frightening when you've no money, nor a place to lay your head. I was slung out of the room we'd taken down Oyster Street, and me goods thrown after me. One night I slept in St Thomas's Church and got froze to the bloody marrow. Next morning I walked up to the market at Charlotte Street and stood there singing. Me teeth was chatterin' so much I could hardly get the notes out.'

'My stars,' Beattie gasped.

Cook seemed not to have noticed the interruption, her eyes were staring into the fire. 'One of the costers give us a cup of broth and it weren't in appreciation of me singing. 'Twas pity at the poor whey-faced little runt that I was.'

'What happened then?'

'Next night, I slept in a doorway. In the mornin' I was going to try and beg some food and walk out to Portchester, where my old granny lived, but then me luck turned. I met up with Elizabeth Hobbs, out walking with Samuel, a baby in a perambulator. Years back, we'd been girls together, in a little singing glee down Landport way. She told me as her employer wanted a woman for rough work and it would be a live-in position. I walked home with her. She sneaked me into the kitchen, gave me some food and a halfway decent dress and apron.

Elizabeth put in a good word with the doctor and I was hired. It was a close shave, I tell you.'

'How can you keep a picture of him, all this time, when he was so despicable?' asked Beattie, in amazement.

'To remind me of where a handsome face can take you. Up in the bows, we was, all kissing and cuddling, then wallop, back down in the hold, with Clem whispering his nonsense in another doxy's ear.'

Beattie blew her nose again and threw the rag into the fire. She couldn't imagine little cook, with her whiskery chin and fingers like knobbly carrots, in the grip of passion. When she had threaded through another row of clippings Beattie said, 'D'you fancy another cup?'

'Well, since you're twisting my arm,' said Cook. 'Then I'll have forty winks, while the family's out. There'll be supper to get later. Mildred'll be back in an hour, full of God and Hallelujah.'

'What's Mildred's Lionel look like?' asked Beattie. 'Is he handsome, like an angel?'

'Never met him. Bin away in Egypt all the time I've known Mildred. Sixteen she was when he went off. Mind you, I got a picture of him in me mind's eye from what she tells me.' Mrs Frostick screwed up her eyes in disapproval. 'A skinny, domineering little whelp is how he comes over in 'is letters. Reckon it'll be out of the frying pan into the fire for Mildred.'

'How d'you mean?'

'Her dad was a mean, nasty piece of work and his Lionel sounds to be a bloke out of the same mould. And as for his mother she's a tartar of the first water.'

Beattie loved listening to Cook when she was in full swing. She had a way of mixing her words as she did her pies, making them rich and salty. 'Poor Mildred,' she said, before blowing her nose and throwing another rag into the fire.

'Daft happerth,' said Cook; 'she's cast herself as a doormat and playing the part for all she's worth.'

After draining her cup, Mrs Frostick, unbuttoned her boots, tucked her feet up under her and settled for an afternoon nap. Beattie finished her tea and took herself up to the nursery, stowing her mat under the bed. The room was cold and dark. She pulled back the curtains to their fullest extent to make the most of the afternoon light. From her attic room she could see the gold flag on the weathervane of St George's Church twisting back and forth. Wrapping herself in the counterpane, she perched on the window ledge and took up her pencil and diary. It was time to draw a few conclusions about number two St George's Square and its occupants.

I am getting to understand this place and the people in it.
We are like two different tribes. Cook and Mildred and me
are the 'Hiddens', who live in the back of the house, and are
the slaves of the 'Uppers', who live in the front. We are
allowed to wash their clothes and cook and clean, scrub
floors, empty their chamber pots, but we must always know
our place. I love Cook for she is a jolly battler and I love her
even more since telling me of all her early trials. Mildred is a
wet lettuce.

Mrs Augusta Pragnell is 'Upper' through and through.
She is a pretty woman and loves fine things about her. I am
not sure if she speaks to us 'Hiddens', purposely, as if we
were stupid or whether she is unaware of her condescension. I
think that Doctor Pragnell is only 'Upper' by marriage. He
can be quite friendly. After I had been here only a few days,

*he stopped me in the hall and asked if I, 'had settled in
happily.'*

   *Master Samuel is big and hearty and laughs a lot but is
like a horse with blinkers on, only interested in farming. If I
were a pig or a parsnip he would be quite sociable. Since I
am the lowest of the 'Hiddens' he only nods at me.*

   *Master Albert is my favourite. He is able to be himself
and moves freely between the tribes. Albert is only here on
leave, and will soon join a ship and be away for years.
When he is home we talk, especially when his mother is out.*

Beattie sighed and closed her diary. Mrs Augusta Pragnell
would be furious if she knew about their friendship. Even
Mildred accused her of getting above herself when she
expressed a liking for Master Albie.

'Better than settling for the leavings,' she had snapped,
referring to Lionel's widowed status.

'That don't make 'im leavin's,' Mildred had protested, near
to tears.

Mrs Frostick had made her apologise.

'To err is human,' said Mildred, unctuously, 'to forgive
divine.'

Thinking of Mildred always made her angry. She hated her
way of settling for the least that could be had. Where was her
gumption?

Again she shivered and climbed off the window ledge.
Before she went to bed Beattie determined to bring up a hot
water bottle. It would be possible to light a fire, but Cook said
the chimney had not been swept for years, better to be cold
than smoked out, she thought. After four months of sleeping
in the nursery Beattie was familiar with every nook and cranny.

She loved the pictures pasted on the nursery screen; the chrysanthemum tiles beside the grate; the dressing-up box with its dusty clothes and hats with faded ribbons. On a whim she drew it out from under the bed and began to rummage inside. She pulled out the slippery green folds of a dress, and draped it about herself like a cloak, promenading up and down the room, swirling the material back and forth like a banner.

'Bravo,' called a voice from the doorway.

Beattie jumped in fright and began tearing the dress from her shoulders and thrusting it back into the box. 'What you doin' in my room?' she blustered, 'You spyin' on me?'

'Of course not, Beatrice,' Albert's face was flushed with embarrassment. 'I had no idea this was your room. I'm sorry to have frightened you.'

'What do you want?' she asked, feeling foolish.

'I wanted one of my old books from the cupboard.'

'Well, it's locked,' she said, putting her left foot on top of her right one so that he would not see the hole in her stocking.

'Allow me,' said Albert, standing on tiptoe, while he ran his fingers along the picture rail and brought down a key.

'Why don't you light your candle? It's rather gloomy in here.'

Beattie went over to the chair beside her bed, lit her candle and carried it, in its holder, over to the mantelpiece.

Albert knelt down in front of the cupboard. 'Open Sesame,' he said as the lock clicked open. Like a conjuror, he flung back the doors before standing up and brushing the dust from his navy trousers.

Beattie was astonished. Here were bricks and toy soldiers, playing cards, a kaleidoscope, marbles and at least twenty children's books. 'All these toys and books and things, it's not fair,' she burst out.

'Beatrice, what's wrong?' Albert said, looking puzzled.

'All this shut away and then there's, there's . . .' She could hardly speak. 'Children with not even a marble between them.'

Albert looked down at his shiny boots. 'What would you have me do with them, Beatrice? You decide.'

'What will your mother say if you start giving them away,' said Beattie, still angry at the mountain of locked toys but awkward at venting her feelings on Albert.

'But gifts belong to the person to whom they are given, don't they?'

'What about Master Samuel? These are his things too, aren't they?'

Albert scratched his head. 'Sammy's off to Canada soon, so I shouldn't think he'll be the least concerned.'

'Don't want your mother to think I put you up to it,' said Beattie, feeling that her burst of temper may well cost her dear.

'We'll leave it to Pa,' said Albert. 'In the meantime, if you want to read any of the books or play any of the games you are most welcome.' He knelt on the floor and began reading the titles on the books. 'Here's one for you, Beatrice,' he said, picking up a thick red volume. 'Please, take it as a gift from me. *The Last of the Mohicans*. It's very exciting. Have you got some ink and a pen?'

'On the table by the window.'

He opened the book and wrote on the title page: 'To Beatrice from her friend, Albert, April 1870.'

'Thank you,' said Beattie taking the book in her hands and staring down at it. Her anger had evaporated, leaving her feeling ill at ease standing there in her stockinged feet. She wanted to blow her nose but had no more bits of rag left.

'I shall want to know what you make of it.'

'Make of what?' she asked.

'The Mohicans,' said Albert. 'Here is my address on my new ship the *Audacity*. I shall be joining her quite soon.'

'Oh, yes,' she said, trying not to sniff. 'What were you looking for when you came up here?' she asked trying to distract attention from her runny nose.

'*Aesop's Fables*. Do you know it?'

'I remember the story about the dog and the bone. He saw it in the water and he thought it looked bigger than the bone in his mouth, so he let it go and ended up with nothing.'

'That's it,' said Albert. 'Ah, here it is, I promised it to Major Spooner's little girl.'

'What's this?' asked Beattie, turning her head to one side and reading the words, 'Snakes and Ladders' down the side of a box.

'It's a game. Have you never played it?'

She shook her head.

They settled down on the floor by the empty grate. Beattie set the candle beside them. Albert opened up the board and got out the counters and the dice.

She loved the changing fortunes of the game, one minute up and the next down. Albert shook the dice with such gusto and was so delighted when Beattie reached the top of the ladder and commiserated with her when she fell back down the snake. He was not handsome, in the accepted sense, having a thin face and sharper features than his brother, but had grey eyes and full soft lips that Beattie wanted to touch. He was a person who watched and waited. When he spoke he looked directly at her and listened as if what she said was of great importance. When he smiled or chuckled she couldn't help being caught up in his gaiety. Every so often, she tried to rub her nose across her sleeve while Albert was shaking the dice. She had thought her sniffs and wipings had gone unnoticed, but then, as she was putting her counter at the top of the ladder, Albert drew out his handkerchief and laid it on the floor beside her.

'My turn, I think,' he said, taking the dice and shaker from her.

Beattie thrust out her hand and closed her fingers over the cotton square and drew it towards her, while Albert made much of shaking the dice.

'A six, a six,' he crowed.

Hastily Beattie blew her nose then slid the hankie up her sleeve. As she took the shaker from Albert she looked up and smiled at him.

He smiled back at her, his eyes crinkling up at the corners. She felt as if her prickliness were being smoothed away and all sorts of possibilities were there between them. The game ended with Beattie climbing the last ladder just as the candle was beginning to gutter.

'Why don't you take it downstairs?' said Albert. 'You and Freddy and Cook could play it some time.'

'Will you write on it and say as it's for Freddy before the candle burns out?'

'It will be my pleasure,' he said, taking up the pen again. When the ink was dry he handed the game back to her along with the key to the cupboard. 'Please,' he said, 'use the cupboard as your library.'

As they left the nursery together he took her hand. 'Thank

you, Beatrice, I haven't had such fun in ages.' And then there was the sound of the front door opening.

'Albie, darling, where are you?'

He smiled at her and hurried downstairs to join the 'Uppers' and Beattie felt as if she had fallen back down the snake.

June 5th 1870

Dear Master Albert,

I think 'The Last of the Mohicans' is quite good but ever so long winded. I like the bits about tracking and how Hawkeye and Chingachgook can almost read the forest as if it were a book. Perhaps for the natives nature is their bookcase. You will be surprised to know that I have never been in a wood and know very little about trees or plants or animals. I had a tiny patch of garden at the Mariners and I managed to grow runner beans. I thought about them when I read the book because I had to build wigwams of canes and string for the beans to climb on.

What I like best is looking at the sea. It is always different in colour and mood isn't it? I like watching the ships pass by the Round Tower with their sails like fat bellies. I would like you to tell me all about the life of a sailor. How wonderful it must be to see different lands and peoples and taste all manner of strange food. I think I would like to climb the rigging and be the sailor who calls out, 'Land Ho' as he spies a tropic island.

Cook and Freddy and me are most pleased with the Snakes and Ladders that you gave us and play it often on a Sunday afternoon with lots of laughing and shouting. Mildred goes off to Bible Reading or to see Lionel's mother who is a proper tartar according to Cook. She comes back all ratty and full of sermons.

I have my own ideas about God and I think he must be very different to Mildred's angry, crotchety old man. My God would be like a male Miss Sankey full of wonderful ideas and laughing. I should think he gets really down in the mouth with all Mildred's mournfulness.

I have this strange idea that we are like wells and most of us never know all that we can do or be. The more we meet people and read and look at things the deeper they get. Then when we're in trouble or lonely we can dip into the well and see what comes bubbling up. I suppose that makes God a man with a big jug always filling us up.

Your Ma and Pa are fine though I think Madam is sad at the news that your brother wants to go to Canada. Still, she will have you home for Christmas and that will cheer her up no end.

Please address your letter to Freddy at the Mariners, as I want our correspondence to remain a secret.

Yours in Friendship

Beatrice

'Fancy a trip down the beach?' asked Freddy, coming in the back gate as she was on her way to post Albert's letter.

'Yes, yes,' she said 'I'll be back in a second. I just want to post this.'

'What you two plannin'?' asked Mrs Frostick, when they went back into the kitchen.

'Goin' to have a look at the briny, Cookie my dear,' said Freddy, kissing her on the cheek.

237

'You're just butterin' me up 'cos you wants to take some vittles with you.'

'You're too sharp for yer own good,' laughed Freddy.

'Right, Beattie, you get the basket out the larder and fetch a blanket out the hall cupboard. I'll cut you up some Madeira cake and there's a couple of apples in the bowl in the dining room. And Madam, you're to be back by four. Madam's got friends in for supper and I shall save you the onions to chop.'

Beattie climbed up beside Freddy and set the basket between them. He flicked the reins over Dapple's back and they were off. Apart from the joy she felt at seeing the sea, she enjoyed Freddy's company. They were easy with each other, having so much shared experience between them. This time he stared moodily at the sea and told her about Sally, Mrs Spooner's maid, and his wanting to walk out with her.

'I likes her something cruel, wonder she don't hear me heart beating like a drum when I sees her.'

'What does she think of you?'

'Well, she smiles and blushes an' all,' he said, red-faced at the memory.

'Why don't you ask her out for a stroll next Sunday?'

'You'll think me a real daft bugger,' Freddy said, 'but I don't know what I'll do if she turns me down.'

'You'll have to smile, like it doesn't matter, and have a good howl where no one can see you.'

'There's another thing,' he mumbled; 'it's the kissing.'

'What about the kissing?'

'I wants ter kiss her but I ain't never had any practice.'

'Neither have I,' said Beattie. 'Matron loved us, but she didn't ever kiss us; that wasn't her way, was it? Besides, that would have been a different sort of kiss.'

'P'r'aps no one never kissed her. You gotta face it, she ain't exactly no oil painting.'

Beattie was always hurt on Miss Sankey's behalf when mention was made of her appearance. 'If people looked like their true nature she'd be beautiful,' she said.

'Could I kiss you?'

'Why?'

'It'd be a sort of practice for both of us.'

Their mouths seemed to bounce off each other and then they tried again. Fred's lips were rough and dry and Beattie was disappointed. They tried cuddling, but they were awkward and stiff with each other.

'Didn't feel nothin',' said Freddy, equally disillusioned.

'I suppose you have to be all fired up first and then it feels different. It won't work with us because we're like brother and sister.'

'S'pose you're right,' said Freddy, tossing a stone into the water.

'Only the brave deserve the fair,' Beattie said, wondering what she would do if ever Albert kissed her.

Chapter Twenty-five

*I wonder what Jesus would make of Christmas in this house.
There's the Uppers in their finery out buying candied fruits,
clementines and Cuban cigars. They send off cards, eat rich
food and stay up late. Down below there's us Hiddens
plucking maggotty-pheasants, starching evening shirts,
goffering the frills on a tea gown and washing the earth from
swedes and carrots. Cook says, our moment comes tomorrow
when we get called into the drawing room like a bunch of
obedient pets to get the annual pat on the head, the few coins
and a present. Perhaps in heaven Cook will have Madam
peeling her an orange; and Mildred will be fed chocolate
mousse by Doctor Pragnell from a silver spoon and I will
have a kiss from Albert.*

Beattie shut her diary and blew out the candle. In two days it
would be Christmas Eve and Albert would be coming home.
How would they be with one another? she wondered. When
she thought about it, they had only spent a few hours
together, and those in secret. She had been a scullery maid

now for over six months and her first impression that there were two distinct tribes in the house had been underlined by Cook and Madam. Albert's friendship with her was a little diversion for him, but for her it could mean dismissal. Sighing, she sat up and felt for the matches and relit the candle. She needed just one more read of Albert's letter before she could possibly go to sleep.

August 10th 1870

Dear Beatrice,

Thank you a thousand times for writing to me. Your letter was delightful and it was as if you were whispering in my ear.

It is difficult to convey to you what it is like living and working on the Audacity. I suppose it is like a floating village, without of course, any women to civilise us. We are over 700 souls, each with our own task and our own little niche in the scheme of things.

I suppose, in your eyes, the upper yardmen are the heroes, racing barefoot up and down the rigging furling and unfurling the sails in all weathers. They are brave splendid fellows. Sadly, sometimes there are accidents when they fall into the sea and drown, or on the deck and break their bones.

The Audacity is a steam ship as you know and has huge boilers that need constant feeding with coal. My heroes are the stokers who shovel coal and ash in the stokehold feeding the massive boilers in temperatures of over 100 degrees Fahrenheit. The dirt and noise are appalling. I want to be an engineer officer so I am often in the stokehold or making detailed drawings of our massive engines or doing complicated mathematical calculations. I also have to keep a journal which is inspected once a month by the Captain so I am kept busy all the time.

It is also our home and so we have free time to eat and sleep and write letters. Sometimes the sailors sing and dance together and generally make merry.

The most important people for our well being and cheerfulness are the cooks. You can tell Mrs Frostick I have found nothing to compare with her roly-poly pudding or her gingerbread.

Dear Beatrice I am greatly looking forward to seeing you again and having Christmas at home.

I send you my very good wishes.

Your Friend Albert.

Christmas Day dawned and Beattie, Cook and Mildred flew about like agitated mice, clearing grates, laying fires, cooking, washing up and scraping mountains of vegetables. At eleven they were called into the sitting room, so that Madam could bestow the gifts. Beattie looked around her. It was like a picture from the *London Illustrated* that she'd looked at once when Mildred brought it into the kitchen to throw away. In the corner, reaching almost to the ceiling, was the tree, aglow with candles, and baubles shining in the light. On one of the lower branches, almost at eye level, was a little bell made of wire covered in tiny pearls. Her fingers itched to slide it from the branch and take it to her room just to have a sliver of that beauty for herself. The mantelpiece was smothered with cards and the gilt-framed mirror was bedecked with red satin ribbons.

Beattie looked up to see Albert watching her. He must have arrived while she'd been in the kitchen, slaving over the vegetables. They smiled at one another and it was like a wonderful secret between them, unnoticed by anyone else.

'Beattie, this is for you,' said Mrs Pragnell, handing her a package wrapped in shiny green paper and tied with matching ribbon.

Carefully she untied the bow and peeled back the paper, wondering what it would reveal. She wanted something extra-ordinary; something she couldn't possibly have imagined for herself. Inside was a little sewing basket with a set of lace-making bobbins and a reel of thread. They frightened her. Without taking them in her hand she knew the sound they made. Click, click, click – it was the sound from her dream. She felt dizzy and afraid. Holding the basket tightly in her hands she managed to say, 'Thank you, Madam, and you, Sir.'

'Oh, they are not from me, Beattie,' Dr Pragnell said, smiling at her. 'I have something entirely different for you.'

And it had been different. It was a perpetual calendar such as he had on his desk in the surgery. 'Thank you, Sir,' she said, looking at the carved wooden box and the little cards with days, weeks and months written on them. She hoped she had sounded sufficiently grateful. What she needed was not some-thing to mark the passage of time, but some happenings worth recording.

Cook was thrilled with her little tray with its matching cup and saucer, while Mildred exclaimed at her pair of pillow-cases.

'Oh, I'm ever so pleased, Madam,' she cried, bobbing and smiling. She and Cook also received five shillings and Beattie half-a-crown. The three of them stood there sipping sherry and making clumsy conversation. When she thought no one was looking, Beattie edged towards the Christmas tree. The little bell was held on the branch by a wire hook. She stared at it until the outline became fuzzy through her tears. She was relieved when Cook began moving towards the door.

'If you will excuse us, Madam,' Mrs Frostick said, 'we'd best see to the dinner.'

Once inside the kitchen Beattie was swamped in dirty dishes, saucepans, roasting pans and ladles brought to the scullery in an endless procession.

'They're all right, in the dining room, for half an hour or so,' said Mildred, wiping her face in her apron. 'Doctor's carving the birds and Albert's pouring the wine.'

'Right you are,' said Mrs Frostick. 'I'll give the pudding another fifteen minutes' steaming, then it's on to the plate, a sprig of holly on top, and a good dousing with brandy.'

Beattie had just got the scullery sink cleared when the bell rang.

'Mildred and you, Beattie, take the pudding plates, the brandy butter and that jug of custard. Set them down on the sideboard and bring back the dinner plates.'

'Tell Cook that was splendid,' said Dr Pragnell smiling at them both. 'Those pheasants were done to perfection.'

'And the roast potatoes,' said Albert.

'Well done, all of you,' said Mrs Pragnell.

As she stacked the dishes onto her tray, Beattie wondered if there was a word for the way that she spoke to them. It was painted-on politeness with an appearance of care and interest. Underneath it all was a reminder of the distance between them.

Samuel nodded and raised his glass.

As they turned to leave the room Albert got to his feet and held the door open for them. 'Happy Christmas,' he whispered behind Mildred's back.

'Tell Cook to bring in the pudding in ten minutes, please, Beattie,' said Mrs Pragnell, looking at her sharply.

'Yes, Madam,' she said, almost staggering under the weight of the laden tray.

Albert went ahead of her and opened the kitchen door.

'Thank you,' she said, smiling at him and feeling her spirits lift.

Everyone cheered as Cook set fire to the brandy and rushed the flaming pudding into the dining room.

'I'm nearly too tired to eat,' gasped Beattie, taking her seat at the kitchen table, for their roast chicken, at nearly five o'clock.

'Thank God they're all out to supper,' said Cook, 'it'll give us a breather.'

'Can I slip away at six?' said Mildred. 'I promised Lionel's ma I'd be round for tea.'

'I think Beattie and me can hold the fort,' said Cook. 'Freddy's droppin' in for a game of Snakes and Ladders once he's taken everyone to Commander Wentworth's.'

'You go up and rest your legs for a while, my duck,' she said later to Beattie, as the front door shut behind the Pragnells. 'I'll lose myself in the armchair.'

Beattie toiled up to the nursery. Outside the door was a small flowerpot filled with earth. In the centre was a twig from the Christmas tree. Hanging from it on a satin ribbon was the bell and a card.

'A little tree to hang your bell on. Happy Christmas, Albert.'

Beattie blushed. All the time she had thought herself undetected Albert had been watching her.

Chapter Twenty-six

May followed her husband Nathaniel up the gangway onto the *Crocodile*, along with all the other passengers bound for Canada. Behind her came her mother Anne. Her father, Thomas Norris, had died of pneumonia four months ago in February. His death had been a turning point, that and the lay-offs in the dockyard. After his funeral the three of them had talked long into the night.

'We've got the chance of a new life,' Nathaniel had said. 'We've spoken of it before, but now, what kin have we to bind us to England?'

'I don't know, Nat,' May had said. 'It's a fearful big step. If we don't prosper, we shall be poverty stricken miles away from home.'

'Home don't abide in sticks and stones, Jewel, it's in your heart. You'll be taking all your treasures with you that you can set out again in your new home.'

May laced her fingers over her belly. She had told neither of them of her pregnancy.

'The Emigration Board have spoken to us dockyard

workers and are willing to pay our passage to Quebec and then on to Toronto. In the countryside around there they are crying out for labour. Won't be the trade I'm used to but I'm young and strong and you women can sew and bake. We shall not starve or go ill clad.'

Finally it was her mother who swayed her. 'I'm sick of this place,' she had said. 'Dockyard men, thousands of them thrown on parish relief. Only last week I saw one of them selling salt from a cart, a man that was once head of the sail loft. Let's up sticks and make a fresh start.'

'Are you sure?' May asked. 'You'll leave Pa's grave with no one to attend to it.'

'I have done my duty to him over and over.' Her mother startled her with her vehemence. 'I looked after your father and yielded to his every wish. If I'd not traipsed round after your granddad, too, I'd not have lost your sister. We might even have been able to take in that Beattie as you were so fond of.'

Beattie! May felt tears pricking her eyes. How she still missed her. Even now, she would not be parted from the box of letters and the little frock she had dragged off that cart in Golden Lion Lane. She remembered walking up to the work-house and taking Beattie's dolly for her. The man at the lodge had said he would see that 'the child got it'. Ma, she knew, still kept the little Weymouth jug she had used to feed Beattie and the gown that she had been wearing in the boat.

'Three of us to stand against the wilderness,' said Nathaniel.

'Don't be such a windbag,' said his mother-in-law, cuffing him affectionately. 'Of course we shall go. And as for Quebec being a wilderness that's stuff and nonsense.'

'Am I to be given no say in all this?' asked May, feeling herself swept along with no sounding of her wishes.

'What's to keep us here?' asked Nat, shrugging his shoulders.

'I am bearing your child.' May smiled; they were all attention, now.

'May, dear, dear May! Oh, I'm that excited,' said Nat dancing her around the room. 'No, sit down,' he said. 'I must take care of you.'

'Am I only worth caring for because of your son or daughter?' Her temper once more flared to the surface.

'I'm weeping tears of joy,' said her mother, holding her close. 'Whatever you decide, I shall stay with you. Whether it be Canada or Cosham makes no difference. I want to be there at the birth of my grandchild.'

'May,' said her husband, kissing her on the cheek. 'I've been a mite hasty. The next sailing is in June. Perhaps 'twould be wiser to delay till the child is with us.'

May smiled, realising that they were looking to her to cast the final vote. 'Yes, we shall go, and this year, too; all of us. I shall be over the sickness and on dry land for the birth.'

Everything raced forward from that moment. Nat honed and polished his tools and May sewed garments for their coming child. Anne Norris packed her herbal remedies, her samplers and keepsakes. And then, suddenly, it was 11 June, 1871, their last day in England.

May smiled to the well-wishers gathered at the jetty, took a deep breath and stepped on board the *Crocodile*. They gave their papers to an official and after some scrutiny they were handed over to a young sailor who showed them to their quarters.

★

The ship reeked of tar and old timbers as they made their way along dimly lit passages and down ladders deep within the ship.

'Are we to have no privacy?' protested Anne Norris.

May sunk down on the nearest bunk, too shocked to say anything.

'I expect you and the other families can come to some arrangements,' the sailor said. 'We can rig up a canvas curtain with men one side and women t'other.' He looked harassed. 'There's sheets and pillows and such on each bed and a list of all the bowls, basins and cutlery what you've been given. Through that doorway is the space for your belongings. That sailor over there will show you how to stow them. When you're ready, make your way aft.' He smiled apologetically. 'I mean to the back of the ship, on this deck; there's tea and vittles waiting for you. You can go back up top and wave good-bye to your friends if you've a mind to.'

This was worse than all May's imaginings. They were herded together like cattle. What did they do for washing? How were they to keep their clothes clean? Where did they pass water or open their bowels? Ma and Nathaniel would have to sort everything out, it was all beyond her. She was exhausted. If only she could stay asleep for the whole of the voyage and not open her eyes until they were safe in Canada.

'Don't you want to wave goodbye to anyone?' asked her mother.

'I'm so tired, Mother,' she said. 'Maybe when I've had a doze I shall feel better.'

'Nat, you go aft and fetch your wife some tea and bread and butter – that'll hearten her.'

May shut her eyes. She wished that Ma had not reminded

her of Beattie. Going to Canada was like she was deserting her little friend. *'I'll be back Beattie, one day I promise,'* she whispered into her pillow.

Anne Norris stood on the deck looking down at the press of people bidding them Godspeed. Well, she was done with England. This was a new start, not only for May and Nathaniel but for her. She recognised a group of pauper boys coming up the gangway by their rough clothes and cropped hair. Little Beattie would be fifteen by now, and likely earning her own living. Anne thought of her friend Ruth Salter. Strange, she missed her almost more than her dead husband.

They had been like sisters, sharing their joys and sorrows, exchanging recipes and flower seeds. She had let her down badly, not taking little Beattie into her home. P'raps God had taken her little Martha from her as a punishment. One thing she was certain of; if May was safely delivered of a daughter, she would call her Beatrice.

Thank God it was Sammy that was going. Augusta could just about manage to spare him. Naturally, she was tearful. Canada was on the other side of the world. If it had been Albie it would have broken her heart. It was bad enough to have him in the navy, but at least he came home, from time to time, on leave. Thankfully, too, Britain was at peace, otherwise she could not have borne the separations.

Manitoba! Augusta had been ashamed to admit to Obi her total ignorance of the place. He had spread the atlas on the carpet and they, all three of them, had studied it carefully.

'The wheat lands of Canada, they stretch for miles and miles, further than the eye can see. I shall learn so much there,' Sammy said. 'And when I come back, in five years' time, I shall be of real help to Uncle Hector. We shall be able to expand Dovecote Farm and make it really profitable.'

'"Fair waved the golden corn in Manitoba's land, when full of joy, one shining morn, went forth the reaper band."' sang Obadiah, adapting the old harvest hymn.

'It was very good of Hector's friend to pay your passage for you,' said Augusta. 'He must think well of you.'

'Uncle sent him glowing reports,' laughed Sammy. 'He described me as a Samson in strength and George the Third in knowledge.'

'Why George the Third?'

'He was known as Farmer George, Ma, in his saner moments. Loved to roam about his estates and talk to his tenants about crops and pig-rearing and such. Even contributed to the agricultural journals. Mr Grey wants my youth and strength and willingness. I doubt we'll have many parlour teas and conversations.'

'You will write to us, often, won't you, darling?'

'When I'm not earning my keep and my passage money home,' he said.

'If it doesn't suit you,' said Obi, 'you will promise to let us know, won't you, son? I will send you your return fare posthaste, should you need it.'

'Pa,' Sammy brushed his offer aside,' I want to stand on my own feet. It's good of you to offer, but it would only be the direst of emergencies that would make it necessary.'

And now the day had come, 11 June 1871, Sammy's twentieth birthday. Augusta slipped her hand through Obi's arm as they stood on the jetty looking up at the *Crocodile*. At any moment Sammy would appear on the upper deck and wave to them. They stood there for an hour or more watching the passengers go on aboard. What a motley collection they were: dockyard workers, farm labourers and pauper children.

'Great Scot, there's Mrs Norris,' said Obadiah, looking up to the top deck where a matronly woman in a plaid shawl was looking down at them. 'You remember her, dearest, the wife of the constable in Old Portsmouth? She was the woman that I took the foundling baby to, all those years ago, when I found it on the beach. Surely you remember, Gussie?'

'Vaguely,' said Augusta, impatiently. 'But look there, further along, it's Sammy. He's waving to us. Do pay attention, Obi. This may be the last time we shall see him.'

Obadiah waved, his eyes filled with tears.

Augusta took his hand and squeezed it. 'Come on, my darling,' she said. 'You must take the advice you gave me when Albie set off for *Britannia*. See this as a proud moment. Your work is done and you have sent a fine young man into the world.'

'I'm not very good at taking my own advice,' he said, his voice unsteady. 'Gussie, we're on our own, now? How shall we fare, d'you think?'

'We shall do very well, Obi,' she said, slipping her arm through his as they walked back through the dockyard.

Later, as he stood at the dressing table, taking the collar stud from his shirt, Obadiah was deep in thought. It had been a turbulent day. In spite of his best efforts tears kept welling up. He couldn't escape the feeling that he would never see Sammy

again. Did he know how much he loved him? He hoped he
did.

And then there was the sighting of Mrs Norris. It brought
back that moment at Point Beach when he had found little
Beattie. How often he had regretted not taking her into their
home as their daughter. If he had been really determined, a way
could have been found, once Augusta had recovered from the
measles. There was a long period when Ruth Salter would have
been glad to part with her. Seeing her pale and unkempt, at the
workhouse, had been one of the worst moments of his life.
Almost as bad as when Merle died of diphtheria when he was
six. His exaltation when he and Mrs Norris had managed to
save Beattie had felt like a recompense for the loss of his sister.
Now, the lively dark-haired girl was a member of his household, in spite of Augusta. In fact, she had no knowledge of the
connection between the foundling on the beach and her own
scullery maid, and neither did Beattie.

Chapter Twenty-seven

Mildred looked almost pretty. Her sharp features were softened into a smile and her white skin tinged with pink. 'Lionel's home and we've named the day – 28th of June.'

''Bout time,' said Mrs Frostick, busy pouring vinegar over a dish of herring. 'What has Madam to say about it?'

'She says I'll have to take a letter to the registry on Monday so she can get my replacement organised.'

Mildred was leaving. Beattie almost danced around the kitchen. This was her chance, a step up from being a scullery maid and at everyone's beck and call. It was three years since she had started work at the Pragnells, and she was eager to advance herself. But she would have to act quickly. It was Friday night, giving her two days to perfect her plan. Two days to present herself to her employer in the most favourable light. 'Congratulations,' she said, pecking Mildred on the cheek and trying to sound sincere.

She and Cook sat sipping their cocoa, listening to Mildred droning on about hat trimmings, Lionel's new job on the railways and what the vicar said to the pair of them.

'I hope you'll be very happy,' she said, yawning and stretching. 'You'll have to bring him round to meet Cook and me.

'It's all the Lord's doing,' said Mildred, suddenly rushing across the room and hugging Beattie. 'I'm so happy,' she cried.

Beattie tried not to recoil. She was not used to being touched or held, least of all by Mildred. It wasn't that she disliked her but that she was out of sympathy with her way of going about things. She wanted to make something of herself, get up off her knees and use abilities other than kindling fires and scrubbing kitchens. Mildred had no ambition or spirit, being content to leave all decisions to the Lord and Lionel. Where was her pride?

Later, in her room, she sat composing a letter to Mrs Pragnell, mulling over the final details as she finished her cocoa. She looked critically at her effort. Yes, she was satisfied. There was a twinge of doubt about some of the spellings, but she had no time to go to the Mariners' for a dictionary. Sealing it up in an envelope she placed it in her treasure box until she was ready to sneak into the dining room on Sunday and leave it on the sideboard. Augusta Pragnell would have a whole twenty-four hours to consider her suitability before the registry was even open. The last thing she wanted was for a stranger to come in and queer her pitch.

'My stars, our Beattie,' said Cook, watching her performance with the bread knife the following morning. 'You bin here three years and you still can't square off a loaf proper. Looks like a bloomin' helter-skelter now.'

The bell rang in the sitting room. 'Oh Gawd, Mildred's in the lav, you'd better take up Madam's lemon tea. Take off yer scrubbin' apron and try and look shipshape.'

This was her chance. She carried the tray up to the nursery and set it on the floor to pick up a blouse she had sewn, which she folded over her arm before hurrying down to the sitting room.

'Beattie, thank you,' said Mrs Pragnell, looking up from her book. 'Put the tray on the table by the window.'

'Madam, I have something to show you,' she said, trying to keep the excitement from her voice.

'Oh, yes,' the interest was mere politeness.

'I made this blouse myself. I copied it from a picture in the paper.'

'Really, Beattie?' Her tone changed. Mrs Pragnell was examining it closely, turning it inside out and looking at the seams and the buttonholes. 'It's very fine. You are a good needlewoman.'

She stood in front of her employer, the picture of humility, debating her next move. Turning her head sideways she read the title of the book Mrs Pragnell was reading – it was *Adam Bede*.

'I loved that book,' she said. 'I cried buckets over poor Hetty Sorrel.'

'That will be all, Beattie.' There was a note of irritation in her voice.

You've overreached yourself, Beattie thought, cross at having spoilt the earlier good impression.

Mildred was watching her from the bottom of the stairs. 'What you up to?' she asked, her eyes sharp with suspicion.

Beattie smiled. 'Nothing,' she said. 'Nothing at all.'

'Fancy that Lionel popping the question,' said Cook, busy cutting up some stewing steak. 'I thought it was all in her dreams. She'll be more a slave to that Lionel and his mother than ever she was here.'

'It's having a house of her own that's lured her into it,' said Beattie, helping herself to the last of the bread.

'Hope to God she don't fall for a baby straight off or she'll be well and truly trapped.'

'Are you sure it's falling over that does it?' said Beattie, winking at Freddy coming in through the scullery. 'If that's the case, half the women in Portsea need to watch their step.'

'Ain't you sharp?' he laughed. 'Reckon you must've slept in the knife drawer.'

They all chuckled.

'You fancy going up the Theatre Royal to the music hall? We could just make the first house at six. Doctor and his missis is at Colewort Barracks tonight. He's going to drive himself over. I'll be free by half five. What d'ya say?'

'Can I, Mrs Frostick?'

'Tell you what. I'm nipping over to see Queenie early on. If you two stays here till I gets back, you can go to the second performance at half eight. No good sulking, Frederick, you know as Doctor don't like the house left unattended case there's an emergency.'

'How's things?' asked Freddy, busy cleaning the family's shoes while Beattie curled her hair.

'I'm moving up in the world,' she said, taking Mrs Pragnell's curling tongs from the top of the range and testing their heat on the evening paper before using them on her hair.

'What you up to besides burnin' the paper?' he asked.

'I'm scheming to be Madam's personal maid,' she said,

setting her hat on top of her ringlets and cocking it at a jaunty angle.

'May not be the shift up you think it'll be,' said Freddy, putting away the shoe brushes under the sink.

'How do you mean?'

'Well, Mildred reckons she can be a tartar if you don't get things just so. You'll 'ave to keep your temper.'

Beattie shrugged. 'I'm a hundred times neater and quicker than she is. Madam will have nothing to find fault with.'

'You watch your step, my gal,' said Cook, who had stepped unnoticed through the back door. 'Pride comes before a fall.'

'It's time to go,' snapped Beattie, furious at being found out. She ran out of the house closely followed by Freddy. They were both breathless by the time they joined the queue at the Theatre Royal.

In the road facing them was a man with a straw hat and a carnation in his buttonhole, singing to the crowd.

'It's that Italian, Carmenatti,' said Freddy.

His voice caressed the words, his eyes full of pleading. It soared above them and then died away like a sigh. Listening to him, Beattie was filled with longing. She wished Albert were with her instead of Freddy in his shiny suit and hair plastered down with Macassar oil. He'd cut himself shaving and his collar was crumpled.

It was ages since she'd seen Albert, almost three years. His ship had been travelling around the world. 'Showing the flag,' Doctor Pragnell had called it. Letters came from wonderful sounding places like Valparaiso and Barcelona; with drawings of men fishing and exotic fruit and flower stalls. 'Oh, Albert, hurry home,' she breathed to herself.

The man stopped singing and walked up and down the theatre queue holding out his hat, bowing and smiling.

'*Grazie, grazie,*' he said as pennies and halfpennies were tossed in his hat.

'Going to meet this singer from the show afterwards,' Freddy said. 'Name's Zelda Corday. She's beautiful.'

'How d'you know she's beautiful? Have you seen her up close?'

'Been in her dressing room with the doc,' said Freddy. Sore throat, she had. I went back there with the gargle what he give her. She was in this silky frock and laying on this sofa. Had eyes as green as her frock and she smiled at me.

'"You're a darling,"' she whispers. '"Come and see me after the show on Friday and I'll thank you properly."' Freddy was like a puppy in his eagerness.

Beattie didn't want to dampen his enthusiasm, but she doubted that Zelda Corday would be much interested in a penniless cab driver. Wasn't it toffs in evening dress and white silk scarves, offering champagne suppers, that took up with actresses?

Mr Carmenatti was replaced by an old woman in a hat with Prince of Wales feathers. She played the concertina and soon had the crowd singing with her.

'The show had better be good,' she said to Freddy. 'We've had a feast out here for nothink.'

'Threepence each,' said the woman in the box office.

The queue swarmed up the stairs like a colony of ants, past the dress circle, then the upper circle and finally arriving breathless at the gods high in the roof.

Here we are again, thought Beattie. The Uppers with all the chandeliers and velvet seats and us Hiddens stuck under the roof on wooden benches. There was a smell of cheap perfume, sweat and mothballs. The excitement trembled between them. There was a gasp as the lights dimmed and down below them the velvet curtains glided apart.

'Ladies and gentlemen,' said a man in evening dress and white gloves, sweeping off his top hat and bowing low. 'You are most heartily welcome to a veritable feast of entertainment. You will have your ribs tickled by Snitcher Smith and his droll observations, thrill to the nightingale tones of Zelda Corday, delight in the rich timbre of Courtney Fitzroy's tenor voice. And that is but a small selection of the cornucopia of delights we have to lay before you for your further delectation.'

'Fer Gawd sake, put a sock in it,' roared a sailor, sitting down below Beattie. 'Bugger off, you old twerp.'

The gods erupted. 'Get on with it,' they roared.

Beattie was dazzled. There were rousing choruses, with girls in sequinned gowns and hats with swirling feathers and men dressed in uniforms resplendent in gold braid. Between the singing were animal acts. Dogs with frills around their necks jumping through hoops, doves fluttering from the magician's hat. Beattie held her breath when a woman in a glittering costume and spangled stockings walked across a slender rope strung from one side of the theatre to the other. Acrobats flung themselves into the air and formed themselves into a human pyramid.

At the interval some of the men dislodged themselves from the benches and fought their way down to the bar in the dress circle.

'I'm staying put,' said the woman next to them, 'else I shall be trampled underfoot.' She opened her handbag and took a genteel swig from a blue medicine bottle. 'Very restoring,' she gasped, her breath coated with whisky. Beattie remembered her calling at the surgery only the day before, saying she was a martyr to her chest.

Freddy took a bag of humbugs from his pocket that Cook had given him.

'I wonder what Zelda Corday's going to be like?' she said, crunching her sweet between her teeth.

'Oh she'll seem like the moon and the stars from up 'ere,' said the woman with the medicine bottle. 'Up close she'll be a raddled old tart.'

Fortunately for her, Freddy was distracted from her comments by a song sheet descending from the ceiling. Everyone linked arms, swaying back and forth in time to the music. Freddy stared at the curtain as if willing them apart.

And then she appeared. The one thing that impressed Beattie was Miss Corday's belief in herself. She strode onto the stage and bowed low, giving everyone the benefit of her low cut dress and generous breasts. Her voice was thin but husky, teasing and promising by turns.

'Like a bleedin' fisherman,' whispered Medicine Bottle. 'She's got them hook, line and sinker.'

Fred was mesmerised.

Then Courtney Fitzroy sauntered onto the stage.

'"Come into the garden Maude,"' he warbled, fluttering his hands in entreaty.

'Maude, yer wastin' yer time,' roared Medicine Bottle, ''e ain't got it in him.'

Poor Courtney's confidence was severely dented. He tried singing 'Drink to me only with your eyes' but received the same savage reception.

'Push off, you pansy,' another voice shouted, 'we wants Zelda, we wants Zelda,' they cried.

Miss Corday reappeared to thunderous applause.

After the final curtain when they had clapped and shouted themselves hoarse the residents of the gods descended to the street.

'See you tomorrow,' said Freddy, walking towards a flower seller.

'Right you are,' said Beattie, 'good luck with your goddess.' She left Freddy, standing nervously outside the stage door, having spent his week's wages on a box of chocolates and a wilting bunch of flowers. Looking at the other men waiting there, Beattie did not hold out much hope for him. They were all more moneyed and self-assured. Poor Freddy looked what he was, a young lad in borrowed clothes. She remembered Cook's words when his last romance had foundered. 'Poor nipper, that young minx won't give 'im the time o'day. That lad is pure gold but 'e just gotta set his sights more realistic.'

What would she think of her hopes of Albert? thought Beattie uncomfortably. She was halfway down Queen Street about to turn into St James's Street when she heard footsteps. No, she must have been mistaken. Looking round her she could see no one. She hurried into St George's Square and turned to the back gate. There it was again. Beattie got the key from the flowerpot but before putting the key in the lock, she turned round. Someone drew quickly into the shadows.

Could it be a patient? No, they wouldn't hide, what would be the point? Her hands were shaking and it took a while to get the back door open. She was about to close it firmly behind her when a woman pushed past her into the house.

Beattie screamed.

The woman putting her hand over her mouth muffled her cry instantly. 'Fer Chrissake, be quiet.'

'Molly, Molly Horrabin. It's you, isn't it?' Beattie stood on Cook's box and lit the lamp. What was it that made her recognise the thin bedraggled creature as her old friend?

'Had a bit of bad luck,' she said. 'Bust up wiv my feller. I'm potless and 'ungry.' She began to cough.

Quickly shutting the door from the kitchen into the hall Beattie turned back to her. 'Sit down, I'll find you something. Would you like some hot chocolate?'

'Ain't got nothin' stronger, 'ave yer?'

There was nothing in the kitchen but cooking sherry. All the wines and spirits were locked in a cupboard in the dining room. She knew where the key was but she didn't want to leave Molly on her own. Experience had taught her that her present passivity could turn to violence at any moment. 'Sorry, it's all locked up.'

Molly shrugged. She sat in Cook's chair and looked about her. 'You struck lucky,' she said.

'It's hard work,' Beattie felt a flash of temper. Whatever she had she had earned. Then she looked at Molly's hollowed out cheeks and dull, rusty hair. 'Yes,' she said, 'I was lucky. What about you?' She had heated the hot milk and poured it into the jug before Molly answered.

'Charlie was a bad 'un. Only wanted to fuck me and work me into the ground. All any of 'em wants.'

Beattie was shocked. It wasn't the words but what they conjured up. How little she knew of the lives of girls like Molly, living on the street and prey to violence and disease. Sex had, for Beattie, been only imagined or read about in books. How worldly wise she had thought herself until this moment. She was warm and safe with every meal accounted for. 'But,' she said, turning to her friend, 'it was ages ago that you went off with Charlie. What's happened since then?'

'Well,' said Molly, holding the cup in both hands, 'you don't get no references for fuckin'. Had to bob and weave a bit – live on my wits.'

'Where are you living now?'

'Here and there.' Molly was evasive. 'I'm bit desperate. If you could just let me kip here tonight, won't trouble you no more, honest. Can't stand to sleep out no more. There was rats in the cellar, they was scrabbling about.' Molly began to cry.

Beattie was amazed. Molly was tough and sparky. Even when she fell out of the pear tree and gashed her knee she'd never shed a tear. She put her arms around her. How thin she was and how cold and in dire need of a bath. Her breath was sour and an unwashed stale-fish smell seeped from beneath her clothes. 'Let me get you something to eat, then we'll think of something,' said Beattie, drawing away from her. Her mind was in a ferment as she sliced some brisket, took the misshapen bread from the bin and spread it with butter. Molly could not have come at a more inconvenient moment. Here she was within grasp of being Mrs Pragnell's maid, and entertaining a whore in the kitchen.

'Christ, I needed that,' said her friend, wolfing down the food. 'Me belly thought me throat was cut. Got any sweet stuff?'

'There's some trifle.' When she handed Molly the little bowl she had been saving for her own supper it was grabbed out of her hand and polished off without a word of thanks. From nowhere Matron Sankey's words came to her.

'If you don't grow up to help other people you're not worth the upbringing.'

'Where can I kip, then?'

'You'd better come up with me, to the nursery,' said Beattie, putting the cups and plates in the scullery sink before lighting her candle.

'Where's the lav?' asked Molly.

Beattie was torn between stopping on the first landing and using the toilet there and taking Molly to the cloakroom by the front door, a place strictly forbidden to servants. She chose the cloakroom on the grounds that the Pragnells would be unlikely to hear the chain being pulled.

'In here,' she said.

'Give us the candle,' demanded Molly. 'I can't pee in the dark.'

Beattie stood outside in a fever of impatience.

'Posh place this. Who's yer guvner?' asked Molly, pulling down her dress.

'Doctor Pragnell. You know, the Mariners' doctor.'

'Oh, yeah. How's old Sankey?'

'She's well,' whispered Beattie as they stopped on the first landing.

Molly began to cough and she hustled her up to the nursery.

As she set the candle on the table by her bed, she was aware of Molly looking around the room, picking up things and putting them down again. 'There's that little sofa over there. I'll give you a blanket and one of my pillows,' she said. 'First I'll get you a nightgown and bring you up some hot water. You'll sleep better once you've had a wash.'

'Bleedin' Florince Nightingale you are,' said Molly,

standing shivering by the sofa. There was scorn in her voice, but affection too.

Beattie handed her a gown from the chest of drawers and took up the candle, ready to go back to the kitchen.

'Don't leave us in the dark. I 'ates it,' Molly cried.

Beattie found her way down through the house by feel and a chink of light between the curtains from the landing window. She filled a jug with hot water and crept cautiously back up the stairs. It would have been easier if she had taken a candle from the kitchen, but . . . she needed both hands to hold the jug of hot water.

Molly had climbed into her bed, fully dressed, and was now fast asleep.

All Beattie's good intentions fled. Selfish, selfish cow, she thought. Were it not for the Pragnells sleeping below she would have dragged Molly out of the bed and down the stairs. Instead, she poured some water into the bowl on the wash stand and gave herself a thorough all-over wash, while Molly snored. She felt invaded by her. This was her room that she had made her own by her books on the shelf, the handmade quilt and rug. Molly had brought a different life trailing into the house, a life that Beattie could so easily have been leading. Why, when both of them had had much the same start, was she warm and safe each night and Molly out in the street prey to violence and disease? Was it luck, or had Molly made her choice back at the Mariners' on the day of the prize giving?

She must have eventually fallen asleep, for when she opened her eyes it was half past five by Miss Sankey's clock. Molly was sat on the floor with a box of picture bricks, setting them out in a row.

'Mornin', she said, smiling at her as if she had every right to be there. 'These is pretty. I've made the picture. Best bit is the little white house on the stick that the doves live in. Look, Beattie, it even got a thatched roof.' She looked around her and said, 'Funny, innit, you and me sleepin' in a posh family's nursery. We could've bin rich kids. Wonder 'ow we would've turned out?'

Beattie was too anxious to be rid of her to take in much of what she was saying. Thank goodness it was Sunday and a late start for the household. If she could get Molly away by six there should be no trace of her by the time Mildred appeared.

'Stay here,' she said, 'I'll fetch us some tea.' When she hurried back up from the kitchen with two cups Molly was still absorbed by the bricks. 'Got another picture on the other side,' she said, holding out her hand for the cup and the slice of bread that Beattie had brought her.

In the early morning light Molly looked even worse than the night before. Her face was pale and pinched with hunger and there were blue smudges under her eyes.

'I'll get you some water for washing,' she said. 'I could look you out some clothes.'

'Right you are,' said Molly holding the cup to her forehead. 'Got a thick 'ead this morning', takes me a while to get goin'.'

Beattie gulped her tea and then whirled down to the kitchen to fill her jug. She emptied the teapot and thought of taking Mildred and Cook a cup each. It would keep them in their rooms while she got rid of Molly.

'Blimey, child,' groaned Mrs Frostick, fumbling to light her candle, 'is it my birthday or 'as the Queen died or summat?' At any other time, Beattie would have smiled at the sight of her peering over the top of the bedclothes like a sleepy mole, but not today. 'Thought you'd like a treat,' she said, waiting impatiently for her to sit up and take the cup. Mildred was sound asleep and so she left the tea on the chair beside her bed. Down she rushed to the kitchen for Molly's washing water. As she moved towards the stairs again with the full jug, she heard the front door click shut. Molly had gone. The only reminder of her visit was the unmade bed and a pair of boots with the soles gaping from the uppers. Hastily she washed and dressed and flung open the nursery window. Beattie cursed her friend when she discovered that Molly had left the boots in replacement for her own. She would have to wear her old ones that she had been on the point of throwing away. No, she would not let Molly distract her from her plan. 'How was your evening, both of you?' Mrs Frostick asked, as she doled them out bowls of porridge.

'It was good,' said Beattie, feigning enthusiasm.

'How was Zelda Corday?' she asked Freddy, winking at Beattie behind his back.

'Had a lovely voice when she was singin' but when I went round to speak to her afterwards, she turned nasty and told me to bugger off. Had her eye on this toff wiv a bouquet. I wasn't even in the running.'

'Well,' said Mrs Frostick, comfortingly, 'them artistes are a rough crew. When you're settled with a nice family, that Zelda will be a sad old whore. Ain't that right, Beattie?'

Beattie escaped into the scullery. Would that be the fate of Molly, she wondered – a sad old whore?

Chapter Twenty-eight

Augusta turned to her sleeping husband and whispered in his ear, 'Albie is coming home.' She smiled to herself in the darkness. In a few hours she would see her son, hold him close and note the changes in him.

It was almost three years since he had taken his sea chest from the hall and joined *HMS Audacity* on its tour around the world. Since then he had been immersed in the world of men, ships and oceans. There had been letters and drawings from the Bay of Naples, the Cape of Good Hope, the Galapagos Islands and the West Indies. His voice had spoken to her from the pages and pages of excited observations. There were also sketches of the ship, and the men high up in the rigging; sailors turning the capstan; the seamed face of a seaman, with a monkey on his shoulder; vibrant pictures of native women with fruit piled high on their heads – all of them demonstrating his talents as an artist. He would have so much to tell her and she was greedy for every detail.

Samuel was also far away. She missed him, too, and he sent her the occasional letter full of how many bushels of wheat had been harvested and all the new ideas he would be able to share with Uncle Hector. But he was not her Albie.

'He's coming home,' she whispered again into Obi's ear. When there was no response she began to stroke his moustache and to outline his lips with her fingers. Smiling to herself, Augusta began to seduce her husband. She made a trail of kisses across his chest and walked her fingers down his ribs.

'Grrrrhhh!' Obi awoke with a growl and rolled her over onto her back. 'What a shameless baggage you are,' he chuckled, smiling down at her and kissing her on the mouth, drenching her with dizzying kisses.

From the awkward exchanges of their early marriage, Augusta and Obadiah had fumbled their way into lovemaking. They giggled and nibbled; sucked and stroked; voyaging together to uncharted territory. Now she twined her legs about him, drawing him deeper. They were caught up in a rhythm – advance, retreat; advance, retreat; climbing together, then falling back into a shuddering content.

'Albie is coming home,' he whispered in her ear.

'You were awake all the time,' she accused him. 'Why didn't you answer me?'

'I would have missed being seduced by Salome,' he said, pulling his dressing gown around him.

Augusta giggled. 'I hardly recognise myself,' she said. 'Why was it so difficult for us and why were we so long in discovering each other?'

'We were still our parents' children,' he said. 'Still in their shadow. Now we belong to ourselves and each other.'

'We're so, so lucky,' she said, reaching behind her and tugging the bell-pull. 'And now I am parched. Quick, Obi, get into the bathroom before Mildred sets eyes on your legs.'

'Poor girl. I do hope this Lionel of hers will be good to her.'

'He seemed a poor specimen from what I saw of him. They were walking down the High Street when I came out of the milliner's. He was hectoring Mildred in a horrible, reedy voice. She was shrinking into herself, especially when she saw me.'

'Like a lamb to the slaughter,' said Obi. 'Well, there's little we can do beyond giving her a generous present. Now, I must go to the bathroom before I embarrass Mildred.'

At nine o'clock Augusta positioned herself by the dining-room window, anxious to catch the first glimpse of her son entering the Square.

'Waiting for Albie?' asked Obi, coming across the room and kissing her on the neck in greeting.

Augusta said, turning back to the window. 'He will be a young man now, no longer the boy that went away.'

'I'm sure you'll recognise him, darling. He will still be our Albie at heart, whatever veneer of sophistication the navy has given him.'

'I suppose so,' she said, searching among the churchgoers crossing the Square for a first glimpse of a midshipman's uniform. So absorbed was she in searching out her son that she jumped when Obadiah tapped her on the shoulder.

'You have a letter, Gussie,' he said; 'it's addressed to Madam.'

'I am only Madam to three people in this house and neither Cook nor Mildred can read or write,' she said. I suppose it must be Beattie, though why she has written to me I can't imagine.' Augusta was on the point of picking up her paper knife when there was a tap on the window. 'Albie, Albie,' she cried, dropping the letter in her haste to get to her son. Flinging back the front door she swept him into her arms. 'You're home,' she said, 'Oh darling, let me look at you.' Even as a child he had been appealing, but now he had an assurance and grace that were irresistible. His youthful spots had gone and he was taller, broader and altogether manlier.

Albie chuckled. 'Yes, Mama. I'm home and famished for the sight of a beef sausage.'

'My boy, how good to see you.' Obi hugged his son. 'A sub-lieutenant, I see,' he said, tapping the gold ring on Albie's arm.

'Feels very strange, it was only sewn on yesterday.'

'Darling, how wonderful,' said Augusta. 'I'm so, so proud.'

Arm in arm the three of them went into the dining room for breakfast.

Augusta tugged the bell-pull. 'Oh, Beattie,' she said, in surprise, having expected the mournful Mildred. 'We are ready now. Ask Cook to send in more sausages for Master Albie.'

The girl nodded, turned, and looked at Albert.

'Good morning, Beatrice,' he said, smiling at her before taking up his napkin and spreading it in his lap.

The girl reddened and withdrew her gaze. Well might she blush in front of her son, thought Augusta, Albie was now quite splendid.

Beattie felt sick. Her joy at seeing Albert was hedged around with thorns. She'd not been prepared for this complication. All her energy had been focused on setting out the letter, and making a good impression on Madam. She had taken so much trouble over her appearance too, making sure her hair was pinned securely, and washing under her arms. She remembered

Mildred being reduced to tears one day after a lecture about stale perspiration. For all the impression she had made this morning, she might as well have worn a sack on her head. Albert was home, everything else could go hang as far as his mother was concerned. Even so, she was glad to have made that extra effort. Oh, how contrary she was; as if there were a fork in her belly whisking her feelings this way and that. And what did it matter anyway, because the letter, over which she had taken such care, was lying unopened on the floor.

'Master Albie home, that is good news.' Cook beamed when Beattie told her. 'I do like that lad. Got his pa's nature. Seeing him will please her ladyship no end. Here you are, sausages, bacon, eggs and fried bread. That boy always did relish my cookin'. Can you manage all of it on your tray?'

Beattie nodded, not wanting to make any more journeys into the dining room than she could help.

'I'll go ahead of you and open the door.'

'Set the tray on the sideboard, Beattie, please,' said Mrs Pragnell. 'Albie will serve us. Toast in ten minutes, if you please.'

'Mrs Frostick, how well you look.' Albert stood up and held out his hand.

'Master Albie, we've missed you sorely,' said Cook twisting her apron between her hands.

'And I have missed your cooking.' He moved over to the sideboard and took the silver covers from the breakfast. 'Splendid, splendid.'

They were stood together almost touching and yet Beattie could not look at Albert. He was concentrating on filling his mother's plate. Deftly he set a sausage and a slice of bacon on a plate and slid a fried egg beside them. 'Here you are, Mama,' he said, stepping on the letter on his way to the table.

'That will be all, Beattie,' said Mrs Pragnell, 'Don't forget the toast.'

'Yes, Madam,' she managed to say before backing out of the room.

'Oh, ain't he turned out 'an'some?' said Cook when they were back in the kitchen. 'Went away a boy and 'as come back a man. He'll set the young girls a-flutter and no mistake.'

Beattie bent over the sink to hide her tears.

'Will *Audacity* be part of the naval review?' asked Obadiah.

'Oh, yes, Pa,' said Albie, slicing into a sausage. 'We will be well to the fore, after which we shall be in the yard for a refit. They're turning *Audacity* into a hybrid: part steamship, part sail. What with that and an engineering course, I shall be at home for at least six months.'

'Shall we be invited to meet your captain and see your quarters?' asked Obadiah.

'Certainly. I'm sure I could arrange a place for you both on one of the launches going out to see the illuminations.'

'Perhaps Pa would like that,' said Augusta. 'I shall wait until your ship is firmly tied up to the jetty. I am no seafarer.'

'I'm sure, Ma, there will be many opportunities for you to tell the captain what a splendid fellow I am,' said her son teasingly. He got up from his place and gathered up the plates, stacking them neatly on Beattie's tray. He swooped down and picked up something from the floor. 'What's this?' he said, turning over the envelope.

'It's only a letter from Beattie, nothing important. Though

why she has written to me I have really no idea. You may read it if it amuses you.'

'It may be something personal that Beatrice would not want me to know,' said Albie, wiping his mouth on his napkin.

'Yes, Gussie,' said Obadiah. 'We don't want to embarrass her.'

'Fiddlesticks,' said Augusta, somewhat annoyed at her son's defence of her scullery maid – and why did he call her Beatrice? 'Read it to us, and then we'll be done with it,' she insisted. 'Beattie's affairs have nothing whatsoever to do with you, Albert.'

'She has a very fine hand,' he said, 'and it's well set out.' He began to read.

May the twenty third 1873.

Dear Madam,

As Mildred is leaving to get married a vacancy will occur for the post of Lady's Maid to yourself.

I wish to apply for the post and think myself eminently suitable. Since childhood I have made all my own clothes and have a good eye for what is stylish. I can study a garment and see how it is put together.

I know how to wash and press garments, look after silk and lace and about stain removal. I can read and write and I am the sole of discression.

'Oh, poor Beatrice,' he said, 'she has some way to go with her spelling. She has got the fishy sole instead of the spiritual one and discretion looks somewhat peculiar.'

'Hush, put it away,' said his father, as there was a knock on the door.

Beattie came into the room with the toast racks. She put them down on the table and went over to the sideboard to collect her tray.

Augusta looked at the girl. She had grown since first coming into her employ. In fact, she was now quite a beauty. Her black hair was swept up off her face into a coiled knot, showing her oval face to advantage. But it was her eyes, dark and thickly lashed, that were Beattie's best feature. She moved with greater confidence, and could almost pass herself off as a lady. Her speech was careful too, with none of the slovenly diction of most girls of her class. 'Thank you, Beattie, that will be all for the moment,' she said, turning her attention to the toast.

'Thank you, Ma'am,' the girl said, glancing at Albie before closing the door behind her.

Taking up the letter again, Albie began to read.

If you could see your way clear, to employing me in this post. You will not have to look at any references, as you must know my character through and through.

I would not expect the same wages as Mildred, being inexperienced and so perhaps I could be employed on a temporary basis. If I don't suit I can go back to my old position with nothing lost.

Your Faithful servant Beattie.

'What do you think, Obi?' Augusta asked. 'It would be a neat solution. I'm sure you can find me another of Margaret Sankey's protégées to replace Beattie as scullery maid.'

'I think we should receive a retainer from Miss Sankey for employing her children. Isn't Freddy one of her pupils?' asked Albie.

276

'Enough, enough,' said Augusta, wanting to be done with the subject. 'Albie, knock on the kitchen door and tell Beattie I want to speak to her, before you take your things upstairs. Obi, church is in fifteen minutes. Make yourself scarce while I speak to the girl.'

'I suppose you will want to parade me in front of the local mamas,' he teased her. 'Perhaps there will be an admiral's daughter among them.'

Beattie was scraping the plates into the pig bucket. As she straightened up she became aware of Albert watching her from the doorway. Startled, she combed her hair back from her face with her fingers. Stood there in her sacking apron, her face shiny with sweat, Beatrice could have howled.

'Why didn't you knock?' she snapped, furious at being caught unawares.

'I'm sorry, Beatrice. I did knock, but you didn't hear me.'

'What do you want?' She looked at him, immaculate in his uniform: his shirt starched and boots gleaming.

'Mama, would like to speak with you.'

'Yes, Master Albert,' she said, turning her back on him and tugging at the strings of her apron.

'How are you, Beatrice?' he asked, perching on the edge of the dresser.

'Well, thank you,' she mumbled.

'I thought about you a lot when I was away.'

'Very kind of you, I'm sure. Now, if you will excuse me, I will go and see what your mother wants with me.'

'Of course,' said Albert, 'we'll talk another time.'

All the time that he had been away Beattie had imagined their first meeting: bumping into him along the sea front, or being found cutting roses in the garden or serving tea in Miss

Sankey's sitting room. Instead, the setting had been out of her control and she had felt angry and exposed. Flinging the cutlery into the drawer she left the kitchen and knocked on the dining-room door.

'Come in,' called Augusta. 'Ah, Beattie,' she said drawing on her gloves. 'I have received your letter.'

The girl blushed but still held her gaze.

'I have considered what you have said and I am prepared to engage you as my maid for a trial period only.'

'Oh thank you Madam,' Beattie said.

Augusta was irritated that she expressed neither surprise or gratitude. She had a moment of doubt as she looked at her. The immaculate picture she had presented earlier had gone and she looked somewhat slovenly. Perhaps she had been caught in an unguarded moment. In any case she wanted to be done with the interview and revel in parading Albie at church.

'You have six weeks to learn my requirements,' she said briskly, 'and I'm sure Mildred will happily show you all that she has learned. Now, I must set off for church.'

'Yes, Madam.'

Dismissing the girl from her mind she waited in the hall for Albie to join her.

Why wasn't she triumphant? Beattie wondered as she set off that afternoon to see Miss Sankey. It was what she had schemed for and yet now the position had been given her she felt let down. Perhaps the arrival of Albert, so handsome in his naval officer's uniform, had eclipsed her sense of achievement.

'Beattie, my dear, come in and welcome. You are just in time for some rock cakes.'

'They're very good,' she said to a tall girl with a ribbon in her hair who carried the tray. She didn't want to eat anything, only to pour out her disappointment.

'Thank you, Ethel, that will be all, my dear. We will bring out the crockery later.'

'Now, Beattie, what is the matter? You look as if you have lost a sixpence and found a halfpenny,' said Miss Sankey, settling herself in her armchair.

Out it all came. the care with which she had written the letter, how she had pinned her hair, Albert treading on the envelope and then finding her in the scullery and, last of all, having to take orders from stupid Mildred.

There was a pause after her outpourings. Miss Sankey looked at her and Beattie began to feel uncomfortable.

'It all seems to be a storm in a teacup. You have received a dent to your pride, that is all. But my greatest fear is that you are in danger of becoming a snob,' she said.

'I only want to better myself,' Beattie protested, stung at her words.

'And what does that mean? Using your skills to greater advantage or aping the manners of the gentry. I think you have shown great aptitude in that direction. Your contempt for Mildred has placed you well on the path.'

Beattie stared at the globe of the world, wishing herself anywhere but in Miss Sankey's sitting room.

'Your intelligence is God-given but wisdom has to be worked at. How easy it is to puff oneself up by odious comparisons. Mildred has not had your advantages and because of that she is deserving of your kindness and courtesy.'

'But she's had a home and a family.'

'You have had a home and a family. You were rescued and

cherished, your gifts recognised and striven for. If the pinnacle of your ambition is to attract the attention of Doctor Pragnell's son and acquire a wardrobe and a carriage I have wasted my time.'

'I think I'd better go. Thank you for the tea,' Beattie said, feeling worse than when she had arrived.

'Very sensible of you,' said Miss Sankey. 'I hope I shall find you in better spirits the next time that you honour us with your presence.'

Everything was dull and hateful. Mildred was droning on about Lionel when she got back to the kitchen, and Cook was asleep.

'I thought you'd've wanted to be in with them this evening,' said Mildred when she handed her the tray, 'now you've bin promoted.'

'Got a bit of a headache,' Beattie said, wanting to avoid Albert. 'See you all in the morning,' she said after they had cleared away the supper.

Thankfully, she closed the door of the nursery and lit her candle before confiding in her diary.

*A hateful day. I started out full of hope and now I am like a
ruined sandcastle, my wonderful battlements and flags
washed away by the tide. I don't know which is the worst of
my defeats: being mean to Mildred, puffing myself up with
pride or the exposure of my petty ambitions by Miss Sankey.
And then there was Albert seeing me in the scullery looking
what I am, a skivvy. I want to be so much more.*

Chapter Twenty-nine

Beattie stood in the doorway of Mrs Pragnell's bedroom. She was supposed to be putting the ironing away, but she lingered there, looking around her, at the little gilt tables strewn with ornaments and the dressing table littered with perfume bottles and necklaces hanging out of the drawers of the jewel box. She opened the wardrobe and hung up the green brocade gown next to the ivory satin, running her fingers over the different fabrics. It was as if she were in a dream as she drifted to the dressing table and took the stoppers from the bottles and rubbed them along her arms. The scent of lavender, patchouli and attar of roses mingled on her skin. Taking a necklace from the jewel box she held it up to the light and watched the colours glinting from darkest amber to palest lemon. She took a pair of pearl earrings from a velvet-lined box and held them against her face watching herself in the mirror. The pearls glowed against her skin. Reluctantly she returned them to their box. Beattie sat for a moment in the pink chair with the spindly gold legs imagining the outraged expression on Mrs Pragnell's face were she to catch her rifling through her things. But she had disturbed nothing, simply savoured a few stolen moments away from the kitchen.

The last few days had been exhausting. Beattie felt as if she were a ball being batted back and forth between Cook and Mildred. When she wasn't upstairs bedmaking, dusting or emptying chamber pots she was scrubbing the front doorstep or peeling vegetables.

Even Mrs Frostick had been getting snappy. 'If we don't get some more help down here we'll be worn to a frazzle,' she'd said slapping a wet fish down on the table and going at it with her knife.

Albert had hardly spoken to her beyond their exchanges in the dining room as he passed the plates to her or greeted her as he ran down the stairs and out of the house. He had become just a navy blue blur in her life.

On the next Saturday evening Mr and Mrs Pragnell were invited to a party on board Albert's ship. Mildred and Beattie were run off their feet helping Madam to appear to her best advantage.

'Here, quick, sew this collar back on her dress,' said Mildred rushing out of the kitchen. 'Come straight up when I tugs the bell.'

Beattie settled herself in the corner with her sewing basket, feeling like Cinderella. How she wished she could go to the party. Albert's return had been a great disppointment. She had had more communication with him via their letters than they seemed capable of making face to face.

'Beattie, rouse yerself,' snapped Cook. 'Get up them stairs, Mildred's rung for you twice.'

Mrs Pragnell, looking as if she might faint at any moment,

was gripping the brass rails of her bed, while Mildred tugged at her corset strings.

'Ah, Beattie,' she gasped, 'lay the dress on the bed and assist Mildred, if you please.'

Her hair hung down her back, like a gold rope, almost to her waist. Mildred parted it in the middle and swept it up and back, securing it with numerous pins, handed to her by Beattie. 'The tongs, quickly, over there on the coals,' she snapped. 'Test them on that paper.' The smell of *The Times* scorching mingled with Madam's perfume and Mildred's sweat.

'Quick, here,' demanded Mildred holding out her hand. With a few practised twists of the tongs she had produced three golden ringlets on either side of Mrs Pragnell's face and went on to pin them back with green ribbon rosettes. Beattie stood behind her holding the tongs, full of admiration.

'The bustle, Beattie, fetch the bustle,' demanded Mildred. 'There, there,' she snapped, pointing to a cage made of straps and wire coils. She showed Beattie how to attach it to Mrs Pragnell's waist before draping her petticoat into it. The gown was arranged over the top. The flat front and draped back gave her the look of a ship's figurehead, with the folds of material resembling curving timbers.

There was a tap on the door and Albert came in, immaculate in his dress uniform and starched shirt. 'Good evening, ladies,' he said.

'Albie darling, it's you,' said his mother. 'Sit over there out of the way. How do I look? I hope I won't disgrace you.'

'You look splendid, Ma. Captain Forsyth will be speechless.'

'Is your captain married?'

283

'Oh yes,' said Albert, 'to a round, red-faced woman. She's wonderfully cheerful. She is known among us as the Christmas pudding.'

Beattie, bending down to pick up the crimped paper, couldn't help smiling.

'I hope there will be some young ladies present,' Mrs Pragnell said, turning her head this way and that to see her best reflection. 'You must ask your friends to introduce you to their sisters, darling. We shall have to have a party for your birthday.'

'I hope you are not going to turn into one of those dreadful predatory mamas who prey on young girls. Watching them from behind the potted palms, looking for good childbearing hips.'

'Albert,' Madam said, striking him on the hand with her fan. 'Don't be indelicate.'

Beattie looked up from tidying the dressing table and Albert winked at her behind his mother's back. Further exchanges were prevented by the chimes from the carriage clock on the mantelpiece.

'Six o'clock,' he said. 'I must go and winkle Pa out of the surgery and tell Freddy to bring Dapple to the front door.' He turned to Mildred and Beattie, 'Good night, ladies,' he said before running down the stairs.

'That will do, I think,' said Mrs Pragnell, taking her evening bag from the dressing table: 'thank you, both.'

'What a palaver!' Beattie said later, as she and Cook and Mildred sat over their cocoa in the kitchen. 'I don't think I'll ever get to grips with her hair.'

'You'll just have to watch and learn,' said Mildred, heaping sugar into her cup.

'Only three weeks and you'll be wed,' said Cook, dipping

a biscuit into her cup. 'Then all Madam's antics will be behind you. You'll be a madam yourself. Mrs Rutter of Rosemary Lane.'

Mildred blushed. 'I hope you're coming to the church,' she said shyly. 'I would've liked you to come back with us to the house, but Lionel says it's to be family only.'

'We'll be there with every hair on duty,' said Cook; 'wouldn't miss it for worlds.'

The wedding was on the last Saturday in June; a hot airless day with not a leaf stirring. Cook, in a large brown hat that gave her the appearance of a mushroom, paced the kitchen while Beattie threaded a red ribbon through her straw boater.

'First time I been got up in me best for bloomin' ages,' she said. 'And as for you, well you looks lovely. Red's your colour, my girl. Makes you, like, fiery and dramatic.'

Beattie laughed and took Cook's arm as they crossed the Square and walked through the gate into St George's Church. The little congregation was scattered among the first two pews.

'You fer the bride or the groom?' asked a tall sailor, having difficulty in focusing on them as he shoved a hymnbook into Beattie's hand.

'The bride, of course,' snapped Cook. 'You wants ter sober up,' she whispered fiercely.

'Shut up, you dressed up midget,' the sailor shouted.

'Percy, sit down and behave yerself,' said a woman dressed all in black and smelling of peppermints. 'Sorry, I'm sure,' she said, grabbing the sailor and thrusting him down into a nearby pew.

'My God,' whispered Cook, as they hurried up the aisle,

'what a rum collection. Don't look to be one of them worth fourpence.'

It seemed that Lionel had the majority of wedding guests. Even with Beattie and Cook the bride's family ran to only half a dozen women.

The Reverend Merchison stood in front of the altar staring short-sightedly down the aisle. He wore a starched surplice with a lace fringe over his faded cassock and twitched nervously at his sleeves.

'Look at his hair,' muttered Cook, 'Looks like it's bin done with a gofferin' iron.'

Beattie tried not to giggle.

'Hark, the wedding march,' said the woman beside her, turning her head.

Clutching her father's arm, Mildred entered the church. It was difficult to form an impression of her feelings, as her face was covered in an almost impenetrable veil flowing almost to her feet. It was fixed to her hair by a coronet of yellowing wax flowers. Her dress was too big and the hem at the back had come undone, revealing a raw edge.

Poor girl, thought Beattie, it's so unfair. All the hours Mildred had spent over Madam's hair and clothes, making sure she was immaculately turned out, while she herself looked creased and uncared for.

'Makes yer heart bleed,' whispered Cook; 'she looks a sketch. Her mother would have cried her eyes out.'

Beattie looked at Lionel dressed in a red military jacket and black trousers. His hair was combed in greasy strands across his head and from the sideways view she had of him he looked much older than Mildred.

'Dearly Beloved, we are gathered together here in the sight of God

and in the face of this congregation to join together this man and this woman in Holy Matrimony.'

The Reverend Merchison's voice had no light or shade and he seemed to have no regard for the rhythm of the words either. Beattie's attention wandered. When he made his vows, Lionel had a reedy tone and poor Mildred's words came out in anxious gasps.

Voices were important to Beattie. Miss Sankey's was clear, giving due value and expression to each word. Madam's was apt to be high and fluty and a little too precise. Albert's was low and sometimes tentative, but often full of humour. He had a wonderful ability to mimic different characters. What she loved above all was to hear him say her name, giving it the full three syllables.

'Quick,' said Cook, nudging her with her elbow. 'We gotta get down the aisle and be ready at the gate to throw our rose petals.'

As she came towards them Mildred looked almost transparent, her pale face not flattered by her white dress and bunch of wilting lilies. There was a desperation in the way she clutched the arm of her Lionel, and smiled at everyone. Beattie stared at him. Lionel Rutter was a scrawny figure, with pale eyes and a mean mouth. 'Good luck,' she said, pressing an embroidered hankie into her hand.

'You take care of her, young man,' said Cook, staring up at Mildred's husband. 'You drop in and see us, my duck, whenever you're passing.'

'She'll be too busy looking after her own home to be idling her time elsewhere,' said an angry looking woman, presumably Lionel's mother, who appeared from behind the bridal pair.

Mildred smiled uncertainly about her.

'God bless you,' said Cook, reaching on her tiptoes as Mildred bent towards her to exchange a kiss.

'Here,' she said, 'your turn next,' handing her flowers to Beattie before being swept away by her new family.

Cook shivered as they went back to the kitchen. 'I gotta bad feeling about that fellow, narrow-gutted and mean spirited.'

Beattie put the lilies in water. 'Your turn next,' Mildred had said.

Even when Freddy called in that evening their spirits had not lifted. 'You two looks as if you bin to an execution,' he said, taking off his jacket and settling himself at the kitchen table.

'I never liked Mildred,' said Beattie, 'but I felt sorry for her today. It was as if she knew she'd made a mistake and was trying to make the best of it.'

'Blimey, I come in for a laugh and a bit of a skylark,' said Freddy, tamping down the tobacco before lighting his pipe. 'Cheer up the pair of ya. Here, Beattie, get out the Snakes and Ladders and, Cook, any chance of a piece of cake?'

'Freddy, you're a tonic,' said Mrs Frostick, taking her box into the larder and stepping up on it to reach the cake tin.

Sitting with them in the kitchen, eating cake and shaking the dice, Beattie felt happier than she had for ages. Cook and Freddy were her family or as close to a family as she could get; they and Miss Sankey.

'Here, I gotta bit of news for you both. It's a bit of a step-up.'

'What, what? Don't drag it out, Freddy, tell us.'

'I got a new position and I gets to wear a uniform.'

'You ain't gone and joined the colours 'ave you?' asked Cook.

'No,' said Freddy, 'something nearer home.'

'Is it still to do with horses?' asked Beattie, sliding her counter down a snake.

'Yes, and it takes me all over the place; into the dockyard and on board all the ships.'

'My stars, Freddy, what is it?'

'I'm the new Collector for the Mariners' Children's Home. I shall get that little bedroom and living room over the stable, all found and five shillings a week.'

'Freddy, lad, that's wonderful,' said Cook. 'It couldn't happen to a nicer lad. I'm so glad, I'm like a dog with two tails.'

Beattie leapt from her chair and hugged him.

'Blimey, leave off, Beattie,' he gasped, red in the face.

'This calls for a drop of something special,' said Mrs Frostick, kicking her box over to the larder then returning with the bottle of cooking sherry. 'Beattie, in that tin on the top shelf there's some broken ratafia biscuits I was savin' fer just such a celebration.'

'To Freddy,' said Beattie and Cook, raising their glasses.

'Course,' he said, 'the only fly in the ointment is I won't be able to drive for the doctor no more.'

'Who is he going to have then?' asked Beattie, taking a sip of sherry and sieving it through her biscuit.

'Some soldier what's retired from the army, used to work wiv 'orses. Widower lives in Hawke Street. The doc once mended his broken leg. Nice old cove, name's Jonas Samways.'

'It's all chop and change in this house, lately,' said Cook. 'I'll be glad when we're all settled down again into a proper routine.'

They both kissed Freddy good night and Cook went to her

bed while Beattie sat up to wait for Madam's return. She took her diary down into the kitchen and tried to make sense of the day.

> Poor Mildred, even the lilies she gave me looked as if they'd come from off the top of a coffin. When she gave them to me she said that I should be next to marry. Marriage is as much a mystery to me as home and family. The only example I have is that of Doctor and Madam. They seem happy together but their path is smoothed with money and servants. Cook's tales of her own passion, disappointment and fall into beggary have made me cautious.
>
> And yet I want to feel passion, I want to be swept away by it; to have a moment that I will never forget for the rest of my life. I looked at my body in the mirror and wondered how a man would view it. I ran my hand over my breasts, imagining someone else touching me, I will not put his name here. It felt good but I was not ecstatic. Perhaps I need words whispered in my ear or to have drunk a lot of wine. It is all a mystery that I hope to solve before I become ancient like Miss Sankey.
>
> I know now that I have been foolish dreaming about Master Albert. Wishing for his friendship is like wanting to catch a moonbeam in your pocket. I am resolved to learn my new job, keep up with my reading and get out and about the town as much as possible. Marriage is something I will consider again when I have seen more examples of it.

On the Sunday the Pragnells were off to Nursling and Cook took the opportunity to visit a friend in Gosport. Beattie could have gone to see Miss Sankey, but although she had made her peace with her she wanted to be on her own. After Mrs Frostick had departed with a laden basket, Beattie sat out in the back garden with a book. The bench was near Mrs Pragnell's herb garden and the mingled scents of rosemary, sage and lavender wafted towards her. She had washed her hair and it made a warm tent around her shoulders, as it began to dry. She laid her book aside and drifted into sleep. The dream came. She was a child again and being swung up in the woman's arms, the air rushing past her. Beattie was laughing, wild with joy, and the woman too was laughing, her face suffused with love. But who was she? Beattie called her – what? The name hovered on the edge of her mind. It trembled on her lips. Footsteps came towards her and a shadow covered her face.

'Hello, Beatrice. I have brought us some tea, and ginger cake.'

She opened her eyes somewhere between sleeping and waking.

It was Albert. He placed the tray on a rough wooden table and set the cups in the saucers. 'Milk and sugar?' he asked.

Beattie nodded. If she spoke the tears would come. She had so nearly recognised the face smiling up at her, had spoken her name, and then the shadow fell and the dream collapsed. Always, on waking, she was desolate.

Albert handed her the cup of tea. He took his own from the tray and sat beside her on the bench. 'What is wrong, Beatrice? You look so sad. Can I help you?'

Beattie shook her head.

'What is it?' he asked, setting his cup on the ground and turning towards her.

Beattie blinked hard and swallowed. The grief washed over her and she was helpless to stop it. He took her cup and set it down beside his own, then he held her hands in his. She cried and cried. Someone had loved her, then the shutter had come down, leaving her tantalised by that glimpse of belonging. Always she was on the outside peering in, never, never at home. Albert handed her his handkerchief and when she began to shiver he took off his jacket and draped it around her shoulders. When she had stopped crying he took her face between his hands and kissed her. It was all so different from the fumbling experiments between her and Freddy on Point Beach. Albert's lips were soft and his kisses tender.

'Why are you sad? Can you tell me?'

'No,' she managed to gasp.

'I have neglected you,' he said. 'I have been so involved with my work on board and Mama has monopolised me. But today I told her I had other plans.'

Beattie looked questioningly at him, still not trusting herself to speak.

'I came looking for you. The parents are not due home until seven and I am not required for duty until eight. We have two whole hours, What shall we do with ourselves?'

Beattie shrugged.

'Would you like to go for a stroll or stay here for a while?'

Beattie shook her head.

'You know,' he said squeezing her fingers, 'I liked you from the first, and even more when we used to talk together. And your letters were so alive and full of wonderful details. I wondered how I would feel when I came home. Even, if you would be here still.'

'I don't have a lot of choice,' she said, finding her voice.

'I know that.'

'You don't know nothing about me. I am your mother's

292

maid and I read books and make you laugh. That's the sum of it.'

'I know that this is not just your job but also your home. You are a dear, dear friend, Beatrice. The last thing I want to do is create problems for you.'

'Or for yourself with your mother.'

Albert stared down at his feet. 'Whatever I think or feel, she is your employer. I don't want to put you at risk of losing your position here. Ma is possessive, I know, but I still want to be with you, to talk to you, and be your friend.'

Beattie looked at Albert, not knowing where the kisses had led them, willing him to be honest with her.

'I want to get to know you.' He busied himself emptying the dregs of cold tea into the lavender bush and pouring them both some more. 'But what do you feel?' he asked.

Beattie hesitated. 'When you're away it's like you're someone in a book I've read.' She hesitated, choosing her words carefully. 'You're not in the real part of my life, but in the bit that runs alongside, full of dragons and castles and happy-ever-after. I want to believe in you, but . . .' Her voice trailed away.

'Tell me what you feel for me — now, at this moment?'

'I want us to be friends,' she said.

'That seems a very good place to start,' said Albert, squeezing her hand. The warmth of his fingers was healing and she so wanted to trust him. But it was a dangerous warmth, promising so much, and it was not Albert who was taking the risk.

Chapter Thirty

'Should be an easy day today,' said Mrs Frostick.' Madam's up in the dispensary and Master Albert's not back again till Thursday. Got some nice beef; what with that fresh horse-radish sauce and mashed potatoes it'll set us all up a treat.'

Beattie smiled to herself. After Albert's kisses, nothing could spoil her day.

They were both startled by repeated knocking on the back door.

'Hold your noise,' Cook shouted, before opening the door to a rosy-faced girl in a black bonnet.

'Pearl Skinner,' she announced, pushing her way into the kitchen. 'I come from the Mariners' fer the job. Good at scrubbin' and I've a cheerful disperzishun.' She put an envelope on the table and her bolster case on the floor.

'Well, Miss Skinner,' said Beattie, trying not to laugh. 'It's the custom in this house to wait at the door until you are invited to step inside.'

'Oh. I knows you won't take me on,' said Pearl. 'I'm a noisy

294

mare, gets up folks snouts. Wanted ter see inside and fawt you'd give us a bit o' cake.'

'What sort of carry-on is this?' demanded Cook, glaring up at her. 'You bin sent out to get yourself a job. Get outside and ask proper.'

Pearl's blue eyes stared at Mrs Frostick as if she were speaking a foreign language.

'Start again,' she demanded. 'Knock the door softly and when it's answered you say, "Good morning, Madam, I've come for the position of scullery maid. May I step inside?" Now, out you go.'

'You're never taking her on, are you?'

Cook chuckled. 'I likes the look of her. Oh, she's raw, make no mistake, and she'll take a deal of moulding. We've had mournful Mildred. Let's have a cheerful savage. Unless,' she looked questioningly at Beattie, 'you're not up to the challenge.'

'How will we get Madam to accept her?'

'Let's just win round one,' said Cook. 'Quick, she's a knocking. Go and see what she has to say for herself.'

'Good morning,' said Beattie. 'How may I help you?'

'I come for to be the scullery maid,' shouted Pearl. 'Let me in.'

Cook seemed to fly across the kitchen. 'You will do this proper, if we gotta take all day. "Good morning, I've come for the scullery maid's job."' She punctuated the words with swipes of her tea towel at Pearl's arm. '"May I come in, please?"'

Pearl was shoved back into the yard and Cook returned to the stove.

They had almost forgotten her when there was a faint tapping on the door.

'I wants ter come. I'm gonna be your maid. If you don't let me in I shall pee in me drawers,' Pearl gasped.

Beattie turned to Cook who was spreading the stuffing onto each piece of beef and appeared lost in her work.

'Take her to the cloakroom,' she said, 'Don't let her out of your sight.'

Beattie stood in the hall while Pearl used the lavatory, wondering what Mrs Pragnell would have made of such an exhibition. 'Come on, Pearl,' she said, as the girl reappeared pulling her coat straight.

'Do you want to work here?' she asked her.

'Don't matter 'cos she'll not 'ave me.'

'This is a good house where you'll be fairly treated. Isn't that worth the effort to get it right?'

'She don't like me.'

'If she didn't like you she wouldn't have shouted. Cook will be making some hot chocolate soon. If you give it one more try, you could be sat inside with a nice drink in two shakes of a lamb's tail.'

'Tell me again,' sniffed Pearl, her eyes swimming with tears.

'"I have come about the maid's job. Please let me in."'

'What if she gets it wrong again?' Beattie asked as the back door closed once more.

'She won't,' said Mrs Frostick pouring the gravy over the beef. 'Knows she'll be in clover, here.' She held her hand to her ear. 'Hark! I think we've got a caller.'

'Please may I come in and be your maid?' Pearl looked at Cook's face.

'We all deserve a cup of chocolate,' said Mrs Frostick, picking up the milk jug.

'You're a jewel,' said Pearl, swinging Mrs Frostick around the kitchen.

'Put me down at once,' said Cook, her face scarlet with rage.

Beattie had difficulty keeping a straight face. 'I'll read the references,' she said, taking up the envelope and recognising Miss Sankey's graceful script. Inside was a letter addressed to herself and a sealed envelope for Mrs Pragnell.

July 30 1873

Dear Beattie,

    As you will have observed, Pearl Skinner is a girl with many raw edges. I am hoping that you will see beyond them to the warm hearted, hard working creature beneath. How you present her to your employer is a test of your ingenuity.

    Pearl came to us after a miserable, violent childhood. She can read and write, with help, and responds to kindness. If supervised, she will be a useful scullery maid.

    Call soon for Sunday tea, or I shall forget what you look like.

    Kindest regards,
    Margaret Sankey.

I'll take up Madam's chocolate,' said Beattie, 'and the letter.'

Mrs Pragnell was busy pouring hot water over a bowl of leaves.

'Your chocolate, Madam, and a letter from Miss Sankey,'

she said, putting the cup on the table at some distance from the bowl.

'Ah, thank you,' she said, 'I am just making a tea of Bergamot leaves to relieve the doctor's cough. Did you know they were greatly favoured by the Oswego Indians? That is, according to the first settlers in America.'

Beattie wondered if Chingachgook had used them. There was no mention in *The Last of the Mohicans*, but she supposed they couldn't put in every detail or there would be no room for the story.

'What has Miss Sankey to say to me. Have you any idea, Beattie?'

'She has sent a new scullery maid for us. I think it must be a reference.'

Mrs Pragnell sipped her chocolate and read the letter, then replaced it in the envelope. 'I should think that you and Cook would be able to assess the girl sufficiently. After all, she will be in your care. You have been here now long enough to know my requirements.'

'Yes, Madam,' she said, picking up the empty cup and returning to the kitchen, wondering what they were taking on with Pearl.

She found Cook stood on her box in the scullery supervising Pearl's potato peeling. 'That's it, not too thick. You just carry on till the pot's full. That's the way.'

'She's leaving it to us,' said Beattie, looking doubtfully at Pearl.

'Well, we'll have to tame her a bit before Madam sees her. You'll have to keep an eye on her when she's upstairs. Don't want her wandering into Madam's bedroom or nothing. Might be as well for her to share your room for the first few nights.'

Beattie's spirits sank. Her bedroom was her refuge. The last thing she wanted to do was share it, least of all with Pearl.

'Don't go all sulky on me,' snapped Cook. 'We'll see what the day brings forth.'

Beattie took her housemaid's box upstairs and began tackling the bedrooms, starting with Albert's room. As she took out a clean duster it crackled. She shook it and a piece of paper fluttered to the floor. '*Beatrice*' was written on one side. She sat on his bed and smoothed out the paper.

Dearest Beatrice,

I shall be at Miller's Bookshop in the High Street at 3 o'clock on Thursday afternoon. Perhaps you might meet me there and we could walk and talk together.

Your Friend Albert.

She was thrilled with the secrecy of it all. So, it was not just a stolen kiss in the garden, he wanted to see her away from the house. They were going to have an assignation. She slid the letter down inside her chemise for safekeeping, then patted herself, delighted at the crackling sound beneath her apron. Picking up his hairbrush from the dressing table Beattie drew a hair from it and wound it around her finger. 'Albert,' she breathed against the mirror. With infinite care she dusted between the shells, pieces of knotted rope and driftwood on the top of his bookcase and then moved with reluctance into his parents' bedroom. Thursday, Thursday, Thursday she whispered to herself as she changed the sheets and smoothed the pillowcases. It was twelve o'clock when she returned downstairs, in time to lay a cold luncheon in the dining room.

'When do we get to eat anything?' Pearl asked. 'Me guts is rumblin'.'

'You got those pots done and I'll set you up a place, next to Beattie.'

Pearl came to the table, her apron drenched with water, and fell on her food as if she were starving.

'Take Pearl upstairs, Beattie, and show her where she'll be sleeping,' said Cook when they had finished eating. 'Get her fixed up in some dry clothes, then she can help me with some cake-making. That dress is sodden.'

'I'll put you in Mildred's room,' said Beattie. 'You'll be right next door to me,' she said, determined to keep her privacy.

'As long as she stays put,' whispered Cook, as Pearl gathered up her things. 'Don't want her disturbin' the household. She don't know the meaning of quiet.'

Pearl looked around her. 'It ain't got no colours,' she declared, picking up her bundle and marching out of Mildred's room and into the nursery. 'I'll sleep in here.'

'No,' said Beattie. 'This is my room.'

Pearl sat down on her bed and said nothing.

Honey, not vinegar, that was what Cook had said, when she had fallen out with Mildred. Some big gesture was called for. 'Pearl, I want to give you a present for your room to cheer it up.'

'I wants ter stay here.'

'Stand up, and let me take this quilt off. There,' said Beattie, when she had spread it on Mildred's bed. 'This is yours. It makes it Pearl's room, now.'

'Wants a picture.'

Keeping hold of her temper, Beattie went back into the

nursery and looked around the walls. She was about to take down a small painting of sunflowers, when Pearl pointed to Beattie's favourite, a Noah's Ark with all the animals crammed on board; it had been painted by Albert.

'That's the one I'm havin' or I'm not goin'.'

'Nothing more, or you can go back to Miss Sankey,' said Beattie, glaring at her.

'You won,' said Pearl, picking up her bag.

Fortunately, she had a clean Mariners' uniform in her bolster case and Beattie left her to put it on. Mildred's old black dress was far too small. But that was a problem for tomorrow. Getting through the next few hours was enough to think about.

'Jesus, it's bin a long day,' said Mrs Frostick as the clock chimed eleven. 'We'd best be away to our beds.'

'Good night, Pearl,' said Beattie, after she had settled her into her own room. 'You've got your po under the bed. There's no need to leave this room at all. I'll knock on your door in the morning. Remember, no noise.'

'I'm fagged out,' said Pearl, lying fully dressed on top of the bed.

Beattie fell asleep the moment after she'd blown out the candle. And then she was shaken awake violently in the middle of the night.

'Don't like it on me own,' blubbered Pearl. 'I wants ter come in with you. Ain't never slept on me own.'

'Get back into your bed and I'll come in with you,' Beattie sighed, dragging a blanket off her bed and taking the clock next door with her. She curled herself on the floor and was woken, it seemed, only minutes later by the light creeping through a gap in the curtains. 'It's six o'clock,' she cried, shaking Pearl. 'Get up, get up.'

The girl was sulky and sluggish. 'I'm tired. You get up if you wants to. I'm going back to sleep. Aggh, you cow, watcha do that for?' she shouted after Beattie had poured water from the jug over her.

'Out of that bed if you want to eat today,' she snapped, 'and keep your voice down. You do as I say or I'll tell Cook and she'll wallop you.'

Pearl burst into noisy tears. 'Don't let her 'it me, please, oh, please.'

'Get up or I'll give you such a smack.'

Beattie bullied Pearl into getting dressed and carrying a bucket and scrubbing brush out to the front steps. She followed her with a broom and dustpan. After showing her how to sweep all the dust and leaves into the pan, she left her scrubbing the bottom step. Beattie was about to go into the kitchen when it happened.

'What a friend we have in Jesus' [Pearl bellowed]
All our sins and griefs to bear.
Oh what peace we often forfeit.
Oh what needless pain we bear.'

The hymn was accompanied by much clanking of the bucket.

Beattie rushed out and smacked Pearl hard on the arm. 'Shut up, shut up,' she hissed.

'*Owhh!!* Look what you done,' gasped Pearl, as she let go of the bucket in her fright and it clanged down the steps. ''Ere, stop 'ittin' me. *Owhh!!*'

'Pearl, get up these stairs,' demanded Mrs Frostick in a fierce whisper from the top of the steps, as she dragged her coat over her nightgown. 'What in God's name is goin' on? You'll have Madam down here, and all hell will be let loose.'

They had all three of them crept back into the kitchen when the bell for the Pragnells' bedroom jangled vigorously.

'Beattie, what is all that noise about?' asked Dr Pragnell, meeting her at the top of the stairs, hair on end and his smoking jacket dragged on over his night shirt.

'It was a tramp. He knocked into me and my bucket tipped over,' she lied.

'Remarkable,' he said. 'To me it sounded for all the world like Pearl Skinner.'

Beattie blushed and Dr Pragnell smiled. 'Fortunately for her, Madam is still asleep. Please try and curb her enthusiasm, or she'll have to go back to the Mariners'.'

'That was a narrow escape,' she said, relating the conversation to Cook.

'Could have been worse,' she said philosophically. 'We've got through the first twenty-four hours without too much uproar, and for that much praise.'

The repentant Pearl had been sent to the cellar with the coal bucket.

'I'll get on and finish outside,' sighed Beattie. 'I think we've had uproar enough for my liking.' She swished the water down the steps. How long it seemed until Thursday afternoon and her meeting with Albert. Between now and then lay hours of washing, ironing, meal-serving and hair-brushing, not to mention overseeing Pearl. Thankfully, the disturbed nights were magically cured when Beattie found a bedraggled sailor doll in the nursery cupboard and gave it to the girl.

'I'll call him Jonah,' she said, ''cos he was in the sea an' I shan't never be parted from him.'

At a snail's pace the week crawled along towards Thursday. 'I'm taking this afternoon off. I need to buy some trimmings for Madam's hat and if I don't get away from Pearl I shall be wanted for murder,' she said to Cook while Pearl swept the yard.

'Well, ducks, you go and have a breath of air,' said Mrs Frostick, getting out her mixing bowl and pastry cutters. 'We're going to make jam tarts this afternoon. Pearl, get your apron on and wash your hands.'

'You looks lovely,' said Pearl when Beattie emerged from her bedroom wearing the lilac dress that Madam had given her. She had made a new collar of purple silk and matching buttons.

'Thank you,' she said, tying the lilac bonnet strings, well pleased with her reflection in the hall mirror.

'Can I come wiv yer?' asked Pearl.

'We got our baking to do, my gal,' said Cook.

Beattie got to the High Street at ten to three by the clock on St Thomas's church. Dawdling along the street she looked into the windows of the jeweller's and wine merchant's before opening the door of the bookshop.

The bell clanged loudly. Flustered, Beattie kept her eyes on the bookshelves. She stared at the gold titles on the blue spines, the letters jiggling about in front of her.

'Good afternoon, Miss Salter,' Albert took off his cap and nodded towards her. 'Let me take you for a strawberry lick,' he whispered.

Beattie giggled once they were safely on the pavement. 'What's a strawberry lick?' she asked.

''Tis all the rage, my dear,' he said. 'We need to go to Cremona's Tea Rooms in Grand Parade.'

They walked to the end of the High Street and into an

elegant row of villas and hotels. Written in gold on one of the bow-fronted windows were the words: Cremona Brothers – Artistes in Ice.

A smiling moustachioed man in a striped apron and straw hat held the door open. Albert ushered her into a small booth upholstered in green velvet. Between them was a marble-topped table.

'*Signore*,' said the waiter, bowing before them, 'What is your pleasure?'

'Two strawberry licks, please, Carlo,' said Albert.

The little man disappeared behind the counter and Albert took her hand. 'I'm so glad to see you,' he said. 'It's been an age since Sunday, hasn't it?'

Happiness flooded her. She wanted to stop time and be in the moment for ever. 'Glad to see you, glad to see you,' the words sang in her head.

'*Signore, signora*,' said the waiter, holding two cone-shaped glasses in front of him topped with pink swirling cream, 'your licks.' He gave Beattie a napkin with which to hold the lick and then placed it in her hand. 'For you, *signore*' – he did the same for Albert.

She watched him lick the top of the strawberry ice and then did the same. It was cold and smooth and fruity.

'What do you think?' he asked.

'Delicious,' she said, licking around the sides and then the top.

'This is fun, isn't it?' he said.

Beattie nodded and smiled at him and watched a returning smile spread across his face.

'I want to make time stand still for us,' he said. 'I want to talk and talk to you until my words run out.'

I want to kiss you, she thought. I want to reach across the table and touch your lips and have you suck my fingers.

'What are you thinking?' he asked.

'This doesn't feel real. As if we're in a magic parlour and when we get up and leave, the spell will be broken.'

'In that case, we must stay for ever.'

'Oh, no,' she said, putting down the empty lick on its saucer. 'We must see the sea.'

Albert tossed a sixpence into the saucer and went to the door and held it open for her. '*Grazie, signore*,' he said to the waiter as they stepped back into Grand Parade.

He offered her his arm and she rested her gloved hand on it as they made their way towards the Victoria Pier, on Point Beach. A ferry was just leaving for the Isle of Wight and they had the place to themselves. She could feel the heat transferring itself from his arm to her fingers. Kiss me, kiss me, she wanted to say.

Albert took off his cap and set it on a ledge before dipping his head beneath the brim of her bonnet and brushing her lips with his. 'Take off your hat,' he said.

Her fingers were so clumsy.

'Chin up,' he said, helping her undo the ribbons.

He kissed her again and Beattie stood on tiptoe and wound her arms around his neck. His lips were cold and tasted salt and sweet. They feasted on slow, dizzying kisses. At the sound of footsteps crunching over the shingle they drew apart.

'Do you know,' he said, 'I was counting the time until we sail again, and now I don't want to go at all.'

'I want to cut off my hair and sail away with you,' said Beattie. 'I want to hold a cutlass between my teeth, climb the mainmast and be a common sailor.'

'You would make a most uncommon soldier, my darling,' he whispered against her neck.

'When will you go? she asked.

'In January,' he said.

'For how long,' she asked.

'Four years or so,' he said. 'But I shall think of you every waking hour.'

Beattie thought of the hundreds of days that would have to pass before he returned. How many hundreds of yards of sewing thread would she have used, how much washing soda, furniture polish, candles, before his ship came back over the horizon. How many millions of breaths and sighs and words scratched onto paper would be expended before 1879 dawned and Albert stepped ashore once more.

'Let's walk home through the elm trees along the ramparts to King William Gate. We can stop and kiss at every tree we pass.'

Beattie put on her bonnet and stood like a child while Albert tied the ribbons. They laced their fingers together and left the beach. Beattie felt bewitched as they moved among the trees, one moment in sunlight and the next in shadow. They were too immersed in each other to see Dr Pragnell pass them on his way to a patient in Grand Parade.

Chapter Thirty-one

Beattie looked out from the dormitory of the Mariners' Home across the garden to the bricks of the new school. In an hour's time she was to give the welcoming speech, before the foundation stone was set in place. There was even a silver trowel with the date inscribed on the blade.

'I want you to do it, Beattie,' Miss Sankey said. 'You have grown and flourished here and it is only fitting that you should pass on the torch of learning. Besides,' she said, 'I want to show these old armchair sailors and their wives what we can produce. You are a credit to us.'

'I had a wonderful example,' she said, shyly.

'I had excellent material to work with,' Miss Sankey said.

Beattie looked at her, noticing the grey streaks in her hair. Her teacher was growing old and the thought frightened her. How would she cope without Miss Sankey's wisdom and bracing common sense? Nobody else challenged her as she did. There was no one else with her rocklike integrity. She must not grow old, not yet, not while she still needed her.

'I shall be proud to do it,' she said.

'That's settled then. Five minutes will be ample. There is no need to show me first; I have every confidence that you will strike the right note. I have arranged everything to start at four o'clock. That way, we avoid the expense of giving them luncheon. A glass of sherry beforehand and a substantial tea will suffice. Let's get all the huffing and puffing out of the way first and then we can all relax and tuck in together.'

In the dining room would be all the big wigs and their wives, the committee and the children. The Pragnells would be there too, with Albert. How handsome he had looked when she had seen him earlier. They had all walked down the road to the Mariners' and he had fallen behind to talk with her. 'My hero,' she had whispered and he had laughed and squeezed her hand.

'Beatrice, you look delicious,' he had said. 'I could eat you. I wish I could run away with you this very moment. But tomorrow we shall have the whole evening to ourselves.'

Beattie sighed. Most of the time she delighted in the secrecy of their love, the snatched moments: the letters found in her sewing box, the tender kisses and whispered regrets. But today she would have liked him to stand beside her and give her courage. Hand in hand with Albert she could have dealt with the sherry and small talk.

'You do whatever is comfortable, Beattie,' Miss Sankey had said, patting her arm. 'I have to go. I shall send Freddy over in five minutes, before the start of the proceedings.'

Taking a deep breath, Beattie took out the crumpled sheet of paper on which her speech was written. She felt that today was going to be one that she would always remember and one that would require several pages in her diary. Just one last glance and then it would be time to go. There was a tap on the door.

She opened it to find Freddy standing there, combed and polished almost out of recognition. His hair was plastered down with water and he was trying to ease the starched collar away from his neck.

'You looks a picture,' he said, giving her one of his lop-sided grins.

Beattie gave a quick glance in the mirror as if to confirm his words. She had chosen the purple dress again and threaded some Michaelmas daisies through the band of her hat. Impulsively she took his hand in hers.

'Good luck wiv your speech. I'm proud of you, gal,' he said, giving her hand a returning squeeze.

'Oh, Freddy, I'm so glad you're here. You're the nearest I've got to having a family.'

'And me,' said Freddy. 'We've got to stick together, through thick and thin.'

They walked arm in arm across the lawn to the stage, erected for the occasion. Standing waiting for them was Miss Sankey.

Beattie looked around her at the big bluff Admiral Hawksmoore, red-faced and dripping with gold braid. His wife was a small woman weighed down with a brown hat, on which was nesting a stuffed bird and a mass of oak leaves. Facing the stage were Albert, the committee, and his parents. He smiled and waved, crossed fingers at her. Dear, dear Albert, she wanted to jump off the stage and into his arms.

Miss Sankey's speech was at an end and she was introducing her. 'Before the moment we have all been waiting for I should like to call upon Miss Beattie Salter to welcome our dis-tinguished guests.'

Beattie took one last look at Albert and then began:

'*Sir Peregrine, Lady Marcia, Matron, committee and friends how proud I feel to be welcoming you to witness the beginning of our new school.*

'*The Mariners' Home for Children was my home for ten years. I came here at the age of four from the workhouse, rescued by Doctor Pragnell. How frightened I was. But, stood at the door to welcome me was Matron Sankey and then I was even more frightened.* [Everyone laughed and Beattie's tension eased.] *How lucky I was to be here. How much I learned, so much more than reading, writing and arithmetic. Miss Sankey instilled in us a belief in our own worth and a responsibility towards others. To her our education was as important as that of a Duke or Duchess's son or daughter. We were as entitled as they were to appreciate good music, literature and works of art. This was balanced by realism. We were all orphan children needing to make our way in life and she made sure that we learnt skills that fitted us to make an honest living for ourselves.*

'*The Mariners' is much more than an institution for foundlings, it is as its name suggests our home. Every Sunday you will find past pupils: now soldiers, sailors, waitresses, maids all coming home to tea. Before handing the trowel to Sir Peregrine I should like to call on you all to give three rousing cheers for Matron Sankey under whose guiding spirit the Mariners' Home for Children has gone from strength to strength. Hip-hip hurrah! Hip-hip hurrah! Hip-hip hurrah!*'

Obadiah wanted to cry, he was so proud of her, his (almost) daughter. The fulsome words of old Hawksmoore passed him by. He waited impatiently while the admiral gave the prepared mortar a perfunctory smoothing with the trowel and two workmen in shiny suits lifted the stone into place before he hurried to Beattie's side.

'That was splendid, splendid,' he said, handing her a glass of wine from the buffet table nearby. 'I do believe I saw a tear glistening in Matron's eye.'

Beattie was standing beside Albert, helping herself to a sandwich from the plate he was holding.

'Thank you,' she said, smiling up at the doctor. 'I was so relieved when it was over, and now I could eat a horse.'

The three of them were laughing and talking easily together when Gussie walked over to them. 'Well done, Beattie,' she said briskly. 'You did us credit.' Then she tapped her son on the arm with her parasol. 'Albie, I want you to come over and meet Sir Peregrine and Lady Marcia. You too, darling,' she said to Obadiah.

'Augusta, I have a call to make shortly. You will not need me. You go and be the proud Mama. Albert, I'll see you back at the house when the admiral has done with you,' he said, winking at his son. Albert waved at Beattie behind his mother's back.

Obadiah offered his arm to Beattie. This is the right moment, he thought. I know why I have hesitated before, but now I shall tell her. Once his wife and son were out of earshot, he turned to Beattie. He could see that she had been hurt by his wife's curt dismissal and Albert's instant capitulation. 'Beattie,' he said, 'I would like you to take a walk with me.'

She seemed not to have heard him and was about to drift away and lose herself in the crowd.

'Beattie, I would appreciate it if you gave me a little of your time,' he said, anxious not to lose the moment.

'All right, Doctor,' she said, 'but I must say goodbye to Miss Sankey.'

'We can go into Matron's garden. You can see her after we've talked.'

She waved to her teacher before taking his arm.

'I will see you before I leave,' she said. 'Doctor Pragnell wants to talk to me.'

Margaret Sankey looked at him. It was a cool, assessing look. 'Very well, Doctor. I shall see you both later. Thank you, Beattie,' she said, shaking her by the hand. 'You were a credit to us all.'

They settled themselves on a bench screened from the rest of the garden by a privet hedge. This was Margaret Sankey's own little enclave and Obadiah had chosen it especially, knowing that he would not be interrupted. The blinds were down in the sitting room and even the bird table was deserted. Their only witnesses were the white jasmine climbing the trellis by the window and a crimson rose bush.

'Is it about Albert and me?' asked Beattie, turning towards him after a lengthy silence.

Her directness shamed him. 'No, Beattie,' he said, 'that is none of my business. It is about what happened here some seventeen years ago.'

'Oh,' she said, kicking at a stone with the toe of her boot.

'You mentioned in your speech our journey together from the workhouse.'

She nodded. 'But that was thirteen years ago. Seventeen years ago, I was just a baby.' He waited for her to come to an understanding of what she had said. 'You knew me as a baby?' she gasped. 'Why did you never say?' There was an angry flush to her face.

'Lack of courage, I suppose,' he said.

'Why courage and why now?' she demanded.

'I saw you today for the first time as a woman in your own right. I decided that I had to tell you what I know of you, and accept whatever judgment you might make of my part in it.'

Beattie stared at him. Her dark eyes probed his face. 'You have always been kind to me but I have not taken that for anything special,' she said. 'You are a kind man.' She looked away from him and then said in a whisper. 'You're not my father, are you?'

'No, Beattie, I am not,' he answered her, 'although I have always taken a fatherly interest in you.'

'I haven't felt that. Why have you hidden all you know about me? I've always hungered for a family.'

'Just listen to me, Beattie,' he said. 'I shall tell you now and then you must make your own judgment.'

She nodded.

'It was the day of the victory celebrations after the Crimea. The town was wild with rejoicing. In the midst of all the marching and flag-waving there was a sudden violent storm. Everyone rushed from the common for carriages and I found myself in the company of some soldiers bound for Point Battery. I returned with them and took a glass or two of champagne. When the storm abated I took a stroll along Point Beach to clear my head. I intended to hurry home afterwards. Augusta was busy looking after Samuel and Albert, who were fretful and spotty with the measles.'

'I don't see where all this . . .'

'Patience,' he said, not wanting to be interrupted. 'There was a sudden, fearful storm that drove a boat aground at the foot of the Round Tower. The boat was called the *Beatrice*. She was a tender for a larger vessel.'

Beattie was all attention, now.

'In the boat was a young seaman. He was dead, but in his jacket was a small bundle. Something made me take a look at it.'

Beattie looked up at him. Her face had become pale and she put her hand to her mouth.

'Inside was a baby barely alive.'

'Was it – was it me?' she gasped.

'Yes,' he said. 'I rushed you up the beach to a policeman's house in White Hart Row.'

'What number?' she asked.

'Number seven, I believe,' he said.

'Was she the woman who died? Was that the place I was taken from to the workhouse?'

'No,' said Obadiah, 'it was a woman in Golden Lion Lane, a soldier's wife, who had lost her own baby. Her name was Ruth Salter.'

He watched her chewing her fingers and his heart was wrung with pity.

'What was she like?' Beattie asked.

'A sad young woman when I first saw her,' he said, 'but you brought her such joy. She and Anne Norris, the policeman's wife, were great friends. There was a little girl, May Norris, who doted on you. She cried when you had to be taken to Ruth for feeding. She wanted you to be her sister. But Ruth loved you. I saw her with you when you were a little toddling girl. You were holding her hand and laughing up at her.' He was about to tell Beattie how he had, at that point, almost dismissed her from his mind, thinking her happily settled.

'The man who had me in his jacket?' Her eyes searched his face. 'Could he have been my father?'

'I don't know, Beattie. He was dark, as you are. I thought he might be a French seaman, as the constable found some centimes in his pocket.'

'Where is he buried?' she asked.

Obadiah could not look at her. 'He will have been put in an unmarked grave in Kingston Cemetery, in the north of Portsmouth.'

'Did no one go to his funeral?'

It was hard for him to tell her the bare details, but she deserved nothing less than the truth. 'There would have been a minister and some followers from the workhouse, and I believe Constable Norris attended.'

'You believe?'

'I had Augusta ill with the measles and the boys still not recovered.'

Beattie looked at him. Her face was ashen and her eyes full of tears. 'Where d'you think my mother was?' she asked.

'I think she must have drowned.'

Beattie gasped and turned away from him. She wrapped her arms about herself and stared at the rose bush, tears running down her face.

Obadiah handed her his handkerchief and tried to gather her into his arms, but she would not be comforted. 'Beattie,' he said, 'let me take you home.'

'I want to stay here,' she said, 'and think of them.'

'Beattie,' he said, 'I truly have a call to make near here. I don't like leaving you so distressed. Can I get Miss Sankey to talk with you?'

'No, thank you, I want to be alone,' she said, refusing to look at him.

'Beattie, I have loved you as if you were my daughter,' he said, touching her arm.

'But not well enough,' she said, turning away from him.

Her words stung him. He stood beside her in an agony of indecision. 'Beattie, I tried my best for you.' How paltry the words sounded, how lame and futile.

'You'd best go and make your call, Doctor,' she said, her face shut against him. 'I will be back at the house later.'

Obadiah hurried away. The midwifery case in Grand Parade could not be delayed.

'Margaret,' he said, clutching at Miss Sankey's arm and taking her away from helping to clear the tables, 'I must go. I have spoken to Beattie of her childhood. She is upset. Can you go to her? She is in your garden.'

'She will seek me out if she needs me, Obadiah. Likely she will want to be by herself for a while.'

Later, when Miss Sankey returned to her garden, the bench was empty.

Chapter Thirty-two

Who am I? Who am I? The words pulsed through her as she ran into Kettle Street. Beatrice Salter was a complete invention. Her name had been taken from a broken boat and the woman she had believed to be her mother was no relation at all. Gasping and stumbling she ran on. A painful stitch in her side halted her and she resumed her journey half-walking, half-running. At last she reached Point Beach.

There was a corner where the Round Tower and the town wall met and Beattie rested there on a heap of shingle. It was a dank refuge reeking of seaweed. The water seeped into her clothes making her shiver. She closed her eyes and listened to the waves dragging the stones and flinging them back; the clamour of sea birds and shouted orders from the nearby gun battery. They connected her to her father. They were the last sounds that they had shared, as she lay in his jacket; the sea and the beating of his heart. The heat would have gone from his body as now it was leaving hers. Beattie wept for him. She had found and lost her father in little more than a pulse beat. His bones lay in a pauper's grave, unmarked and unmourned. How

courageous he had been wrestling with the sea in order to bring
her to safety. He was dark-haired like her, Dr Pragnell had said,
and French, perhaps. How easy it would have been to jump
into the sea after his drowned wife, taking her with him. But
he had wanted her to live.

'Mama, Papa,' she whispered.

Even then her life had hung in the balance. All that effort
could so easily have been lost. It was only by chance that Dr
Pragnell walked across the beach, and the greatest good fortune
that he was a medical man. Yet she had sent him away with
not a word of thanks. It was all too much. All the bright
promise of the day was gone. Beattie bent her head down to
her knees, wrapped her arms around herself and wept.

Still the question gnawed at her. Who was she? Who had
decided to call her Beatrice? Was it the constable's wife, or
Ruth Salter, Dr Pragnell or even little May Norris?

She was so, so cold. Pushing against the wall she got herself
into an upright position then staggered across the beach, her
legs stiff and awkward. Dimly she was aware of other people
sauntering arm in arm in the twilight.

'You wants to take more water with it, my young doxy,'
called a soldier.

His companions jeered.

One even touched her arm.

Angrily she flung his hand away and returned to her
thoughts. So often she had imagined how she would find her
family, and how she would feel, but even her imagination had
failed her. They had been dead all the time. And Dr Pragnell
had known that, almost from the first moment he had set eyes
on her. Why, why, why had he kept silent? He had said that
he loved her as if she were his daughter. That being the case,

why had he not taken her home with him? He had muttered something about his wife and sons being ill, but later, when they were better, he could have got her back from Ruth Salter. But perhaps, by then, she had not wanted to give her back. His talk of Ruth loving her had been the one crumb of comfort. Once she had been loved and held close. There was such joy in that dream, the happy one, where she was rushing through the air. Was it 'Mummy' she called out or was it 'Ruth'? How would her life have been if Dr Pragnell had taken her home and Augusta had not had the measles? Albert would have become her brother. Beattie sighed. It was such a tangle and she was so tired and sad. Soon it would begin to get dark. Her dress was too thin for the night air. She had cudgelled her brain to the point of exhaustion. If only she could lie down and lose herself, then wake later, with all the questions answered. Once it was dark, no one would see her. She would stay here until she had calmed herself. Beattie stood at the edge of the shingle, throwing stones into the water. How strange it was that she had been so drawn to this place. Did her body remember? Was that possible? The sound of the sea, it had been her accompaniment. She had not been totally alone, it had spoken to her when her father could speak no more. This was her dwelling place regardless of where the journey had begun. One day she would come back when she was happy and bring her joy to this place; until then she would stay away.

It was now almost dark and Beattie began to shiver. She threw a last stone. Someone was coming down the beach towards her. Taking to her heels she tried to run away from them up the shingle. Instead, she ran straight into the man's arms.

'Help, help!' she screamed, struggling with her captor.

'No, stop. Beattie, it's me, Freddy.'

'Oh, Freddy,' she cried clinging to him. 'Freddy it's you.' She could say no more.

'Come on, let's get you home.'

They stumbled across Broad Street to where Dapple was patiently waiting. 'Up the steps – that's it; pull the blanket round yer shoulders. Have you home in two shakes I will.'

'Sit with me a minute,' she begged him.

'What's happened?' he asked. 'You was Queen of the May this afternoon. How come you're down here on your own? Saw you go off with the doctor. What did he say to set you off?'

'Too much to tell now,' she said, still shivering. 'Put your arms around me, hold me close like I really was your sister.'

'"By baby bunting, Daddy's gone a-hunting, to get a little rabbit skin to put his baby bunting in."' Freddy sang.

He smelled of horses and old clothes. He was so dear to her and so familiar. She could feel his heart beating beneath his shirt. 'Why are you singing that?' she whispered.

''Cos I can't think of nothin' else,' he said. 'Course there's always, "What a friend we have in Jesus, all our sins and griefs to bear."'

Beattie giggled, reminded of Pearl's early-morning recitals.

'That's better,' said Freddy, 'that's my girl. Let's get you home. Whatever it is 'twill all seem better in the morning. Poor old Dapple's tired and wants to be back in her stable.'

'Why have you got her? Where's Jonas?'

'I went round your place jist now and they was in an uproar not knowing where you was. Poor old doc just come in from a childbirth, done up 'e was. When Cook says as how you ain't bin seen since you set off in the mornin', he was all for searching the whole town fer you. I told him as I would get ya.'

'You rode to my rescue,' she said, giving him a watery smile.

'Course I did. We're family; besides, I knew where to find you.'

'I want to go to the Mariners' please, Freddy,' she said. 'I can't cope with the Pragnells tonight.'

'I shall 'ave to drop off there first and tell the doc as you're safe, first. Pearl reckons you've bin took by pirates.'

Beattie sat in the trap in the dark while Freddy ran round to the back door and gave the news of her being found. She was almost asleep by the time they got to the Mariners'.

'Straight up to bed in the sick bay,' Miss Sankey said when she saw her tear-stained face and thin dress. 'Freddy, thank you, you have been a trouper. Have you let the doctor know? He has been so anxious.'

'We just come from there,' said Freddy. 'I'll be off now. Old Dapple wants his stable and I wants mine.'

'Off you go, Beattie. You know where everything is.'

The familiarity of the little room with the white beds and pictures of old sailors enfolded her like a blessing. She was putting on a nightgown when Miss Sankey came in carrying a stone hot-water bottle.

'Get into bed and tuck down. I will get you some hot milk and then it's off to sleep with you. Explanations can follow in the morning.'

Gratefully, Beattie rested her feet on the bottle and pulled the blankets up to her shoulders. She was glad the sick bay was empty, she needed the sanctuary to herself. After she had drunk her milk Miss Sankey blew out the candle.

She fell into an exhausted sleep. And then, the sound of

clicking bobbins came jolting her awake. Sweating and terrified, she lay in the darkness, too frightened even to search for
the matches. What did the noise mean? In the last few years she
had felt as if she were climbing out of the fears and sorrows of
her childhood and now it was as if the ladder had been kicked
away. 'Lighten our darkness,' she whispered to herself, over
and over again.

The sun was glinting through the curtains when there was
a knock on the door. 'Good morning, Beattie,' said Miss
Sankey, briskly. 'I will go and get us some breakfast while you
wash and dress, there's hot water in the jug. You will have to
wear one of our uniforms, I'm afraid,' she said, putting a clean
dress and underwear on a chair beside the bed. 'Your finery
from yesterday will need a good wash.'

Beattie didn't want to go back to St George's Square, she
wanted to stay at the Mariners' and be looked after just as she
had been when Rosie had diphtheria. Reluctantly she turned
back the covers and did as she was told.

Later, there was another tap on the door and she opened it
to Miss Sankey, bearing a loaded tray. It felt luxurious. She
poured the tea, for both of them, from the little pot into the
cups with the rosebuds in the bottom. On the plates were two
slices of toast wrapped in a napkin to keep hot. There was a
dish with curls of butter and another with plum jam. Lavishly
she spread her toast with both.

Miss Sankey nodded approvingly. 'That's it, a good breakfast will always help one back into the saddle.'

Beattie looked at her. How much did she know of what
had taken place yesterday in her garden?

'I believe you talked with Doctor Pragnell and he gave you
some news of your background?'

'It was all such a shock,' she said. 'It wasn't what I had thought at all,' she said haltingly. 'I'd always hoped one day to find my family.'

'You and Freddy and all our other children, my dear,' said Miss Sankey. 'You have had, as you say, a shock. But you are incredibly lucky to be alive at all.'

'I know. It's just such a surprise that Doctor Pragnell knew so much about me and yet he'd never told me anything.'

Miss Sankey shrugged. 'Men are strange creatures,' she said. 'They will do enormous feats of gallantry and yet run from a woman's tears.'

'Why d'you think he didn't take me home with him if he is so fond of me?' she asked.

'Many very good reasons. His children were ill and then his wife caught the measles from them. You urgently needed a wet nurse. How was he to know that the woman who loved and care for you would die?'

'I don't know.'

'Once you were safely settled, as he thought, he was plunged in work. All the wounded veterans of the Crimea needed his care. The Mariners' Home was in a parlous state and he had his own family to deal with.' She looked at Beattie and said, 'Whatever your grievance with your treatment at the hands of Doctor Pragnell, remember, he was the one who made your life possible.'

Beattie blushed. 'I'll tell him that I'm sorry I ran away,' she said softly.

'He'll be glad to hear it.' Miss Sankey smiled. 'You were bound to feel sluggish, for a while, but life goes forward, not back.'

'Sluggish?'

'Oh, sad, lonely, unhappy and grief-stricken. All those capitals spell out sluggish to me. And the best cure for a sluggard is activity.'

With her purple dress and straw hat wrapped in a paper parcel, Beattie set off for St George's Square.

'Thank you for looking after me,' she said as she took her leave of Miss Sankey.

'Think nothing of it, my dear. Whatever you make of them, your adventures will fill a good few pages in your diary. Now off with you, and send Pearl along for her tea this afternoon. Tell her I'm looking forward to some singing.'

Obadiah saw the determined figure approaching the house as he looked out of the bedroom window. He wanted to rush out and fold her in his arms, but he knew that he must wait for Beattie to signal her readiness to talk.

He had been anxious about her all night, in spite of knowing that she was safe in Margaret's care. When he returned drained from a midwifery visit he had been alarmed to know that she was missing. There was not even the consolation of knowing that he had been gainfully employed. After hours in labour the young mother had given birth to a dead child. Her screams and her husband's silent tears still haunted him. And then, to come home to Beattie's absence and Augusta's petulance had been a severe test of his patience. To stand in the bedroom having to undo his wife's ridiculous corset while she railed about Beattie's negligence had been the last straw. 'If your father could hear you now, he would be ashamed. Gussie, this childishness is unworthy of you,' he had snapped.

'If you're going to be horrid, you can go away,' she said, her face red with temper.

Obadiah, sighed. Perhaps if he had explained to Gussie the cause of her maid's distress she would have been more understanding. But he didn't understand his own actions, let alone Beattie's.

Thank God she had Freddy for a friend. His rough kindness was the balm Beattie needed. Now, he must brace himself for luncheon with the Spooners.

'Sorry I'm late,' said Beattie as she shut the back door and walked into the kitchen.

'Least said soonest mended, my duck,' said Cook, her face red and shiny with sweat. 'You go and speak with her ladyship. There was a real set-to last night. Doctor gave her a good talking to. He was that upset that you was missing. You best go upstairs and speak to the pair of them.'

'Ah, Beattie,' said Mrs Pragnell when she tapped on her door. 'This brown silk dress Miss Nevatt has made for me. It's not right.'

'Could you walk around for a moment,' said Beattie, glad that Madam had not mentioned her absence the night before. 'It's the shoulders, I think, and the waist is set too low.'

'Is it possible that you could alter it for me?'

'It depends when you require it,' she said guardedly, knowing her employer's tendency to want things done with magical speed.

'For a luncheon on Tuesday.' She smiled at Beattie coaxingly. 'Is that a possibility?'

'Provided I can leave the buttonholes on the cream blouse until later, then I could almost guarantee it.'

'Thank you, Beattie,' she said, looking directly at her. 'Perhaps if you went to bed earlier you would not be so tired.'

'Thank you for your concern,' said Beattie, with chilly politeness before gathering up the dress. She rushed upstairs and flung it on her bed before running downstairs to lay the dining table.

'Ah, Beattie,' said Dr Pragnell, putting down his newspaper as she came in with a tray of cutlery. 'I am so very glad to see you.'

'Thank you,' she said, looking down at her tray.

'Enough said for the moment?' he asked.

Beattie nodded.

'I was ever so worried,' said Pearl when she went back into the kitchen. 'I thought you was drownded. You all right, now?'

'I think so.'

'Good, then you can give us a hand with the taters, there's mountains of 'em.'

Beattie smiled. 'Glad you missed me,' she said. Later, when she went up to the nursery to change out of the Mariners' dress and put on her black dress and starched apron she found a letter in the pocket.

Darling Beatrice,

I cannot meet you tonight, which is a great pity. If you can slide away, next Sunday afternoon, I have in mind something quite special. Look out your best bonnet.

Best Love

Albert.

Beattie was surprised at how relieved she felt at not meeting Albert. Tonight she wanted to sit in the kitchen with Cook and Pearl. To read to them about the goings-on of the gentry from Madam's discarded *London Illustrated*. To sit and sew and gossip and for everything to be as before. What she had learned of herself, lay like a wound inside her. She needed time to recover from the shock and to find her own means of healing.

Chapter Thirty-three

Beattie left St George's Square by the back gate. She had said nothing of her destination. Everyone would think she was off to see Matron Sankey. It was not a lie; more an evasion. What had Albert told his parents? she wondered. She had not seen him, alone, since the ceremony and the speech-making at the Mariners' and doubted that his father would have told him of their conversation in the garden. She, too, would say nothing. Albert would not understand. How could he? Secure, always, in his parents' love, how could he make the leap of the imagination needed to stand in her shoes?

Albert was there, outside Denby and Shanks, the naval tailors on The Hard. He raised his cap to her. There was always a feeling of disbelief for her at their meetings, as if they were actors in a play. The first few moments were awkward. Her words fell over themselves and she could not look directly at him. Then, he would take her hand and say something quite foolish and make her laugh, after which they would be easy with each other.

'Beatrice, you look so pretty. Can it be me that you have come to see? No, it must be some prince or hero.'

'Don't be so silly,' she said. 'I am having a holiday from princes. I fancied a sailor for Sundays and perhaps an admiral for the rest of the week.'

'What audacity,' he said, taking her arm.

'Ah,' she cried, 'is that a clue to our destination?'

'Just a few moments more,' he said like a conjurer, about to produce the white rabbit, 'and all will be revealed.'

Beattie was fizzing with excitement as they approached the policeman at the dockyard gate.

'Good afternoon,' Albert said. 'Sub-Lieutenant Pragnell of the *Audacity*. I am taking a guest on board for tea.'

'Carry on, Sir,' the man said and nodded to Beattie.

'Ooh!' She gasped, squeezing his arm. 'I can't believe it. Will your captain be there? Will the band play? What will we have to eat?'

'My captain is in Chichester today with his family. As for the band, if you ask him nicely, I'm sure Rollo Reed would give us a tune on his penny whistle. It's my fellow subby Inky Pen's twenty-first birthday, so the refreshments are down to him.'

'It sounds more and more like Alice in Wonderland than a proper ship,' she said, skipping to keep up with him.

Albert laughed. 'The ship is our world, especially when we're at sea. I want to show her to you and have you meet my chums. They are tired of having me sing your praises. They want to see you for themselves.'

'And I want to see them,' said Beattie, trying to sound bold and unconcerned.

What would they think of her? she wondered. Did they

know she was Albert's Mama's maid? She remembered Miss Sankey's words: 'People can only make you feel inferior if you give them permission to do so.'

What's the good of having an adventure, she thought, if you don't rise to the occasion. No, she would throw herself into the afternoon and savour every moment. As they trotted through the dockyard she was surprised at the Sunday quiet of the place. How different it had been when she and Freddy had come bowling through the gates, to return the empty dishes to the Naval College, after the grand French banquet. Then, the yard had throbbed with the sound of the steam hammer and the competing cries of sailors and mateys hurrying back and forth. She could not have imagined herself, at that time, strolling through the gates on the arm of a sub-lieutenant.

As they walked deeper into the dockyard she began to feel cold. The wind blew in her face and her eyes began to water. 'We seem to have been walking for ages,' she said.

'There she is. *Audacity* – every sail and spar of her.'

Beattie was astonished. The ship was a vast expanse of yellow and black with sails and ropes towering above them. The figurehead personified Audacity being a woman with a laurel wreath in her hair and a carelessly draped gown, which exposed a generous wooden breast. Her eyes were brown and bulging and her nose sharp as a needle. What gave the figure its character was her smiling scarlet mouth. Beattie gasped. It seemed a legendary vessel. Never had she been so close to a ship of such size. Her experience of ships so far had been waving to them from the distance of the beach.

'It's wonderful,' she said clutching his arm.

'She is rather splendid, I must admit,' said Albert.

Looking high up among the furled sails, she was surprised

to see a figure in naval uniform sat on a platform clutching hold of the rigging.

'What's that boy doing up there?' she whispered.

'Oh, poor Osborne,' he said, 'fell foul of the Commander, failed to salute him when he passed him in the dockyard.'

'That's not fair,' said Beattie, 'he must be shrammed to the bone.'

'He won't be up there much longer. You'll probably meet him later. It's all a part of the life of a snotty.'

'Weren't you a snotty, once?' she asked. 'Isn't it the name for a midshipman?'

'Yes,' laughed Albert, 'and jolly glad I am to be one no longer.'

'Is it because they're always out in the cold and their noses are running that they have that name?' But Albert didn't answer. He was already going ahead of her up the gangway to the ship. Beattie followed after him, trying to look as if she had tea on warships every day of the week.

'Permission to come aboard and bring a guest, Sir,' he said, to an officer at the top.

'Permission granted, and a good afternoon to you. I hope this young man takes good care of you, my dear young lady.'

She nodded, too overawed to speak. It was wonderful and strange. As they walked along the deck she was fascinated by all the activity. There were barefoot sailors everywhere. Some sat on strange low tables, with square cut holes in them, smoking their pipes or mending their clothes. It fascinated her to see men with needles in their hands. Others were laughing and talking or playing penny whistles. There was a group with a monkey scurrying between them and others were making complicated knots with pieces of rope.

'Our living quarters are in the Gun Room. Let me go ahead of you and help you down the ladder,' said Albert.

She must have looked anxious, for Albert smiled reassuringly at her.

'Turn around and face the ladder and catch hold of the ropes on either side.' She watched him climb nimbly down and then it was her turn. She faced the steps and clutched at the ropes. The gap from one step to the next seemed very long and she was terrified of losing her footing. At last she was on the next deck and Albert guided her to another ladder.

She followed Albert past yet more sailors. This time they were sat on benches at long tables writing letters or playing draughts. There was even a squawking parrot in a cage. And then they faced another ladder at the bottom of which was the Gun Room.

Standing waiting for her was a tall blond youth. He smiled at her.

'Good afternoon, dear lady,' he said, taking her hand and kissing it.

''Tis Leonardo with the light of his life,' said another officer, moving his chair away from the dining table and coming towards her.

'Beatrice, these are my comrades,' said Albert.

Beattie found herself the subject of amused scrutiny by the men sat around the table. The atmosphere was different from that of the sailors on the deck above. There was a tablecloth, patterned crockery, even a pot of jam.

'Sub-Lieutenant Rollo Reed,' said a tall man, holding out a chair for her.

'This is Beatrice,' said Albert.

'Come and sit next to me,' said a freckle-faced man with ginger hair. 'It's my birthday and I get to choose my neigh-bours.' He shook her hand vigorously. 'Hello, Beattie, my name is William Pen.'

'You must be Inky?' she said shyly.

'The very same,' he said.

Albert disappeared through a door saying, 'I'll rouse the steward.'

Beattie felt abandoned and at a loss for words. She stared at the blue and white china plate in front of her, praying for Albert to come back. Someone tugged at her sleeve. Beattie turned to see a blonde, doll-like creature on the other side of Inky Pen who looked no more than twelve years old.

'I'm Charlotte, Inky's sister,' she said in a fluty voice. 'Pleased to meet you.'

'You too,' said Beattie, smiling nervously.

Albert returned with a man in a white jacket carrying a tray laden with cakes, sandwiches and a large teapot. 'Good after-noon, Ma'am,' he said nodding to her.

'Beattie, this is, Boggy Marsh, our steward.'

'Pleased to meet you,' she said, not knowing whether to call him Boggy or Marsh. She had to stop herself from getting up and helping him set the food on the table.

'Will you be Mother?' said Rollo as the steward set the teapot in front of her.

For a moment she was puzzled, then she realised he wanted her to set out the cups and fill them.

'Young lady, I have not had the pleasure,' said a deep voice behind her.

Beattie turned to see an older man smiling at her with grave dignity.

334

'The name's Sub-Lieutenant Finlay.'

'I'm Beattie Salter,' she said shaking his hand.

'Not an artist like your young man, are you?'

'No, I read and keep a diary,' she said, determined not to be overawed by his manner.

'Have you made any watercress sandwiches?' Finlay asked the steward, appearing to ignore her words.

'Yes, sir,' said Mr Marsh. 'I'll bring them in directly.'

'So what d'you think of our young Leonardo?' asked Finlay, returning to Beattie.

'I think of him all the time,' she said, trying to calm her shaking hand as she poured the milk into the cups.

'How very sweet,' said Charlotte.

'I believe you play the penny whistle, Rollo,' said Beattie, anxious to turn the attention away from herself.

'Ah, yes,' said Rollo. 'When we have eaten our fill I might manage a tune or two. Beattie, do you sing?'

'Like a frog?' she said, blushing as the conversation once more focused on her.

'Has Leonardo a tune in him, I wonder?' Finlay asked, his voice suggesting something more intimate.

Albert laughed easily. 'Not a note, but Beatrice is an accomplished juggler.'

'And who taught you such a skill?' asked Rollo, passing the plate of sandwiches around the table.'

'A lady does not reveal her secrets,' said Beattie.

'Quite right,' said Charlotte, winking at her. 'Do have a piece of chocolate cake. I brought it from Mama. It's Inky's favourite, that and macaroons.'

Beattie was about to take a piece of cake for herself when there was a cheer.

'Hurrah, it's Osborne. Come in, you young scapegrace,' cried Albert.

The midshipman came shivering into the room.

'Sit next to Beattie,' said Finlay, 'she may, if you are a good young snotty, teach you to juggle.'

'Let me pour you some tea.'

'Th-th-thank you,' said Osborne, his teeth chattering.

'Well, I must leave you young puppies,' said Finlay, 'I'm off to see my Sophia.'

'Has she a tune in her, I wonder?' asked Beattie, looking innocently at her plate.

Everyone laughed but Sub-Lieutenant Finlay.

Once he had left the room the atmosphere lightened.

'Would you like a piece?' Beattie asked Osborne, putting the last slice of chocolate cake on his plate.

Osborne smiled gratefully.

It was a new experience for her to sit still and have others clear the table. Rollo got out his whistle and played a hornpipe and Inky danced. Charlotte sang 'Barbara Allen' and 'Greensleeves', then all the men gave a chorus of 'Hearts of Oak'.

'What about the juggling?' said Rollo. 'What have we that you can use?'

'What about apples?' suggested Osborne, who was beginning to thaw out.

'Steward,' called Albert, 'have we any apples or oranges?'

'Here you are, Sir,' he said bringing in a bowl and setting it on the table.

There were three of each.

While Beattie practised, the steward cleared the table. Rollo and Inky lit clay pipes and Albert sat smiling at her. She started off with the three oranges and then he threw the apples

336

to her one by one she added them to the other fruit flying through the air. Everyone began to clap. Beattie was flushed and excited. She couldn't remember when she had been so happy.

'I have a present for you,' Albert whispered getting up from the table and leaving the room, while Osborne was entertaining them playing the spoons.

Inky smiled at her. 'Thank you for coming, Beattie, he said, 'it's been the best birthday yet.'

Albert returned with a large package wrapped in string and brown paper.

'You've finished it, Leonardo,' said Rollo, 'Well done, old chap.'

Albert held his finger to his lips. 'It's a surprise,' he said. 'You can open it later.'

'We'd best go now,' said Charlotte, 'the carriage will be here for me at any moment. May I set you down at your home, Beattie?'

Her heart lurched in alarm. The sight of her and Albert stepping out of a carriage together in front of his house would outrage his mother and likely lose Beattie her job. She looked imploringly at Albert.

'Beatrice lives in St George's Square, not a stone's throw from here, Charlotte. Thank you kindly. I shall walk to her home with her.'

Beattie shook Inky's hand. 'Thank you for inviting me,' she said, then kissing Charlotte on the cheek.

'It was my pleasure,' said Inky, 'we must do this again. It's Rollo's birthday next.'

'Glad you could come,' said Osborne, 'we were all agog to see you.'

Albert cuffed him playfully around the head. 'Not wanting to climb the yards again, are you?' he asked.

Climbing back up the ladders was an easier task.

'Permission to escort a lady home through the yard, Sir?' Albert asked, saluting the officer at the gangway.

'Granted Pragnell. Good day, to you, Madam,' he said, shaking her hand.

'Goodbye,' said Beattie, 'and thank you.'

'Did the *Audacity* live up to your expectations?' asked Albert, as they hurried towards the dockyard gates.

'It was much bigger than I expected,' she said, 'and there were so many sailors. It was all so lively. What a strange smell it had, too, like old bacon. I suppose it comes from tar and rope and salt water. I liked meeting your friends and seeing where you live. Now, when you are away, I shall be able to picture you in the Gun Room with Inky and Rollo and even the horrible Finlay.'

'Should you like to be a sailor, Beattie?'

'Oh, yes, Albert, I've told you before, I would cut my hair and be an upper yard man, climbing the rigging as agile as a monkey.'

'Beatrice, you're wonderful,' he said, swinging her round in his arms and kissing her.

This display of affection drew admiring whistles from a group of passing sailors.

Beattie hugged him. He was so dear to her. Their friendship opened a door beyond which no idea was too fantastic and no dream impossible to realise.

'I can't wait to open my present,' she said, skipping along beside him.

'It comes with my fondest love,' he said, squeezing her hand.

As they left the dockyard and crossed The Hard they saw a group of wild looking women following some sailors towards Queen Street. Beattie hurried past, looking fixedly at the pavement. She thought she saw Molly Horrabin among them.

'Well, bugger off, you tight-assed bastard,' shouted a familiar voice.

'I must be back,' she said, 'there's supper to get.'

They stood by the back of the church and Albert held her close and kissed her tenderly on the lips. Beattie kissed him back, loving the softness of his lips and the scent of him, a mixture of soap, bay rum and a faint odour of *Audacity*.

'I'll glimpse you at supper,' he said, 'and perhaps we could meet on Thursday afternoon?'

'I thought Thursdays were for making and mending the sails,' she teased.

'You can always bring your thimble,' he said laughingly before handing her the parcel.

They separated, Albert running up the front steps with his key, and Beattie slipping around the side of the house to the back door.

'Hello, Cook, I'll just go and get changed,' she said, holding her present behind her. 'I'll be down in two ticks.'

'No need to rush,' Mrs Frostick said, looking flushed.

Sat opposite her in a chair by the fire was Jonas Samways, looking very much at home.

'How do,' he said, puffing great clouds of smoke from his clay pipe.

'Mr Samways,' Beattie said, nodding to him before running

up the stairs, glad that Cook had a caller; it would distract her from asking her any questions about her own afternoon. Talking would somehow take the gloss from her time with Albert. Hastily she took off her Sunday clothes and donned her black dress and starched apron before opening her parcel. It was a framed drawing of herself sat in the Ice Parlour eating her strawberry lick. She gasped, it was so lifelike. Her joy shone out of the frame. All the details of her bonnet, even the buttons on her dress, were noted. In the bottom right-hand corner Albert had written '*To darling Beatrice, from Albert, with love.*'

He loved her. She hugged herself with the knowledge. Impulsively, she took down the painting of the sunflowers over her bed, and replaced it with Albert's drawing.

It had been an afternoon she would never forget.

Chapter Thirty-four

'I'm afraid, Beattie, that you have the mumps,' said Obadiah. 'It's not surprising. The sick bay at the Mariners' is full to overflowing.' He poured her out a glass of Augusta's lemon tea, well laced with honey. The poor girl looked a sorry sight with her swollen face and lank hair. 'You'll be able to get up tomorrow, although I think you should stay in your bedroom for a day or two.'

Beattie nodded. If only she'd not visited Miss Sankey last week. It had been Freddy's twenty-fifth birthday and he had been so delighted with his party and the silk tie she had made him.

'I shall look a real swell,' he'd said, hugging her warmly. 'Might even catch the eye of a rich young widow.'

'Who knows what's round the corner?' she had said. 'You might even have met your true love already and not noticed her.'

'I'm on the look-out all the time.'

'Perhaps she will find you,' Beattie had said, kissing his cheek.

She brushed a strand of hair from her face and looked anxiously up at Dr Pragnell. 'Will anyone else catch the mumps from me?' she asked.

'Cook and Pearl have both had them in childhood.'

'How about you and Madam and Master Albert?' she mumbled.

Obadiah smiled at her. 'We are all past members of the mumps society,' he said.

Beattie nodded. Sometimes Dr Pragnell sounded just like his son and yet he was nothing like him in appearance. Albert had his mother's neat features, although his hair was darker than hers and he had not the intense blue of her eyes. She wondered if his own grey eyes were inherited from one of his grand-parents. When would she be able to see him now, imprisoned as she was in the nursery? Not that she wanted him to see her in the state she was in, looking like a full moon.

'Try and get some sleep, my dear. I'll look in on you tonight after supper.'

Beattie turned over her pillow to the cooler side and slipped the sheet and blanket down to her waist. She was so hot. After one more painful swallow of the lemon tea she settled down to sleep.

Augusta had not visited the nursery for years and yet when the boys were small it had been her second home. She tapped on the half-open door, but there was no reply. Looking inside she could see that Beattie was asleep. The girl looked flushed, and when she tiptoed into the room she saw that her forehead was wet with perspiration. Beattie's hair was spread out on the pillow in a black cloud. Never had she studied her at such close quarters. In spite of her swollen face the girl was comely. There was something almost exotic in her dark hair and eyes. Where had she come from? She was not at all like the usual ragbag of children from the Mariners' Home. The girl was intelligent and carried herself with a natural dignity. She was certainly a skilled needlewoman and a vast improvement on Mildred. In fact she quite liked the girl and had even felt a certain pride when Beattie had made the speech at the Mariners' the other week.

Although she had visited the nursery primarily to enquire about Beattie's health, Augusta began to look around the room, noticing the little changes the girl had made. There was a red and blue rag rug, two embroidered cushions and a collection of books on the shelf beside her bed. Idly she read the titles: *Madame Bovary, Oliver Twist, The Moonstone* and *The Last of the Mohicans.* She recognised the last book as one that she and Albert had read together. How had she come by it? Carefully she reached across the bed, picked it up and read the inscription on the first page.

> *For Beatrice Salter,*
> *From her friend*
> *Albert Pragnell,*
> *February 1870*

How charming, she thought. Albert was so like his father, impulsive and kindly. As she put the book on the shelf she noticed the drawing hanging above it. It was of Beattie. The girl was laughing and eating an ice cream. As she looked more closely Augusta knew that Albert was the artist. It had the delicacy and attention to detail that was his. She saw that there was a signature in the corner belonging to him. '*To darling Beatrice from Albert, with love.*'

He was in love with her. Augusta could not believe it. Her earlier fond approval was gone and all her good intentions towards Beattie quenched in an instant. She wanted to shake her awake and scream at her. 'How dare you, how dare you take my son's affection.' She wanted to haul the girl's possessions from the room and drive her, with a whip, if necessary, back to the orphanage from whence she came. The violence of her anger frightened her and Augusta rushed from the room, slamming the door behind her.

Obadiah was astonished. He had just bid good night to his last patient and had been looking forward to a peaceful evening with Gussie when she hurtled into the surgery.

'Did you know about Beattie's deceitfulness?' she demanded.

Unprepared for her onslaught, he stood there dumb-founded by her attack.

'She and Albert are having an affair behind our backs, and who knows what else?' Gussie glared at him. 'Well, what have you to say for yourself?'

'I think you are blowing a simple friendship between them out of all proportion,' he said.

'You knew about it?'

'I knew that they talked together sometimes,' Obadiah temporised. 'That was inevitable since they are living in the same house.'

'Obadiah, what are you saying, that you condoned their

liaison? All the creeping around behind our backs and all their scheming together?'

'Gussie,' he said, taking her arm and trying to persuade her into a chair. 'Aren't you making a mountain out of a molehill?'

'I know what I saw,' she persisted, snatching her arm away. 'He has made a drawing of her and inscribed it with his love. What do you say to that? And it is in her bedroom.'

'Nothing that you have said to me so far, Augusta, proves impropriety between them. As to Beattie having the picture in her room, that is perfectly natural. Where else would she keep it?'

'Only a few weeks ago Lady Marcia Hawksmoore gave Albert an invitation to her daughter's birthday party. Think where that could lead? Albert's career in the navy would be tremendously enhanced. I will not stand for him jeopardising his chances in this way.'

'If Albert could hear you now, Augusta,' her husband said, keeping a firm hold on his temper, 'he would be horrified. He wishes to progress by his own efforts not by toadying to some desiccated old buffer and his family.'

'You are so provincial,' she said scornfully. 'Content in this backwater. Albie could have a wonderful career and a wife who could rise with him.'

'Gussie, you are being quite ridiculous,' he said, attempting once more to calm her.

'No, no,' she persisted, her voice rising, 'it is you that is being blind, blind to the risks he is running.'

'And what are they?'

'Being saddled with a skivvy, being duped by her into doing things he would regret. Having a child. Have you thought of that, a bastard child, disease, madness? Well, I am going to face him with it directly he comes home, I shall . . .'

Crack! Obadiah raised his hand and slapped Augusta hard across the face.

She gasped and put her hand to her cheek.

Obadiah was horrified. 'Oh, Gussie,' he said, attempting to draw her into his arms. 'Gussie, Gussie, I didn't . . . no . . . I didn't mean.' He grabbed her, as she was about to storm out of the room.

She fought with him, kicking and scratching his neck. They gasped and struggled with each other until at length he managed to force her down into a chair. Obadiah knelt in front of her to prevent her escape. He held her hands tightly in his. 'I'm sorry. Oh, my darling, I'm so, so sorry.'

Augusta began to cry and he took her in his arms.

'*Sh-sh-sh* now, my precious, let Obi look at your face,' he coaxed.

She looked at him, her face wet with tears and a red palm mark on her cheek.

'Will you let me help you?'

She nodded.

Obadiah got a handkerchief and poured some water into a basin and bathed her face. He was ashamed at what he had done. Gussie would be mortified if he had left a bruise. Quickly he dabbed the red area with some arnica. 'There, my sweet. Now just sit still and listen to me quietly until I have finished.'

Augusta looked mutinous, but said nothing.

'Before we rush to conclusions let's look at what you saw. A drawing in your maid's room sketched by your son.'

'The words; it was the words. "To darling Beatrice, from Albert, with love."'

Obadiah held a warning finger in front of her.

'You think that they are lovers as we are?'

Augusta looked uncomfortable.

'I think Albert has too much respect for her to have let their friendship go that far. Besides,' he said, 'where would he have the opportunity? Neither of them would choose this house as their love-nest. Albert has very little money to take her to an hotel, and I'm sure neither of them would want to couple on the beach or in the bushes.' His outlandish suggestions were having the desired effect. Gussie was looking doubtful. 'What had you thought of doing to stop the friendship?'

'Dismissing her,' she said.

'And what do you think Albert would have to say about that?'

'He needn't know.'

'I think, Gussie, it is not Beattie or Albert who are taking risks here, it's you. How do you think he will view his mother when he finds out that she has dismissed the girl he loves without a reference and rendered her homeless?'

'I don't know what to do,' she said quietly.

Obadiah sighed. She was calming down and beginning to think. He knelt in front of her and held her hands. 'In less than three months he will be gone from us. We shall not see him for three years or so. Don't let our time with him be tarnished. Darling, if you get off on the wrong foot with him and force him to choose, you will regret it. Darling, I know how much you love him. All I'm begging of you is that you do nothing. Just let them have their few moments together and then he will

347

be gone. Beattie will be out of sight for at least another week and then she will be caught up with the wedding preparations at the Mariners'. After which, we shall be plunged into Christmas.'

'And Naomi Hawksmoore?'

'If you think about it carefully, Gussie,' he said, looking up into her flushed face 'you will see that choosing one's children's sweethearts is rather insulting their intelligence, don't you think?'

'I wish I had never engaged her,' said Gussie as if she had not heard what he said.

'I wish we had taken her in when I found her,' he said.

'I don't understand, Obi. What do you mean?'

Now, he had her attention. 'When she was a baby.'

'A baby, you knew her as a baby?'

'When you and the boys had the measles and I spoke of finding an infant, near death, in a sailor's jacket. Don't you remember? You were adamant that we could not keep her.'

'The little mermaid? You mean that Beattie was that child?'

'I thought her well placed with a poor soldier's wife and dismissed her from my mind. And then, by chance, I found her in the workhouse half starved and filthy. Do you know, Gussie, I felt as guilty as I did when Merle died, and with more reason. After a lot of persuasion, I managed to get her accepted into the Mariners'. What you see now is thanks to Margaret Sankey.'

Augusta said nothing.

'What I venture to suggest, my love, is that you have your supper on a tray. I will bring it up to you and we will spend the evening together. In the morning, after my loving attention, things will seem much less alarming.'

Augusta said nothing. Obadiah's back was beginning to ache. He wanted to get up from his knees. He also felt guilty. If she knew what he had seen that afternoon last summer among the elm trees there would be no calming her.

'It's so ironic, isn't it, Obi?' she said. 'If we had taken Beattie into our home and cared for her as our child. Albert would have treated her as his sister.' She got to her feet and walked towards the door. Obadiah was relieved to see the mark beginning to fade from her cheek. 'I am going to rest now. It has been a most upsetting afternoon. Perhaps a little supper later,' she said.

'Will you forgive me?' he asked her.

Gussie looked at him and he could read nothing from her face. 'I am not ready to do that Obi, it's much too soon.'

Beattie woke up and for a moment did not know where she was. A perfume lingered in the air. She looked around her. Someone had been into her room, but nothing had been brought in with them. Why had they come? Her heart lurched with fright as she identified the perfume. It belonged to Madam. She sprang out of bed and gave her room a closer inspection. At first she noticed nothing and then she saw that on her bookshelf *The Last of the Mohicans* had been put back in a different place. It had been the last book on the shelf and now it was on the other side of *The Moonstone*. She looked up at the picture Albert had given her. Was it her imagination or was the frame a little straighter than when she had last looked at it?

Chapter Thirty-five

Augusta had hoped that their trip to Dovecote Farm would give her the opportunity to talk with Albert and gauge the strength of his affection for Beattie. He was fond of Uncle Hector and had enjoyed going out with him and picking a Christmas tree and gathering swathes of holly. Her opportunities for conversation were few: when he wasn't fetching the greenery he was out sketching. In the evening he had pleaded exhaustion and gone early to bed. Now they were in the carriage together, with Uncle Hector outside, driving his old horse, Beauty, surrounded by the Christmas foliage. It would be a long journey to Portsea and there might yet be a chance to talk with her son.

Albert stared out of the window. 'How different the countryside looks in winter,' he said. 'The trees are like skeletons. I love the way the frost crisps the grass and patterns the windows. Even the air is sharper.'

'Did you manage to make any sketches? While you were out with Uncle?'

'Oh no, we spent all our time cutting holly and mistletoe

and talking about Sammy. He misses him so much and is counting the months till he's back from Manitoba. I miss him too, you know. Sammy is so droll, isn't he?'

'That will be some consolation,' said Augusta. 'To have him back with us next year just six months after you set off again. It seems an age since we were all together.'

'What a celebration that will be with all the Pragnells under one roof.'

'Speaking of celebrations,' she said, 'have you answered Naomi Hawksmoore's invitation to her Christmas party?'

'Yes, Ma, I have sent my regrets to the lady.'

'Oh, Albie,' she sighed. 'It would be such a good . . .' 'Her voice trailed away as she saw the set of his jaw.

'Ma, I am not an Angus bull to be offered to my breeding partner.'

'Albert, how can you be so coarse?'

'You exasperate me into coarseness, Ma,' he said. 'I am a grown man and will do my own choosing.'

'What is wrong with Naomi?' she asked, in spite of the warning tone in his voice.

'She is your choice. Naomi is hard and cynical without an ounce of love in her.'

'And I suppose Beattie Salter is a paragon of virtue,' she snapped.

'What has Beatrice to do with anything?' he asked, no longer looking at her.

'I saw the drawing you made of her and your loving words.'

'You went up to her room, supposedly to care for her, and did a little sleuthing?'

'You are twisting my intentions shamefully, Albert,' she gasped, frightened by the hostility in his voice.

'Beatrice is my friend. She has intelligence and a loving heart and sees beyond the gold ring on my sleeve.'

Augusta was furious with herself. She had upset Albert, and the rest of the journey home to Portsea in the rattling carriage would now be conducted in silence. 'Don't be cross with me, I can't bear it,' she pleaded.

'Not cross exactly,' he said, still avoiding her eyes. 'I'm sad that you still do not value people for what they are. Always rank and position are in your scales.'

'Not always,' she said softly. 'Papa was a penniless doctor when first I met him.'

'Why did you marry him,' her son challenged her, 'if he was such a poor catch?'

'I was frightened of going to India with Ma and Pa, and frightened of staying in England alone. And, because he asked me,' said Augusta, ashamed of her cowardice.

Albert came and sat beside her. 'I never thought of you as a gambler,' he said, smiling quizzically at her.

'It has been a struggle, Albie,' she said, relieved at his friendliness. 'Papa would give his coat away to anyone in need and is, as you know, blind to possessions and society. He is so like your grandfather. But I am my mother's daughter, too. I like pretty things around me and have to be prodded into goodness.'

'Have you ever regretted marrying Pa?'

'Many times, and I am sure he would say the same.' Augusta smiled at her son. 'In recent years we have come to a happy accommodation of our natures, and now I would be lost without him.'

'And Pa without you,' said Albert, taking her hand. 'I think I am your mongrel, having the best and worst of both of you.

We share our love of painting and Pa and I share a love of the sea. I think you and I must agree a chart together, if we are to avoid the reefs.'

Augusta held her breath.

'Whom I decide to marry will be my choice, Ma. Naturally I hope that you and Pa will love her as a daughter. I would be unhappy if you didn't, but I would not be swayed from her. If that meant I should not see either of you again I should have to bear it as best I could.'

The thought of never seeing Albie again was terrible. She would rather see him married to Beattie than to face a life without him. Oh, how simple had been the problems of childhood compared to living with one's children as adults.

'I think I shall go up aloft with Uncle Hector and see Portsmouth from the top of the hill. You can sit there and plan where Pa and I should hang the greenery,' he said, swinging out of the carriage door.

Augusta had suddenly lost her appetite for Christmas. Like Hector she wished that Sammy were home. Dear, placid, uncomplicated Sammy who would dance her around the room and make her laugh at her own foolishness. It seemed that every advance she made was countered by a retreat. The closeness to Obi was now offset by the tension developing between her and Albert. Yesterday she had passed Meadholm, now in the hands of a new family. Seeing strange curtains at the windows and a new carriage at the door had been a shock. Always she had thought her old home to be inviolate. There was now no evidence of her country childhood or place to which she could return, not even a gravestone. It was ridiculous, she was now forty-three years old and her parents had been dead for fifteen years. Why did she feel so desolate? I am nobody's child, she thought, and now Albert wishes I wasn't his mother.

The carriage drew up in St George's Square and Obadiah came running down the steps to meet them. 'The bringers of joy and greenery. Uncle Hector, Albert, Gussie – welcome all of you. Gussie, darling,' he said, opening the coach door and taking her in his arms. 'Let me get you indoors, you are quite frozen.'

'Obi,' she said clinging to him. 'I'm so very glad to see you.'

Time had narrowed to these last sixteen days. Albert was sailing on her birthday. Beattie had hardly seen him. The family had dined out on Christmas Day and this evening they were off to a party at Rollo Reed's family in Southsea. She felt like a jack-in-the-box, let out when it suited Albert and shut in with the lid clamped tight when Mama called the tune. Was she being unfair? Was Albert really protecting her position in the household or was he protecting himself?

She was distracted from her thoughts by a scratching and whining at the kitchen door. It was Bijou, Madam's gift from Albert, a tetchy Pekinese.

Cook had not been at all impressed. 'Yappy, high strung little tyke,' she snapped, 'not a real dog at all. Wants putting back in the oven and cooking proper. He ain't even pretty, face looks as if it's bin sat on.'

Poor Pearl received a thorough scolding from Madam when she accidentally trod on Bijou. Today she had gone to the Mariners' for a Boxing Day party, leaving Cook and Beattie to their own devices.

'Funny, ain't it,' Mrs Frostick said as she came back from

the dining room with a loaded tray, 'how lovely them decorations looks afore Christmas, then after, they gives ya the miseries?'

'What do you mean?' asked Beattie as she stood by the kettle, letting the steam take out the creases in Mrs Pragnell's velvet dress.

'Well, they just makes me think of time passin' us by and nothin' different this year than last. I gets frightened.'

'What of?'

'Getting old and not wanted. When I gets up in the mornin' I cries with the pains in me joints and in me fingers. I dreads the winter. The cold seeps into me bones like damp in a church. Then I gets ter thinking, what if I looses me mind and gets foolish or starts peeing in me drawers? What if I'm not able to do me work and lose me place here? Some old cooks ends up in the workhouse, you know.'

'Doctor would make sure you were all right, you know he would,' said Beattie, saddened by the fear in Mrs Frostick's voice. She had become close to the little woman and loved her bounce and salty humour.

'Makes me think of that verse in the Bible,' Cook said. '"*When thou shalt be old, thou shalt stretch forth thy hands and another shall gird thee, and carry thee whither thou wouldest not.*" When you're young you get's up with the lark and thinks yer energy'll go on for ever. Ooh, I'd give a king's ransom to be able to kick up me heels like I used to.'

'I'll fetch you a sherry and read you the society bits out of the paper.'

'You're a good gal, Beattie. If I was yer fairy godmother I'd wave me wand and find you a handsome prince as would take you to his castle.'

'I'd give you a room there and a golden bell to ring.'

'And Madam as me servant,' laughed Cook, beginning to brighten. 'Mind you, young Albert has growed into a handsome fellow. You gotta prince on your doorstep.'

Beattie blushed.

'I see'd the pair of you looking at one another like a pair of turtledoves, and why not? You enjoy it, my gal. All the sighing and dreaming and up in the clouds like the bloom on a peach, it don't last. But I'd give anything to have them feelings again.'

Was it unreal? Beattie wondered. When she was with Albert she treasured every second. She wanted him to hold her close and whisper wonderful silly things in her ear. Her common sense told her that she was daydreaming. Love between servants and masters only existed in fairy tales. As if to underline her thoughts the front door slammed behind the Pragnells as they set off for Rollo's party.

Beattie went into the dining room and poured two glasses of sherry from the decanter and carried them back into the kitchen.

Cook sat in the armchair, her little doll's feet resting on her box, listening to snippets that Beattie read from a local paper. Her brown eyes shone with sherry and merriment, reminding her of a robin. They both exclaimed at the descriptions of furs and jewels and the gold braided uniforms of the 'toffs', as Mrs Frostick dubbed the society party-goers. 'Fancy dancin' till two o'clock in the mornin' and then bein' able to lie in bed till dinnertime. What a life!' There was a long silence. 'What's up, my duck? You've gone quite pale. Not bad news, I hope?'

Beattie stared at the headline in the paper. 'Young Woman found Dead in Cellar.' It took her some time to calm herself sufficiently to read it out to Mrs Frostick.

*On the twenty second of December a young woman's body
was found in the cellar of a derelict house in Half Moon
Street. Police Constable Waring recognised the deceased as
nineteen-year-old Molly Horrabin, a local prostitute. She
was found in the cellar lying on a mattress made of empty
bottles covered with sheets of newspaper. Miss Horrabin
was wearing a thin cotton dress and no underwear. Her
only possession was a child's picture brick, found in her
pocket. It is thought that the young woman died of
alcohol poisoning.*

'Poor soul, what a sad, sad end,' said Cook. 'What's up with
you, my duck? Don't know her, do you?'

'We were at the Mariners' together,' gasped Beattie, drying
her tears on her apron. 'My first friend, she was. Oh poor, poor
Molly,' gasped Beattie.

'You have a good cry, my duck,' said Mrs Frostick. 'Poor
nipper, least she got you to mourn her.'

'She came here one night after Freddy and me went to the
Theatre Royal. Followed me home. Awful, she looked, thin
and dirty and smelly. I let her stay the night with me up in the
nursery. When she left she took that brick, the one in her hand
when she died. Molly had been sleeping in an old cellar. Said
she was afraid to sleep in case a rat crawled over her face. Poor,
poor, Molly.'

'Well, my duck,' said Mrs Frostick, lifting the kettle on to
the range, 'she had the same chances as you, seemingly, but she
must've taken some wrong turnings.'

'Charlie Mabs,' said Beattie, 'he was her wrong turning.
She ran off with him when she was fifteen. Determined, she
was, though we all tried to stop her.' How hard had she really

tried? What would have happened if she had told Miss Sankey before the prize giving? Would it have made any difference?

'Mother Nature gets us all fired up about each other and she don't care a jot about the consequences.'

'But what about that bit in the Bible about every hair on our heads being counted and not even a sparrow falls without God knowing. Where was he when Molly was frightened and lonely in the dark?' said Beattie fiercely.

'I don't know, my duck,' said Cook, busy filling the teapot, 'it's beyond me. One thing I know. We just gotta do the best we can for each other. Molly's at peace now, she won't never have aching bones, or be frightened or sad or lonely.'

'But she won't ever be having good food or being with friends,' cried Beattie. 'All the things she could have been and done just rubbed out like chalk off a slate.'

'Beattie,' said Cook firmly, 'it's a lesson for both of us to pay more heed to the unfortunate and to count our blessings. Every night I says thank God for a roof over my head, good food in my belly and friends around me. You mustn't waste time in regrets. A river of tears won't bring yer friend back. Now, get down the Snakes and Ladders and fetch me a drop more sherry.'

'Doctor will notice we've had some if we have any more,' she protested.

'Well, I got a remedy for that,' laughed Mrs Frostick. 'Bring the decanter out here.' After carefully straining some cold tea into a jug she topped up the sherry and swilled it around. 'What I always say is that, the Lord helps those who helps themselves.'

'That's just the sort of thing Molly would have done,' Beattie said.

'To Molly,' said Cook, raising her glass.

'To Molly,' said Beattie.

There was a rapping on the back door. Mrs Frostick, with surprising speed, hurried to open it. 'Well, isn't that a surprise,' she exclaimed. 'It's Jonas come to warm hisself at our fire.'

'Evening,' he said, grinning roguishly at Cook. 'Merry Christmas to yer both.'

'Would you like some sherry?' asked Beattie, smiling at Cook's attempt at coyness.

'Yus, my gal,' said Jonas, 'and don't stint the measure. I've a powerful thirst. Just taken old Dapple back to the stable, put on her blanket and given her a good bag of oats. I shall walk home from here, only a step or two it is.'

'What you got in that basket?' asked Cook, twinkling at him.

'Fetched you a bit of pie from that party as I've taken them to,' he said, 'and some chocolate covered ginger, and violet creams.'

'Ooh,' said Mrs Frostick, clapping her hands. 'I'm ever so partial to ginger.'

'Would you like to play Snakes and Ladders?' asked Beattie when they were settled around the kitchen table. Neither Cook nor Jonas seemed to have any interest in the game but sat smiling and nodding at each other. Whatever he said, Mrs Frostick chuckled as if it were the greatest witticism, and for his part, the old soldier listened to her words as if they were pearls of wisdom. Beattie made various attempts at conversation but got no encouragement from either of them. 'I think I'll go up and have a read, if you don't mind,' she said, feeling distinctly surplus to requirements.

'You can take them violits with ya, ducks. Better take the sherry back in the dining room, don't want Jonas gettin' under the influence, do we, my dear?' she said, giving him a broad wink.

Beattie lit her candle and settled fully dressed into bed. She reached down her pencil and diary from the shelf and popped a violet cream into her mouth.

A strange Christmas. I haven't felt a scrap of magic this year. Perhaps I have grown out of it. I long to have a life of my own not dependent on the crumbs thrown from the Uppers' table. I don't want to be Upper or Hidden but me. What that is I am determined to find out. Albert gave me a copy of Wuthering Heights *for Christmas but I shall not read it until he has gone to sea. It will give me something to write about. He has promised we shall have a few hours together on my birthday, the day he goes away. When he is gone there will be nothing to look forward to.*

Then I think of poor Molly Horrabin, lying dead in that cellar and feel so selfish.

I want another violet cream but don't want to surprise Cook and Jonas up in the clouds together.

'Happy birthday, my darling,' Albert said, kissing her hand and holding her chair out for her, as Beattie opened the kitchen door at five o'clock in the morning. 'I wanted to be the first to say it.'

The cloth was spread and there were two places set facing each other. In the middle of the table were silver candlesticks complete with flickering candles.

'Poached eggs, toast and damson jelly, for Madam, and fresh coffee.'

Beattie was enchanted. She unfolded the damask napkin

while Albert slid the eggs from the saucepan onto thickly
buttered toast.

'This is such a treat,' she said.

'That is what birthdays are for, to be spoiled,' he said.

She looked at him, wanting to take in every last detail of
his face. He is so beautiful, she thought, trying to pin down the
essence of his attraction for her. It didn't rest in the arrange-
ment of his features and could not be drawn on paper. It was
a particular way of looking at her, a joy that shone from him
and melted her resistance.

'This is our time, when the world is asleep,' he said, 'just
the two of us. I shall always picture you with egg on your chin,
and those dark eyes watching me.'

Beattie laughed. 'Albert, you are funny. That's what I will
have in a bottle, the sound of you laughing. Then when I feel
sad I shall pour you out and laugh with you.'

'Four years is a long, long time,' said Albert, suddenly
serious. 'How shall we feel at the end of it? I wonder. I hope
that we shall love each other as we do now.'

'I want us to stay the same,' said Beattie. 'I don't want our
love to fade.'

'It's such a temptation to put a ring on your finger and make
you mine. But, Beatrice, I want us both to be as sure as sure.'

'What do you mean – put a ring on my finger?' she asked.

'You must know that I want to marry you, Beatrice.'

'How must I? You have never told me. Your mother would
be amazed that we have even played Snakes and Ladders
together, let alone kissed.'

'Pa has given his blessing and Ma knows that I shall marry
whom I choose,' he said, reaching across the table and taking
her hand.

Beattie was astonished. 'If that is so, why didn't you take me with you to Rollo's, if I am no longer such a secret?' She felt angry. Why wouldn't he defend her?

'When we are both sure that marriage is what we want, my darling, I shall speak to both of them. Mama had already guessed that we are friends. She saw the picture I drew of you and what I wrote to you.'

'When?' Beattie demanded, 'When was she in my room? It's private. How dare she snoop on me.'

'Beatrice, I don't want us to waste our energy in skirmishes. Let's keep the cannon for the big battle, when I come home, when we are certain of our feelings.'

They were nearly rowing. This was not what she had imagined at all.

'Let me kiss you,' he pleaded. 'I love you, Beatrice.' He held her close to him and she twined her arms around his neck. Slowly, he kissed her until her anger melted. 'Darling, I almost forgot,' he said, 'I haven't given you your present.' He took a red leather box from his pocket and held it out to her. 'For you, my sweetheart.'

She opened the box to reveal a silver brooch nestling on a satin cushion. 'Albert,' she gasped, 'it's so lovely. The little forget-me-nots, what are they made of?'

'Sapphires. It was left to me by my grandmother and was her engagement present from her husband, my Grandfather Morrell.'

'Are you sure you should give it to me? It's a family treasure.'

'You are my treasure,' he said. 'I've got a chain for it in my pocket. You can wear it like a necklace under your clothes and then you won't have to worry about it. It will be with you always.' He kissed the nape of her neck before setting the neck-lace in place and fastening the clasp.

'Thank you, my love,' she whispered. 'I'll wear it always.'

'You sit there like a queen,' he said, 'while I wash the dishes.'

Beattie watched him swirling the water in the sink and scraping the eggshells into the waste bucket. It felt unreal, as if they were figures in a doll's house playing at life. She thought of Albert's grandmother. How long ago was it when she was given the brooch? It might be over fifty years ago, before even Queen Victoria was born or Nelson. It had been given and worn with love. 'Where is your grandmother now?'

'They were both killed in India during the mutiny?'

'How awful!'

'Mama was desolate. It was three years before she could go to Nursling and pack up the family home. Grandmother had left all sorts of packages with the family solicitor, each with a name on and a little message. Almost as if she knew she would not come home again. Ma said that when they died she lost her trust in life. When I'm away she can't quite believe that I will come home safe to her.'

Beattie felt a lurch of fear. What would she do if anything happened to Albert?

As if reading her thoughts, he said, 'I shall take good care of myself because I have so much to look forward to.' He held out his arms to her and she sat on his lap.

'I shall imagine you in the Gun Room chattering with your chums like magpies.'

'I shall think of you here in my arms, before even the mice are stirring, or Pearl clanking her bucket. Kiss me. I have to be on board by eight and I must say goodbye to Ma and Pa.'

Beattie kissed him goodbye then ran up to her bedroom before he saw her tears. An hour later she heard the front door slam and looking out of the window saw Albert turn at the corner of the Square and wave back at the house. Was he waving to her up in the attic or to his Mama in the sitting room? she wondered.

Chapter Thirty-six

Dearest Albert,

I wonder where you are? Not a question you ever have to ask me, for I am rooted in Portsea like an aspidistra in a pot. But all is not as you left it. As I was telling you work is finished now on the Harbour Station. We are glad to be done with the dirt and noise with the clattering of shovels and the shouting and swearing of the workmen. Pearl threw Bijou out the door the other day and told him to, 'Bugger off.' Unfortunately your mother heard her and she was ticked off soundly. I have grown to love Pearl, she is so cheery and whatever is said to her she bounces back for more.

I love looking out of my window, now, at night and seeing the trains come roaring in and out of the station, like great iron monsters, trailing clouds of steam. What delights me is that the old toll house and entrance to the stations and jetties is now called The Royal Albert Steam Packet Pier. Of course everyone thinks it is named after the Queen's husband but I know it is for you.

Mildred has been transformed since Lionel's mother died and quite inflated with her own importance. I suppose inflated in more ways than one since she is carrying a child. Doctor says she must be careful having a baby so late in life and she is taking his words to heart. Lionel is now her slave taking her cups of tea in bed in the morning. Mrs Frostick thinks if we call around to see her, Lionel is likely to open the door wearing an apron. Because of his work on the railways he is being sent up the country to Eastleigh so this may be where the Rutters exit from the Salter saga.

My latest adventure is to go skating with Pearl at the rink in Pelham Road. It was quite expensive, one-shilling entrance and sixpence each for the hire of the skates. When we arrived the band was playing and people gliding around on the little wheels ever so gracefully. When Pearl and I took to the floor it was a different story. We were falling about all over the place and helpless with laughter and went home covered with bruises.

I have enclosed a cutting from the paper about Captain Nares's Arctic expedition as you requested. It all sounds very thrilling.

I am sealing this letter with a kiss and am counting the days until I get your next letter.

All my Love,
Your Beatrice.

Obadiah watched his wife sitting at the dressing table unfastening her birthday pearls. She was still beautiful, even at forty-seven, and at this moment infinitely desirable.

'It's been the best birthday, my darling, thank you,' said

Augusta, taking off her necklace. 'Didn't Sammy look happy? I quite liked Olive – oh, she's a bit of a country mouse but if that's what Sammy wants. It's all been quite wonderful. Those plums were so juicy and that cake so light. I feel as if we've just returned from Paradise.'

Obadiah laughed. 'Come to bed, my sweet. Your birthday is not over yet.'

'What other treats have you in mind?' she asked teasingly.

'Patience,' he said, drawing her into his arms. 'I want to talk to you first before I give you your final gift. You know, Gussie, I was watching you today as we got off the train at Nursling, you were like an excited child, or a fish in water.'

'Obi,' she said, laughing at him, 'what a strange thing to say. What do you mean?'

'You were in your element, where you are at your best.'

'A happy mackerel?' she asked.

'Perhaps,' he said, kissing her upturned face. 'You were so much a part of country living. Noticing all sorts of things that I am totally unaware of. I have come to a decision that I want to share with you.'

'That sounds ominous,' said Gussie, sliding her hand between the buttons of his nightshirt.

'Behave yourself, Madam,' he teased, kissing her on the tip of her nose. 'You have been such a loyal wife to me. All these years you have made your home with me in Portsmouth and tried to share my enthusiasm for the old town. But I know that you always hoped we would go back to Nursling one day.'

'Where is this leading?' asked Augusta, stroking his chest.

'As I said, I've come to a decision. When I'm sixty we shall sell the practice and find somewhere in Nursling. You shall do your sketching and I shall learn how to be a country gentleman.'

'Oh, Obi, I don't know what to say. Are you sure you could be happy away from the sea and all the hurly-burly?'

'I can always be a day-tripper and come down and walk along the promenade and buy some jellied eels, if the mood takes me.'

'We would be near Sammy and Olive and the grand-children. Oh, darling, you don't know how much I've needed something to look forward to.'

'I rather think I do,' he said, kissing her neck. 'Ever since you came back with Albie from Uncle Hector's I knew you were in mourning. You'd seen your home taken over by another family and lost your influence on your little boy.'

Augusta kissed him, leaving him no doubt as to her intentions. 'It's hard to move away from the centre of their lives, isn't it? Hard to believe that they can manage for themselves,' she said.

'Isn't that a tribute to us, that they have ventured out?'

'I suppose so,' she said doubtfully.

Obadiah was about to mention Beattie and then Gussie trailed her fingers over his belly and he rose to her coaxing.

'If my children no longer need me I shall just have to concentrate on you,' she said, kissing his neck.

'I shall not complain,' he whispered, as he undid the buttons on her nightgown.

'Going home, I'm going home.' The words sang in Augusta's head as she left a trail of kisses over her husband's body.

October 1877

Darling Beatrice

We are approaching the equator and we are slippery with heat. Tomorrow we shall have the ceremony of 'Crossing the Line'. It is like a wild and rumbustious pantomime. It involves a sailor dressed as Neptune and a great deal of horseplay and ducking into a sail filled with seawater. Lieutenant Finlay is the barber and shaves the victims, firstimers, to the tropics, with a rough piece of wood covered with soapy lather. He asks them questions and each time they speak shoves the shaving brush into their mouths. The final indignity is being ducked backwards into the canvas bathing pool. Everyone is involved from the Captain to the youngest seaman. For some obscure reason I have been cast in the role of Neptune's wife Amphitrite and have an itchy straw wig and painted lips.

I miss you so much it seems a lifetime since we were together that morning in the kitchen. I keep the drawing I made of you from memory in my Bible. Rollo and Inky must think me very devout for I am always to be seen looking at the Bible whenever they come into the Gun Room.

Mama sounds happier than I have ever known her, she is so taken up with Sammy's wedding. Have you seen the bride? Tell me what she is like. Mother says she is a country sparrow. She also told me that the odious Naomi Hawksmoore has married an old post Captain twenty years her senior.

Another fifteen months of separation from you and I am longing for it to be at an end. I am heartily sick of all my companions and they are equally tired of me. I kiss this letter and will be waiting, as soon as we dock in Rio de Janeiro, to find a letter from you awaiting me.

I am looking at the stars and thinking of you, wonder if you look at the stars in far off England and think of me.

Good night my love
Ever yours,
Albert.

Chapter Thirty-seven

It was going to be a day of celebration: 23 May 1878, Queen Victoria's birthday and the opening of the People's Park. The Pragnells had been invited to attend, with some naval bigwigs, and Cook and Pearl had set off already. Beattie could have gone with them, but she made taking Bijou for a walk an excuse to stay behind. Lately, she had felt suffocated by her small domestic world and wanted something more. She wanted to go and join in the celebrations without Pearl clutching her arm and squealing with excitement or Cook moaning about her aching feet. Beattie wanted to be on her own.

The celebrations would be the perfect opportunity to wear the jacket she had been slaving over all winter. The materials had come from the dressing-up box. A green brocade dress cut down to size and embellished with braid from an abandoned uniform. She paraded in front of the hall mirror like a young Hussar, in the bright boxy jacket with its swirls of gold braid on the sleeves and bands of frogging across the front.

'All credit to you, Beattie,' Mrs Frostick had said. 'You've brought them clothes back from the dead, and no mistake.'

Beattie had written and told Albert about it. He had called it her resurrection jacket. The name also applied to her gown made from the green dress. Setting her beribboned boater at a jaunty angle she went into the drawing room and prised Bijou from his nest of cushions. 'Come here, you moth-eaten old thing, and let me walk the legs off you,' she said, holding him away from her clothes. Putting some liquorice comfits in her pocket, she took down the dog's lead from the hall stand before securing it to Bijou's collar. 'The front entrance, I think,' she said to the snuffling Pekinese before slamming the door behind them.

Beattie almost danced down The Hard past some whistling sailors and up Queen Street. She blushed at their frank appreciation, pretending to be shocked. But secretly she was delighted to be admired. It had been too long since anyone had sung her praises. Albert had been gone for so long now, she had almost forgotten what he looked like. There were plenty of photographs of him in the house and one she kept secretly in her handbag. But they did not remind her of the exact colour of his eyes or the way his hair fell over his forehead or the way the corners of his mouth crinkled when he smiled. In spite of his wonderful letters she was becoming disconnected. Beattie touched the forget-me-not brooch that she wore around her neck and tried to recreate her feelings of the day that he had given it to her. It was frightening. She thought of the saying: 'Absence makes the heart grow fonder.' It was replaced in her mind almost instantly by the counter phrase: 'Out of sight out of mind.'

At the park entrance, she picked up Bijou and was swept up in an eager crowd and borne up one of the paths towards the bandstand. Seated at their music stands, in their splendid scarlet jackets and white helmets, were the Royal Marine Bandsmen. On the other side of the path was a fountain complete with ornamental swans.

Beattie found herself smiling at complete strangers. The sun glinted on the brass helmets of the fire brigade and the Marine bugles and French horns. The air was scented with flowers. She edged nearer to the fountain and saw in the pond below sudden streaks of silver and gold as the fish swam in and out of the weeds.

'Look at them trees,' said an old lady in a black bonnet with red cherries fixed to the crown. 'My feller 'e works 'ere under the 'ead gardener. Took bleeding months to set it all out. Knows the name of all the trees: laburnum, Kilmarnock willows, chestnuts, almonds, double flowering peaches.' Her face was aglow with pride.

Beattie nodded.

'Bertram, stop scratching. You got fleas or summat?'

'Myrtle, stop jigging about.'

The little girl in the dress with the sailor collar whispered to her thin harassed mother. The woman blushed. 'You'll 'ave to wait till after the mayor gets 'ere. I ain't missing the opening.' She looked around her, then said 'Go round the back of that bush. No one's looking.'

'Oh, Ma,' said the girl, her face scarlet with shame.

'Hark, the band's starting, they must be coming,' admonished a fat man almost bursting out of his suit. 'Gladys, look. There's our boy growed into a man.'

Beattie looked in the direction of his pointing finger but had no idea who 'our boy' was or quite how he had distinguished himself. Down through the main entrance came the mayor and the corporation in their black gowns and hats. Once the mayor had reached the fountain the band stopped playing and he began to speak.

The crowd looked around them restlessly, totally disinterested in his florid phrases. And then came the moment they were all waiting for. The mayor turned on the fountain and the crowd cheered as the water shot up into the air then fell back into the pond.

'Look, Ma, the sun's making rainbows in the water,' gasped Myrtle.

Beattie was thrilled. She clapped her hands. Instantly the lead slid from her arm and Bijou leapt to the ground and disappeared into a forest of legs.

'Oh, Bijou,' she gasped in dismay. 'My dog, my dog.' Pushing through the crowd she looked about her. Desperately she bent down and scanned the paths around her. The little dog would be helpless. He had been so spoiled and petted that she doubted he even knew he was a dog. His sense of smell or direction had never been called upon. Poor stupid little Bijou. The afternoon was ruined.

At that moment a black and white terrier rushed past. Could he be chasing Bijou? Was that how he came to rush away? Oh crikey! Albert's mother would skin her alive. She'd be lucky to keep her job, let alone her home.

Beattie bit her lip to stop herself crying. It was so unfair. In a few seconds her joy was stolen. Dejectedly she walked down one of the side paths to a drinking fountain and held one of the tin cups under the water. She drank thirstily, closing her eyes as the icy liquid slid down her parched throat. Things were bad enough between her and Madam as it was, heaven knows what they would be like if she lost Bijou. No point in crossing that bridge yet, she decided, there was still time to find him. And then she heard a familiar sound – the imperious yapping of a small dog.

There, on the ground in front of her, was Bijou, his lead wrapped around the legs of a sailor. Beattie laughed with relief. 'Bijou, you silly thing. Ooh, what a relief to find you. Thank you for looking after him.'

The sailor swept off his straw hat and made an extravagant bow to her. 'Hello, young maid,' he said. 'Is this creature belonging to you?'

Beattie was dazzled. She looked up at the tallest man she had ever seen. The sun glinted on his flame-coloured hair and beard, seeming to frame his face in a circle of fire. She could not tear her eyes away from him. He was like a figure from a stained-glass window.

'The dog,' he repeated, 'is he yours?'

'Well, yes, um no,' she faltered, feeling a blush creep over her face. 'He belongs to my mistress, Mrs Pragnell.'

He bent towards her. 'Little hound seems to have me lashed up a treat here. Will you rescue a sailor in distress?'

Beattie knelt down and slowly unwound the lead, giving herself time to catch her breath. As she freed Bijou he turned and nipped her fingers.

The sailor scooped up Bijou and shook him playfully. 'You poor excuse for a dog. Good mind to toss you into that laurel bush.'

'Oh, please, I beg of you. Don't do that, it's more than my job is worth to lose him.'

He put Bijou down and tied his lead to the side of a nearby bench before turning to Beattie and saying, 'Let me look at your finger. Small as he is the mutt has likely got a sharp tooth.'

Before she could protest he had taken her hand in his. Slowly, teasingly, he began to peel back her glove, kissing each finger and then her palm. He pressed her fingers to his lips then stroked them down his beard, all the while looking at her. Carefully, as if her hand were made of porcelain, he inserted her fingers back inside her glove.

There was an intimacy to his touch that excited her and sent the blood rushing up into her face. His blue eyes had seemed to look right into her, past the normal gaze of a stranger, as if he wanted more than a casual exchange of words with a girl at a drinking fountain. This is desire, she thought, this pain in my belly, this wanting.

He smiled at her and she smiled back as if something had been agreed between them, a seal had been placed on their meeting by the kissing of her palm. I must know his name, she thought, and he must know mine. 'I am Beattie Salter,' she said.

'Leading stoker Joseph Forrest,' he replied.

'Well, young Beattie,' he said, 'what is your fancy? Shall we sit awhile or are you for walking?'

No, she could not sit still. She wanted to run and laugh and shout. 'I have met the most beautiful man in the world and I won't let him go.' Instead, she muttered, 'I must set out for home,' hating the prim sound of her words. 'Bijou must be exhausted.'

'That nervy inbred little excuse for an animal, more like a bilge mop than a Bijou.'

'Mrs Pragnell says it means a little jewel. She kisses him as if he was a baby.'

'Well, she's never been thoroughly kissed by the right man or she wouldn't throw them away on an animal.'

'Thought you said he wasn't an animal,' said Beattie. Had

she ever been thoroughly kissed? she wondered. Were the kisses between her and Albert thorough?

'Animals should be free to live as God intended. Not robbed of their dignity and treated as playthings.'

'You've got a lot of opinions for a sailor,' she said suddenly, wanting her say.

'How many opinions is a sailor entitled to?' he asked.

'Well,' she considered, 'which way the wind blows, whether to take the sails in or which way to point a telescope.'

'I'm more than a sailor, Beattie, that's just a part of what I am; there is a man beneath the sailor. Or don't you think so?'

'Of course you're a man,' she said, thrilled by the dangerous turn the conversation was taking.

'And isn't there more to you than being a skivvy?'

'I am not a skivvy,' she stormed. 'I'm a cook or will be when Mrs Frostick goes off to Broadstairs with her sister.'

'It's still a servant in someone else's house,' he said.

Beattie gasped. The words stung her like hailstones, stripping away her defences. Tears welled up and with no thought of Bijou she took to her heels.

Joseph followed, calling after her, 'Beattie, come back.'

She ran headlong, wanting to run and run and somehow outstrip the hurt that was overwhelming her. He had struck at her deepest wound. Not even Albert knew how she craved a home and the freedom to cook her own food, to stand at her own doorstep and call her life her own. How could he?

All the long list of hurts struck at her one by one. Waking in darkness to find herself in a cold wet bed, the shaved head and rough clothing of the workhouse child. Then as an orphan enduring the stares of the congregation as she and the others left the church. No pat on the head by the parson or a sweet from the Sunday-school teacher. She had thought herself in clover when she went to live with the Pragnells, but Joseph was right. Whatever fancy name she gave herself she was still a homeless skivvy.

She came to a halt at The Hard having run the full length of Queen Street. A painful stitch in her side slowed her down. Beattie looked about her, wanting somewhere to hide herself. With the throng of sailors and day-trippers there was no chance of being alone. Beattie stood at the bridge between The Hard and the new harbour station looking down at the urchins slithering over the mud below, retrieving pennies thrown to them by the passing travellers. They were like performing monkeys. Those tossing them would quickly forget those coins but to the boys beneath the bridge they bought stale bread to cram into their hungry bellies. She caught her breath and walked on up the causeway to the harbour station, sinking down onto a bench on the platform. Here she could be anonymous. A train started up, hissing and belching steam. Carriage doors slammed and people swirled around her. She wished she could be truly alone to give way to her grief, to cry and cry until there were no more tears – to empty the deep well of hurt inside her. Could it be emptied? she wondered. The thought frightened her. Most of the time she was able to keep the lid tightly shut and to convince herself that she had done well. Yet she knew only too well how precarious was her position. The Pragnells could fall down in the world and she would be the first casualty if they were driven to economy. Her own seemingly abundant health could fail and she would be back at the workhouse on the bottom of the heap. Beattie clenched her fists. No, she must not let her thoughts go down that path. She must take charge of herself. What's the good of moaning, she thought, it won't change anything. The train left the station, the press of people thinned out and the noise died down. Beattie sighed. She'd better go into the ladies' room, rinse her face and rebuild her defences.

But as she walked past the next bench Joseph, with Bijou under one arm, stood up and took her hand. She couldn't trust herself to speak for fear of crying.

'Beattie, I'm sorry,' said Joseph. 'I have a rough way with me. I suppose it comes from living among men. I didn't mean to upset you.' He led her down the other end of the station to a bench on its own away from the crowds.

She would like to have told him to bugger off and leave her alone, as Pearl would have done, but she had not the spirit. He could see that she had been crying – what was the point of pretending?

Beattie wrapped her arms across her chest as if to hold in the panic that was beating against her ribs. 'I don't belong.' The words had rushed from her mouth before she'd a chance to stop them.

'What do you mean, Beattie?'

'I was a workhouse kid. I've got no family or nothing.'

'Don't you have a sweetheart?'

Beattie blushed and fingered the forget-me-not brooch on the chain around her neck. 'I've got an understanding. His name's Albert Pragnell, he's on the *Audacity* out on the China station.'

'Not much of a sweetheart if he doesn't make you feel you belong.'

'What d'you mean?' she protested. 'He's good to me, sends me letters.'

379

'Did he give you that necklace?'

'Yes,' said Beattie, 'and there's a brooch on it that was given to him by his grandmother.'

'Why aren't you wearing this brooch on your dress?'

Guiltily she touched the chain around her neck. 'He wants me to be really sure of my feelings. When he comes home he'll tell his mother and . . .' Beattie's voice trailed away. Even as she said the words she realised how tentative was her understanding with Albert.

'If I were your sweetheart,' said Joseph, taking her hand again, 'I'd hold you tight and tell you that I loved you. We'd tell each other all our hurts and seek ways to heal them. We'd belong to each other.'

'But,' said Beattie, blushing, 'you're not.'

'Tell me about this fellow on the *Audacity*. Didn't you say that the people you work for were name of Pragnell?'

'He's the son,' answered Beattie. While he was talking Joseph had been stroking Bijou. Combing the fur through his long fingers. She wished he were stroking her hair, then blushed at the thought. She looked away in confusion, but not before he had met her glance and, by his amused smile, seemed to have read her mind.

'How long has he been on the China station?'

'Four years,' she said, unwillingly.

'Can you remember what he looks like? Can you remember his kisses?'

Beattie stared down at her boots.

'If I kiss you, you'll never ever forget,' said Joseph.

Still Beattie concentrated on her boots. She was afraid to look at him. Her feelings see-sawed between despair and a dangerous delight. She sensed that Joseph would not be hindered by caution. If she wanted to remain true to Albert she had better make her escape now.

'I'd best be off,' she said, turning towards him and holding out her hands to take Bijou. There was a shrill whistle from the departing train and her words were lost. As the train advanced up the track they were both enveloped in a cloud of steam.

Joseph took her face in his hands and kissed her. It was the merest brush of his lips against hers. It left her wanting more. Again he kissed her. He kissed her eyelids and her hair. Beattie closed her eyes. She was dizzy with desire. Joseph ran his tongue across her lips and she opened them. It was a searching, breathless, drenching kiss.

The clouds of steam evaporated and the train disappeared.

'Am I forgiven?'

She looked at him in confusion.

'Oh,' he said, 'I'm not apologising for kissing you. We both knew it was going to happen, didn't we?'

Beattie nodded.

'I'm sorry that I was careless in what I said earlier. I pierced your armour and wounded you.' He smiled at her. 'We all need to protect ourselves. The world's a cruel place.'

Beattie nodded again.

'So am I forgiven?'

'I think so,' she murmured.

'Certainty's what I'm after, Beattie.'

'I certainly forgive you,' she said, smiling back at him.

'A clean slate?' he asked.

'A clean slate,' she answered.

'May I walk you home, Miss Salter? You and the little bilge mop that is.'

Beattie got to her feet and took charge of Bijou. 'It's only five minutes away in St George's Square. You may walk with me if you like,' she said, trying to sound unconcerned.

Joseph stood up and offered her his arm and they walked back over the causeway.

Beattie could not believe the change in her feelings in such a short space of time. Half an hour ago she had been in black despair and now she was enchanted by everything. 'Stop a minute,' she said. She took a threepenny piece from her purse and threw it over the railings to a skinny freckle-faced boy of about nine years old.

They crossed The Hard and turned left into St George's Square.

'We're here,' said Beattie, leading Joseph through the gate into the back yard.

'Now, Miss Salter, will you walk out with me again?' asked Joseph, smiling down at her.

'Maybe next Sunday,' she said smiling back at him.

'Maybe is not good enough,' he answered, 'and Sunday's too far away.'

'Next Thursday at six,' she said, 'definitely.'

'There's just one thing you have to do,' he said. 'If you're stepping out with me I'll want you to take that chain from around your neck. I want to clear the decks. I'm no deceiver, Beattie, and I don't want you to be. You've got four days to make up your mind.' He bent and kissed her cheek and was gone down the path before she could think of what to say.

Beattie went into the kitchen and settled Bijou in front of a saucer of minced chicken before climbing the stairs to hang up her jacket. She sat in front of the mirror and fiddled with the chain around her neck. Did she remember Albert's kisses? Around her were his drawings and, in an old cigar box, all his letters. Even thinking about Joseph in this room seemed so disloyal. Four days! It had taken less than four minutes to be dazzled. Had she desired Albert? Had her body ever felt before that sweet pain that she experienced when Joseph kissed the tips of her fingers? But it was more than desire, she wanted to tell him about herself and she wanted to know about him. Always she had kept her hurts to herself, always presenting a lively entertaining side to Albert. There had been that time, in the back yard, when she'd awoken weeping from a dream and Albert had comforted her. His kisses had been tender and solicitous but she had not wanted to tell him the cause of her grief. Their love was so tied up with secrets. The excitement of stolen moments and stolen kisses.

Joseph wanted none of that. He wanted to claim her. She wouldn't be surprised if he marched up to the front door on Thursday and demanded to see her.

Beattie smiled at herself in the mirror. She couldn't wait until Thursday – it was a lifetime away.

Chapter Thirty-eight

It has taken me all this time to take off the brooch and necklace Albert gave me but I shall not write to him until after I've seen Joseph again. When I think of what we said to one another before he went off to China there was nothing binding to it. He wanted me to make no decisions until he returned – and yet, and yet? He gave me his grandmother's brooch and said that he loved me. I said that I loved him. But do I? Would I have let Joseph kiss me as he did if I really love Albert?

Joseph is so beautiful, like an angel from a church window. I have always loved red hair and he has such grace for a man so tall. I couldn't stop looking at him. Even my belly ached for him to kiss me. But more than that, he listened to me with such attention, and was so tender and kind.

What will this evening bring for both of us, I wonder.

'Where you off to?' Cook asked, looking at her with a glint in her eye as Beattie walked into the kitchen with Bijou's lead in her hand. 'You looks like the cat that stole the cream.'

'Just taking Bijou for a walk,' said Beattie, blushing under her friend's scrutiny.

'And don't bother to bring him back,' she sniffed. 'Little tyke peed in my slippers.'

Beattie and Pearl burst out laughing.

'I'll give you laugh,' snorted Cook.

'I reckon as Beattie's got a gentleman caller,' said Pearl. 'She don't half look pretty.'

'That she does,' said Cook, smiling at her. 'I haven't seen you so lit up in ages.'

The clock in the hall chimed six and Beattie knocked on the sitting-room door.

'Come in,' called Dr Pragnell.'

'I'm just collecting Bijou for his walk,' said Beattie, glad that Madam was not there.

'Help yourself, my dear,' he said, pointing to the dog asleep in a nest of cushions.

'Thank you, Sir, good night,' she said, anxious to avoid any questions.

Beattie snatched up her gloves from the hall stand and opened the door.

Joseph was standing at the gate. At the sight of her he swept off his hat. 'Evening, my lady,' he said.

Beattie was speechless. With her head down and conscious of him watching her she dawdled to the gate.

'Hello, you old bilge mop,' he said to Bijou before taking Beattie's hand in his.

'I was going to put on my gloves,' she said.

'Leave them,' said Joseph, 'I want to hold hands with you, not your gloves.'

He squeezed her fingers and she felt giddy.

'Shall we take a stroll and then have a drink together?' he asked her. 'We won't have to walk far to tire out little Bilgemop, here.'

Beattie laughed and then it was easy between them. 'I've never been in a public house,' she said. 'Which one would you take me to?'

'There is the Wheelbarrow Castle that's a good stroll from here and we could take a look at the sea before heading back. What do you say?'

'In for a penny in for a pound,' she said, trying to sound unconcerned. They strolled down towards Elm Grove with Bijou scampering along beside them. Beattie glanced in the shop windows at the bonnets and gowns and had mentally spent at least five guineas by the time they neared Castle Road.

'It's been a long four days, hasn't it?' Joseph said. 'I've been impatient to see you.'

'Why?' she asked, staring at her feet.

'I wanted to see you, and find out if I would feel that excitement again. You felt it too, I know you did.'

It was not a question but a statement.

She wanted to be dismissive, but instead she nodded.

He leaned towards her and ran his fingers along the inside of her collar. 'You've taken off the necklace. When did you do that?'

'This morning.'

He kissed her hand and then released it. 'Why did you take it off?' he asked.

'Not because of the excitement,' she said. 'It was what I told you about myself.'

'Have you never told Albert?'

'Once I was crying and he was kind, and asked me why, but I didn't feel ready to tell him.' She shrugged, 'I didn't think he would understand, his life's so different.'

'You said you didn't belong. Perhaps you sensed that I didn't belong either.'

'What do you mean?'

'Let's get up to the Wheelbarrow Castle and we'll find somewhere to sit in peace and talk together.'

Beattie gripped his hand as they walked through the door and into the bar of the public house. She was hit by a wave of sounds: talking, laughter and singing. There were a group of old men, clouded by a fog of pipe smoke, playing dominoes. At another table were a group of sailors each with a tankard of ale listening to one of their companions telling a tale with much gesturing and chuckling. In a corner a man with a rose in his jacket was talking to a woman in a low-cut gown, whose bosoms were much on display. Joseph led her out into a little garden with rough tables and benches.

'What can I fetch you to drink? Lemonade or ginger beer?'

'Ginger beer, please,' she said.

He set Bijou on the ground and tied his lead around the leg of a table. 'I won't be a moment.'

As he strode back into the bar, Beattie looked around her. The garden was deserted. A window to one side was open and she could here a lot of clattering of plates and shouting. There was a large shed at the back and an arch covered by a rambler rose which led into a vegetable patch. She untied Bijou from the centre table and carried him over to another one near the archway.

Joseph came towards her carrying a brimming tankard of ale and her glass of ginger beer. 'Your very good health, Beattie, and to the bilge mop,' he said, clinking his glass against hers.

'It's pretty out here, I didn't expect it to be so . . .'

'Peaceful?' he said teasingly.

Beattie laughed. 'Well, I'm disappointed that there are no press gangs or stabbings or wild women screaming.'

'Not even a parrot,' he said.

They smiled at each other and he said, 'It's all happened so fast, hasn't it?'

'What?' she asked, knowing what he meant but wanting him to say it.

'Our getting together,' he said, after taking a draught of ale.

'Yes,' she said, studying his face and noticing that his beard was darker than his hair, a rich curly copper colour. She wanted to reach out and stroke it.

'I don't want you ever to be afraid of me, Beattie. I'm a big wild man but I can be gentle as a lamb in the right company.' He leaned across the table and held her hands in his. 'I want to tell you about myself and I hope you'll want to share things with me.'

'I might,' she said, sipping her ginger beer. Beattie put down her glass and took hold of his hand once more. 'What d'you want to say?'

'You told me you wanted to belong somewhere. I lost my sense of belonging when my father was drowned off the Guinea Coast fighting against the slavers.'

'How old were you?' she asked.

'Eight years old and my sister Hester, she was nine.

Everything changed. My grandfather, on my mother's side, had been a minister and left his house to us. We had to take in lodgers and Mother taught the piano and sat up late sewing.'

'You must have missed your father,' said Beattie.

'He was a laughing, story-telling father, a giant like me, and I rode on his shoulders everywhere. He carved me ships from driftwood, taught me songs and I loved him dearly. Foolishly, I made him promise me that he would always come back safe to us.'

'And he did promise you?' asked Beattie.

Joseph nodded. 'The dear, foolish man. And so when he was drowned I couldn't believe it. Even as a boy seaman, years later, I was still looking for him. There was a great cloud of anxiety over our house and always strangers sharing our food. I was forever hungry. Hester who used to play with me was sent into service out in the country when she was twelve and I went off to sea as soon as ever I could.'

'Your mother must have been very lonely.'

'I'm sure she was. But I was full of my own hurts and blind to others' troubles.'

'Is she still living?'

'After a fashion, with Hester and her husband George, still in our house by the Royal Marine Barracks. Poor Ma has become muddled and forgetful. My sister is kind and patient with her, but it is their home not mine.'

'I have a home with the Pragnells, or a room,' said Beattie. 'But I have no key to the door and they could walk in at any moment. And my time, well it's leftover time that they don't want.'

Joseph nodded. 'I tried to make a home in the navy but

whatever space you have is shared with other men.' He laughed. 'I'll not deny, I've enjoyed roving around but now I want to settle.'

They sat in silence for some while and then their eyes met. Joseph smiled at her and she felt breathless as if she had been running. He took her hands and held them up to his face and kissed each fingertip. 'What shall we do, my little Beattie?' he said. 'Shall we walk or shall we talk?'

'We could walk and talk,' she said, not feeling able to sit still a moment longer.

They went back through the bar and out across the common. The grass was patchy and bald in places; there were gorse bushes and, in the distance, the sea.

'I suppose we should let Bilgemop use those legs of his,' said Joseph putting him on the ground and giving his lead to Beattie.

'Can we go and look at the water?' she asked.

'We can do whatever we like,' said Joseph, taking her hand. 'You have to be a bit careful, there are some boggy patches here and there.' He pulled at a gorse twig and handed it to her. 'Smell that, it's like honey, don't you think?'

She held it to her face and breathed in the scent.

Joseph leaned down towards her and she stood on tiptoe and they kissed one another.

'Your mouth tastes of honey,' he said. They stopped walking and Joseph slid his foot through Bijou's lead, then turned towards her. She felt drowsy with desire as she wound her arms around his neck. They sipped and tasted each other, the kisses becoming more searching. Joseph undid the strings of her bonnet. She closed her eyes and he loosened the pins from her hair and combed his fingers through it. 'Beattie, you are so beautiful,' he whispered.

They sat down under the shelter of the gorse and he took off his straw hat. She began stroking his hair. It was silky beneath her fingers. She kissed the curls of his beard, coarse and springy to her lips. They kissed again and again. Suddenly he reared up crying. 'Ow, ow, you little brute,' he cried, waving his hand in the air.

Only when Joseph showed her the bite marks on his hand from Bijou's pointed teeth did Beattie realise what had happened. He held her to him and after a few dazed moments she saw how funny it was and they both laughed.

'I'm changing your name from Cupid to Nanny,' he said to Bijou. 'Your mistress whispered in your ear, "Bijou, don't let that sailor kiss her, bite him hard."'

'And would you have?' she asked. 'Had your way with me?'

He took her face between his hands. 'I want to, Beattie,' he said, 'but not now, not here. I want you to invite me into your bed when you're ready. Not have your body run away with you before you've thought what you're doing.'

'I think we should go and look at the sea,' she said, trying to comb her fingers through her hair before putting on her bonnet.

He smiled at her as he tied the bonnet strings. 'I promise you, Beattie, we shall set ourselves on fire, but not yet, not yet.'

'Do you think we would have done, if Bijou hadn't bitten you?'

'I don't know,' he said. 'We must just be grateful to him.'

He smiled at her and kissed her on the tip of her nose. 'What a lot we have to look forward to, my Beattie. Now, let's run and run until we reach the sea.'

They rushed onto the stones, laughing and gasping for breath. After they had been walking some while, she said, 'I was found by the sea, you know. The doctor found me, tucked in this sailor's jacket, in a broken boat. I was just a baby.'

'Who was the sailor?' asked Joseph.

'He could have been my father, I don't know. The doctor thought my mother had likely been drowned in the boat that brought me ashore.'

'What a shock,' he said, 'to find and lose them all at once.' He put his arm around her and she rested her head against his shoulder. They sat together as people drifted past them and Bijou scuttled about at their feet. 'What did you do when he told you?'

'I ran out there to Point Beach and sat on the stones and cried. I'd always hoped that I'd find them or they would come looking for me. It hurt me that I didn't even have a grave to visit.' She smiled and he kissed her hand. 'Strange that when I was at the Mariners' this boy Freddy and me would go there. It was my favourite place.'

'Have you been there since that day?' he asked.

'No,' she said. 'It's too full of sadness.'

'Perhaps we shall go there, together,' he said, 'when you are ready to take me.'

She nodded, shivering, this time with cold as the wind tugged at her hair.

'One more kiss and I shall walk you home very slowly.'

Beattie reached up on tiptoe and he leaned down to her and they kissed each other, their lips cold and salty.

'Where shall we go on our next adventure, my honey flower, and when shall it be?' he asked her as they approached the back gate.

'On Sunday,' she said, 'there's someone I want you to meet.'

Chapter Thirty-nine

She was glad of a few moments to watch Beattie, unobserved, and to get a sense of the man beside her. He was tall and carried himself with a certain grace. They were holding hands and laughing together. Quickly, Miss Sankey stepped back into the hall as they approached. He opened the gate and let Beattie go ahead of him.

Still laughing, her pupil ran up the steps and knocked on the door.

'Beattie, my dear, come in and welcome.'

'Hello, Miss Sankey,' she said, 'I wanted to bring Joseph to meet you.'

'Good afternoon,' he said, taking off his hat before shaking her firmly by the hand.

'I am pleased to meet you. Come into my sitting room, Joseph, and make yourself comfortable. Beattie, fetch us a tea tray, if you please. I believe it's ginger cake today.'

He waited until she had seated herself before taking the chair opposite. 'I've heard a lot about this place,' he said.

'From Beattie, I suppose?'

'Yes, she told me she was happy here and learned a lot.'

'Beattie was always eager to learn. She repaid handsomely any time we spent on her and is a young woman of whom I am justifiably proud. And I may say, Joseph, I am apt to be critical of any of her suitors.'

He laughed. 'I hope I shall come up to your expectations, Miss Sankey. I'm sure if I fall short you will let me know, and quickly.'

Margaret Sankey smiled. So far, so good, she thought.

'But leaving Beattie aside, it was some of my shipmates that spoke of you. Over the years, lots of them were ex-Mariners' lads; smart boys who took a pride in themselves. Used to tell me about Christmas Days here and learning rowing and navigation in the Mariners' boat.'

Margaret warmed to him. He was not just a handsome flatterer, there was a genuine note of interest in his voice.

'My best chum, Mark Cousins, was one of your lads, I believe. Due home from the West Indies on the *Dauntless* any day, now.' He gave a rich rumbling laugh. 'Mark said you used to terrify him.'

'Running a home has some comparison to seamanship, I often think,' said Margaret Sankey. 'How much rope you pay out is a matter of judgment and experience.' She looked at the man. 'Where was it that you met Beattie?' she asked.

He smiled at her. 'It was in the People's Park a couple of weeks ago. We ran into each other. That little dog belonging to the doctor wrapped his lead around my feet and acted as Cupid, you might say.'

'What do you think of her?' she asked, watching him carefully.

'She is bright and quick and brave. I think she has a warm heart and I feel that I could tell her anything.'

'You didn't notice her beauty?' she teased.

Joseph laughed. 'That was there for all to see, but it's how she makes me feel, Miss Sankey. I'm proud to be walking out with her and I want her to feel pride in me.'

There was a knock on the door and Beattie came in with the tray. She looked at Joseph and smiled. 'Have you passed the Sankey test?' she asked.

'I think I'm only halfway through my grilling,' he said.

The atmosphere relaxed as they drank their tea and ate the ginger cake. Margaret watched them. She could see that they were besotted with each other. But they were not, all the time, gazing into one another's eyes. They talked together and included her in what they said. When the cups were drained and the cake finished she tugged at the bell-pull. 'George,' she said to a tall boy who came to the door. 'I'd like you to take this tray back to the kitchen, and then give Leading-Stoker Forrest a tour, not forgetting the boathouse.'

Without protest, Joseph got to his feet. 'I'll see you ladies after the inspection,' he said. 'George, lead the way.'

She watched Beattie smiling at him as he left the room. 'Have you brought him home for my approval?' she asked.

Beattie was silent for a moment and then she smiled at her and said, 'No, I just wanted you to meet him. It's for me to approve of him, no one else.'

'Well,' said Miss Sankey, 'I think there may be hope for you yet.'

Beattie blushed. 'You sound as if there was a time when you doubted me.' There was real concern in her voice.

'For a while,' she said, watching for a response. Beattie

fidgeted with the sugar tongs. 'I thought you were behaving like a heroine in a penny romance.'

'When did I do that?' she asked indignantly.

'Does the name Sub-Lieutenant Pragnell sound familiar?' Margaret Sankey asked.

'But I wasn't being foolish, Miss Sankey. I really thought that I loved him,' she said. 'For ages I've believed that. And I know he cares for me.'

'Not enough to defy his mama. And why did you never bring him home to me? What is it about this Joseph that you chose to bring him in preference to Albert?' Margaret Sankey watched Beattie struggling with her thoughts. The subject was far too important for her to interrupt.

'I've known Albert for years and I've never thought of bringing him here. I was afraid you would think I was being a social climber. I thought keeping it all such a secret was part of the fun of it. But with Joseph I don't need your approval and there are no secrets.'

Margaret looked at her. There was hardly a trace of the proud little four-year-old who had stood at the gate all those years ago. 'I think my job is finished, Beattie. You have graduated. You are under your own command now and, for what it is worth, you have my blessing.' She was totally unprepared for the hug that Beattie gave her and it was some time before she could extricate herself.

'Thank you for everything,' she said. 'It has been home for me and you have always been my rock.'

'Stuff and nonsense,' she protested half-heartedly.

'What times we've shared,' said Beattie. 'I'll never forget them.'

'And neither should you,' Miss Sankey admonished her.

They sat together talking of past pupils and her future plans for the home until Joseph returned.

'I'd like to come again if I may. Perhaps myself and some of my shipmates could take your lads out in our whaler one Sunday.'

'Excellent, Joseph.' She shook his hand. 'Now off with the pair of you. I have work to do.'

Margaret Sankey watched them going down the street hand in hand, talking away to each other. She went over to the china cabinet and got out the bottle of medicinal brandy and poured herself a celebratory glass.

Chapter Forty

'I'm really curious about your family. I can't wait to meet them,' said Beattie, as they bowled along in the hansom cab on the way to his home in Eastney.

'I hope you won't be disappointed,' said Joseph. 'Ma is apt to be muddled and forgetful and Hester can be scratchy.'

'If they're so strange Joseph why are you taking me to meet them?'

'Because they're the only family I've got,' he said, 'and I want you to meet them. I want you to know all about me.'

She kissed him on the cheek. 'That's why I took you to the Mariners',' she said.

'Our home is nothing like the Mariners'. It's nowhere near as tidy. And with Mother anything can happen.'

'Why are you so nervous?' laughed Beattie. 'What will she do? Run naked down the street?'

'No,' he said, 'Hester will keep the door locked.'

'As for tidiness, I'm not a government inspector. You've told me your mother is confused and forgetful. I'm not

399

expecting lace doilies or pastry forks. Let's just go and meet her and your sister. She hasn't got a gun, has she?'

'Not that I know of,' he said glumly.

'Give me a kiss and stop worrying,' said Beattie, not feeling half as carefree as she sounded.

Joseph laughed. 'And another kiss for courage,' he said, taking her in his arms.

The journey was all too short. After many more kisses in the musty interior, the hansom came to a halt outside a little row of bow-fronted houses.

Beattie looked curiously around her as she stepped down from the cab. Opposite was the flint-stoned grandeur of the Royal Marine Barracks complete with clock tower and a sentry outside. Joseph paid the cabman and then opened the gate and walked towards the front door. As she stood on the path, waiting for him to put his key in the lock, Beattie could hear someone playing the piano.

He had barely opened the door when his sister came down the passage towards them. She put her finger to her lips. 'I'm Hester, pleased to meet you,' she said, smiling at her and stretching out her hand. 'We'll go out into the kitchen first. Best not disturb her while she's playing. I'll just lock the door behind us or she may get it into her head to wander off.'

Beattie's first impression was of a well-scrubbed freckled woman with a faded resemblance to Joseph. Her hair was not so red-gold as her brother's and hung down her back in a plait. She followed her down a passageway with the piano music ringing in her ears and visions of the mad Grace Poole in *Jane Eyre*, flickering through her mind.

'Sit yourself down and I'll pour us some tea.'

Hester busied herself with the cups and saucers and Joseph

put his hat on the dresser before pulling out a chair for Beattie. The little kitchen was clean and tidy, with a red-tiled floor and a black-leaded range. At the window looking out onto a tiny garden hung a starched net curtain and on the table was a vase of marigolds and a well-risen sponge cake on a blue plate.

'Thank you,' she said, as Hester passed her the sugar basin. There was a long silence in which the sound of her spoon stirring seemed to fill the room.

'Where's George?' asked Joseph. 'Are we going to see him?'

'He'll be over from the barracks at four,' said Hester. 'Let me cut you a piece of cake, Beattie.'

'Should we wait until he comes in?' she asked. 'I'm looking forward to meeting him.'

'Oh, no, we must make the most of Ma being occupied. Once she's on the go, I'll not get a moment to breathe.'

Beattie watched Hester cutting the piece of cake into tiny squares before she handed one to her. Joseph looked questioningly at his sister and then, blushing, she took the plate back.

'I'm so sorry. I'm just so used to doing it for Mother.'

'Please don't worry,' protested Beattie, trying to smile reassuringly. She bit into her second slice and tried to swallow, but her mouth was dry with anxiety. His description of his mother, as muddled and forgetful, was beginning to feel like an understatement.

'You're honoured,' said Hester, 'Joe's never brought anyone home before.'

Beattie was amused to see him blush and fidget in his seat, but she was irritated at Hester calling him Joe. It reduced him somehow to an ordinary man pushing a cart or shovelling earth. Perhaps that's what people did in families. After all, to their parents Albert and Samuel were Albie and Sammy.

'You work for a doctor, don't you?' asked Hester, spooning sugar into her cup.

'Not exactly,' said Beattie. 'I'm Mrs Pragnell's maid, I look after her clothes and keep their rooms clean and tidy.'

'I could do with a maid here,' said Hester, looking angrily at Joseph. 'Mother has me on the go from morning to night.'

'I'm sure she appreciates all you do for her,' said Beattie, not knowing what to say, just wanting to fill the angry silence.

Hester snorted. 'You don't get appreciation from your family. Might as well go whistle for it.'

'George and me,' said Joseph, glaring at her, 'we do what we can. I send you money and, George, he never stops from the moment he steps over the doorstep.'

Beattie felt imprisoned between them, an unwilling spectator to their raised voices and bitter looks. It was a while before she became aware of the door handle rattling. After some moments it opened and a small woman in a cotton nightgown pattered across the floor, her feet bare and her white hair loose about her shoulders.

'Oh a party,' she said, 'and my Clem come home to me.'

She rushed around the table and threw her arms around Joseph.

'No, Ma, it's me, your son Joseph.'

'Then where's Clem?' she asked.

Beattie was startled. Mrs Forrest was like a beautiful wayward child. Her blue eyes filled with tears. 'Have you seen him?' she asked, peering into her face. 'Please say you have.'

'Was it you playing the piano?' Beattie didn't know why she had said that, but it had a magical effect.

'I'll play for you,' she said, taking her hand and pulling her towards the door.

Hester tried to intervene. 'Sit down, Mother, the front room's not fit to be . . .'

'I don't mind,' whispered Beattie.

'But I do,' said Hester, fiercely. 'I mind that you should see it.'

'I've come to see your mother, I'm not concerned about the house.' Beattie had no chance for further conversation as Mrs Forrest snatched at her sleeve.

'Come on, come on, the concert's just about to start.'

Nothing could have prepared her for the chaos of the front room. The floor was littered with hundreds of strips of torn up newspaper. On a couch was a broken plate with the remains of a meal congealed on it. There were no chairs, just a rickety brown piano stool. Mrs Forrest plumped herself down on it. She played without a single false note, her fingers rippling over the keys, one melody flowing on from the other. She closed her eyes and began to sing, her voice in perfect harmony with her piano playing. Beattie watched her from the doorway, thinking how irresistible she must have been when her Clem first set eyes on her. She could see traces of Joseph's grace and charm in his mother in spite of her confusion. Poor Hester seemed to have none of their joy or enthusiasm. But that was unfair, Beattie chided herself, for she has all the responsibility.

Joseph came and stood in the doorway with his arm around her.

'You sing,' demanded Mrs Forrest.

'Will you sing with me?' asked Beattie, not knowing what his mother would make of her lack of talent.

'"I dreamt that I dwelt in marble halls",' Mrs Forrest began.

It was a difficult tune and Beattie struggled to keep up with the piano.

'Stop, stop,' screamed Mrs Forrest, getting up from the piano and shaking Beattie fiercely by the shoulders. 'You've no idea. Tell your mother she can save her sixpences, there is not a tune in you.'

'Mother, come on,' Joseph coaxed, 'there's cake ready for you.' He sat her on a chair in the kitchen and put a plate in front of her. She fell on the food as if starving and crammed one piece after another into her mouth without seeming to swallow.

Beattie felt utterly at a loss and Joseph looked at her with tears in his eyes. She wanted to hold him in her arms but Hester was there, clattering angrily with the washing up. Picking up a tea-towel, Beattie stood beside her at the sink drying the cups and setting them back on the dresser. She wondered how long they needed to stay before they could decently leave.

Like an answer to her prayers there was a rapping on the front door.

'That's my Clem,' screeched Mrs Forrest, leaping off her chair and trying to run down the passage.

'Beattie, quick, open the door. It'll be George,' whispered Joseph.

'Hello, my gal, you must be our Joe's lass,' said a cheery man in the dark blue uniform of a Royal Marine.

'And you're George, Hester's husband,' said Beattie, holding out her hand.

'Welcome to the family,' he said. 'Where's my beautiful Charlotte,' he called as he followed Beattie down the passage.

'Clem, it's my Clem, home at last,' cooed Mrs Forrest holding out her arms.

'I'm going out in the garden, said Hester. 'You can see to her now,' she said, slamming out of the back door.

Beattie went to follow her but Joseph shook his head.

'Leave her, Beattie, she likes to sit out there for a while. That's her kingdom.'

'Come on, Charlotte, now you tell me all that's happened since I've been away,' said George kindly, as he cut himself a slice of cake.

The whole atmosphere changed and Charlotte Forrest chattered away to George quite happily.

Joseph signalled to her to sit beside him and put his arm around the back of her chair.

'She likes you,' said Beattie, watching the little woman kissing George's hand.

'Good old girl, is Charlotte,' he said. 'I've only ever known her as she is today, so I'm not disappointed. Joe and Hester,' he said, smiling at Joseph, 'grieve for what she's lost. Keep trying to draw her back to the mother she was. I can take her as I find her. There's not an atom of harm to her, poor soul.' He laughed. 'If you was here some days you'd think you was at a pantomime. I plays all the parts. Sometimes I'm Clem, her husband, or her father, the old vicar, or even her own mother. Never knows who I am for two minutes together.'

'It must be tiring for Hester,' said Beattie, smiling at George.

'Course it is,' he said. 'Her salvation's the garden. Loves dibbin' about in the earth and watching things grow. An hour out in the garden soon gets her to rights.'

'Who's that girl over there?' asked Charlotte. 'She looks like a gypsy. You got Spanish blood, my proud beauty.'

Beattie didn't know whether to laugh or cry.

'Let's have a song together,' said Joseph, taking his mother's hand.

Charlotte suddenly snatched his sailor's straw hat from the dresser and put it on.

> *'Ye banks and braes o' bonnie Doon.*
> *How can ye bloom sae fair!'*

She sang and Joseph and George joined in, their voices blending together, a deep complement to Charlotte's clear soprano.

> *'How can ye chant, ye little birds*
> *And I sae fu' o' care.'*

Beattie felt included in a warm circle of affection. Charlotte caught hold of her hand as Joseph led them into the second verse.

'I'll finish washing up and clearing the table,' Beattie said, wanting to contribute something to the afternoon.

'Thank you,' said George. 'Hester will appreciate that.'

'Kind girl,' said Charlotte. 'You are a kind girl.'

'I'll take Hester out another cup,' said George, 'then I'll be in to sit with my best girl. You two can set off, then, it's a long walk back to Portsea.'

Beattie washed and Joseph dried the tea things while Mrs Forrest sat shredding a newspaper into long strips.

'Thank you for coming,' whispered Joseph. 'I'm sorry it's been so hectic.'

'It's been strange,' said Beattie, 'but next time I'll know what to expect.'

'You'd come again?' he asked.

'Of course,' she said, 'as long as I don't have to sing.'

'I hope George comes back soon,' said Joseph, 'because I badly want to take you away and kiss you.'

They sat down either side of Charlotte. She looked up from her tearing and said, 'My Joseph and his Gypsy Rose.'

'You are my lovely old Ma, aren't you?' he said, kissing her cheek.

Charlotte nodded and beamed at him.

The back door opened and Hester came in with a bunch of sweet peas in her hand. 'Take these with you, Beattie,' she said. 'It was good of you to come. Sorry I've not been any company, but that's how it is.'

'Thank you ever so much, Hester. Aren't the colours pretty. Look, Charlotte.'

'I am your mother, young lady,' she said, smacking her hand.

'Get along with you,' said Hester, shooing them down towards the front door.

They had barely got out of the front door when Joseph kissed her. 'Ooh! I've been dying to do that all afternoon,' he said, swinging her round in his arms.

'Poor Hester,' said Beattie as they strolled along towards Portsea. 'It must be hard work looking after her mother.'

'I'm sure it is,' said Joseph, 'but she doesn't make it easy for herself. The woman next door offered to sit with Ma sometimes, but Hester must do it all herself, that way she can play the martyr. But that's families for you.'

Beattie nodded. She thought that her earlier imaginings about families needed a lot of revision.

They had almost reached the back door of the Pragnells before he kissed her again. They stood under the shadow of an oak tree at a street corner, almost hidden beneath the branches.

Beattie stood on tiptoe and Joseph leaned down towards her. All the frustrations of the afternoon dropped away. He held her face between his hands and kissed her eyelids and her lips and then her neck. She felt a tender ache in her belly and wanted so much more than kisses.

'I want to be alone with you next time,' whispered Joseph. 'Can you think of somewhere where we can meet?'

'Yes,' said Beattie, 'I know the perfect place.'

Chapter Forty-one

July 7 1878

Dear Albert,

*I am sorry that I have not written to you for so long.
There is not an easy way for me to tell you what has
happened. For so long you have been the dearest person in
my life and the thought of causing you pain saddens me.*

*Albert, I have met and come to love a man called Joseph
Forrest. He is a Leading Stoker who lives on one of the
harbour hulks, called the 'Asia,' and has a family living in
Eastney. I don't know what will happen between us. Maybe
we shall marry, maybe we shall go our separate ways, I
don't know.*

*What I am certain of is that I no longer love you as I did.
Always I shall have a deep affection for you as a dear, dear
friend. I hope you will be able to look on me as your loyal
friend, too.*

*I no longer wear your necklace and forget-me-not brooch
but I shall keep it safe until you return. I thank you Albert
for all your kindness to me and shall never forget you.*

*I hope that you will not be sad for long. Somewhere over
the horizon is your perfect partner and soul mate.
Ever your true Friend,
Beatrice Salter.*

She slipped the envelope in the letterbox and hurried off
towards Old Portsmouth. The decision had been taken and she
was happy now that she had been able to be honest with Albert.
Her day with Joseph lay ahead of her with all its possibilities.
They would have hours and hours in each other's company –
time to kiss and time to talk. Beattie had packed a picnic of
bread and cheese and slices of pork pie in a basket along with
a bottle of Mrs Frostick's lemonade. She passed Cambridge
Barracks, at the top of the High Street, and walked slowly
down to the George Hotel for their meeting at ten o'clock.

'Boo!'

Beattie screamed half frightened, half excited as he leapt out
at her. 'Joseph, do you want me to drop down dead?' she
protested.

He laughed at her, 'No, my honey flower,' he said, 'I've
got other plans for you today.' He took her basket and hand in
hand they walked down to the town walls and through the
Sally Port arch. Point Beach was deserted save for a few gulls
busy at the water's edge.

'You've brought me to meet your family,' he said, setting
down the basket on the stones.

Beattie nodded. Joseph stood behind her with his arms
around her waist and held her against him. She took his hands,
held them up to her face, and peered at the sea through his
fingers. Today it was dark grey-blue and boisterous as it flung
itself at the shore. Slowly she steadied her breathing in time

410

with its rhythm, as she had always done, since that first visit
when she was nine years old. Why had she stayed away so long?
How different it seemed from the last time she was here. Then
she had crouched, alone in the corner by the Round Tower,
shivering and crying with neither hope nor belief in anything.

'I want us to go over there, where I was last time,' she said.

Joseph picked up the basket and followed her up the beach.

He took off his hat and filled it with stones before sitting
down with his back against the tower. He drew her down into
his arms. 'Tell me what you are thinking, my honey flower,'
he said.

'I'm wondering what my father would think of you,' she
said.

'I don't know,' he said. 'If I was him, I would be looking
for someone who would care for his daughter and keep her
safe. Who would love her with his heart and with his body;
who would lie with her and give her children; who would
listen to her woes and laugh at her joys. He would want a man
for his daughter who would value what had been given into
his caring. I could promise him all those things.'

Beattie could not speak. She felt tears pricking in her eyes.

'And what could I say to your mother?' Joseph took off her
hat and began to stroke her hair. 'Your daughter is comely and
I desire her. I want to be with her always, even until she is an
old woman. I want her to tell me her hurts and fears and I shall
tell her mine. You would be proud of your daughter.' He took
the pins from her hair and it hung loose about her shoulders.
Beattie closed her eyes and he stroked her hair in a slow, lulling
rhythm. They lay on the shingle side by side. She mapped his
face with her fingers, tracing the shape of his eyebrows, his nose
and the fullness of his lips, fascinated by the coarse crispness of

his beard in contrast to his silky hair. 'I think it would take all day to count your freckles,' she whispered.

'I want to know your hands,' he said, stroking the lines on each palm and pressing his lips against the pulse at her wrist.

Beattie kissed him. 'I know what being happy is,' she said.

'Tell me,' he demanded.

'Being here with you,' she said, 'and feeling that we are at the beginning of something. As if we were setting out together on an adventure.'

'We are,' he said, 'but first I must ask you a question, here where your father brought you and from where the doctor carried you to safety.'

Beattie sat up and Joseph knelt in front of her. He smiled at her and she was breathless. His face shimmered at her through her tears.

He took her hands in his. 'Will you be my wife and my dear friend. Will you share what little I have of this world's goods for now and for ever?'

'Yes,' she sobbed, 'yes, yes, yes.'

'I will be back in a moment,' he said, walking down to the water.

Beattie watched him bend down and dip something into the sea.

'I made this for you,' he said, spreading out a length of what looked like wet string in front of her on a large flat stone. 'It's a necklace. The knot is called a running bowline – see there those shapes joined together? It's called two hearts that beat as one.'

'It's wonderful,' said Beattie. 'Will you put it on for me?' she asked, holding her hair away from her neck.

'Let it dry in the sun first,' he said.

'Why did you dip it in the water?'

'You were brought over the water to me by your father who was a seafaring man and I am a sailor, too. The sea has played her part in all our lives and I wanted to thank her for her gift.'

'We should drink a toast,' said Beattie, 'in lemonade.'

'Quick, before any day-trippers arrive or the sentry peers at us from the tower. To my darling Beattie – I give you my love always,' said Joseph, raising the glass to her.

'To Joseph, my dearest love,' said Beattie. 'Thank you for finding me and choosing me. Thank you for coming here and understanding what this beach means to me.' She laughed. 'Do you know, it must only be about half past ten and yet I'm starving.'

Joseph roared with laughter, then hugged her tightly. 'Oh, Beattie, I can see that I shall have to work from morning to night to keep you fed.'

'It's our betrothal breakfast,' she said.

'It's strange how different food tastes eaten in the open air,' he said. 'This is the best pie I have ever tasted.'

'I shall tell Cook, she will be pleased.'

'I shall tell her myself,' he said, 'when I walk you home later.'

'I suppose I shall have to tell Madam and Doctor Pragnell.'

'We can tell them together,' he said. 'I don't mean burst in today, but you arrange a time and I'll arrive in my number one uniform and a new straw hat.'

'Where will we live, Joseph?' she asked.

'That depends on you and how soon you would like us to be married.'

'What d'you mean?'

'Well, it's likely in the next few months I shall get a new ship and be sent away. If we marry before I go, we will have to live with Ma, and then save up for somewhere better when I come back. If you want to wait until then, which could be three to four years, then we could go straight into a couple of rooms on our own.'

'I want us to be on our own and be married now,' she said.

'Our first disappointment,' he said. 'If you had married Albert you would move straight away into your own little home. But if you choose me your life will not be that easy. Come here and let me give you a hug.'

Beattie felt as if she had been given a prize only for it to be snatched away a moment later. There was no doubt that she wanted to be married to Joseph, but sharing him with his muddled old mother and resentful sister? – that was another question. If she wasn't prepared to make the compromise it meant years more of living at the Pragnells and waiting to be Joseph's wife.

'I don't want to wait years for you,' Joseph said. 'Life is too uncertain. What will you feel if we decide to wait and something happens to me; say I get drowned or die of some tropical disease? Then we will both have missed out on six months of marriage for the sake of having our own front door and a few sticks of furniture. Ma is not going to last for ever, you know.'

'I want you, too,' she whispered. 'It's just more complicated than I thought it would be.'

'We can put Ma in the little middle room upstairs and we can have the big front bedroom,' he said, running his fingers around the neck of her blouse. 'It would probably only be for a few months. And, I promise you, when I get home again we'll have our own place.' Joseph undid the top buttons and pressed his lips against her collarbone.

'Promise,' demanded Beattie, her resolve melting under his determined stroking.

A loud whistle interrupted their caresses and they found themselves the subject of intense interest by a group of lads throwing stones into the water.

'Where's my necklace?' asked Beattie, sitting up and rebuttoning her collar.

'Here on the stone where we left it,' said Joseph. 'It's dry now, let me put it on.'

She held her hair off her neck as he fastened it in place.

'Beattie,' he said, 'we've got our health and our love. Isn't that enough? Think how lucky you've been so far.'

'What do you mean?' she asked.

'You were within moments of dying when the doctor found you and then, twenty years and more later, a little dog leads you to the feet of your true love. Isn't that enough to tell you that someone wants you to be happy?'

She got to her feet and took his hands in hers. The beach had begun to fill with people wanting to catch the steamer from the wooden pier to the Isle of Wight. There were soldiers from the Point Battery and other young couples out for a stroll.

'There are two more places I want to show you,' she said, 'before we're done. Places I hadn't the courage to visit on my own.'

They left the beach and crossed Broad Street and followed the winding White Hart Row until they reached number seven. 'This is where Doctor Pragnell took me in his arms, to a policeman's wife. Here they saved me.' She stood outside the house with the dingy curtains and dull brass knocker, and tried to imagine the drama that had unfolded there twenty-two years ago.'

'It's almost your birthplace,' said Joseph. 'Do you want to knock on the door?'

'No, the policeman and his wife moved away some time ago. I just wanted to see if I felt anything.'

'And do you?'

She smiled up at him. 'I feel lucky,' she said.

'Where else, Honey Flower?'

'Golden Lion Lane, not far from here, beside St Thomas's Church. I was a little girl here in one of these houses. One day Doctor Pragnell saw me toddling along with Ruth Salter, the woman who wanted to keep me. I must have been happy here,' she said.

'You may be standing in your own footprints, Miss Beattie Salter,' Joseph said, bending to kiss her.

'Perhaps I am. I just feel as if something is completed. Well, not exactly completed, as I shall never know where I came from, but I know enough to be going on with.'

'So where to now?'

Beattie laughed. 'It's Sunday and the sun's shining, let's just be trippers.'

The day sped by. They raced across the common to the Ladies' Mile and strolled through the ornamental gardens to listen to a brass band playing then feasted on winkles. At six o'clock they strolled back to St George's Square.

Joseph pulled her to him just before they reached the back gate. 'Have you enjoyed your day?' he asked, resting his hands on her shoulders.

'It's been the happiest one of my life, a new beginning for both of us.'

'Let's not wait, Beattie. Let's get married as soon as ever we can.'

'Yes, yes, yes,' she said. 'Give me some kisses to last me till Thursday.'

'Do you want me to kiss you in front of the girl looking out of the kitchen window? Or will you introduce me first?'

Laughing, they looked towards the window just as Pearl bobbed her head down below the sill.

Beattie took Joseph by the hand and knocked on the back door, which was immediately bounced back on its hinges by Pearl, who whooped delightedly at them.

''Ere, Cook, it's our Beattie and a feller. Told you she had a follower.'

'Happy to meet you, Pearl,' said Joseph, sweeping off his hat with a bow.

Giggling, she sank into a chair and threw her apron over her face. 'If I'd seen you first,' she gasped, 'I'd have run off with you myself.'

'Pearl, pull yerself together,' said Cook, starting up from her chair. 'What will the young man think.' She stood up on her step and nodded her head to Joseph. 'Good evening, young man. So you're the fellow as has our Beattie all lit up?'

'Joseph Forrest,' he said, 'pleased to meet the woman who made that excellent pie.'

Cook beamed. 'I was just thinking about supper. If my memory serves me right, there's a heel of pie in the larder. Pearl, set the table, we'll see what we can scrape together.'

The meal was a noisy affair with Pearl continually seized with the giggles, and often in danger of choking. When every crumb had been eaten Joseph whispered to Beattie, 'Shall we tell them?'

417

Beattie stood up and tapped on a glass with a fork. 'We've got something to tell you,' she said. 'Joseph has asked me to marry him and I have said yes.'

Cook burst into tears and Pearl leapt up and knocked over her chair before almost crushing Beattie with a hug.

Mrs Frostick got onto her step and demanded a kiss from Joseph, then sent Beattie into the dining room for the sherry. 'To the happy couple,' she said, when four glasses had been poured.

'To Beattie,' said Joseph, 'the queen of my heart.'

After many more toasts they were able to extricate themselves, and walked together to the back alley. They dizzied themselves with slow drenching kisses.

'Till Thursday,' she whispered.

'Thursday,' said Joseph.

Chapter Forty-two

I am to be married. Each time I write the words I feel a new burst of excitement. I shall be Mrs Forrest, a name I have chosen to take. Since we said 'Yes' our plans have taken wings.

Last Sunday we went again to Joseph's home and took his mother out for a stroll. I took George's advice and became whatever character she wanted me to be. Most of the time she doesn't know who or where she is but I am certain there are moments when she is purposely mischievous just to annoy Hester.

She is going to be the bigger test of my patience. Hester simmers with resentment at every turn. Only when she is in the garden does she come close to being agreeable. I can see I have much to learn about families.

Joseph will be joining a new ship in January called the Hermione. 'My Honey Flower,' he said, 'we shall have to make the most of every second we have together.'

Tonight at six o'clock we will be meeting with Doctor and

*Madam to tell them of our plans. Our wedding will be on
September 21st, Joseph's twenty-fifth birthday, at St
George's Church. How glad I am that Albert and I made
no promises before he went away. How different my
feelings are for Joseph: everything is in the open and
discussed between us. Even my body feels the change from
Albert to Joseph. I did not realise that there is a language
without words that is communicated through touch. It
would be so easy to follow where my feelings are leading me
but I want our full knowledge to come, as the final signature
of the wedding day, when all the public declarations are at
an end.*

'Great heavens, Obi, it's Beattie and a sailor walking up the
front steps.'

'Gussie, come away from the window,' said Obadiah going
towards the door, 'she'll see you. We shall know their news
soon enough.'

Augusta was stunned. For weeks she had noticed a change
in Beattie, a tendency towards forgetfulness and a habit of
smiling to herself. Did this mean that her friendship with Albert
was at an end? She felt a guilty relief.

'Good evening, Beattie, and to you, Sir.'

'Doctor, this is . . .'

'Come in, come in,' he interrupted, 'you can make the
introductions to both of us.'

'Doctor and Madam,' said Beattie, 'this is my fiancé Leading
Stoker Joseph Forrest.'

'I'm very pleased to meet you, Joseph,' said Obadiah
smiling at him, 'and this is my wife, Augusta.'

'Good evening, Mr and Mrs Pragnell,' said the sailor, shaking them both firmly by the hand.

'Sit you both down and I'll get the sherry.'

Well, he certainly doesn't lack confidence, thought Augusta, looking at the sailor as he settled himself in a chair by the window. His height and grace gave the man a compelling presence. She could quite see why Beattie was taken with him.

'To Beattie and Joseph,' said Obi raising his glass. 'Good health and happiness.'

'So Joseph, where and when do you intend your marriage to take place?' she asked.

'At St George's, as it's Beattie's parish church, on the twenty-first of September,' he said. 'I know it's only a couple of months away, but I may well be at sea, by January, so I don't want to waste a moment.'

'You will be married from here, of course,' she said, smiling at Beattie.

'I am being married from the Mariners', Madam. It's where I grew up and it's always been my home.'

Augusta was astonished. How could she be so ungracious? After all she had done for the girl. Anger flamed in her cheeks.

'Quite right,' said Obadiah. 'I'm sure Miss Sankey will be delighted.'

'Oh, she is.' Beattie smiled at him. 'She's arranging it like a military operation. There is one important thing I wanted to ask you, Doctor. I wondered if you would give me away.'

This is outrageous. Augusta was about to protest when she caught Joseph smiling at her. He seemed to be reading her thoughts. Flustered, she fiddled with her bracelet. Am I being unreasonable to feel so angry? she wondered.

421

'I would be delighted – no, I would be honoured,' said Obi, rushing over and kissing Beattie and shaking Joseph by the hand. 'Isn't that wonderful, darling?' he said, coming and standing by her chair.

Beattie was looking at her with none of the deference Augusta expected from her maid.

'It would be so appropriate,' Beattie said, 'since he found me all those years ago. I am the little mermaid from your sons' stories.'

'Of course, of course,' said Augusta, forcing herself to smile. 'So you will be leaving us, Beattie, but not before you have trained your replacement, I hope.'

'I shall be here until the Friday before my wedding, Madam. I can take a letter tomorrow to the registry. Oh, and I have written to Albert and told him my good news.'

Augusta fumed. Whatever protest she made would look petty and ridiculous. Why was she so angry, anyway? It was the best of solutions. After all, she could have been announcing her engagement to Albert. What rankled was that she had been found out. She had not cared for Beattie and had been paid back in her own coin. 'Where will you live?' she asked, trying to simulate interest.

'With Joseph's family in Cromwell Road near the Royal Marine Barracks.'

'Have you contacted the Reverend Merchison?'

'Oh, yes, Madam. I had to be christened, because Miss Sankey had no baptismal certificate.'

'Well,' said Augusta, desperate for the interview to be at an end, 'I must congratulate you both. Refill our glasses, Obadiah, will you, please? To Joseph and Beattie every happiness.'

'Thank you, Madam,' said Beattie, 'you have been very kind. We will go now and not interrupt your supper.'

Augusta had the distinct impression that it was she who was being dismissed.

'Goodbye, Mrs Pragnell,' said Joseph, shaking her hand. 'And to you, Sir. I shall see you both in church, I hope.'

'Certainly, my boy. Let me see you to the door.'

'Goodbye Joseph, I am pleased to have met you.' She nodded to Beattie. 'I shall see you in the morning.'

'I don't know when I've been so pleased,' said Obi coming back into the room.

'Well, I don't know what to think,' said Augusta. 'I did not appreciate having my hospitality flung back in my face.'

Obadiah looked puzzled. 'Whatever do you mean, Gussie?'

'I thought she would be only too pleased to be married from here. We are practically next door to the church. She would look so pretty coming down the front steps in her wedding dress. I feel quite hurt.'

'Do you really, Augusta?' he asked, giving her one of his searching looks. 'Aren't you just a tiny bit relieved that she is no longer interested in Albert?'

'Well, of course, I am,' she said, piqued at the acuteness of his understanding. 'It's just that . . .' Her voice trailed away.

'. . . She is not being sufficiently deferential or grateful to her employer? Is that it? *Owh!*' he exclaimed as the pillow hit him in the face. 'Gussie, my darling, you really can't have it both ways. Given that you have been a mite condescending to Beattie and unjust over her friendship with Albie you can hardly expect her to be gracious in return.'

'Why must you always be so infuriatingly logical,' snapped Gussie.

'Oh come on my sweet, simmer down. I have an invitation from the Admiral of the Dockyard to attend his daughter's christening at St Anne's on Sunday with luncheon afterwards at his splendid house.'

'I'm not really mollified,' she said, trying not to respond to his pleading.

'Perhaps you could be Gussified then,' he said, kissing her on the mouth in a most unhusbandly fashion.

She laughed. 'Obi, you are so silly.'

'Pleased to meet ya,' said Freddy, shaking Joseph by the hand.

'It's good to meet her family,' said Joseph. 'You must have known her longer than anyone. Let me get you an ale. Beattie, what would you like?'

'A ginger beer, please, darling.' Beattie sat out in the garden of the Wheelbarrow and watched Freddy and Joseph going back into the bar. She was glad that they had met at last. She couldn't believe that everything was going so smoothly. Even Mrs Pragnell had been quite agreeable lately.

'Beattie,' she had said, only yesterday. 'You must give me your address in Cromwell Road. I will have your wedding present delivered there for you.'

'That's very kind of you, Madam,' she had replied.

'I might as well tell you now that Doctor and I thought a sewing machine would be a most useful gift. You are such a skilled needlewoman, I am sure you will put it to very good use.'

'I don't know what to say,' Beattie had mumbled, feeling guilty for all her earlier criticism.

'I have appreciated your talents and your loyalty, although you may not have thought so.'

'Thank you, Madam,' she had said, at a loss for words.

'Now off with you, here's a list of my requirements from the draper's that should occupy a few moments of your time; then I have my winter pelisse for you to look at. I really think the fur needs renewing, it's looking quite drab.'

'Saw the old doc the other day,' said Freddy, sitting down beside her with a brimming glass. 'He's like a dog with two tails. Pleased as Punch to be giving you away.'

'A good man,' said Joseph. 'I can see why you're so fond of him. Madam's another story.'

'She's like a thoroughbred,' laughed Freddy. 'Needs careful handling. Only a month and you two puts your 'eads in the noose.'

Joseph laughed. 'I'm getting enough of that on board. All the old Jonahs trying to frighten me off with tails of rolling pins and petticoat government.'

Freddy smiled at both of them. 'Don't you listen,' he said. 'All the beer and sing-songs in the world don't make up for havin' someone to come home to and to be there for you through thick and thin. We knows that, don't we, Beattie?'

She nodded and squeezed his hand. 'You will drive us to the church, won't you, Freddy? Jonas is a nice old fellow and I know he's got his eye on Cook, and would love to get all dressed up, but you're family.'

'So's Dapple,' he said; 'she knowed you as long as I have. Fetched you from the workhouse. Course I shall drive ya. Who you havin' as bridesmaid?'

'Rosie Siddons. You remember the girl that was so ill, just before I left, nearly died of diphtheria?'

'Oh, yeah, she's workin' at Denby and Shanks now, saw her the other day when I was down The Hard. Says they're right slave drivers, looking for something else, she is.' Freddy laughed. 'I've saved the best bit to last. Me and Clara is courtin'.'

'Freddy,' she cried, hugging him fiercely. 'I'm so, so glad.'

'What's Clara like?' asked Joseph, smiling at the pair of them.

'Big and bossy, but a great cook,' laughed Freddy. 'She's a widow, you know, with a little boy called Harry. Not 'alf as bossy as she was, but her grub is still as tasty as ever.'

'You must bring her to the wedding,' said Beattie.

'She'll likely make you a cake,' he said. 'Got a little bakery in Hawke Street.'

The three of them sat talking and laughing until the land-lord called time.

'You'll have to come on a run ashore with me and my chums, the night before the wedding,' said Joseph, shaking Freddy's hand.

'Wouldn't miss it for the world,' said Freddy. 'I'll leave you two lovebirds to see each other home,' he said. 'I'm off to see my Clara.'

'Ooh, won't it be good when we don't have to say good night at the door?' said Joseph, as they stood in the alley by the back door. 'Give me a kiss, quick, before Pearl spies us.'

Beattie stepped up on the two loose bricks they had hidden behind the hedge especially for the purpose, and drew herself level with his face. 'Oh, Joseph, I can't wait to be married,' she sighed.

Chapter Forty-three

Beattie held up her arms while Miss Sankey helped her into her wedding dress. She shivered as the slippery satin folds fell into place.

'I haven't done that since I was four,' she laughed.

'What a fierce little girl you were,' said Matron, smiling at her. 'You have come a long way since then.'

'I have, haven't I?' said Beattie, holding out her arms again for the buttons to be fastened at her wrists.

'I'll leave you to do your hair while I gather some flowers for your hat.'

Beattie smoothed her hand over the bodice of her dress and smiled to herself. She was simmering with excitement. In an hour's time she would become Mrs Beattie Forrest, a name she had chosen for herself. Picking up the brush, she drew it through the full length of her black hair, then divided it with a comb into three sections. Carefully, she plaited it, weaving in a narrow blue ribbon as she did so. It had been a present from Pearl. Cook had lent her a lace handkerchief. They had both hugged her and bade her a tearful goodbye when she left St George's Square last night.

'Don't you forget to wave to us when you comes back down the aisle,' Mrs Frostick had said.

'Can I kiss yer 'usband?' asked Pearl, bursting into fits of giggles.

Even Madam had kissed her and seemed genuinely sorry she was leaving. 'I hope you will be happy, Beattie, and I am sure you will be a beautiful bride.'

And she was, she hardly recognised herself in the high-collared long-sleeved dress. The satin lent a glow to her skin and her black hair shone.

Miss Sankey came back into the room bringing the white wide-brimmed hat Beattie had chosen in preference to a veil. The thought of being trussed up in muslin and not being able to see every detail of Joseph's face as she walked up the aisle towards him was unbearable.

'Sit still now, and let me skewer this in place with a hat pin,' said Miss Sankey, standing behind her and smiling at her in the mirror.

'Ooh! Don't they smell delicious?' said Beattie, turning around and holding her hat up to her face and inhaling the rich scent of white jasmine and pink roses, that were threaded through the hat band.

'Perfection,' said her teacher.

Beattie looked at Miss Sankey in her blue Nursing Sister's uniform, complete with the short cape and Crimea medal. 'Thank you for everything,' she said, 'you were my mother and father and teacher all rolled into one. You saved me.'

'You were well worth the saving, my child,' she said gruffly. 'Now, you be a credit to yourself and you won't go wrong. I shall go and fetch Rosemary and your bouquet. I hope she will have calmed down a little by now.'

Beattie walked up and down Miss Sankey's bedroom, a place severely off limits to her charges. It was full of books and paintings and interesting shells and rocks, testimony to her teacher's enquiring mind. She was about to open a volume of poetry when there was a tentative tap on the door.

'Oh, Beattie,' Doctor Pragnell stood in the doorway smiling at her with such affection. 'You look beautiful.'

'You look splendid yourself,' she said. 'That waistcoat really suits you.'

'Are you anxious?' he asked.

'Impatient to claim my prize,' she laughed.

'Good, good,' he said, smiling at her. 'Your Joseph is a splendid fellow. I have seen him this morning with Freddy, deep in conversation. He asked me to give you his love. Oh, and to hang on to your flowers.'

Beattie laughed. 'How mysterious. This is going to be a very different ride today from our first one from the workhouse all those years ago. You rescued me twice, didn't you?' said Beattie, taking his arm. 'Once from the beach and once from that awful place.'

'It has been a joy to me,' he said, 'watching you grow into such a splendid woman.'

'Thank you,' she said, kissing him on the cheek. 'I almost forgot,' she said, picking up an envelope from the dressing table. 'I have something to return to you. I want you to open it now.'

Dr Pragnell tore it open and took out a small crumpled card and turned it over to read the two words written in his own hand.

'"Beatrice Salter,"' he read out her name. 'Oh, my dear, child,' he said, kissing her hand. 'We have come full circle, haven't we? I shall treasure this and never be parted from it,' he said, tucking it into his waistcoat pocket.

Arm in arm they went out into the hall where Miss Sankey and a very excited Rosie Siddons were waiting for them.

'Ooh!! You looks like an angel,' said Rosie, bursting into tears as she handed the bouquet to Beattie.

'Rosemary, you get along this minute to the church porch and calm yourself,' said Miss Sankey, sternly.

'Rosie you look so pretty in that blue dress,' said Beattie, and was rewarded by a shy smile.

Miss Sankey nodded to all of them. 'I shall see you after the ceremony,' she said, closing the door behind her.

'My stars, Beattie, you looks like a duchess. Here, take me arm and let me get you settled,' said Freddy as they walked down the steps of the Mariners'. He was resplendent in a black suit, top hat and scarlet waistcoat. The hood of the trap had been folded back and filled with green leaves and heaped with white flowers of all kinds. Dapple's harness was covered with bells and ribbons. 'Bin up half the night I have scouring out the seats. Looks good, don't it?'

'Fit for a queen.'

They trotted down Queen Street and around The Hard past the Dockyard Gate and on to St George's Square.

'I feel like royalty,' laughed Beattie, as passers-by waved at her and shouted their good wishes. Another crowd was waiting outside the church.

'You looks a picture,' said little Mrs Frostick before she hurried into church.

'Are you ready, my dear?' Doctor Pragnell asked.

Beattie nodded, suddenly close to tears.

They stood at the entrance by the prayer books and hymnals while the vicar nodded up to the organ loft. There was a great wheezing and clashing of chords and the wedding march began. Heads turned towards her, all of them smiling. She felt herself wafted up the aisle on a great wave of affection. And then Joseph turned to look at her and it was as if the church were empty.

The clergyman was talking away in a solemn, fluty voice. All she was conscious of was the warmth of Joseph's sleeve next to hers. In a silence between his words they sneaked a smile at one another.

'Wilt thou, Joseph Matthew Forrest, have this woman, Beatrice Salter, to thy wedded wife?' asked the vicar. 'Wilt thou love her, comfort her, honour and keep her, in sickness and in health, so long as ye both shall live?'

'I will,' said Joseph, his voice loud and sure.

'Wilt thou, Beatrice Salter, take this man, Joseph Matthew Forrest, to thy wedded husband. Wilt thou love him, comfort him, honour and keep him in sickness and in health, so long as ye both shall live?'

'I will,' she answered, looking into Joseph's blue eyes, now swimming with tears.

'Who giveth this woman to be married to this man?'

Dr Pragnell placed her hand in the priest's hand and he in turn gave Joseph's hand to her. And then Joseph was making his vows, looking directly into her eyes. She had to be prompted to, 'Love and cherish, till death us do part, and thereto, I pledge thee my troth.'

431

And then Joseph was slipping the ring on her finger. 'With this ring I thee wed, with my body I thee worship, and with all my worldly goods, I thee endow.'

'Those whom God hath joined together, let no man put asunder,' pronounced the priest, holding both their hands.

There was a triumphal clash from the organ and they were led into the vestry where she signed her new name with a flourish. Joseph signed his and Dr Pragnell and Hester were the witnesses.

Rosie handed Beattie back her flowers. There was another discordant wheezing from the organ and she and Joseph were walking hand in hand down the aisle, laughing and smiling at everyone.

At the church door there were four sailors making an archway with gleaming new coal shovels. Laughing and holding hands they ran underneath and into the sunshine where they were hugged and kissed and pelted with rose petals. As they approached the trap the old pony deposited a steaming heap of manure in the road.

'A present from Dapple,' laughed Freddy.

Joseph helped her up beside him then leaned forward and whispered to Freddy, who drove them in a leisurely fashion back to the Mariners'. 'Give me a kiss, Mrs Forrest,' he said, taking her into his arms. They were flushed and slightly dishevelled when the trap arrived at Nile Street.

There, at the front gate, stood Miss Sankey. 'Welcome, Mr and Mrs Forrest,' she said. 'Let me escort you to your wedding feast.'

Beattie and Joseph gasped as the doors were opened into the dining room. Its long tables were covered with red cloths each trimmed with swags of green and gold ribbon. Around the walls were paper chains. The tables were heaped with plates of sandwiches, jugs of elderflower wine and bowls of trifle.

'Take your places,' said Miss Sankey, blowing her whistle.

'Freddy, will you take the flowers?' said Joseph.

'What are you up to?' asked Beattie.

He tapped his finger to his nose. 'All will be revealed later.'

Another blast on the whistle created silence. Dr Pragnell tapped his glass with a fork and said. 'Welcome, everyone, to Beattie and Joseph's special day. There is no need to ask if they are happy, it is written all over their faces. Thank you all for being here today to make this such a joyous occasion. Let us raise our glasses to the new Mr and Mrs Forrest.'

Everyone cheered. There were whistles from the sailors, clapping and cheering from everyone else.

Beattie drank her wine and tucked into the ham and cheese sandwiches.

'What a feast,' said Joseph. 'Doctor, here, let me fill your glass. My turn now,' he said, taking a piece of paper from his jacket pocket.

'Ladies and gentlemen, may I have your attention. My wife and I thank you for celebrating our wedding with us. It has been a wonderful occasion. I should like to thank my beautiful Beattie for saying yes and making me the happiest of men. I should like to thank Doctor Pragnell for his fatherly services and last but by no means least Miss Sankey for making this all possible.'

There were deafening cheers. 'Sankey, Sankey,' everyone cried.

'Beattie and Joseph,' she said. 'This is a proud moment for me, watching the two of you setting out together on the great adventure of life. Now you are a couple, you must work

433

together as a team. Look after one another, be honest, respectful and kind. And remember – blame poisons love and a pinch of humour will season the dullest meal.'

Everyone cheered, and Miss Sankey came over and kissed Beattie and Joseph.

Beattie hugged her tightly.

'Now,' she said, when she had at last extricated herself, 'we will push back the tables and Horry Dashwood will organise the concert.'

One turn followed the other in rapid succession. Freddy did bird imitations, two of the sailors did a hornpipe and Rosie Siddons sang a soulful ballad. Miss Sankey did some conjuring with coloured flags and paper flowers. And then, somewhat flushed with wine, Pearl got up and insisted on singing a song entitled, 'The Mad Butcher', with lots of mention of chops and suet and clashing knives. When she sat down again to noisy applause, Joseph nudged Beattie.

'We need to sneak away now,' he whispered.

'Where are we going?' Beattie asked as he hurried her outside towards the waiting trap.

'Another ceremony, Mrs Forrest,' he said. 'Just enjoy the ride.'

Freddy touched the reins and Dapple set off at a steady trot towards Old Portsmouth.

'Happy?' Joseph asked, drawing her into his arms.

'Happy and curious,' she said, kissing him again.

'Whoa!' called Freddy as they reached Broad Street.

Joseph helped her down and they walked, hand in hand, through the Sally Port, onto Point Beach. Beattie breathed in the smell of wet seaweed and smiled at her new husband. 'What happens now?' she asked.

'I shall escort you down to your barge, your majesty, and we shall take a little trip along the Solent.'

'Joseph,' she cried, 'I've never been on a boat. Oh, how wonderful!' She held her skirt in one hand and her flowers in the other as they made uneven progress over the shingle to the little wooden pier.

A cheer went up from a group of sailors in a large boat, and the petty officer, standing on the jetty holding a rope, nodded to Joseph.

'Are you ready, Mrs Forrest?' asked Joseph.

As they drew near to the boat Beattie saw that the sailors were all sat with their oars upright in front of them. The petty officer helped them aboard.

'Good afternoon,' said Beattie, smiling shyly at the sailors, and they nodded and touched their straw hats respectfully.

The man ashore leapt nimbly aboard and stood between Beattie and Joseph, holding the tiller. 'Out oars,' he snapped, 'and give way together.'

Beattie was enchanted as the oars were set in the water in one fluid movement. The sun sparkled on the water and the oars dipped and lifted rhythmically as the boat left the shore and swept out into the Solent. She watched the beach getting smaller and smaller as they left the Round Tower behind. The oars creaked against the rowlocks and splashed in and out of the water in a steady pattern of sound. Beattie could not draw her eyes away from them.

'Where are we going?' she whispered to Joseph.

'I thought you would like to scatter your flowers on the sea,' he said. 'They might float back to where you came from. It would be a message to your mother and father.'

Beattie gasped and her eyes filled with tears. 'Oh, Joseph,' she said. 'I hadn't thought. Oh, thank you, thank you.' She was overwhelmed. He had understood how much she grieved over her lost parents and had given her the means of remembering them and making them part of her wedding.

'Would you like to do that, Beattie?' he asked her.

He is my angel, she thought. I knew that when I first saw him with the sun glinting on his hair and now I am certain.

'Cease rowing,' said the petty officer, and the boat drifted with the tide.

She handed half the roses to Joseph and together they began to cast them one by one into the Solent. 'Goodbye,' she whispered as she watched the flowers floating away on the tide. 'Wherever you are, my parents, I thank you for bringing me here. I shall never forget you. Now I have a new life here with Joseph. Goodbye, goodbye.'

Beattie sat beside Joseph, holding his hand as the boat made its way back to the jetty. There were no words to express her thankfulness. When the boat reached the jetty again the petty officer leapt ashore and held the boat steady for her and Joseph to climb out.

'Thank you, all of you,' she said, smiling at the sailors. 'I shall never ever forget you.'

'Our pleasure, 'Ma'am,' they said, once more touching their hats.

Joseph stepped onto the jetty and helped her after him.

'Thank you,' he said to the petty officer, 'and you, lads. Here's some ale money for your trouble.' He reached into his pocket and fetched out a handful of coins, which the petty officer took from him.

'Three cheers for the happy couple,' he said.

'*Hip-hip hurrah, hip-hip hurrah, hip-hip hurrah*,' they roared, waving their hats in the air.

''Bye, Joe, and good luck,' said the petty officer, 'and to you, Ma'am.' He leapt back on board. 'Out oars, make way together,' he shouted.

Beattie and Joseph stood arm in arm on the jetty as the whaler took to the sea.

'Oh, Joseph, that was so appropriate,' she said, 'just what I wanted. I do love you.'

'And I love you,' he said, bending to kiss her.

'How can I thank you?' she whispered.

Joseph chuckled. 'I think we will find a way,' he said, before bending to kiss her.

Dr Pragnell stepped through the Sally Port, his head buzzing from too much wine. Appreciatively he sniffed the salty air and looked about him. Over on the jetty he saw Joseph bend and kiss Beattie. He raised his hand in greeting and then let it fall by his side.

His foundling had no need of his services today.